THE
WRONG
GUY

OTHER TITLES BY LAUREN LANDISH

Cold Springs

The Wrong Bridesmaid

Never Say Never

Never Marry Your Brother's Best Friend
Never Give Your Heart to a Hookup
Never Fall for the Fake Boyfriend

The Truth or Dare Series

The Dare
The Truth

The Big Fat Fake Series

My Big Fat Fake Wedding
My Big Fat Fake Engagement
My Big Fat Fake Honeymoon

Bennett Boys Ranch

Buck Wild
Riding Hard
Racing Hearts

The Tannen Boys

Rough Love
Rough Edge
Rough Country

Irresistible Bachelor Series

Anaconda
Mr. Fiancé
Heartstopper
Stud Muffin
Mr. Fixit
Matchmaker
Motorhead
Baby Daddy
Untamed

Get Dirty Series

Dirty Talk
Dirty Laundry
Dirty Deeds
Dirty Secrets

Dirty Fairy Tales

Beauty and the Billionaire
Not So Prince Charming
Happily Never After

The Virgin Diaries

Satin and Pearls
Leather and Lace
Silk and Shadows

Standalones

The French Kiss
Risky Business
One Day Fiancé
The Blind Date
Drop Dead Gorgeous
Filthy Riches
Scorpio

THE
WRONG
GUY

LAUREN LANDISH

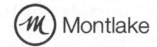
Montlake

Text copyright © 2023 by Lauren Landish

Published by Montlake, Seattle

www.apub.com

Amazon, the Amazon logo, and Montlake are trademarks of Amazon.com, Inc., or its affiliates.

ISBN-13: 9781662515057 (paperback)

ISBN-13: 9781662515040 (digital)

Cover design by Letitia Hasser

Cover photography by Wander Aguiar

Cover image: © MG Drachal / Shutterstock; © Meranda19 / Shutterstock

Printed in the United States of America

THE
WRONG
GUY

Prologue

WREN

"Shit, baby. You're so gorgeous when you come. Show me."

With every word, he thrusts his fingers deep inside me, petting that spot that drives me wild. I ride the wave of convulsions as I throw my head back and clamp my legs closed to hold him there. I writhe against the cheap cotton sheets, the roughness of the fabric adding to the sensations rocking through my body.

He leans down, nudging my thighs open with his scruff-covered chin. His breath is hot over my core as he urges me, "More."

I don't know if he's telling me to keep coming or speaking his own desire for more of my body, because he licks my clit with the flat of his tongue and I fly again . . . or still. I shove my fingers through the wild length of dark hair currently between my legs. "Jesse, if you stop, I'll kill you."

The threat is gasped out, but I feel his smile against my tender flesh. He thinks I'm kidding, but I'm not so sure. I want this . . . need this release. Maybe that makes me greedy, but if so, I'm good with that. Especially when Jesse clamps onto my clit. The feeling is intense, and my cries get louder and louder. I squirm beneath him as he grunts back in a primal conversation between our bodies, fighting to keep our connection. The pressure inside me is building to something bigger, wilder, more out of control, and I don't know if I'm ready for it.

But Jesse is.

I shatter into a million pieces of light, becoming a human firework. Hot, sparkly, all-consuming, and over too quickly.

"Dammit, baby. Can't . . . wait . . . wanna . . . feel you." Jesse is doing his best to awkwardly shove a condom on with his left hand so he can keep my explosion going. Somehow, he manages, and a second later, he replaces his fingers with his cock as he thrusts into me with one rough stroke. I tense, knowing how much he always stretches me, but he's made sure I'm more than ready for him. He shudders at the feeling of my still-pulsing pussy enveloping him.

I'm the one smiling now, loving the power I have over a man like him. I lift my legs to his shoulders, and given our height difference, he drops a kiss to my right ankle. But I don't want sweet kisses, not now. I want to make him come as hard as I did. Using my legs for leverage, I pull him toward me. He's quick to catch himself, one hand on either side of my head as he bends me in half. "Come here."

I grip his face in my hands and pull him farther down to me, stealing his grunt with a kiss. He thrusts in . . . deeper, harder, with a punishing pace as he chases his own pleasure. I'm at the edge of what I can take—my hamstrings stretched, my breath erratic, my pussy full. And it's glorious.

The tendons on each side of Jesse's neck strain, his eyes clench closed, and he bares his teeth in a growl. And then he spasms, bucking into me wildly. I squeeze him, using my inner muscles to pull his cum from him, wanting his pleasure. He thrusts through his own release and then collapses over me, panting to catch his breath. "Holeee shiiit, Wren. You're a damn witch. I think you stole my soul right outta my dick."

I shrug, choosing to take that as a compliment. "I've been called worse. You're welcome." A beat later, he lifts up and peers at me with one eye open and one still closed. "And thank you."

He places a quick kiss on my forehead as he pulls out, a habit of his that I secretly like. As he moves away to take care of the condom in the attached bathroom, I lower my legs and stretch out as long as I can, feeling luxurious even though I'm in a too-small bed, on rough sheets, with beard burn between my thighs. I groan in delight and call out, "I'm hungry. Wanna get dinner?"

Jesse pops his head around the doorframe. His hair is still messy, but I can tell he's run his fingers through it to repair the damage my hands did, and he's brushing his teeth. "Cahn't. Sowwee," he mumbles around the foam that makes him look like a rabid dog. He disappears, and I hear him spit into the running water. Coming back into the bedroom, he heads for the dresser and clarifies, "I'm meeting the guys at Puss N Boots for beer and pool."

"Oh. No worries." I enjoy the view for one more second as he pulls on fresh boxer briefs, and then I get up. I make quick work of cleaning up in the bathroom, and when I return to the bedroom, Jesse is dressed and sitting on the edge of the bed. He holds up my panties with a smile that'd make sugar melt.

"These are sexy as fuck, ya know?"

"I know." They're not a teeny-tiny, ass-chafing string, but I buy quality, with delicate lace that makes my cheeks smackable. I happen to like sexy underwear, especially for times like this. I take them from him, slipping them back on, followed by the rest of my clothes.

Jesse walks me to the front door, and outside, he heads for his truck as I go to my car. "See ya later?"

I nod and climb into my car. His truck roars next to me, and when I look over, he throws me a two-finger wave. We follow each other to the stop sign at the end of his street, where I turn left to head home, and he turns right to go play pool with the guys.

Chapter 1

JESSE

One Year Later

Friday night in Cold Springs is a hotbed of wild debauchery . . . if your definition is playing pool with your aunt, eating a greasy burger piled high with cheese and bacon, drinking a few beers with your buddies from work, and crashing into bed alone by midnight.

And if that's not your definition, you're shit out of luck around here, because that's about all the excitement we've got in Cold Springs.

I lean over the pool table, hoping I can get at least a few balls in before Aunt Etta runs the table on me. I'll be a good sport when she does, same as always. She taught me to play when I was a kid, and I've won only a single game against her in my whole life, and that was a couple of days after Gran passed, so Etta was definitely off her game then. Hell, I don't know how she was upright, but that's how she is. Strong, fearless, badass . . . just like my mom and sister.

Thank fuck. Because if I'd grown up surrounded by a bunch of Hallmark-movie-watching, wine-sipping, emotional women, I wouldn't be who I am. And I'm awesome.

I flash a wink at Aunt Etta, just to taunt her. Another valuable skill she taught me. "You watching, ol' lady? I'mma show you how it's done." I line up my shot, spreading my legs for any onlookers, and peer down the length of my pool cue at the red three ball. If I get it in, I've got just the eight ball, and then I win. I wiggle my hips and take a couple of practice strokes, steadying my breath. Ready and sure, I pull the cue stick back and push it forward sharply.

"Yeah, shake that ass. Show Charlene how it's done," Aunt Etta calls out right as I make contact. The three ball goes squirrelly, hitting the bumper a solid two inches from the corner pocket.

"Shit."

I glare at Aunt Etta, only to find her already gloating. When I sniff in annoyance, her smirk only grows. "No wonder you always strike out with the ladies. No follow-through."

"Oooh, burn!"

"She's gotcha there!"

"Jesse, I think I'm in love with your aunt. That's cool with you, right?"

I stare my buddies down one by one, and though they try valiantly to straighten their faces out, they fail miserably. "All of you are on cleanup duty on Monday."

Mike laughs. "Dude, fuck you. I'm not even on your crew."

He's got a point.

We all work for Jed Ford's construction company, but Mike's an electrician while the rest of us work general contracting. Which means Roscoe and Alan are on the hook. They glance at each other and then back at me. Finally Roscoe declares, "Worth it." He pops Alan in the gut, and they start laughing again.

"Hey, young 'un," Aunt Etta calls, turning my age comment back on me to get my attention.

I sigh resolutely. She's damn near run the whole table, and as soon as I look, she drops the eight ball in the side pocket, winning the game. Again.

"Good game," I admit.

She hands her pool cue to Mike, letting her hand drift over his as she lets go and tells him, "You're a cutie-pie, but a little inexperienced for a woman like me." She pats his cheek a bit too hard and spins to walk away, her dark braid flinging over her shoulder. But I swear there's a little extra pep in her step.

Mike's tongue lolls out like a cartoon dog, but he manages to yell after her, "I can learn!"

Tayvious, Etta's "HR complaint waiting to happen" cook, leans out of the food window. "I can teach you a thing or two, Mike. Things you never knew about yourself."

Mike laughs good-naturedly. "Thanks, Tay Tay. Pretty sure the only thing I wanna learn from you is your famous fancy ketchup recipe."

"You and everyone else," he quips back. "But a man's gotta have some secrets." With that, he disappears back into the kitchen. Recipes are probably the only secrets Tayvious has, given that he tells every-one everything about his life—dates, what he bought at the local swap meet, and even the rash he got last month, which thankfully was just a bit of razor burn and nothing contagious, because I don't think even unknown dermatitis would stop us from eating Tay Tay's food.

Mike racks the balls, and Alan squares up to play a game with him while Roscoe and I sit at a table and watch. "You know Mike ain't really after Etta, right? He just likes giving you shit."

Cutting my eyes over, I see that Roscoe's serious. "You ever meet his last girlfriend?" When he shakes his head, I grin as I watch Mike and Alan battle to clear the table. "Mike's got a type. You heard of cougars? Well, Mike likes jaguars. Less than fifty need not apply. So he's dead serious when he flirts with Etta, but she ain't interested. Or if she is, I don't want to know about it. Her business is her own, and I've got a strong preference for living, so I keep my nose out of it."

He laughs, probably thinking I'm exaggerating, but I'm not.

I pour a glass of beer from the pitcher we're working our way through and hold it up. Roscoe clinks glasses with me and toasts, "To a good week and good-er weekend."

I sigh happily after I take a big sip.

And I know better than to jinx shit like that. You never say *it's quiet* in an ER or restaurant, you never say *what's the worst that could happen* before you do something stupid, and you never toast to a good weekend when it hasn't started yet.

So I shouldn't be surprised when the door of Puss N Boots opens and trouble walks in, but I am.

Chrissy Ford is standing by the door, looking around awkwardly and fidgeting with her bottle-blonde hair. In seemingly slow motion, people freeze as they realize who's here and quietly alert their friends, the wave of recognition and buzz of interest moving around the whole bar until all eyes are on Chrissy.

I know for a fact it's the first time she's been here, because she's persona non grata in Etta's place. Once upon a time, long, long, long ago, the two of them were best friends. Chrissy was even going to be the maid of honor at Etta's wedding.

Until Etta found Chrissy and Etta's soon-to-be groom, Jed Ford, right in the middle of being *real* familiar. The fallout was ugly and continues to this day, which is what makes Chrissy's appearance here all the more concerning.

"Shiiiit." I grab my phone from my back pocket and send a quick text to my sister, Hazel, who's the only person with a chance at refereeing a cat-fight catastrophe between Aunt Etta and her nemesis.

911. Not a drill. Chrissy's at Puss N Boots. Get bail money for Etta ready.

Charlene gets to the door before Etta, narrowly saving Chrissy's life. "Hey, honey-baby, normally this'd be the part where I tell you to grab a seat and offer to getcha a beer. But we both know the only thing you'd best be grabbing is your own ass as you get the hell outta here." Charlene smiles widely and blinks her fake lashes as she offers the free advice with all the sassy fire she possesses.

Chrissy seems unsure what to do with the less-than-welcoming greeting, but I don't know what she expected here. Even people who might be friendly with her or Jed, or work for Jed like I do, know that given half a chance, or a Purge Day, Chrissy would be number one on Etta's shit list. She hates Jed, but I think deep down, Etta was more hurt by her friend's actions than her husband-to-be's.

"Uhm, is Etta here? I need to talk to her," Chrissy tells Charlene.

We can all hear every word at this point, and from somewhere over at the bar, a voice says, "Your funeral."

Tayvious's voice calls out, "Etta, you got some trash to take out up front." He dings the bell signaling an order is ready, but there's no food in the window. I think it's supposed to be the start of round one—Chrissy versus Etta.

My money's on Aunt Etta every time. Hell, Etta versus Stone Cold Steve Austin, my money's on Etta.

"What the hell are you doing here?" Etta snaps as she comes out from the back, drying her hands on a towel, and sees what we're all staring at.

To her credit, Chrissy doesn't run out the door. Though, maybe that's because she's too foolish to save her own life. She even doubles down on her death wish, asking Etta, "Can we talk for a second?" After a swallow, she adds, "Please?"

Etta narrows her eyes, taking Chrissy's measure—probably for a casket—and lifts her chin toward a table by the door. The relief that washes through Chrissy is obvious, piquing everyone's interest more. Etta tosses her rag to the bar, stomps over in her boots, and perches on the edge of the stool across from her old friend, not getting too comfy and staying ready to rumble at the slightest provocation.

Chrissy starts to speak, but Etta holds up one finger and turns to the room at large. "Anybody wanting to be up in my business needs to know it requires six figures, verifiable by bank statement, 25/8 availability, and the ability to recognize the difference between beer and that piss they call Natural Light. If that ain't you, mind your own." She twirls her finger in the air, indicating everyone should go back to what they were doing.

Mike leans over and whispers to me, "Ya think she means her business, like the bar, or her *business*-business?" When I stare at him stonily, he lifts his brows. "I mean, I qualify."

"Roscoe, play a game with this asshole while I try to keep Etta outta jail this time. And explain that six figures means before the decimal point, not including the cents."

He hops up quickly. "On it, boss."

I ain't his boss, not really. And Etta's never been to jail, that I know of. But you could cut the tension in here with a plastic spork, and I've got my aunt's back, no matter what.

I slow walk over to a table close to Etta and Chrissy, lifting my chin at the couple sitting there. I don't know them from Adam, but they know me and Etta are kin, so the guy scoots over a bit, giving me space to sit. I smile my appreciation and tune in to Etta so I can eavesdrop.

"I didn't know where else to go," Chrissy says. She sounds . . . choked, but Etta hasn't had time to wrap her hands around her throat since I last looked over there. Hopefully.

Etta huffs. "So you came to the one place you're not welcome. Genius move, Chrissy."

"I know, but that's why. Because he'd never think to look for me here," Chrissy says, almost sounding depressed and amused at the same time. It's a weird sound. "Hell, he wouldn't dare come here if you rolled out a red carpet and sent him a gold-embossed invitation. That's why I'm here."

Etta's silent long enough that I get worried and peek over my shoulder. But Etta hasn't moved, other than tilting her head a bit as she peers at her former friend.

"He hurt you?" Etta's voice has gone cold steel. She's probably plotted out four new ways to kill Jed Ford in the last two seconds. Which is impressive, not because of the speed, but because she can still come up with new ways to do something she's pondered for decades. I heard her listing them off to my mom one time when they were drunk. Etta got to "strangle him with an anaconda" before she got too carried away with a case of the beer giggles to continue.

"Yes. Well, no. Not like . . . physically. But—"

"Chrissy," Etta sighs, "I don't give a shit if he hurt your feelings or took away your credit cards or whatever else you think I'm going to care about. We're not friends, and I don't feel sorry for you. You made your bed over and over again. You chose this life every night when you went to sleep and every morning when you got up."

"He's cheating on me," Chrissy blurts out.

I cough to cover my chuckle. Not about the infidelity—anyone doing something like that is a piece of shit in my book—but the irony of Chrissy coming to Etta of all people about this is a little too on the nose.

"And this is somehow shocking news? Ever heard the expression 'a leopard don't change its spots'?" Etta answers dryly.

I'm guessing that's not the reaction Chrissy was expecting about her not-at-all surprising news.

"He's not like that. Or he didn't used to be. I'm sorry for what happened all those years ago, but we've been happy. It wasn't until the whole construction thing here in Cold Springs went to hell that everything changed. He was devastated, Etta. Embarrassed and angry. It changed him, and now he's been traveling so much. That's why I went to the hotel to surprise him."

"I'm guessing you were the one who got surprised?" Etta asks, one brow kicked up sardonically. I see Chrissy nod. "So why're you defending him, then? You're sitting here making excuses for him when I can see the tears in your eyes."

Chrissy shrugs. "It's not that simple."

"Sure it is. You gonna put up with that or not? Decide that and go from there," Etta suggests flatly, actually giving reasonable advice. "Way I see it, you got three choices. You can get marriage counseling, you could invite her in and be a throuple, or you get a divorce. It's all your call."

Still arguing, Chrissy repeats, "It's not that simple. She's young. Can't be a day over thirty, and pregnant. Like 'bouncing on top of Jed with her boobs going every which way and her belly big and round' type of pregnant." She gestures at her chest, one hand going clockwise and one going counterclockwise like swinging tassels, and then mimes a pregnant stomach large enough to house a full-term calf.

I hiss. Etta gasps. The rest of the bar is a chorus of cusswords, obviously eavesdropping, too, despite Etta's threat.

"Fuck, Chrissy. Okay, I take it back a *teeny, tiny* bit," Etta says, sounding a little more understanding. "I'm sorry . . . that's . . . wow. I knew Jed was a bastard, but that's a new low, even for him. Is the baby his?"

A couple of months ago, Etta bought a karaoke machine, thinking a sing-along night at Puss N Boots would be fun. We managed to keep to the script for two whole weeks before it turned into a game of How Bad Can You Sing? with a "winner drinks free all night" prize. It made quite a few ears bleed.

But that machine came with a damn good microphone. I wish I knew where Etta stashed that thing right now because I'd prop it up next to the table so the whole bar could hear Chrissy's answer firsthand.

"I don't know. I ran out of there too fast to get any answers. But if I had to guess? Yeah, it's his. He wouldn't do that with someone who had some other man's baby in her. Not because it'd be wrong, but because his ego wouldn't take it." Chrissy's resignation to the situation makes us all feel a little sad for her.

"I think you're right about that," Etta agrees. "So the question's the same. What're you gonna do about it? You signing up to be a stepmama to a baby he's having with another woman or what? I told you . . . you choose your life every day. What're you gonna do with yours?"

Chrissy's head drops, and she stares at her hands, picking at a manicure I don't think I've ever seen look less than perfect. "I'm not like you, Etta. I can't do *this*." The condescension peeks through Chrissy's distress, and I think she might actually go home, pretend she didn't see anything at that hotel, and continue on with her life of luxury as Jed's wife.

"*This* is something I'm damn proud of," Etta says, her voice strong and sure. "I built this life day by day, just like I'm telling you to do. I've got friends, family, and my horse. That's all I really need anyway. And if I decide I want a little more, I got fellas to warm my bed, enough money to go lay on a beach somewhere, and a pool table I can whip anybody in town on. I'm happy, Chrissy." She pauses and adds, "You deserve to be too."

Wow. I never would've thought I'd see the day Aunt Etta told Chrissy Ford that she deserves to be happy. Deserves to be caught up in a hailstorm in a convertible with the top stuck down? Probably. But happy? Nope, wouldn't have put that on my bingo card.

"Thanks, Etta. I think I've got a lot of thinking to do," Chrissy says, getting up.

When Etta stands, too, Chrissy makes a move like she's going to hug her, and Etta steps back, obviously declining the friendly gesture. But she does offer, "Don't make a habit out of it or anything, but if you truly need a place to hide out one day, you can sit in the corner over there. Charlene'll getcha a beer, and Tayvious'll make you a burger—" Louder, she calls out, "And not spit in it."

Tayvious grumbles loud enough for the whole bar to hear, but doesn't argue. He's dead serious about his food anyway and wouldn't taint it, not even for Chrissy Ford.

Chrissy smiles grimly at Etta and heads toward the door.

"Go get 'im, girl!"

"Give him the hell he deserves!"

"Cut off his dick!"

That last one is Charlene, who shrugs and adds, "Well, getting someone pregnant wouldn't be an issue after that, and he'd only be able to use his fingers and tongue for her pleasure. Sounds like a fair punishment to me. No?"

She's got a point, and everyone kinda shrugs along in agreement too.

Once Chrissy's gone, the whole place lets out a collective breath I don't think any of us realized we were holding.

"Get back to your Friday night beers'ing and cheers'ing," Etta declares, knowing that everyone and their damn brother was listenin' in. Hell, half of town probably knows by now. "My business ain't none of yours, and Chrissy's ain't none of yours either."

I try to approach her, but Aunt Etta just tells me wearily, "I'm fine. Think I'll go home and check on Nala. She probably needs some fresh hay."

Her horse is her baby and probably got fresh hay less than eight hours ago, but it's her way of saying she's going to deal with this on her own. I nod and step out of her way, letting her save a little face with her patrons too.

No less than two minutes after Etta disappears, the door bursts open again. "Where is she?"

My sister, Hazel, must've read my text and, instead of getting bail money, decided to go to jail with Aunt Etta. I'm so proud of her.

Hazel's eyes are wild, her hair is piled on her head in something resembling a greasy rat's nest, and there's goopy stuff across her nose that looks half-scrubbed off. She must've been having an even more exciting

Friday night than me. I know a hair mask and pore treatment when I see them after growing up with all women.

"You're too late, sis. You probably passed Etta on the way here," I tell her.

Etta lives in a small house on what used to be Gran's property. It was a way for her to look after Gran when Gran got to the point that she needed it. After Gran passed, Hazel moved into Gran's place, taking it and Gran's foul-mouthed parrot under her care. And when she got married, her husband, Wyatt, moved in. Basically, it means that Hazel and Etta live a few hundred yards from each other, but somehow Hazel still missed her.

"Well, what's going on?" she asks warily. "Did hell freeze over or did a black hole into an alternate timeline open up?"

I look at Hazel in surprise. Sci-fi is not her thing, but that rolled off her tongue like she knows what she's talking about.

"Don't get your panties in a twist. It's some show Wyatt's forcing me to watch," Hazel remarks at my look. She grins, adding, "And by forcing me, I mean he rewards me in tongue licks for every minute I watch. It's pretty devilish if I do say so myself. I think I'm corrupting him."

Only my sister would pop off with that as a good thing.

"I don't want to hear about what you and Wyatt do in the bedroom. Let's play a game and I'll tell you what's up." I spin, heading for the closest empty table.

Right behind me, Hazel clarifies, "Bedroom? We don't have a TV in the bedroom. Studies show that couples who do have fifty percent less sex. Fifty percent, Jesse! No, we watch the TV in the living room like sex-having people do."

I shake my head, mentally singing as loud as I can so I don't hear her.

"Wait, the living room where we all sit on the couch when we come over?"

Hazel grins, and I shudder.

"I'm bringing over a plastic sheet to sit on," I declare. "Or sitting at the kitchen table from now on."

"Been there, done it on that too." She wiggles her dark eyebrows, making sure I know exactly what she's saying.

I drop my head, pinching the bridge of my nose and closing my eyes. I repeat the mantra I have so many times since Hazel and Wyatt got married. "She's not my problem now. She's not my problem now."

But that's not true. My family is the most important thing to me—good or bad, ugly or pretty.

I wait until Hazel is aiming at the cue ball to tell her, "You still have pore shit on your nose."

She makes three balls on the break anyway.

Chapter 2

Wren

"Hey, Mom, sorry I'm late for dinner. Work was crazy," I shout as I enter my parents' home, tossing my purse to the marble-topped table in the foyer and praying it doesn't knock over the vase of fresh flowers. Maria must've made something spicy tonight because it tickles my nose, even over the smell of the bouquet. My stomach growls as I *click-clack* as fast as I can across the tile floor, pulled toward the kitchen.

"No worries, honey." Despite her patience, Mom's sitting at the table with a glass of sparkling water that's ready for a refresh, obviously waiting for me for our Monday night mother-daughter catch-up dinner. I give her shoulders a hug, and then I do the same greeting for Maria, my near–second mother who's stirring a big pot of rice on the stove. There are several other pots, too, but they have lids, so I don't get to sneak a peek at what she's whipped up. And I know better than to try, because she'll whack my hand with the wooden spoon she can wield as well as a knight with a sword.

"Smells delicious."

"Thank you, *mija*. Sit down and I'll get you and Ms. Pamela a plate." She gestures at the table with her spoon and then opens a pot, getting a face full of steam in the process. Maria and her husband, Leo, have worked for my parents since before I was born, and have kept this family going through good and bad. Catching up with Mom might be the reason for my visit tonight, but Maria's cooking is a close second.

"What's happening at work?" Mom asks, genuinely curious, as I sit down beside her.

Her reputation is a lot to live up to, though I try every day. Pamela Ford has officially been "the mayor's wife" for most of her adult life, standing steadfastly at my father's side while raising three kids, acting as Junior League president, volunteering for the PTA, and serving a killer backhand on the tennis court. Despite her lack of "official" work, she's supporting and understanding of what I go through as the newly minted city attorney for Cold Springs.

"Norton's got a case of sticky fingers. I caught him trying to make copies of some of the city contracts. Actual physical copies on the copy machine of entire files." I roll my eyes at the absurdity. Ben Norton has been the city attorney for nearly thirty years, overseeing everything from contracts to helping my dad, the former mayor, with legal advice to keep the city running right and proper, and I've been his right-hand man since I did my internship with him years ago. There was never a question where I'd go to work after law school. My place was in Cold Springs, at city hall, as Norton's heir apparent.

"He said it was 'for old times' sake' and when I called bullshit, he admitted to wanting to have a backup 'in case you messed up.'" I mimic his shaky voice, which despite its weakness had hurt my feelings, given our solid work experience together. "Seriously. Like *I'm* the one who'll mess up city contracts when he doesn't understand a thing about the twenty-first century. He didn't know to include social media clauses in employment contracts, for God's sake." I'm waving my hands around and looking at Mom like *can you believe that?* as I rant.

Maria sets down plates filled with shrimp and rice in front of us and then adds a glass of sparkling water for me when she tops off Mom's. "Eat. You'll feel better," Maria tells me. It's her solution for most things, and I'm not ashamed to admit that I take that advice regularly when she's the one who's cooking.

Mom's smile is gracious as she picks up her fork, taking a small bite. "Mmm," she moans. "I don't know how you do it every time." The compliment makes Maria blush in delight. "And you, honey—" She pins me with a blue-eyed stare. "Be nice to Ben. That poor man has been through the wringer and then some. God rest his Margaret's soul." Mom presses a hand to her chest and looks toward the ceiling. "Retiring is hard when it's the only thing he has left. He's not worried about you. He's worried about not being needed."

I sigh, knowing she's right. "I am being nice. You know I love Ben, and Margaret was always nice to me. But if he doesn't hurry up and retire, I might be forced to help him out the door. With a good, solid shove." Scrunching up my face, I mime pushing old Ben Norton out of city hall like a dog that won't go outside to shit in the rain.

Mom laughs, but quickly covers her mouth. "Wren, you're terrible."

I shrug, laughing too. "You made me this way."

We eat a few bites in companionable silence, waving as Maria disappears upstairs with plates for Leo and her. So when the doorbell rings, we both jump. "You expecting someone for dinner?" I ask, and when Mom's brows lift, I add, "Is this another setup? I swear to the almighty Taylor Swift that if you invited some frat boy fresh out of medical school for a li'l meet-n-greet with yours truly, I will cancel our dinners for a month this time." She's not too worried about my single status with both of my older brothers married, but that doesn't mean she wouldn't be over the moon if I did pair up and find my own slice of happily ever after.

Thankfully, Mom throws her hands out in innocence. "I'll get it."

She disappears, her bare feet silent on the tile, and I eat another bite. My plan is to open-mouth chew like a cow if Mom does reappear with a possible suitor, maybe talk about how eager I am to have an entire litter of kids as soon as possible. That's usually enough to run people off, even with the draw of my last name.

I perk my ears up when I don't hear the shuffle of loafers or the squeak of tennis shoes, but rather the clacking of another pair of heels.

"Have a seat. Let me get you a plate," Mom says as she comes back into the kitchen.

"Oh, no, I couldn't. I don't want to be a bother. Sorry for dropping in like this, I . . ." My Aunt Chrissy's voice grates on my nerves in just the few short sentences before she stops when she sees me.

We're not what you'd call a "close family." She's married to my Uncle Jed, and makes a job out of salon visits, Pilates sessions, and judging others. Of course, she always finds them lacking compared to her own self-ascribed amazingness.

Well trained by the years of my dad's mayorship, I roll my eyes . . . on the inside, while maintaining a bland smile . . . on the outside. "Hey, Aunt Chrissy."

"Oh, I didn't know you had company, Pamela," Chrissy tells Mom, ignoring me and my greeting.

Mom waves her off. "Pshaw, don't worry a bit. Sit down." It's not a choice this time, and Chrissy sinks onto a chair. Mom fills another dinner plate, sets it in front of her new guest, and then takes her place at the head of the table. "How're you doing, Chrissy?"

Mom and Chrissy have never been close. They're polite because their husbands are brothers. But Uncle Jed and Dad couldn't be more different. And though Mom and Chrissy are both behind-the-scenes wives in a lot of ways, they're also as different as night and day.

"Fine," Chrissy answers.

Her expression is blank, not even a practiced smile. But Mom's patient and experienced with hiding the truth when the situation calls for it. I am too. So we can see Chrissy's lie a mile away.

"I hear you've been trying a new Pilates instructor. What do you think of her? I'm usually more of a yoga lover, but maybe we could go together sometime." Mom's chitchatting away as if Chrissy is paying attention to a word she's saying. Mom might as well be talking to a brick wall, though, because Chrissy's vacantly staring at her plate as though the shrimp might pop up and start dancing through the ocean of rice.

"Jed's having an affair," Chrissy blurts out suddenly. "I caught him *in the act.*"

My eyes widen in shock, and I gasp, garnering a sharp look of reproach from Mom, who's taking it completely in stride. Chrissy might as well have mentioned there'll be rain later this week. Then again, knowing Mom . . . she already knew. She might not be the mayor's wife anymore, but she's got a network of friends and acquaintances who keep her in the loop. Not to mention caught up on any town gossip. And even if she didn't know, she would never show surprise or distaste publicly. And that's what Chrissy is . . . the public, not family. Not really.

"Oh! I'm so sorry."

Chrissy sniffles, nodding at Mom's condolences as she wipes her nose with one of Mom's favorite linen napkins. I can almost see the younger version of Chrissy that must've once existed. One that believed Jed Ford was a good man, who'd love her and give her some version of life on Easy Street. And honestly, he has given her that. The rest is in question.

I don't think my uncle is a good man. He's rude, narcissistic, and, just a couple of years ago, tried to railroad a huge subdivision project into Cold Springs that would've destroyed what makes the town special.

All to line his own pockets.

As for loving Aunt Chrissy, I think the only person Jed truly loves is himself. Everyone else is a pawn he can use as he sees fit, including, unfortunately, my father. So I can totally imagine no less than a dozen scenarios where he'd willingly fall dick-first into someone other than his wife.

Mom presses her lips together, and though the corners lift, it's not really a smile. It looks more like pity. She probes gently, "Do you want to talk about it?"

Chrissy takes a shaky breath. "Well, he's been building that subdivision over in Brookstone, which is a huge undertaking that he wanted to be involved in daily. I understood, but that project's been done for a couple of months. Or it was supposed to be." She swipes at her eyes, which don't look particularly teary. In fact, though she squinches them, they seem drier than the meatloaf Maria tried to make one time before declaring that meat in the shape of a cake was against the laws of nature. "But he's still going over there a lot—like every weekend. And I just . . . I don't know. I missed him, so I went over to surprise him on Friday."

"What could go wrong?" I murmur.

Chrissy turns clear and anger-filled eyes to me, and I shrug, pushing a shrimp around my plate. It looks delicious, but it seems rude to eat while she's working through a breakdown of sorts. Though, if I'm honest, it seems like she's working through the *act* of a breakdown more than actually having one.

Her eyes cut back to Mom, offended that I dared question her—or maybe dared to speak—and looking like she expects Mom to do something about it. Does she seriously expect Mom to scold me for stating the truth?

Instead, Mom tilts her head, carefully considering her words. "You already know what you're going to do, don't you?"

"What?" Chrissy's surprise is echoed by my own widened eyes.

But Mom's on a roll, popping a shrimp into her mouth and nodding. I take a cue from her and eat the shrimp on my own plate that's been calling my name. It also keeps me from saying what I'm thinking, which is . . .

She said she caught him in the act . . . I wonder if Jed keeps his stupid cowboy hat and dirty socks on when he has sex?

Blech.

Once she swallows, Mom continues. "You went to find out the truth and you did. That was Friday, and it's Monday now. You've been making plans all weekend." Mom smiles with a knowing glint in her eyes. "It's what any smart woman would do."

Pretty sure she's considering herself in that particular group. Mom and Dad went through it a couple of years ago, and I know it was hard on her. She stood steadfastly by Dad, but I'm sure the idea of life without him crossed her mind a time or two.

Chrissy eats a tiny forkful of rice, considering what Mom said. I open my mouth to add my two cents, especially given I'm a lawyer, and Mom kicks me under the table. "Ow!" I hiss. But instead of apologizing, she gives me that Mom glare that says, *You need to shut up right now or you'll feel my wrath.*

So I do what any smart person does. I shut the hell up.

"You're right," Chrissy admits. "I met with a lawyer on Saturday, and things are already in motion. Actually—"

When Chrissy pins me with a shrewd gaze, I freeze in confusion. I typically think of Chrissy as a bit of an airhead, trophy wife, without a brain of her own in her head. What I see lurking in her blue eyes now is . . . intelligence, anger, and a desire to hit Jed where it'll hurt the most.

I'm impressed.

"Since you're here, I guess I can fill you in, Wren . . . my lawyer is going to contact you. It seems that dividing assets when you're personally and corporately embedded with the city on properties, contracts, and such is not as easy as splitting everything right down the middle. Especially when there's a baby to consider. Brookstone is huge, but it's done, so it shouldn't be a problem to divide proceeds. But the smaller Township build is the real issue." Chrissy sounds annoyed at the speed bump in her drag strip race to divorce.

Township is a much smaller development that Jed's company is building on the outskirts of Cold Springs. It's *nothing* like the one he tried to rush through before. No huge influx of newcomers to destroy the town, no need for rezoning or ramrodding existing owners off their property. Township is actually a nice little pocket of semiattached townhomes that'll provide affordable housing for people who already live in Cold Springs. I kind of think it's Jed's way of apologizing to the town he grew up in . . . in a way that's still financially beneficial for him. Which is, of course, key for my uncle.

"Wait, did you say a baby?" Mom questions sharply.

Chrissy clenches her teeth and inhales loudly through her nose. "Yes. Jed's hussy is very . . . very . . . pregnant. I want this done so I never have to sit in a courtroom with Jed, his new woman, and their child."

I don't know if Chrissy ever wanted children. Never thought about it, I guess. But whether she did or didn't, maintaining civility in that situation would be hard for anyone, so I understand her rush.

"Oliver will be handling the divorce," Chrissy says to me, "but he'll have to work with you and Norton to get everything sorted for Township so that it's split properly."

She's back to all business, and judging by the way she's talking, she's definitely more than a single meeting with a lawyer into this. Unless this Oliver guy is a shark in the deep, emotional, dangerous waters of divorce when there's wealth involved, this isn't going to be easy at all. What Chrissy's suggesting is complex and multifaceted.

"Sure, give him my number. I can meet with him anytime this week," I tell Chrissy, well aware that my schedule isn't that full with Ben still trying to do everything he can.

She nods politely, and I can tell that she's already done that. "And just so we're clear, I know the relationship between you and Jed might be seen as problematic, being as you're both Fords. I trust that you can stay professional, and separate family from law."

I narrow my eyes, peering at my aunt carefully. She knows I have no warm fuzzies for my uncle, but I also don't have any for her. "My oath is to the law itself. My job is to represent Cold Springs. Frankly, your divorce isn't my business. Though I'm sorry." Polite, civil, to the point.

"Good. And, Pamela, I'm sorry, but this is definitely going to involve you and Bill. I can't help it. That's actually what I came to talk about tonight. Oliver will likely want to meet with you too."

Mom raises one perfectly arched and penciled-in brow. "Thank you for the heads-up. Bill and I will tell the truth, whatever's asked of us. Of that, you can be sure."

"I appreciate that," Chrissy says, seemingly oblivious that what Mom and Dad have to say might not paint either Jed or Chrissy in the best light. There's a long moment of awkward silence where I think Mom is supposed to invite Chrissy to lunch or schedule that Pilates class together, but Mom stays quiet long enough that Chrissy gives up. "Well, I'd better let you get back to your dinner. I hear you're doing quite well at city hall, Wren. Hope this doesn't toss too big of a wrench in that."

My focus whiplashes around, trying to figure out Mom and Chrissy's relationship—of which I thought was mainly civil distance—and then centering back on the familiar topic of work. "Thanks. Ben's taught me so much. Hopefully, I can fill his big shoes when he leaves."

I'll bitch about Ben to Mom because she knows I'm venting and truly respect him, but I would never say a rude word about him, or anyone else for that matter, to Aunt Chrissy. She's of the "if you don't have anything nice to say, come sit by me" gossip mentality, and I don't have the time, patience, or manners to put up with that. Especially in a town the size of Cold Springs.

"You just do your best." The motto is less encouragement and more condescension, but I force myself to flash a polite, politician's-family smile.

Mom walks Chrissy back to the door, and though I shovel in a few bites of shrimp and rice while she's gone, I'm mostly thinking about what Chrissy said.

"Holy wowww," Mom drawls out as she sits back down. "That was unexpected."

"Unexpected? The look on your face told me you expected it!"

Mom shakes her head. "Just rumblings at tennis over the weekend."

"Rumblings? Mom, that was some crazy bullshit!" I explode. "Divorce, baby, property division? I mean, when did our family turn into a soap opera? What's Jed thinking?"

Mom chuckles at my outburst. "I don't know what Jed's up to. Don't really give two shits, if I'm honest." I whistle at Mom's uncommon use of a curse word, and she grins behind a hand. "He almost ran Bill into the ground. Did cut several years off his life, far as I'm concerned, and I wouldn't piddle on him if he was on fire." That's a top-tier insult from Mom. Actually, come to think of it . . . I don't think I've ever heard her say anything *that* violent. About anyone. "But if he's up to no good again, especially in the way Chrissy says, she deserves at least half for helping him become the success he is." Mom shakes her head sadly. "She's been wearing rose-colored glasses where that man's concerned for entirely too long. It's about time she sees the truth. I hope she makes him pay for every asshole-ish thing he's done."

"Dayum, go, Mom," I deadpan. "Right for the jugular without a single remorseless cell in your body."

"Wren!" Mom scolds. "You're awful."

But I grin. "It was a compliment."

It really was.

Chapter 3

WREN

"Ben, I've got this. You haven't read a divorce proceeding in forty years. I handled dozens of them during my internships." I'm trying to reassure Ben, but he's not having it. His head is shaking back and forth the whole time I'm speaking.

"It's only been thirty, and this is nothing like whatever amicable splits they had you work on in school. This is the big time, and might affect Cold Springs for decades. Maybe longer." He opens a file folder on his desk, flipping through the pages so quickly, there's no way he can focus on one before he goes to the next.

"Which will be the tenure when I'm here as city attorney and you're enjoying the view from your front porch," I remind him gently. "You've earned that and shouldn't have to worry about this. I won't mess it up. You can trust me."

Ben flops back in his tufted executive chair, the only nod to his stature at city hall. The old, well-oiled leather creaks mellowly from years of use as he steeples his hands beneath his chin and peers at me from behind his thick black-framed glasses. "Walk me through it."

He's handing me the rope to hang myself. It's the way he's taught me everything over the years, which is one of the reasons I chose to work with Ben instead of some fancy law firm where I'd be relegated to years of grunt work. Ben demands greatness from me, and I'm well versed in what he expects to hear.

"First, the contract for Township—it will be the driving force behind the city's position for the property distribution. Want me to quote it to you?" I ask with a twinkle in my eye.

A bushy brow appears above Ben's glasses as he silently and wryly tells me to get on with it. We wrote that contract together last year, and he knows that I could recite the whole thing verbatim, backward and forward, as well as explain every nuanced detail of it. Township might be one of Jed's construction company's babies, but that contract is one of mine, and it's tighter than a one-size-fits-all Spanx bodysuit.

"Second, meet with the lawyers. Jed's hasn't been in touch yet, but that call's gotta be coming. He's probably going for something dramatic, or thinks this whole thing will blow over and Chrissy will lie back down under his thumb." I roll my eyes at my uncle's habit of dismissing anyone of the female persuasion. "As for Chrissy's lawyer, the appointment is later today. Officer Milson's parked on the edge of town, keeping watch. He'll give me a heads-up when he spots the lawyer coming into town, but I'm ready. During the meeting, my purpose is to gain intel for Cold Springs, not share information that could affect the case. We want to know the plan for Township and what they're expecting from Jed for pushback because we all know there's going to be a helluva lot of that."

Ben nods in agreement, and I continue. "Third, represent Cold Springs and the city's interests. Township is important to us, much more than a single person. Regardless of their last name."

I add that last bit for Ben's benefit. Cold Springs and the name Ford go hand in hand, sometimes for good, sometimes for bad, but Uncle Jed should have no more sway with this situation than Aunt Chrissy, and I won't lean one way or the other for them just because we share a name or bloodline.

"And if the shit hits the fan?" Ben queries.

I smile confidently as I lean forward. "I deal with it."

"Good girl," he says with an answering smile of his own. He relaxes in his chair and takes a look around his office.

I wonder what he sees in the green-painted walls, bookcases, and framed certificates and pictures. It's nothing fancy, but when I first came here, I saw my future—and I've worked my ass off every day to make sure it happens. I'm looking forward to doing more of the same for the foreseeable future too.

When Ben's eyes settle on me again, his expression softens. "I'm gonna miss this place. But I want you to know . . . I don't have any doubts about you, Wren. I'm damn proud of the lawyer you've become, and pleased as a pig in muck that I had a thing to do with it."

I can feel the blush rising in my cheeks. I haven't been lacking in male role models most of my life. Starting with my dad, who selflessly served Cold Springs as mayor for many years. And when he made a mistake, he stepped down for the good of the city, owning up to his part and taking responsibility when it mattered.

My two brothers have dealt with shit in their own ways, both strong in their own right, either starting over fresh when it was warranted or doing the hard work from within the faulty system.

But despite their good characters, Ben has been a role model for me professionally since I interviewed him for a high school project when, impressed with my questions and fortitude, he encouraged me to go to law school. His support has been instrumental in my growth, so his compliment means a lot to me.

"Thanks, Ben. I wouldn't be here if it wasn't for you."

"Pshaw, girl. You'd be wherever you dang well pleased with that brain and backbone of yours, and we both know it. I'm glad you decided to stick around here instead of going to one of those fancy firms that was wooing you. Now, you go give this big-shot city lawyer a run for his money. I *guar-un-tee* he doesn't have a clue what he's getting himself into with you. Use that." He smirks, pointing a bony finger at me.

Ben's right. I'm underestimated a lot, usually based on my appearance. At barely five-foot nothing, with blonde hair, green eyes, and my mother's good looks, I'm often taken for being either young or stupid. I'm neither.

I'm an analyzer, looking at situations from every angle, which lets me be strategic. I'm mouthy and confident, seeing no need to put up with bullshit unless it's to serve my own purposes. And despite my good looks, my best asset is my brain.

It didn't take long for the know-nothings at law school to drop their attempts at nicknaming me "Legally Blonde." Most of them at least.

"You got it." My phone buzzes in my pocket, and I look at it, quickly reading the message. "Milson says a black Lexus LS just rolled into town. Betting that's Chrissy's guy." My eyes meet Ben's, confirming that he's going to let me handle this on my own.

He stands, pulling his suit jacket from the back of his chair as he pushes it in, and I have a moment of disappointment, thinking he's prepping to meet the incoming lawyer. "Well, if you need anything, I'll be sitting on my front porch, getting reacquainted with Mr. Samuel Adams till about nine. Otherwise, I'll see you tomorrow."

I exhale in relief. Ben is ready for retirement, but the intersection of that milestone with a huge negotiation makes it extra hard for him to let go. But he's doing so because he trusts me.

I follow Ben out the door to the lobby of city hall, telling Joanne that it's showtime with the lawyer. "I'll send him to the conference room when he gets here, Wren."

I retrace my steps, grabbing my laptop and the Township files—yes, the paper copies that have the original signatures on them—and sit down in our multipurpose conference room. It's nothing special, just an oversize room with a long, laminated wood-top table and blue-cushioned, stackable chairs that were probably new in 1995. The ceiling is one of those grid-patterned, acoustic-tiled, drop-down deals, and the walls were freshly painted white about three years ago. City residents can reserve the room for baby showers, book clubs, or Tupperware-sale parties when it's not being used for official city business.

I've chosen the space intentionally. I know my office isn't impressive, but it's telling . . . with pictures of my friends, family, and Finnegan, the not-so-stray, orange-striped cat that my entire street has adopted as a mascot. I don't need Chrissy's lawyer to know that much about me, though she can and probably has told him as much. But if not, I'm not going to volunteer the information.

Promptly at three thirty, there's a knock on the conference room door, and a moment later, Joanne pokes her head in. "Ms. Ford, your three thirty is here." God bless Joanne and her sense of propriety. I don't think she's called me anything except Wren a day in her life, but she knows this is a big meeting and goes for formality.

"Thanks," I say, knowing she understands that I mean for more than just playing greeter. I stand and walk around the table as she opens the door.

The man standing with her is . . . not what I expected.

Divorce lawyers are usually one of two types—smarmy guys in cheap suits or smarmy guys in expensive suits. I expected Chrissy to go with the latter, someone experienced and successful enough to have made a name for themselves with divorces of this caliber. And I figured he'd look something like Ben—older, glasses, potbelly.

Assuming was my first mistake.

Because the man standing before me is none of those things. He's tall, at least a foot taller than me, in his midthirties, with meticulously styled blond hair, a clean-shaven face even given the late hour in the day, and I'd bet a plate of my favorite nachos that he's cut as hell under his crisp three-piece gray suit. His appearance screams *money, city,* and *power.*

This guy just walked off the set of Suits, *didn't he?*

He smiles, his teeth worthy of a Crest commercial, and I realize I'm staring a bit. He holds his hand out, and I take it, shaking politely. "I'm Wren Ford, Cold Springs' city attorney. Nice to meet you."

The greeting I practiced, but instead of confident, it comes out sounding robotic because my brain is going *hummina-hummina-hummina*.

"Oliver Laurent, and it's lovely to meet you." His eyes never leave mine, but I sense he's checking me out and likes what he sees too.

Joanne clears her throat. "Coffee? Water? I'm happy to get either of you some."

"Oh, uh . . . none for me. Thank you. Mr. Laurent?"

"Oliver, please. And no thank you."

Joanne's eyes miss nothing as she closes the door, and I already know she'll be on the town grapevine in a minute, telling everyone about the hot, young lawyer and my ridiculous reaction to him.

But it's not interest.

It's surprise.

That's it. Or at least that's what I tell myself, hoping the repetition of that lie will make it sound a bit like the truth.

I invite him to sit and take my place at the head of the table. It's a calculated move, not sitting across from him as though we're on opposing teams, while also showing myself to be in charge. Subtle psychology in action.

"I appreciate you taking the time to go through this with me. I understand it must be a difficult family matter for you as well, Wren," Oliver says kindly.

"Thank you," I answer, immediately catching that though he asked me to use his first name, he's taken the liberty of using mine without invitation. I open my Township file. "Shall we get started?"

Serious. Professional. Think about Cold Springs.

"Sure." He agrees with a slight smirk, like he thinks I want to get to business for an entirely different reason—the effect he's having on me.

Narrowing my eyes, I scan the contract that I have memorized, and Oliver follows my lead, pulling a folder out of his leather briefcase. "This will be relatively straightforward. We certainly didn't expect this situation when drafting the contract, but it's ironclad as to what falls under city expectations and Ford Construction responsibilities regardless of the situations that arise during build-out."

"Did you write this?" he asks, tilting his head as he holds up the stack of papers. I think he intends it to sound complimentary, his own demonstration of psychology in action. But if he's impressed by my ability to write anything beyond a bare-boned, beginner-level contract, it's telling that he's already deemed me that stupid, and set the bar that low.

Rather than being charmed by his flattery, it's an instant buzzkill on any attractiveness I thought he possessed, and my initial instinct is to prove him wrong by showing exactly who he's dealing with, but everything with lawyers is a dance—of power, of information, of advantage. More than once in my life, being underestimated has served me well, so there's no need to avail him of his assumptions about me—yet.

Plus, I want to do some recon on who I'm dealing with too.

"What's your take?" I ask, not answering his question and instead, giving him an opening to share . . . or overshare.

Unfortunately, that's not the case.

Oliver is concise, intelligent, and accurate as we begin working our way through the contract, which he again compliments, making me wonder if I jumped to a conclusion too soon with him. I hate to think the chip on my shoulder might've led me to misjudge someone, considering it annoys me when it happens to me, so I'm being cautiously watchful of Oliver—open-minded but aware of his reason for being here.

As we read through the clause about dissolution of Ford Construction, he offers, "The hope is that we can settle things without a full dissolution. More likely, there will have to be a buyout deal reached so that one party retains sole proprietorship."

He's speaking in generic terms, but this is a chance for me to get a read on his plans.

"If Jed buys out Chrissy, he'll be short on funds, but Township is already fully financed, so its completion wouldn't be affected," I note, specifically mentioning who would do the buying out, and see the tiniest flinch in his blink. Interesting. "So that would work, meeting the construction company's responsibilities under the contract with the city."

Oliver nods, his face blank. "As for the rest of the property owned by Mr. and Mrs. Ford, there will need to be a complete reporting and analysis on value before division can be properly ascertained."

Right. Because this is more than just the Township development. Jed basically owns half of Cold Springs in one way or another, and his company employs a fair portion of tradespeople at various sites in the area.

But while we, as a town, have concern about who owns what, as the city attorney, I don't have a vested interest in the outcome of that. My focus is Township.

Admittedly, though, as a human, I'm curious as hell.

We're still working our way through the details of page eight when Joanne pokes her head in. "Wren, I'm heading home for the day, unless you need anything?"

After reassuring her that I'm perfectly capable of conducting a meeting without her to get drinks for us, she leaves begrudgingly. I suspect she's been doing walk-bys all afternoon to listen in at the door and giving half-hour updates to her husband, Ben, and Francine, the mayor.

"Is it after six already? I'm sorry for keeping you so late," Oliver says as he looks at his chunky silver watch. I can't see the face, but I wouldn't be surprised if it's a Rolex or something comparable. "Actually, I'm staying in town for a bit to handle this case. Is there somewhere you'd recommend for dinner?"

Yawn. He's not fooling anyone, least of all me. I know he's inviting me out. It's on the tip of my tongue to tell him to stick with room service when I remember Ben's advice. *He doesn't know what he's getting into. Use that.*

Maybe a beer or two would loosen Oliver's tongue about what he plans to do with the case. That might give us an opportunity to better prepare as a city for the change of ownership of Ford Construction and Township.

"There is. What's your opinion on hole-in-the-wall places with overly flirty waitresses, cooks who make food that'll clog every artery in your body, and pool tables you'll never win on because the owner doesn't take mercy on anyone? Not even her own family." I smile invitingly as I sell the best dinner spot in town.

This is perfect. Oliver should understand what's at stake with this case. Cold Springs is a special place, and we want Township completed regardless of who owns it.

Plus, neither Chrissy nor Jed would dare go to Puss N Boots.

"Am I dressed appropriately?" he asks, straightening his already-perfect tie.

I laugh. "You could go in wearing underwear and a T-shirt and nobody would bat an eye. A three-piece suit? You'll be the best-dressed diner Puss N Boots has ever seen."

"Perfect," he answers, "though I suppose I could strip down if that'd be better." He grins, his eyes even brighter than they have been while we worked. I guess he does have a sense of humor after all, not only the dry, serious legalese he's been using all afternoon.

"We'll see," I tease back. "I think the local *Magic Mike* competition isn't until Thursday. That's ladies' night with half-price margaritas. The winner gets a free dinner." I'm not kidding. There is a for-real dance competition this week, though Etta doesn't let anyone get on her bar to do their thing. It's strictly dancing around the tables to see who wins, which is usually the silliest dance, not the sexiest.

He follows me to Puss N Boots, parking his rental Lexus LS next to my Tesla. When he gets out and sees me looking at his car among the lot filled with beaters, jacked-up dirty trucks, and SUVs, he says, "Didn't intend to look so funereal, but it was this or some pregnant roller skate of a subcompact." He scrunches his shoulders and ducks his head down, grimacing. It's a charming way of saying he's too tall for the small-car option. I also notice he's removed his jacket and vest, as well as lost the tie. In his button-down, I can tell that I was right about his workout habits.

Inside, Charlene greets us. "Hey, Birdie! Who's the stiff?" Quieter, but not quiet enough, she adds, "And is he stiff all over?". Her eyes drop to his groin pointedly, as if we wouldn't know what she was talking about otherwise.

Rolling my eyes to the wood-beamed ceiling, I remind Oliver, "I told you about the overly flirty waitress? This is Charlene. She's not serious, unless you'd like her to be."

Oliver smiles, holding out his hand to Charlene, who shakes it like she might never let go. "Nice to meet you. I'm Oliver."

Charlene's eyes flick from Oliver to me and back again questioningly. I'm honestly surprised she hasn't already heard the scoop. "He's Chrissy's lawyer."

She waves a hand dismissively, nearly clipping me with her long nails. "Honey-baby, I *know* that. *Everybody* knows that. What I'm trying to figure out is if this is one of those meet-cutes they talk about in those spicy books I definitely do not read, no matter what Ms. Nash says."

Ms. Nash is the town librarian, who took over after Francine became the mayor, and she's sworn to secrecy about everyone's reading preferences, though she did let it slip that our resident green thumb, Fernanda, once checked out *How to Keep Your Plants Alive*. It'd been a scandal for weeks when Fernanda admitted that some of her prized cacti in the planters by her driveway were actually fake because while she's a pro with flowers, the less-needy plants were dying on her left and right. Turned out, she'd been smothering them . . . literally, with too much water.

"Strictly professional," I assure her, certain she doesn't believe me. Charlene loves love—the idea of it, the daily living with it, and, most of all, the act of making it. Despite her sexualized, flirtatious nature, she might be the most romantic person in Cold Springs.

She walks her fingers up Oliver's arm to his shoulder, stepping closer so that she's looking up at him. "Too bad for you, and all good for me," she declares. "Follow me, Ollie. Make sure you get a good look while I'm not watching too. Plenty more where this came from." She pats her hips and turns, strutting toward a table.

Oliver grins, looking at me in surprise, and I shrug. "Welcome to Cold Springs." When we sit down, Charlene hands us menus, but suggests, "Tay Tay made chili today. You definitely want that. Just let me know if you want it in a bowl, on a burger, on Fritos chips, on my tits. Your call, Ollie."

I don't need to look at the menu. I knew what I wanted as soon as Charlene said "chili." "Can I get chili nachos? And a water with lime?"

Oliver stacks his menu on top of mine. "Sounds good. I'll do the same, Charlene."

She nearly melts at Oliver saying her name, and I can't help but smile. I like Charlene. She's bold, honest, and makes no apologies for taking care of her needs and wants. But when she walks away to put our order in, Oliver turns back to me, and there's more than humor in his eyes. There's heat. "Nachos? Are you my soulmate?"

I find it hard to believe that the man sitting across from me has ever eaten nachos in his life. Messy finger foods don't seem like his type at all, and I wonder if I'm about to witness him eating nachos with a knife and fork. But to my surprise, he digs in a few minutes later, though he wipes his fingers on his paper napkin instead of licking them clean, but he does seem much more relaxed as we chat. And while he wasn't particularly interested in Charlene's aggressive moves, he's definitely dropping all pretense of professionalism between us for this dinner, making it feel more like a first date than a work deal.

"What's Cold Springs like? Other than the whole family thing, what makes Wren Ford want to live here?" he asks.

Oh, he's done his homework on me alright. And now it's my turn to do a little on him.

Chapter 4

Jesse

"Nah, I'm not playing tonight," I tell the guy asking if I want to call next on the table he's owning. Almost literally, he's at five games in a row, and even Etta's given him a glance to see if she wants to take on a challenger. "Eating and heading home after a long day."

"Sure thing, man. Maybe next time." He's off to play with someone else before I shove another fry doused in Tayvious's famous fancy ketchup into my mouth.

I need the simple comfort of the fry, which is God's perfect food as far as I'm concerned. Forrest Gump might've waxed poetic about shrimp, but he should've focused on potatoes—chips, fries, baked, mashed, soup, salad, and more. Today physically *sucked*. My crew is busting ass to meet deadlines, and the overtime is taking its toll on us all. Tonight, my plan is to eat, shower, and sleep. In that order, as quickly as possible before my five thirty alarm goes off.

I'm basically face down in my plate of steak and fries, trying to hurry because my bed has been calling my name since quitting time.

"Did I hear you turn down a game? That's not like you." I lift my eyes to see Hazel looking at me curiously. "If nothing else, the money's always sweet."

Hazel and I have played pool since Etta taught us how as kids, and we've both made more than our fair share betting on games. We don't hide our skills—no sharking and conning people—but if they want to take us on, knowing what they're getting into, far be it from me to refuse their cash. Except tonight.

"Not feeling it," I grunt.

She hums thoughtfully, and I brace myself for whatever she's gonna say. Hazel isn't exactly gentle with her words, especially with me. She prefers to punch me in the face with whatever she wants to express. "Have anything to do with a certain someone sitting over there with a guy who's not you?"

That gets my attention. "Huh?"

When I drag my head up and meet Hazel's eyes, she nods to the right. I look that way, and my heart skips a beat in my chest. "What the fuck?"

It's not a rhetorical question, I really want to know what's going on because Wren Ford is sitting at a table with some asshole. I don't need to meet him, don't need a "get to know you" conversation or anything else to know he's an asshole.

One, he's having dinner with Wren. Automatic asshole.

Two, he looks like the type of douchebag who gets his eyebrows waxed, has a multistep skin-care regimen, and has never worked a day of hard labor in his life. Extra asshole-y for sure.

Hazel props her drink tray on the table, leaning over it, to share, "Charlene said his name's Oliver, he's Chrissy's lawyer, and Wren said things are strictly professional. Buuuut . . ."

She trails off, and I look over again. They're both eating nachos, and Wren licks her finger, her red-painted nail disappearing into her mouth for a moment. I have a flashback of her doing the same thing, but in a much different situation, and take a deep inhale to steady myself when I see this Oliver asshole zeroing in on Wren's mouth too.

Strictly professional, my ass.

"Hazel, getchur ass up here for this Fat Pussy!" Tayvious yells from the window to the kitchen. He's serious about his food and won't let one of his infamous burgers die in the window because Hazel or Charlene is too busy chitchatting to deliver it. "Or else Harold can get it himself, and you know he won't tip for shit if he has to get off his ass."

"Keep your panties on, Tay Tay. I'm coming as fast as I can," Hazel shouts back. She taps her tray to the table, letting me know her work with me is done, and strides off, weaving her way through the tables and people with expert ease, though she warns, "Coming through."

A lady bumps into Hazel, and rather than apologizing, Hazel glares at her until the customer apologizes.

Customer service isn't exactly first priority around here, but nobody seems to care much.

My attention returns to Wren, and I watch closely.

What the fuck is she doing here? With another man?

Seriously? Is this some sort of ploy to get my attention? Because if so, it damn well worked.

But in the next second, I know the truth. It has nothing to do with me. That woman has had me in knots for nearly a year, easily ignoring me even when we're in the same room, and I'm a complete nonissue to her.

Like she's forgotten the way I could make her body sing. Like I don't know what she feels like wrapped around my cock. Like she didn't mark me up with those red nails she always has.

I don't make a conscious decision to get up, but suddenly, I'm striding across the room straight toward Wren's table. People hop out of my way, creating a clear path, until I'm looming at the table's edge. The Asshole glances up and mistakes me for a waiter despite my dirty T-shirt and rough appearance. "Hey, man, I could use some more water. Thanks."

I scoff as he looks at Wren and asks, "Would you like anything?"

I drop down to my elbows on the table, stealing a chip from Wren's plate. "Yeah, Birdie. You need anything?" Eye to eye with her, I crunch on the chip that, despite being covered in Tayvious's delicious chili and homemade queso, tastes like sawdust.

"He's not a waiter, Oliver. This is Jesse . . . uh, my . . . brother's wife's brother. Jesse, this is Oliver." She's glaring at me, her eyes sparkling with anger her congenial tone doesn't express.

She meant to say I'm the man who's made her come so hard she nearly passed out. Okay, I don't say that aloud, but I think it as I look deep into Wren's green eyes, withstanding every bit of her fire. Hell, enjoying it. It's damn sure better than the indifference she's been giving me.

"Brother's wife's . . . what?" Oliver repeats, laughing at his own confusion.

"It's not that complicated. My sister, her brother . . . married." I clasp my hands to show their connection, and not at all because I desperately want to touch Wren. Nope, that's not it at all. "No worries about the waiter thing, though. This one"—I lift my chin toward Wren—"thought I was a caterer the first time we met."

Flashing a grin her way, I know Wren is remembering too. It was the day of her brother's wedding, and Wren was making sure everything was perfect for Winston and Avery. I was setting out cupcakes under the big tent in the back garden of the Ford home, and she came barreling in with a mental checklist and an iron will, determined to complete it to perfection in record time. She'd bossed me around a bit, and when I suggested she take a breath, it'd gone over like a fart in church. She'd reared up, popping her hands on her hips and reading me the riot act. I'd bravely challenged her, saying that I knew exactly who she was, but did she know who I was . . . and we'd become friends. It was a while later that we became *friendly*.

And then . . . nothing.

Everything went well for a while, both of us on the same page about what we did and didn't want, and then I texted her and she claimed she was busy. A couple more times and I found myself basically ghosted. Even in a town the size of Cold Springs, she avoided me. When Hazel and Wyatt invited everyone over, I'd hoped to rekindle things and had watched her like a tiger, ready to pounce at the slightest opportunity, noting every detail that had changed in the months since we'd spoken, but Wren was civil, polite, and somehow totally unaffected by the fact that I'd been inside her mere months ago.

I can take a hint. I know who and what she is, and I'm all too aware that she's about ten notches out of my league. She slummed it with me for a bit, but moved on. And judging by Oliver, she's moving up.

But just because I understand doesn't mean I have to like it. She might be over us, but I'm not, and the months since I've had her beneath me feel like years.

"You're never going to let that go, are you?" Wren rolls her eyes about the tease she's heard before, and then she tells Oliver, "He'll probably remind everyone about that at my funeral, even though I apologized profusely. It was a stressful day, and you were wearing an apron and holding a tray of cupcakes." It's the same go-round we always have. At this point, I'm just giving her shit. She knows I don't hold a grudge for her entirely logical conclusion that day.

"Wh-what?" Oliver sputters, confused by the history in our conversation. History he's not privy to.

"It was Winston's wedding. My mom's a baker. I was helping her out." Short and to the point is all he deserves.

"Winston?"

Wren answers, "My brother." At the same time, I register that he doesn't know her family. I'd expect him to know the Ford family tree if he's Chrissy's lawyer, but maybe it hasn't come up. "Not the one married to his sister, but the other one."

"Right, the three Ford kids—Wyatt, Winston, and you," Oliver answers as if he's quoting a spreadsheet. "Children of Bill and Pamela Ford, nephews and niece of Jed and Chrissy."

So he does know. Clearly the asshole just wanted Wren to explain. I don't like the way he's trying to play her like a puppet on strings. It smacks of one of those tricks insecure guys play to make themselves seem two steps ahead.

But I'm 100 percent sure that Wren is ahead of him in every way under the fucking sun, and doesn't need any tricks to prove it. She's smarter than one of those chess-playing computers.

Wren doesn't move, but I can sense the sudden tension in her. She didn't like what this guy said any more than I did. When she doesn't immediately fire back, I draw Oliver's attention, giving her time to calculate her next move. Feigning that I'm impressed, I smile ferally at Oliver. "A-plus for the Boy Scout. Chrissy prepped you well. Did she give you CliffsNotes on everyone in town and tell you to study up for the big visit?"

Oliver's eyes narrow as he looks at me shrewdly. He didn't like me making him sound like Chrissy's lapdog. Score one for me, but that ties it up after his "who's Winston" deal.

Oliver's voice is steady, but tight, as he informs me, "My client and case are no concern of yours."

Is he for real? Jed and Chrissy's divorce is the talk of the town. There's even an unofficial newsletter with updates and theories. Whoever's running it has chosen to stay anonymous, but given the tone of the reports, I'm reasonably certain Tayvious is the author behind the keyboard because the latest discussion is about Jed's teeny weenie not being enough to impregnate a rabbit, much less a woman.

But the overall consensus around town is that we all hate Jed, so though we don't like Chrissy, we're mostly on her side and hope she takes Jed to the cleaners. I'm not going to share that with this guy, though.

I grunt, not agreeing or disagreeing, as I casually steal another nacho from Wren's plate, knowing that Oliver's analyzing my familiarity with her. If I could, I'd claim her in a much more obvious way—throw my arm around her, take her hand, or kiss her. But I don't have the right, as much as I wish I did. Crunching loudly in the growing silence, I keep my attention on Wren, effectively ignoring Oliver as though he doesn't matter and is the interloper into our conversation instead of the other way around.

"Yeah, but we look out for each other around here, don't we?" I ask Wren.

"Maybe we should continue this tomorrow, Wren?" Oliver offers, dropping his napkin to the table in irritation.

She plasters on the fake smile I hate. "Of course. I'm heading out too." She pulls two twenties from her purse and lays them beside her half-eaten plate of nachos.

I start to follow her toward the door, but Wren stops, putting her hand out, and I walk right into it. "What are you doing?" she demands.

"Walking you to your car," I answer.

She shakes her head. "No, thanks. I'm okay."

I inhale sharply, my chest pressing against her palm, and even that small contact makes my heart pound. I can't let her leave with this guy, but I know that look in Wren's eyes. If I push her, she won't just push back. No, she'll annihilate me.

"Wren," I try again, covering her hand with mine to hold it to my chest a little longer. Surely she can feel what she does to me. That has to count for something, right?

"Jesse," she warns.

She turns, heading for the door where Oliver is waiting for her. He holds the door open, making a big show of looking at her ass as she walks through. Damn well aware that it'll piss me off, he meets my eyes with a victorious smirk that I want to swipe off his face with my fist.

Motherfucking asshole.

I stand there until the door closes and Hazel comes up beside me. "Smooth moves, dipshit."

I glare at Hazel and head for the door myself. All I wanted was a quick dinner, and now my brain's completely fucked up and my dick's rock-hard. I'm never gonna get to sleep.

Chapter 5

WREN

Stomping up to the door of the little cottage, I almost trip over the crack in the driveway that I've stepped over dozens of times. Probably should've put on something other than UGGs with my pajamas, but it's too late for that now.

I yank open the screen door and sharply bang on the door three times. Arms crossed and foot tapping, the anger I've been working up for the last hour at home is still raging hot and ready to unleash on the person who screwed over my meeting.

The door opens, and I blink in the light that comes blaring out, startling me momentarily.

"Hey, Birdie, what's up?" Jesse drawls out, using his nickname for me. He's completely unbothered by my unexpected appearance, casually leaning against the door with one arm lifted over his head and a stupid smile on his stupid face.

"What's. Up?" I repeat. "Are you serious right now, Jesse Sullivan? You interrupt my work meeting, where I was *trying* to finagle some information out of Oliver, and then you're all 'what's up?' like you didn't fuck me over?"

His grin falters for a second but then returns with cocky arrogance. "Fuck you over? Is that what you're here for?"

The question is loaded with dirty promises I know he can keep. Once upon a time, I would've said yes. Hell, I would've shrieked it as I was halfway down the hall to his bedroom, dropping clothes along the way like bread crumbs so he could find his way right to me.

That was then, and this is now. That hasn't been our arrangement in a long time, and it's definitely not what I'm here for tonight.

"No, and don't try to distract me with all . . ." I wave my hand around at him in general, suddenly realizing that while I'm in a semirespectable shorts and T-shirt pajama set, Jesse is half-naked, wearing only gray athletic shorts and a sheen of sweat across his bare, muscular chest.

Jesse shifts, his stance matching mine with his feet spread wide, arms crossed over his chest, and a scowl on his face. "All what?"

I blurt, "Were you working out?"

That is *not* what I meant to say. But now that I've asked, I'm curious if he was pumping iron or pumping something else. Memories assail me of that image, and I'm reminded that I'm not wearing a bra beneath my shirt when it brushes over my hard nipples.

Jesse snorts, turning around and walking toward his kitchen. "Yeah, should've been in bed hours ago, but had some shit to work out. Throwing around some weight seemed preferable to throwing fists."

I hear the fridge open and close, and debate whether I should go inside. Are we at the point where I need an invitation now, like a vampire? Or can I barge in uninvited like a regular visitor? I don't know.

While I'm still deciding, Jesse reappears, slamming back a bottle of water. I watch as his throat works with each swallow and a single drip runs down his chin to his chest, making a trail I'd like to trace with my tongue. He finishes the bottle in one go and sighs as he wipes his mouth with the back of his hand.

"You coming in or not?" he asks.

This is a bad idea. I shouldn't have come. I'm playing with fire here. The only problem is, where Jesse's concerned, I might as well be an arsonist. I think I'd happily set my world ablaze for him, burn myself to ashes, and while I'd be a shadow of my former self, he'd simply move on like nothing happened. It's who he is—casual, fun, carefree. At least about his women, of which I'm just one of many.

"I . . . don't . . . know . . . ," I stammer. I glance down to my boots, the toes right at the threshold of the door.

Jesse moves closer, and I look up to find him scanning me from toes to head, not paying nearly as much attention to my boots as I was. No, his eyes are locked on my legs, hips, boobs, and then his eyes meet mine. He licks his lips, and for a split second, I think he's going to kiss me. But instead, he inhales deeply. I wonder if he can smell me from there. He used to love burying his face in my hair—"breathing me in," he called it.

"Well, if you're gonna yell at me some more, could you do it in here so Mrs. Capshaw doesn't complain to the police? I can't afford another 'disturbing the peace' call." As he says it, he drops a bottle onto the coffee table. "Peace offering."

It's a small bottle of my favorite Naked Mighty Mango juice, set right on the edge of the table like it's going to lure me inside. "Why do you have that?" I demand. "I know you don't drink them. Or do you think every woman you bring here will want some postcoital fruity drink? I'm surprised you don't offer them a beer or water and be done with it."

I never decided, but I've entered his home, scooping the bottle from the table and holding it out accusingly like it's proof of his sleeping with any woman who'll follow him home. And I know there are dozens. He can't help it when he looks like a work-hardened sex god and can actually back it up by being amazing in bed.

Jesse holds up his hands, protecting himself from my rage that I refuse to call jealousy. Jesse can do anything or anyone he wants. It's none of my business. And if you believe that, I've got some oceanfront property to sell you. It's right in the middle of Arizona.

"Jesus, Wren. What the hell?" Jesse asks, sounding genuinely surprised and maybe a little hurt at my uncharacteristic outburst. "I keep them because you like them."

Shocked, my mouth drops open and I stare at him, waiting for the punch line where he says *gotcha* or some shit like that, because there is no way he has this because I drink them. I haven't been here in months.

He runs his fingers through his hair and explains, "I dunno, I guess I got used to getting them with my groceries, so I just . . . never stopped. If they get close to expiring, I give 'em to the food pantry and restock the fridge."

He's trying really hard to make that sound like no big deal, but it is. It's a Big Deal with capital letters and little glittery sparkles. Nobody does stuff like that for me. Not even my friends and family. Not because they're not awesome people, but because I'm the one who doesn't need to be taken care of. I'm too independent and strong, preferring to handle things on my own to prove myself.

Needing to see with my own eyes, I push past him to the kitchen and pull open the fridge door. Right there on the top shelf are five more of my favorite juices.

I really thought he was fucking with me, because there's no way he's done that this long. But the proof is staring me in the face.

Jesse's followed me, his presence at my back feeling like a physical touch. I'm a shorter woman, and sometimes tall guys can be intimidating, especially when they loom over me. But Jesse's presence has always felt protective, not dangerous. Or at least not dangerous to me physically.

Emotionally is another story altogether.

"These are expensive, Jesse," I say quietly. "You didn't have to do that."

Though I can't see it, I can feel the air disturbance when he shrugs. "I can afford it. And the food-pantry people appreciate them."

I'm quiet for a moment, relishing the feel of him behind me. So close, but so far away.

I could lean back. It'd be so easy. I know he'd catch me. He'd pick me up and take me down the hall, fuck me hard until I'm a mess of bliss and cum. And then I'd leave, and we'd go back to not talking because nothing's changed.

I still want what he doesn't have to give. And if I go back, I'll only be hurt again. It's taken a while to get my guards back up, and I can't let a moment of weakness shatter them. Even if it would feel so good.

"What was that tonight?" I finally ask, spinning in place. Jesse puts one hand on the counter and one on the refrigerator door, effectively trapping me.

It's what I came here to yell about, but now, I'm more curious than angry. Jesse has barely talked to me for ages and then tonight, he's barging in like some overly protective big brother.

But that's not it and I know it.

He interrupted like a jealous boyfriend. But he's not my boyfriend. Hell, he's not even a boy. Jesse's all man. From the top of his head, which is covered with dark hair that gets too long and flops down in his eyes, to his bare feet, and everywhere in between.

"I was checking on you," he answers, but he can't look me in the eye as he lies. He's trying to downplay the scene tonight, but it wasn't some casual check-in with a friend you happened to see out.

I shake my head. "You don't have to do that. I'm fine."

Arguably, I might need to see a doctor about my body's temperature regulation because while my ass is colder than a winter's morning from the open refrigerator blasting over it, my body is burning up. That might have something to do with how close Jesse is to me, though. He's always a furnace—a warm, cozy one I want to curl up beside.

"I do when you're having dinner with douchey guys right in the middle of Puss N Boots," he growls, taking a step closer. I duck under his arm to escape, and he turns to keep me in his sight. "Wren—"

I hold up a finger and shake my head vehemently. "No, you're making a business dinner sound like I was on a date. Or basically screwing the guy on the table." I choose to ignore the way his breathing has increased, his chest rising and falling as though he's barely holding himself back from the mere suggestion of me with another man. "I needed that dinner to go well. This case is a big deal for me and for Cold Springs. I hoped to get Oliver to relax and share some intel on what Chrissy's strategy is. But instead, now he's going to be on alert and tight-lipped. Thanks for that," I finish sarcastically.

As I've spoken, my anger has returned full force, and I'm digging my nail into his chest, stepping him backward toward the living room. I know he's letting me push him, but that he does is important. He doesn't fight back when he easily could, but rather, lets me have my moment, even though he flinched when I said Oliver's name.

He lifts his hand, pressing my nail into his chest a little harder. I watch goosebumps break out over his bare chest as he takes a shuddering breath. Pinning me in place with his dark eyes, he says lowly, "Fuck, I've missed you marking me up with these nails of yours."

I wasn't expecting that response, and it takes me a moment to process what he said. But when I do, I jerk my hand out of his grip. "I'm not here for an angry fuck, Jesse. I'm actually mad."

A blankness washes over him, turning his face to stone and his voice to a flat monotone. "I know. I'm sorry. I didn't realize you were working an angle with that guy." He shrugs and with zero remorse adds, "Even if I had, I probably would've interfered because of the way he was looking at you . . . like he wanted a *whole* lot more than a business chat." His gaze dips down over my body, looking like he wants more too.

"He wasn't looking at me any sort of way," I argue. Jesse raises a brow, silently disagreeing. "Look, we're gonna pretend tonight never happened. You can go back to ignoring me and I'll go back to focusing on my work." I clod across the floor in my boots toward the door before he can distract me any further. "I need to focus on my work."

"Heard," Jesse clips out.

I turn back one last time, knowing that I'll be tormented by the image of Jesse tonight the same way I was all those months ago. The way his face changes as every emotion flicks across it, his muscled chest that I left marred with nail marks more than a few times, his arms that are strong enough to entirely lift me, and his rock-hard cock that's not remotely disguised by his shorts.

But also, I'll be thinking of Jesse trying to protect me from Oliver, even if I didn't need it. And I'll remember the months of Naked Mighty Mango juice he's bought on the off chance that I came over.

I walk out the door into the cool night, telling myself that this is what I want. What I need. What I deserve.

Go home, get a good night's sleep, and get to work early so you're ready for the next round with Oliver.

Even as I tell myself that, I have to force my feet to keep moving toward my car and not walk me right back into Jesse's house and into his arms. Even if only for tonight.

Chapter 6

Jesse

"Move your ass, Roscoe. We're getting this shit done today or you can fuck off tomorrow."

I mean it to be a threat, but he pauses, leaning on a stack of lumber propped in what will be the second-story bedroom of this house. "So what I'm hearing is that if I take it easy this afternoon, I'll get tomorrow off?" He scratches his belly lazily. "I'm not seeing a downside here."

"How about when your gut is grumbling and you ain't got a dollar to get a gas station burrito that gives you the runs for a solid twenty-four hours?" I suggest before slamming my hammer toward a nail, finding my target expertly. It drives flush with the wood on a single strike, like it'd been fired out of a nail gun.

"Well shiiiit, no need to get that serious about it. I don't want that out there in the universe. Take it back." Roscoe points a thick, dirty finger at me, and I roll my eyes, keeping my pace.

When I don't hear an answering hammer behind me, I look over my shoulder. Roscoe's not budging, so with a sigh, I say to the lumber above me, "Dear Universe, I take it back. Don't give Roscoe the runs, 'kay?" I look at him, asking if that's enough with a glare, and after he dips his chin, he gets to it, though he mumbles something about my piss-poor attitude today.

If only he knew that I'm Mary Fucking Sunshine on the outside compared to the rager I've got slamming around on my insides.

Why did I tell her about those juices? It's stupid to still be buying them because she's right, they're expensive shit and taste nasty. What did she mean about me ignoring her? I'm basically stalking her at this point.

We work for hours, doing the same shit as yesterday and the same as it'll be tomorrow. That's how it is when you're building cookie-cutter homes all in a row. New house, same as the last house. But rather than feeling bored, I love my job.

I get to be outside, work with my hands, never tied to a desk or wearing a necktie noose. For all the shit we give each other, I like the guys on the job site, and as cliché as it may be, I like the idea of something I made becoming someone's home.

Except today, it's giving me too much time to think, and that's dangerous.

From my current perch atop a ceiling joist, I nail in the next rafter tie before walking along the thin length of wood without a wobble to do the same thing again. We're getting the framing done on this roof today so we can start framing next door tomorrow morning.

I scan down the row of homes, all in various stages of completion. The ones closest to the front are nearly finished, only missing some internal touches. The ones farther back are still dirt lots with brightly colored flags marking lot borders and the underground mains for water and power. But the houses aren't all I see.

There's a shiny black car that I don't recognize driving in from the front of the subdivision.

Knowing he's here for an electrical install precheck, I call down into the depths of the house I'm working on. "Hey, Mike, your girlfriend got a new car?" I laughingly tease because a Lexus like that has got to be an old-lady car. But I'm watching the car as it draws closer. When it gets to the area we're working on, it stops in the middle of the road, blocked by various work trucks, concrete deliveries, and a grouping of trailers.

The doors open, and out step Oliver and Wren. They look around, perplexed at the blockade.

Wren is wearing a black pencil skirt, a short-sleeve pale-blue blouse, and heels. Her blonde hair hangs in perfect curls down her back, and she looks good enough to spread butter on and gobble up like a biscuit.

The Asshole is wearing a suit-and-tie combo that I don't give a shit about.

What the hell are they doing here?

I'm no dummy. I know exactly what my most attractive parts are, and why Wren chose to slum with a man like me. To highlight myself, I prop a boot on the joist across from me; spreading my thighs out, I rest an elbow on my knee and flex my biceps a bit before whistling sharply, knowing Wren will look around for the source of the noise. She shades her eyes, scanning the surrounding homes at first-floor level, and then finally looking up higher. I know the instant she finds me because I see her chest rise when she sucks in a breath.

I don't bother to hide my smirk as I shout down, "What the hell are you doing here?"

Wren doesn't hesitate to be loud either. "We need to talk."

We . . . as in me and her?

We . . . as in her and Oliver?

We . . . as in all three of us?

There's only one of those options I'm willing to entertain. But Wren lifts one brow, reminding me of our conversation last night. She needs this case for some reason.

I don't get what the big deal is. It's a divorce, something that happens to more than 50 percent of marriages. Divide the money, split the company on paper, and Jed can buy Chrissy out, and that'll be that. Done deal. Chrissy's only in it for the money anyway. Always has been, always will be. And Jed can go on being the self-righteous narcissist no one likes, the way he's always been, with a new little mini-me to fuck up.

But I'll do this for Wren. Shit, I'd do damn near anything for her. I wipe my forehead with a sigh. "I'm coming down. Gimme a second."

I swing my legs a couple of times for momentum and hop down to the second-story plywood subfloor with a thud. Plodding down the stairs, I stop halfway to call back up, "Roscoe, finish up those rafter ties, will ya?"

"Aye, aye, boss," he answers crisply, for once not backtalking or giving me a hard time. I never told anyone who I was seeing when Wren and I were doing what we were doing, but everyone knew when it stopped because I was a bastard—more than usual— for a long while after that. Hell, I probably still am. A woman like Wren will do that to a guy—fuck your brain up for the rest of your life.

Downstairs, I find Wren and Oliver standing in what will be the living room of this house. They look ridiculous in office attire, surrounded by wood framing and concrete. "Out," I bark as I point toward the doorframe they came through.

"What?" Wren mutters in shock.

Oliver clenches his jaw tight, his eyes narrowed as he glares at me. "We need to go over a few things. Now."

Oh, he wants to be the boss? That might work in his fancy city office, but not here. "We can do that . . . outside." I push past him, bumping his shoulder and leaving a smudge of sawdust on his pristine suit. I have zero regrets.

I keep walking, out to my truck by the curb, trusting that Wren and Oliver are behind me. If they came all the way out here to talk, they'll follow me wherever I go. I lean back on the lowered tailgate, steeling my nerves.

For Wren, I tell myself.

Oliver strides up like this is some scripted performance of how to be intimidating. Too bad for him, it doesn't work in the slightest on me. "This property is partially owned by my client, and we've come out here to discuss it. I will not stand for you barking orders and bullying us around."

He lifts his chin an inch so he can look down his nose at me.

Sometimes, the power move is to rise to the occasion and meet your opponent face-to-face. Other times, it's to seem completely unbothered by someone's loud barking and bleating about. That's the route I take here.

"It's Jed and Chrissy Ford's property. And you work for them, same as me. But it's my job site, and I'm responsible for every person on it, including ones who show up in open-toed, thin-soled shoes"—I glance down at Wren's peep-toe heels—"and dumbasses who don't have the common sense God should have given them about safety." I look back at Oliver, baiting him to blow up and show his ass.

For an uptight suit-and-tie type, he seems to be hiding a lot of entitled brat anger right below the surface. If this case is as important as Wren says it is, she needs to know what she's up against.

"You're right. Sorry, Jesse," she says, interrupting the stare fest between Oliver and me.

I drag my eyes to Wren. I'd rather look at her anyway. She seems worried, and I hope I haven't fucked up her meeting again, because I'm actually trying to help this time. It might not be information on strategy, but knowing who's behind the strategy is important too.

"Apology accepted. Now, what's up?"

Wren glances at Oliver as though checking if he wants to explain. When he stays silent, she tells me, "We've been going through the Ford Construction Company contract for Township this morning. And Oliver asked to see the development to know what he's negotiating for beyond the contract, because I've been telling him about how important this development is for Cold Springs."

He wanted to drive Wren out here alone in his rental car is what he wanted. But fine, I can go along with this . . .

"Township is based on a suburban neighborhood design, mixed with brownstone-type connections. Each pair of homes shares a wall down the middle"—I point to the central wall of the one we left a moment ago—"but have their own yards, driveways, and garages. So they're not your typical duplex. They're small starter homes meant to be affordable for the people of Cold Springs. We're on schedule to finish framing the row of homes on this side of the street this week, starting the other side next week. Finishers are already working over there." I point to the street behind us that's nearing completion. "And we'll repeat, repeat, repeat till the end of the neighborhood." I gesture toward the rest of the streets that have prepped lots ready for construction to begin.

I look at them both to see if that's all they want to hear. Wren could've told Oliver that. Hell, she probably did.

Oliver nods as he looks around. If he could kick the tires on the subdivision like a used car, I think he would, because he's analyzing everything like he's going to buy a house here himself and is picking out the perfect lot to see the sunrise over his daily cappuccino.

"What's the ETA on finishing the whole thing so the investment begins returning a profit?" Oliver asks.

"Six months to full load out. Once we're a few streets down, the ones up front can be sold, though. You'd have to ask Jed for the details on that," I answer with no more detail than he could've gotten from the sales sign over by the turnoff.

His look is shrewd as he locks onto me again and hums in acknowledgment of what I said. "I think I've got what I came for. Shall we?" He touches Wren's back and holds his other arm out in invitation, ready to escort her to his Lexus for the drive to city hall. "Look out for the mud there," he tells her, pointing at the ground in front of her. "Wouldn't want you to get dirty when you're dressed impeccably."

There's barely any veil to his words. He's flat-out talking about me. I'm the dirty mud that'll soil her. Hell, I already have. And I don't need him to explain to me that he's more Wren's type—smart, wealthy, clean.

She smiles appreciatively and takes Asshole's elbow before giving me a professional look and a sweet-as-ice-cream smile. "Thanks, Jesse."

Wren has to know that she's driving me fucking crazy with this shit. I told her that this Oliver dude is after more than a contract and a divorce settlement. Or maybe she doesn't realize. Or believe me.

"Hey," I say, and she stops, looking back at me.

I lean around her, scowling at Oliver, and Wren has the decency— or maybe the fear of what I'm about to say—to tell him, "I'll be right there. Just give me one second, 'kay?"

Once he's climbing in the car and can't hear me, I speak quietly to Wren. "Hang out for a little bit and I'll take you home. Or the office, or whatever. Just don't go with him."

She looks up at me, and there's something in her eyes that looks like pain, but I don't know why. I'm not trying to hurt her. I'm trying to spend time with her, same as Oliver is.

"I can't," she finally answers. "I've got to get back, and maybe Oliver will share some thoughts after this little visit." She looks toward the car hopefully.

I grunt in annoyance and sarcastically inform her, "I'm sure he's got quite a few of those. Not a damn one having to do with Township." She frowns at me in disappointment. Fuck, this asshole has her on a hook. "Yeah, sure. I get it," I say as I step away, putting inches between us that feel like miles. "Have fun."

She hesitates for a split second but then turns and walks to Oliver's car. At least she opens the door for herself because him doing it for her would seem waaaay too much like a date, and I'm on the edge already. As the door slams and the Lexus pulls away, I try to stop myself from imagining what they're talking about . . .

That Jesse guy's a real jerk, huh?

Jesse, the sweaty, stupid building contractor.

Do you actually have a past with a guy like that?

He's probably staring at her thigh, maybe putting his hand there to comfort her from the upsetting interaction. And then slowly, slowly working her skirt a little higher so he can touch her skin.

Motherfucker.

I spin on a worn boot heel, needing to get back to work. I need a sledgehammer or a crowbar or something. But what I find is the whole crew standing stock-still watching the entire exchange among Wren, Oliver, and me.

"If you ain't got enough shit to do, I can give you some more," I snipe. Most of the guys hop to it, returning to their work so as not to have more.

Except Alan. He holds back and tells me, "There's a construction pile over by the dumpster that needs to be tossed."

I sigh, knowing I need to get back up on the joists to finish the rafters. But I nod in appreciation and head toward the dumpster. If there's a pile of trash to be dumped, someone has the usually exhausting task of tossing it all into the dumpster, which is no easy or quick job. Right now, throwing shit around sounds like exactly what I need.

I grab the first chunk of pallet wood and wind up, swinging it out and up into the hollow dumpster, where it settles with a clang. "Me too, dumpster. I'm just as empty as you are."

Only issue is, by quitting time, while I've made a good dent in the trash load and the dumpster is well beyond half-full, I still feel empty as hell.

Chapter 7

WREN

Three full days of silence is at least one too many. I haven't heard any-thing from Oliver about how he and Chrissy plan to proceed. And even though I'm sure Jed has met with his lawyer, they haven't contacted Ben or me at all. Oliver's hands-on approach is unusual, but Jed's team's complete hands-off approach is worrying too.

There's an informational loop here, and I need to be a part of it.

And equally bothersome, though I'd never admit it, is that I haven't heard a word from Jesse since I left his job site. Not even a *you get home okay?* text, and he always sent me those.

That's bare minimum, Wren. Not some stellar gesture of care.

That might be true, but I've never had a relationship with anyone who did things like that—caring texts, stocking my juice, making me come until I was a puddle of wiggly Jell-O. Except Jesse.

Too bad that's all it was.

The knock on my door pulls me from my memories and I call out, "Come in."

Oliver opens the door, and I smile happily, pleased to see him at first. But my lips falter when he waves his arm for Aunt Chrissy to come in with him.

This doesn't look good.

She's dressed in all black—heels, slacks, blouse, and sunglasses . . . inside. Anyone who didn't know the situation would think she's mourning her dead husband, not divorcing her lying, cheating, mistress-impregnating one. Though maybe she's grieving the man she thought Uncle Jed was?

Surely he didn't have her that fooled? Everyone knows who Jed Ford really is. That I share at least some DNA with the man is a badge of shame for me.

I stand to greet them, noting that since my office is already a small space, with the three of us, it's downright claustrophobic.

"Hello, Oliver, Aunt Chrissy. Did we have a meeting this morning?" I know the answer—we definitely don't, and my hackles are already up because this smacks of a surprise attack. I'm just not sure why. I don't have a dog in the fight between Chrissy and Jed, other than to represent the city's interest.

"No—" Oliver frowns, his eyes flicking to Aunt Chrissy as if to blame her for this interruption. "But we were hoping for a little of your time?"

Given that they're already helping themselves to the chairs in front of my desk, they don't care about my answer.

Oliver's sitting tall and still, like a military-esque statue. He's definitely tenser than usual.

"Of course." I glance at my morning coffee that's long since gone cold, wishing I'd chosen something other than my favorite coffee cup, a gift from Hazel, that reads I'M HOT, STICKY, AND SWEET with a cat dancing on a stripper pole. "What can I help with?"

"I'm going to take that no good, cheating jerk for every penny he's got!" Chrissy bursts out as she yanks her sunglasses off to reveal perfectly made-up eyes that obviously haven't shed a tear in days. "I've had to put up with him for years. His grumpiness—" That gets an overexaggerated scowl that bears an uncanny resemblance to Uncle Jed.

"His expectations—" That earns double air quotes and a sneer. "And his grunting like a wild hog in rut when we . . . *you know.*" Thank goodness she doesn't demonstrate that because there's not enough eye bleach in the world for me to unsee it. "I'm done with all of it. He's gonna get what's coming to him." Chrissy's rant is surprising, not in content, but in volume. I'm sure people all up and down the hall can hear every word. "He's not using what we built to take care of some home-wrecking baby-mama whore. I want it all."

Holy shit. Aunt Chrissy has gone off the deep end. She's usually the "seen and not heard" type, though I guess that's maybe at Uncle Jed's direction. If that's the case, she's definitely out from under his thumb now, ready to be loud and demanding. I'd applaud it normally, but Township muddies my "I am woman, hear me roar" mentality this time. Especially in city hall, in my office.

Oliver places a firm hand on Chrissy's shoulder. "Remember what we talked about?" She settles, though I can see that she has loads more she wants to say. "Of course, her anger is understandable." He directs that at me, justifying Chrissy's tirade. "From a legal standpoint, we're seeking a forensic accounting of Ford Construction so that Mrs. Ford can receive her fair share."

"I'm not sharing anything! I want it all!"

Oliver takes a steadying breath, his eyes begging me for indulgence.

I take a deep breath myself. "This is going to be an issue for Cold Springs, isn't it?"

That's why they're here. I can see the train barreling down the track, but I want to hear Oliver spell it out for me. Officially and straight from his mouth.

"We believe Jed is hiding personal funds that belong equally to Chrissy and him inside his corporate LLC accounts."

I'm surprised Oliver is sharing that with me, but truth be told, I wouldn't be shocked in the slightest to find out Jed's doing exactly that.

It's the type of slimy, self-serving thing he'd come up with, and assume he could get away with regardless of its legality.

"Okay, and . . . ," I lead.

Oliver looks at Chrissy, a question in his eyes. She nods once firmly, and he turns back to me. In clipped and unemotional tones, he tells me, "You're aware that the Fords are prominent landowners in Cold Springs. Separating their assets is potentially going to be messier than we anticipated."

Chrissy interrupts. "Yeah, Jed owns property all over Cold Springs. I mean . . . *we* own property." As she says "we," she presses a hand to her chest, clearly meaning *she* owns it, or plans to.

"What exactly does that mean?" My eyes jump from Chrissy to Oliver and back.

Oliver firmly sets Chrissy back in her chair and gives her a punishing glare. She answers with a huff but then seems to realize what she's said and clamps her mouth shut. Interesting.

And terrifying.

This is my town, my home, and my responsibility in so many ways.

"What's going on?" I demand.

Making a concerted effort to appear remorseful, Oliver reveals, "It means Township will need to be put on pause. No further building until we can account for every penny of the company's money and this is settled."

My jaw drops. "You can't be serious. There are people lining up to get in those homes, families who need them waiting on them to be completed. And the people building it. They need to work so they can support their families." Incredulous, I stare wide-eyed at Aunt Chrissy. "What are you thinking?"

I've known for years that my Uncle Jed is basically the villain of Cold Springs. He's proven it time and time again, and there's no love lost between us. Aunt Chrissy's basically been a nonentity, important only in relation to her husband. She's simply "Jed Ford's wife," not herself. With this move, she's going to instantly become *That* Chrissy Ford, the woman making people homeless. It won't be completely accurate, but little things like precision don't matter with town gossip.

"That I have to take care of myself first," Chrissy says haughtily. "And I deserve every penny."

"Mrs. Ford." If Oliver could slap duct tape over Chrissy's mouth right now, I think he'd do it.

"Every penny? Or Jed buying out your equity in the company?" I clarify.

Oliver tilts his head casually, or more likely, wanting to seem casual as he glazes over what Chrissy said. "That is one possibility. Another is that Mrs. Ford will buy out Mr. Ford and retain ownership of the company."

"You want the construction company?" I honestly never considered that. Why in the hell would she want a construction company she knows nothing about running? She's never set foot in the door, or onto a single job site. I don't think she'd know the difference between a screw and a nail, though it sounds like she's about to use both on Uncle Jed to fuck him over.

"Those are ongoing discussions, but at this stage, we simply wanted to notify you that building at Township will need to stop. Immediately."

"I see." I don't see a damn thing other than a long night poring over the contract with Ford Construction Company looking for any loophole I can find to keep things moving while Jed and Chrissy figure their shit out. There are provisions for delays, of course, related to materials, labor, and market fluctuations. There are clauses for the construction company going bankrupt or closing completely.

But a legal battle over ownership that puts the entire project at risk for an undetermined length of time?

I don't think I ever considered that when drafting the contract. And it's coming back to bite me in the ass in a big way. Like a crocodile chomp.

Oliver stands, and Chrissy copies him, though she has a toothsome smile while his lips are pressed tightly together. "We're on our way to the courthouse to file the paperwork, but wanted to give you a heads-up."

I nod, not thankful in the slightest. But the good manners my mother taught me take over, and I escort them to the door.

Chrissy straightens her face to something akin to sadness as she slips her sunglasses back on and strides down the hallway. Oliver pauses, moving in closer to me and saying quietly, "I hope you understand that I have to keep my client's best interests in mind. This isn't personal."

"Of course," I say robotically. It might be strictly professional to him, but it's hugely impactful for the town, and for my success as the city attorney. That makes it extremely personal to me.

He must take my answer as agreement, because he visibly relaxes and smiles warmly in relief. "Good. In fact, I'd hoped that maybe we could have dinner tonight and talk about something other than the case? Mixing business with pleasure is difficult, but it can be done . . . with delicate care." His voice has gone husky and intimate, almost breathing the words to me.

I look up at him in shock. He can't be serious, right? But he's staring at my lips hungrily, like he might kiss me right here in the doorway of my office.

Have I fallen down some rabbit hole into weird world? One where Chrissy Ford of all people becomes an evil mastermind? And lawyers who cut my knees out from underneath me one moment ask me out in the next like that was some sort of twisted foreplay?

I know that happens. I've seen married attorneys, one of whom is a prosecutor and one a defense lawyer, battle it out in a courtroom, engaging in all sorts of verbal warfare, and then go home together like it was just another day at the office. But I've never experienced it.

Can I separate what Oliver is doing for Chrissy's interests from his obvious interest in me? Do I even want to?

It's on the tip of my tongue to tell Oliver that he can take his invitation and shove it up his ass and around the corner, but a tiny voice in my head stops me.

It's dinner, Wren. Don't make it into such a big deal.

That's true. And maybe I can direct some conversation to work talk and get a better idea of what the hell Chrissy is thinking. I'm smart enough to do that slyly without him being any the wiser. And if not, a nice dinner with someone who wants to go out with me isn't the worst way to spend an evening.

It's not like anyone else is asking you out, I remind myself bitterly.

Still torn, and using everything from *do it for Cold Springs* to *hey, he is hot* for my reasoning, I force a fake smile onto my face and coyly slip my hair behind my ear in the universal sign of flirtation. "That sounds great."

He isn't surprised at my acceptance. In fact, he seems cocky about it, like it was a foregone conclusion, which irks me. I'm no one's sure thing. Not anymore, not ever again.

"I'll call you later, and we can decide when and where? I'm not sure how long this is going to take with Mrs. Ford."

"Sure," I force out.

"Till later, then," Oliver whispers into my ear, his lips brushing along the shell. A shiver runs through my body, but not for the reason he thinks. Rather, it feels wrong. Like I'm betraying someone . . . or something. But that's ridiculous. There's no one and nothing to betray.

Besides myself.

As he spins and walks down the hall, I let my smile fall away. It's only when Oliver waves to someone that I realize who's standing at the other end of the hallway.

Jesse.

He looks downright murderous. And is heading right toward me.

Shiiiit.

As he gets closer, he grits out through clenched teeth, "Tell me I didn't just fucking see you flirting with that douchebag."

I whirl to go back into my office, not wanting to admit that I was. And definitely not willing to explain why. But Jesse follows me . . . or rather, he stops me.

His rough hand wraps around my upper arm and in one smooth move, he has my back pressed against my office door and is crowded into my space just as close as Oliver had been. But it feels entirely different with Jesse. He feels big and dangerous, not because he'd ever hurt me physically, but because my whole body is alight with need, straining to get closer to him on a molecular level.

"Jesse . . ."

"Tell me, Wren. Please fucking tell me what the hell is going on in that beautiful, brilliant mind of yours. You have to know what kind of guy he is." He thrusts a finger harshly, pointing down the hall where Oliver disappeared. "And that he'll leave as soon as this case is over."

That sends me from needy to pissed in 0.04 seconds. I dig the point of my nail into his chest, knowing full well that it drives him crazy. Deep down, that's probably why I do it—to punish him.

For not calling.

For not being ready for more.

For not wanting . . . me.

"And that's exactly none of your business," I snarl, planting both hands on his chest to shove him away.

It's like pushing a brick wall. For a full second, he doesn't budge, only moving aside at his choice. Hurt flashes through his eyes, and I wonder if I was too cruel, but it's the truth. It's not Jesse's business what I'm doing, or who I'm doing it with. He chose for it to be that way.

"Are you serious?" Incredulous, Jesse throws his hands out, as if he's the wronged party here.

I might be nearly a foot shorter than he is, but I stare him down with cold eyes that hopefully hide all the thoughts and feelings threatening to let me fall under Jesse's spell again. "Completely."

He huffs and clips out, "Whatever, have it your way."

With that, he stomps down the hallway. I bite my tongue to keep from calling him back to explain, but my need to have the last word surges. "That's right. You can call me Burger *Queen*, I'll have it my way, however I want it."

I see his shoulders go tight with tension, but he doesn't slow. I'm still standing in my doorway, staring at the empty hall, when Joanne peeks around the corner. "You good, Wren?"

Great, just what I need—another tale on the gossip grapevine.

"Fine. Thanks."

I slam my door shut behind me so she doesn't ask anything else, and lean up against it. My breath is too fast, near panting.

What just happened? With Oliver and with Jesse?

And then a moment later . . . *Oh yeah, and what the hell is Aunt Chrissy thinking?*

Chapter 8

JESSE

I should've known better. I was in town to file permits on the few houses we're starting later this week, and thought I'd stop in to see Wren. I was hoping she'd be pleasantly surprised to see me, maybe blush a little and smile. If things went well, I thought I'd ask her out. As much time as we used to spend together, we've never done *that*.

I definitely hadn't expected to see her cozied up with that slimeball. I hadn't believed my eyes at first, and then I didn't want to. My instinct was to rip him away from Wren and stand between them to protect her. Not that she needs protection.

Or wants it.

I must growl in frustration, or make some sort of noise, because Bea suddenly jumps in surprise. "I'm almost done, Jesse. Just need ya to gimme one more jiffy and I'll have these all filed for you."

She adds a well-practiced, soft smile. Bea has worked for the Cold Springs permit office since the day after she graduated high school, which was only a few years ago, but she'll likely be in the same desk chair till the day she retires. She deals with grumpy, dirty construction guys just about every day, and somehow does it without bitching us out for coming into her office smelling like sweat and sawdust. She's sweet as can be and doesn't deserve to feel any of my frustrations and anger, especially when they have nothing to do with the permits she's rubber-stamping for me. They're the same as the previous ones, but she's gotta be careful that every detail is correct so we don't have any issues.

I force an answering smile to my lips. "Ah, sorry, Bea. I'm not pissed at you, just having a rough day. Take all the time you need."

"I heard," she answers with a sly look in her eyes. "You be patient. Wren will figure out that she doesn't belong with some city slicker, even if he is hotter'n an egg on the sidewalk in August. Women have wild oats to sow, too, ya know?"

I don't answer, not wanting to consider Wren's wild oats . . . with Oliver, but also that maybe she already sowed some with me, and that's all it was.

When I'm silent, Bea adds, "At least I did. I dated a bit before I found my Prince Charming."

"Prince Charming" is a stretch. Bea's boyfriend, Sawyer, works for the city, too, doing road repairs. I don't think I've ever seen him without a cigarette in one hand and a Coke in the other, and he probably weighs a buck twenty-five soaking wet. But if Bea's happy with him, I'm happy for her. Besides, it's not like I have any room to talk given my current situation.

"Sure. Uh . . . you done with those?" I lift my chin to indicate the last of the permits in the stack. She glances down, scans it quickly, and stamps it.

Putting it in her inbox tray, she smiles. "Yep, good to go. Get those places built right and fast. I think me and Sawyer might see if we can move out there."

"Will do," I tell her, tipping an invisible hat in a gentlemanly manner that I hope makes up for my grumpiness the rest of the time I was in her office.

Turnabout is fair play. Or that's what I tell myself as I knock on Wren's door.

If she can show up on my doorstep unannounced and read me for filth, then I'm damn sure entitled to do the same to her. That's why I'm here—to get her to see reason. She can't go out with that Oliver guy.

Wren opens the door with a huff, holding on to the doorknob as she bends down to pull one stiletto on. "Sorry, I thought you said you were going to call first. Give me two minutes." Only then does she glance up through the veil of her curled blonde hair. "Jesse?"

I swear she looks behind me like I might be hiding someone.

"I don't have time to fight with you, and I don't wanna hear it anyway," she says bluntly. Considering me dealt with and dismissed, she yanks her other heel on and swings the door, expecting it to close in my face.

I stop it with a hand and walk in like I belong here, closing the door behind me. My focus stays locked on Wren, but I notice the changes since I was here last.

The living room walls are painted a peachy-pink now. Her couch pillows are different and so is the rug. And there's a huge gold-framed mirror propped against the far wall of the foyer.

It's in that mirror that I meet Wren's eyes as she fusses with her clothes and hair, getting ready to go out with another man. Stepping behind her, I smooth her hair back from her shoulders and place heavy hands on the bare skin there. Fingering the strap of her silk top, my voice turns to gravel.

"I don't want to fight with you," I murmur.

Her eyes close as she takes a slow, deep breath. By increments, she sinks back into me until her shoulders are pressed to my chest. I walk my arms around her, holding above her breasts, and she rests her chin on my forearm.

"What do you want?" she whispers.

Does she really not know? How can that be?

I step around to face her, cupping her cheeks. Her soft skin feels like silk against my rough hands, and I can't help but gently run my thumb over her full bottom lip. She parts her lips, letting me feel her breath, and that small give tells me everything I need to know. I bend down, and just before I kiss her, I answer, "You."

The kiss is gentle as I taste her, memories flooding back to my mind and my body. I remember our very first kiss—full of sparks and hunger as our hands explored each other. But oddly, I don't remember our last kiss. It's one of those things you don't recognize the importance of at the time because it's one of many. It's not until later that you realize you've forgotten to file that memory away.

I won't make that mistake again.

I make note of her every nuance—the slickness of the gloss on her lips, the minty breath she's breathing into me, the tiny noise she makes in the back of her throat.

God, I've missed her.

I've dreamed of this hundreds of times over the past year, but now, it's real. This is my chance to remind her why we're so good together.

I let my hands trace over her curves as I drop to my knees before her. Sitting back on my heels, I look up the length of her body, and I'm not ashamed to say, I beg, "Please . . ."

She bites her lip, uncertain, but shifts her legs apart for me.

Relieved and eager, I run a fingertip up her inner thigh until I reach the silkiness of her panties. They're soaked through. That slickness had better not be for her date because it's mine, all mine. Hunger rises up in me, swift and strong. I need to taste her . . . now.

I push her skirt up, revealing her. She's wearing her usual silk panties, not her extra-sexy ones. The knowledge that she wasn't dressing for sex with Oliver is the slightest balm to my heart, and then the idea floats away as I inhale her, breathing her in.

I nuzzle into her cleft with my nose, easily finding her clit and burrowing my face there. "Mmm . . . ," I groan. I pull the wet silk to the side to look at her heaven, and spread her slickness over her clit with my thumb, circling it gently.

I hear her sigh of pleasure as she lets go. I slip my arm beneath one thigh, lifting it to my shoulder and holding her securely. She steadies herself with both hands dug into my shoulders, with those damn nails fucking ruining me.

I tease over her whole core with my tongue, lapping up her hot sweetness. "Fuck, I've missed this," I confess and then sink my tongue between her lips, thrusting it inside to get more. I lay a gentle kiss to her clit, a promise to take good care of it, and then circle it with my tongue the same way I did my thumb.

I drink her down, driving her wild with my tongue and mouth until her hips are bucking into me for more. I want to drag it out so this never ends, but at the same time, I want to remind her why we're so good together. I can help her come now, and then do it again . . . and again . . . and again. Surely then she'll see.

She's meant to be mine.

Because I'm already hers. I have been for so fucking long.

I'm focused on her sounds of pleasure when a sharp ring interrupts. "Oh, that's . . . my phone," Wren pants. "I have to get that." She moves her leg from my shoulder, stretching to reach her phone on the hallway table.

Seriously?

She scrambles to push the button on the screen and answers with her work voice, "Hello, this is Wren."

She's quiet for a moment, listening, and then begins trying to right her clothes one-handed. Like she's done with what we're doing.

"Oh, of course. No problem, Oliver."

My entire body goes tight with those three syllables. *Ol-i-ver.* She's talking to him? She stopped me from giving her pleasure to answer his call?

Fuck that.

I grab her leg and throw it back on my shoulder, yanking her panties to the side. She makes a sound of surprise and looks down. I glare up at her from between her legs, daring her to stop me.

"I'm fine. Just . . . uhm, stumbled in my heels a bit," she lies. To me, she mouths, "Jesse!"

I keep her pinned in place with my arms and our eyes locked together as I lick her again. I devour her roughly, giving her no time to build up or for me to savor the tease. I take her right back to the edge as quickly as I can.

"Huh?"

"Uh, yeah . . ."

She can't follow their conversation, too lost in what I'm doing to her. So I keep doing it, wanting her to focus on me . . . on us.

Wren fights to hold back a moan, losing the battle spectacularly as I slip two fingers inside her and her pussy clenches around them. I pull them out to grip her thigh punishingly. "Quiet," I order and she nods, biting her lip so hard, it's gone white.

I thrust my fingers back inside, fucking her hard as I flutter my tongue over her clit. Her body's going lax, and I have to lift my shoulder to give her more support. She's so close I can taste it.

"I'm fine, Oliver. Just a long day, as I'm sure you understand."

She's saying his fucking name while she's impaled on my fingers? I growl against her flesh and nip her clit with my teeth. She quivers instantly, drenching my fingers as she flies apart, coming in waves.

"Ungh . . . ," she moans, trying her best to be quiet. But I've decided that maybe I want Oliver to know exactly what she's doing, who she's doing it with, and how good I can make her feel.

I keep going, giving her no mercy as I make her come again.

"I have . . . to go," Wren says, and the phone clatters to the floor beside me.

Smiling in victory, I thrash my fingers into her as fast as I can. "One more, give me one more, baby."

Wren curls in reflexively, her hands on my shoulders. But it's not for balance . . . she shoves me away so hard that I fall on my ass, sprawling in her foyer floor.

"What the—"

Wren has gone from shameless sex goddess to pissed-off honey badger in a blink. Panting and wild-eyed, she steps between my legs, the point of her stiletto dangerously close to my cock, which hasn't gotten the memo about the mood change. She bends down and snarls directly in my face, "Do not call me that. Get out, Jesse."

Trying to make sense of what changed, I ask, "Don't call you what? Baby? I always call you that when we're—"

Thankfully, I don't have to decide on what to call what we're doing because Wren interrupts me. "*I know.* That's what you call everyone. Get out."

She yanks me up from the floor, pushing and swatting at me as she shoos me toward the door. "Wren, I don't—" I stop, realizing that I'm about to lie. I do, or I have, called other women "baby" before, but there's been no one since Wren. She's the only woman I've been with since we started whatever we were, and I've been hung up on her ever since. My dick doesn't even notice anyone else. "I haven't been—"

"Shut up. I don't need to hear whatever charming excuses you're about to pull outta your ass."

The next thing I know, the door is slammed shut in my face. I blink, still not sure exactly what happened. I lean on the doorframe, knowing she can still hear me. "Wren, it's not like that. I swear."

I hear her heels clicking away from the door, and then the lights turn off. Angrily, I slam a palm to the door once.

Fuck!

A tiny, evil, petty voice inside me says, *At least she's not going out with Doucheboy.*

Small consolation.

Chapter 9

WREN

It'd seemed fairly innocuous—a simple manila folder of paperwork—
something I receive every day. It wasn't until I opened it that I realized it's a copy of Chrissy's injunction filing to stop construction at
Township.

But that's not the worst part.

I stare at the Post-it note on the front of the injunction. I can almost
hear Oliver reading it inside my head, with all the naughty innuendo.

Sorry I missed seeing you for dinner last night. I hope you're
feeling loads better after such a long, hard day. I was up all
night thinking of you. —Oliver

"Thinking of you" is underlined twice, like I wouldn't read between
the lines. He might as well have written that he jacked off to the spank-
bank version of my sounds of pleasure.

I slam my head to the desk, feeling exposed and vulnerable as reality slaps me in the face again. I had an explosive orgasm with Jesse
between my thighs while on the phone with Oliver. And there's zero
chance Oliver didn't know exactly what was happening. He had to have

recognized the noises I was making and probably heard Jesse whispering in the background too.

What was that? Other than crazy.

Who does that? Not Wren Ford, that's for fucking sure.

I wonder if that counts as a threesome? Or is "aural" sex a thing? I have no idea, and I'm not googling it at work. Probably not at home, either, because there's no telling what I'll find out, and there's no going back to unknowing.

After kicking Jesse out last night, I'd walked a million miles on a loop from the front door, to the living room, to the kitchen. My brain had been going ninety to nothing, jumping from Jed and Chrissy, to Jesse and Oliver, to Township, and, oddly, to a video I saw of a whining dog who demands to be tucked in every night like the queen she is. Eventually, it was that dog that got me to go to bed. If she could go to bed at seven o'clock with no guilt, I could go to bed at midnight with a clear conscience even with everything falling apart. Still, sleep had been slow to come.

But I did work out some shit during my mental marathon.

Focus on the priority.

It's the simplest, most important thing right now—Township. Everything else is a distraction.

Like this Post-it note.

I yank it off, wadding it up to toss in the trash. Gathering my laptop, the stack of papers from my desk, and my mind, I head down the hall. I knock on Ben's door twice and then open it a crack.

"Hey, Ben?" When I see him look up, I jerk my head. "Come on, we've got work to do before you escape this place for a life of leisure."

He leans back in his chair, his brows furrowed behind his glasses. "What're you talking about?"

I shake my head. "Only explaining it once, so c'mon, unless you've already quit on us."

I don't close the door, so I hear Ben's chair squeaking as he gets up quickly and shuffles after me, but I'm already at the base of the stairs. "Going to see Francine if you want to hit the elevator instead," I suggest.

"I'm not that old, young lady. I can manage a flight of stairs."

He absolutely can, but this has become a love language of sorts—him calling me young and me calling him old. We end up doing a quasi-race up the stairs—him hanging on to the handrail for dear life as he propels himself up and me trying not to trip in my heels or plant face-first onto my laptop. Ben wins, and I'm glad to see that I only had to let him by a little.

In Francine's office, her assistant tells us to go on in. As we do, I can feel his eyes following us curiously. Last-minute meetings between the mayor and two city attorneys scream *bad news*. Add in a very public and particularly sketchy divorce that affects the whole town and it's likely front-page, headline, awful news.

Francine Lockewood became our city mayor after my dad stepped down a few years ago. She's a true believer in the magic of Cold Springs, previously serving as our librarian and self-proclaimed town historian. She's done a great job fostering our community back to a better place, especially through the negotiations with Jed over the Township development. She was the one who said we should hear him out and not squash the idea outright because Jed had a history of shady shenanigans.

Of course, she also said she got that idea from an owl while she was sitting under a full lunar eclipse, drinking hard kombucha. But we don't hold that against her. In fact, everyone appreciates that Francine is a little bit out there.

She's sitting behind her desk, her oversize glasses perched on the tip of her nose and her frizzy curls clipped back, which gives her an owl-like appearance. I've never told her this, and I never will, but Francine reminds me of Ms. Frizzle of *Magic School Bus* fame. She has the hair, but it's really more about the knowledge in her head. She knows every-thing about everything. In fact, I bet she would know if last night qualifies as a threesome. Not that I'm going to ask.

"Well, hiya. How's things?" Francine says, smiling easily as she waves us in. I'm pretty sure I'm about to ruin her good mood. Maybe I should've brought bagels or something to soften the blow.

"I don't know. Wren hasn't told me a thing yet," Ben grumbles as he helps himself to a chair. "Floor's yours, girl. Get to gettin', because Francine and I aren't growing any younger."

"Buckle your seat belts. This whole Jed-and-Chrissy thing has gone off the deep end," I warn, and then dive headfirst into explaining my meeting with Oliver and Chrissy yesterday, including Chrissy's ridiculous appearance and outbursts, and ending with the petition for an injunction to stop the building at Township completely until the divorce is settled.

"They can't be serious!" Francine exclaims, getting up to stare at the city map behind her desk. "After everything we went through to make Township possible?"

It wasn't all owl magic to get that deal done. Francine had to meet with Jed numerous times, fighting through the early stages when she called him a "sneaky land shark" to get to a point of actually listening to him enough to evaluate the Township plan objectively. Even then, there were a lot of naysayers she had to deal with too.

This whole debacle is going to be lighter fluid on an already burning fire, making the entire town angry with not just Jed and Chrissy, but Francine on top of it.

"Afraid so. I wouldn't be surprised if Jed is hiding money, and with construction ongoing, he could easily hide more, so I can understand where Chrissy's coming from. But hitting pause is going to hurt. Badly." Letting that sink in, I tap my fingers on my notes. "There's more, and all that's not even the weirdest part."

"Money stashes and letting construction sit idle because Jed couldn't keep it in his pants isn't the weird part?" Ben asks. "What else could there be?"

I look at him wryly. "Remember, you asked." Francine swats at the air as though backhanding Ben for jinxing us. It's not his fault, though, so I drop the bomb. "Chrissy wants the construction company in the divorce."

Francine laughs as though I told a hilarious joke, sounding like Muttley as she runs out of oxygen. "She hasn't worked a day in her life! I don't begrudge her that, seeing as I could happily spend my days in a lounge chair with a good book and a margarita. But now she wants to start working?"

That's not it at all. Chrissy's reasoning is all about hurting Jed the way he's hurt her, and taking away something that means everything to him. But the "why" really doesn't matter in the scope of what we need to focus on.

"What's our move?" Ben goes straight to the point, only concerned with one thing . . . what can we do to help mitigate the impact of this on our town?

"I've got a call in to the property tax assessor's office requesting a full list of properties owned by Jed, Chrissy, and joint holdings. Both lawyers are going to want that, so we might as well speed the process up a bit, given that they're public records." I wait for Ben and Francine to nod their agreement. "And Oliver is requesting a forensic accounting of their bank and business accounts. We can't do anything to speed that up, unfortunately. That's totally out of our hands, but I could try filing an amicus brief with the court to see if they'll urge things along a bit—"

Francine interrupts to ask, "Can we have the bank pull records on properties too? We know where the loan is held for Township at least."

I shake my head. "Against banking laws. They can't share any of that without a court order or consent, so it'll have to come from Oliver. Which leads me to the other thing worrying me . . . I still haven't heard a peep from Jed's lawyer. Not even a name, and we all know Jed's making plans. Ones that will serve him best, and fuck all the rest."

Ben offers to call a few old friends and see if he can figure out which firm is representing Jed. "There's not many of that caliber, and even less of the style he'd go for."

"Expensive, cutthroat devil," Francine summarizes.

I look through my notes. "I think that's all we can do for now, but we need to stay on top of this. This has the potential to go bad really fast, especially with Jed involved."

We're all thinking about the myriad of ways Jed always looks out for himself, no matter the cost to anyone else. Cold Springs has paid the price before, and I won't let that happen again.

"Agreed. I'd really like to hit that man where it hurts," Francine adds, doing a few air punches for good measure. There's a bang beneath her desk, and I realize she must've been doing some knee strikes and kicks, too, with her air-fighting moves. "Ouch!" she hisses. Frowning, she glares at the desk like it attacked her instead of the other way around. "This isn't over, Mr. Ford."

I kinda wonder if she thinks the desk is actually Jed, or if she's simply pretending. With Francine, there's no telling for sure.

"Good job, Wren."

I dip my chin in acknowledgment of Ben speaking, but don't truly accept his approval. His praise usually reassures me, giving me a boost to keep at whatever I'm doing. This time, despite my proactivity this morning, the compliment doesn't feel earned, not after the Oliver fiasco. That's another thing I figured out during my midnight moment of clarity. Ben would never pull some legal-spread-eagle shit during a case. Now is not the time to play attorney privileges with Oliver.

I'll stick to professional, focused, and politely civil. That's it, nothing more.

The same holds true for Jesse. I know what I want, and I'm not going to settle for less. I don't want a casual, uncommitted man who's only after sex, no matter how amazing that sex might be. And not someone who wants me only when he thinks someone else might.

Baby. He fucking called me baby.

"It's okay, we'll get it all worked out," Francine reassures me, mistaking my fresh anger for frustration over the divorce situation.

Heading back down the stairs, I tell Ben that I'm going to grab some lunch and offer to pick him up something too. "Nah, I'm good. Thanks, though."

I worry he's not eating enough sometimes, especially since I know Margaret made his lunch every day since they got back from their honeymoon all those years ago, and she's no longer here to do it. I'll probably grab him something anyway. If he doesn't eat it for lunch, he can take it home and have it for dinner with his nightly beer.

I walk the few blocks over to the deli on the downtown square, greeting people along the way. It's definitely not my imagination that I'm getting more than a few curious glances. Are people wondering about Jed and Chrissy's divorce or Township? Or have they heard some rumor about Jesse and me? Maybe Mrs. Capshaw did hear me banging on his door and told everyone I showed up late at night in my pj's. Or Oliver and me?

My break is only serving to make me angrier . . . with myself. This is not who I am. I'm "Don't Fuck With Her" Wren Ford, not "Gossip Girl" Wren, and I've worked hard to earn that reputation.

By the time I get to the deli, I'm scowling at everyone, and though I get a couple of friendly looks, they're efficiently put off by my apparent willingness to be a full-fledged bitch today.

All except for one person. Avery Ford, my sister-in-law.

"Why so grump-a-potamus?" she asks, bumping my shoulder playfully with hers and offering an easy, warm smile.

We were initially in school together, but hung with different crowds, so we were never friendly then. It wasn't until my brother Winston started dating her in college that we became friends. She's quite literally the best person you'll ever meet, sweet as can be with a heart of gold. I'm not sure what she sees in my brother because he married way, way up, and that was after he climbed several rungs on the ladder of maturing beyond teenage dirtbag.

"Work," I answer, knowing it's too clipped and short and instantly feeling guilty. Avery doesn't deserve my bad mood.

Plus, it's not fair to complain about work to Avery. She's a nurse who takes care of her grandpa, so she literally works all day, every day. When she gets a rare break, she works fill-in shifts at a nursing home. She's the last person to whine about work to, but she takes it in stride.

"I've heard," she teases, wiggling her shoulder at me. "But I'd love to hear more."

She's keeping things light, which I appreciate more than she'll ever know. And though she'd love to hear the latest scoop, she's too kind to push for any information I don't share freely. "You and the rest of the town."

I slide my eyes left and right, and when she follows the move, she sees as well as I do that the whole deli is listening in on our conversation, hoping I'll let some morsel slip out that they can spread around like wildfire.

But Avery is a good friend, and will go to bat for her people. Louder, she tells me, "Yeah, Grandpa Joe's been doing well. If I could just keep him regular. I've tried everything . . . prunes, Ex-Lax, and one of those fizzy tonic waters from the pharmacy. That one gave him gas worse than a dog. But he's still plugged up like a tub drain. Might have to call a plumber to do a little *whoop-de-do* on his butt." The last bit gets a finger swipe through the air that makes me cringe in Grandpa Joe's honor. "It'd serve him right for sneaking all those oatmeal cookies. He knows he's only supposed to have two a day."

I'm smiling before she's half-done with her story, laughing by the end of it. As far as I know, Grandpa Joe hasn't had a bit of trouble with constipation, and he'd tell you if he had. I don't think he knows the meaning of the word *secret* or *private*. Or *people don't talk about that at the dinner table*. He's unfiltered in the best, and worst, way.

"Who can blame him? You do make damn good cookies." I wink, going along with her story because it's definitely turned people off from eavesdropping. Quieter, I whisper, "Thanks."

Avery steps up to the counter and orders two turkey sandwiches to go, one for her and one for Grandpa Joe. I lean over, adding, "Make it three and it's my treat." I hand the cashier my card before Avery can argue.

"Aww, thank you. That's sweet. You know what I think you need?"

"A massaging showerhead with ten speeds?" I suggest when the cashier steps away to grab our food.

"Maybe, but I was thinking a girls' night. I'll text Hazel, kick out Winston and the baby for a little bit, and we can get together at my house tonight." Her place is an automatic choice because of Grandpa Joe. She can't leave him alone, so if there's not a night aide to keep watch over him, she won't go anywhere. "I'll make cookies and pop a lasagna in the oven."

She won't take no for an answer. But she's probably right—a night with Avery and Hazel is always fun, and will hopefully be just what I need to forget about all this craziness with Jesse and Oliver and the divorce.

I hold up a pinkie finger, offering, "Only if you promise that Grandpa Joe bit was fake. I can't listen to him talk about poop over dinner. Again."

She laughs and grabs my pinkie with her own, shaking. "Promise. He might try to have you look at a spot on his testicles, though. He's decided he's got mesothelioma because of a late-night lawyer commercial, and no amount of telling him it's a lung cancer caused by asbestos will convince him otherwise."

"Ew, definitely won't be checking that out for him. If he asks, I'll tell him the doctor might have to cut 'em off and see if that makes him change his tune."

Avery points a finger at me, grinning. "You are an evil one, and I like it."

We laugh, and I'll admit, I do feel better on my way back to the office. People still give me second glances, but I'm looking forward to tonight too much to care.

Chapter 10

JESSE

My phone rings for the third time in less than five minutes. And for the third time, I don't answer the damn thing because I'm busy. This town house isn't going to build itself, and I'm on a deadline. Even if I wasn't, I'm not climbing down from this scaffolding to talk to some telemarketer who won't take *fuck off* for an answer.

"Uh, boss?"

Still running my drill, I shout, "What?" Once the screw is seated in the base of the ceiling fan I'm hanging—which should be Mike's job anyway but he's wiring another house today—I glance down to see Alan holding up my phone. "My sister spamming me again?"

He shakes his head. "Big Boss."

That pulls me up short. Why would Jed Ford be calling me? We're nowhere near close to one of his "inspections," as he calls them. He doesn't actually inspect anything, usually just makes a show of walking around, points out a few things for us to address that are totally fine as they are, tells us "good work," and is on his way.

That's what Jed Ford is good at—show-and-tell. Past that, he's a pit of ugliness and self-absorption. But sometimes you have no choice but to work for the devil, so I do.

Dropping the drill to the scaffolding, I climb down and take my phone from Alan. "Thanks, man."

He nods and leaves, closing the door of the primary bedroom I'm working in to shut out the noise of the job site. Double-checking to see if Jed texted or emailed me a heads-up about what he wants, I only see the missed calls.

I take an annoyed breath, hit "Redial," and wait for the ringing.

"About time, Jesse. I don't like having to call my site lead more than once," Jed snaps in favor of *hello*.

Helluva greeting, I think. But what I say is, "Sorry about that. I was midhang on a ceiling fan and couldn't let go or it'd crash to the floor fifteen feet below."

He chuckles heartily, and I can picture his cheeks reddening and belly jiggling, but he's no Santa Claus. "Yeah, those bedrooms with the vaulted ceilings are gonna be a real moneymaker, ain't they?"

"Yep, sure are. Can I help you with something?" I have zero interest in shooting the shit with him and would prefer to drill into the live electrical running under the house than have a little chitchat about selling features.

"All business, boy. I like that. Yeah, I need you to meet me up at the 101 place in a few minutes. I've got a little surprise for ya."

It pisses me off when Jed calls me "boy," but I can't do anything about it. He's the boss and an asshole to boot, so calling him on it wouldn't do me any good. Add in that my family has bad blood with him from his failed relationship with Aunt Etta, and I pretty much live on thin ice with him regardless of the fact that I'm the best site lead he has.

And a surprise from Jed is bound to be a kick in the nuts. Possibly literally.

I look up at the fan that's hanging on by three of its four screws. It won't fall, at least. "Yeah, I'm on my way."

The line goes dead when Jed hangs up on me, and I sigh, wishing I could deal with anything else today than him. Out in the living room, I point to Alan. "Finish up that fan for me, will ya? I'll be back as soon as I deal with Ford."

"Better you than me. That's why you get the big bucks, boss." He points finger guns at me. "Pew-pew-pew." When I stare blankly at him, he adds, "Ceiling fan, on it."

"Thanks," I say, trying not to take my instant bad mood out on my crew.

By the time I drive up to 101 Fairfield, the town house Jed mentioned, his truck is already parked out front. This is the first of the first in the subdivision, right after the main entryway, and will eventually serve as the model home once we're to the rental and sales stage. As it sits now, it's gorgeous, if I do say so myself—fully landscaped with sod and flowering bushes, a black metal lantern light by the wood front door, and coordinating shutters around the windows.

Not seeing anyone outside, I park and head inside. The door's unlocked, which is unusual, but I'm not surprised Jed has master keys. I shut the door behind me, but right as I'm about to call out, I hear a distinctly feminine voice squeal, "Really? Are you serious?"

There are a few claps and then the distinctive sounds of kissing, complete with moaning.

Who the hell is in here?

"Hello?"

"Mmm—in here," Jed's voice booms.

I walk down the hall to the primary bedroom, much like the one I just left, and find Jed and a much younger woman with a very round, very pregnant belly. And despite calling me in here, he's midmake-out session with her leg wrapped around his calf while he's basically hoovering her lips into his mouth. I swear I actually see his tongue slip between them like a fat, pink slug.

Holeee shiiit! Is this the other woman Chrissy told Aunt Etta about? Here?

It has to be.

"Oh!" she says, wiping her mouth. "Hi!" she squeals in an unnaturally high voice. Untangling herself from Jed, she stays close to him, nearly glued to his side.

She's definitely younger, probably thirty at the oldest, with long blonde hair, heavily lined eyes, and a huge, happy smile that she's directing at Jed. Can't say I've ever seen that before. Most folks barely grimace when looking at him. She's wearing a sweetly floral, midthigh-length dress that's swinging out below her baby bump and flip-flops with big, fake rhinestones.

Jed looks happier than I've ever seen him, if I'm honest. He's still wearing the stupid cowboy hat that's part of his signature look, a snap-front shirt, jeans that haven't seen a day of actual labor, and snakeskin boots that cost more than a month of my salary. But there's a light in his eyes that I don't think I've seen.

Jed kisses her on the cheek, nuzzling up to her ear. "Jesse, this is Lucy. Lucy-Juicy, this is Jesse." She places one hand over her belly protectively and holds the other out to shake mine, though she's still nearly making out with Jed.

I lean forward and take her hand gently, correctly assuming she's not much for full palm-to-palm contact. "Nice to meet you."

I don't really care, but it seems like the polite thing to say. And at least I can corroborate Chrissy's story to Aunt Etta later.

"Surprise!" Lucy shouts unexpectedly, jumping a bit to grab Jed's shoulders. Thankfully, he catches her by the hips so she doesn't crash to the floor, especially in her condition. But it hikes her dress up so high that I can see the curve of her ass, which I quickly look away from.

They go back to a full-on face-sucking session like I'm not even here. After a painfully long two seconds, I shuffle my boots on the floor so they squeak, praying it's enough to stop them.

He wraps an arm around Lucy's waist, holding her tightly to lower her feet to the floor, and then presses a finger to her lips, shushing her. "I haven't told him yet. Gimme a teeny-tiny, itsy-bitsy minute, Lucy-Juicy."

The high-pitched baby talk from Jed might hold the record as the weirdest-slash-grossest thing I've ever heard, and I will never tell a soul about it because then I would have to repeat it myself.

"Oh!" Giggling, she covers her mouth with both hands, but I can tell she's grinning widely behind them. "Sorry, I'm too excited! This place is gorgeous, Jeddie."

Blech. Did [she seriously call him "Jeddie"? I think I just threw up in my mouth a bit. Still not as bad as Jed's baby talk, though.

Swallowing thickly, I ask outright, "What's going on?"

But Jeddie and Lucy—again, puke—ignore me, too busy rubbing their noses together, baby talking, and holding hands. "Not as gorgeous as you are, my pretty girl."

If someone told me they saw Jed Ford cooing sweet nothings, I'd have laughed my ass off. Hell, I'm seeing it with my own eyes and still don't believe it. But as they press their open lips together again, I clear my throat pointedly, afraid I might see even more than I want to if I don't interrupt them again. Thankfully, they stop.

"Ahem, that's the surprise I have for you . . . Lucy is going to be the on-site security here." He winks cartoonishly, his mouth open and eye spasming. "Obviously, it's in name only, but she'll be here if anything hinky goes on."

"Uh . . . what?" There should be more running through my head right now, but that's all I got . . . "What?"

Jed talks to me like what he's proposing is completely logical and I'm slow for not coming up with it myself. "With everything going on"—he raises his brows, and I take it to mean the situations with Chrissy and Lucy—"I want to have some type of security here when the crews aren't on-site. Just in case."

I wonder if he thinks Chrissy is going to go crazy and burn the place to the ground or something. "And you think Lucy is the right person to provide this security?" I repeat, looking at the young woman who's resting her hands on her belly and staring at Jed like he hung the moon and she can't wait to climb him like a tree again. "Out here?"

"It's perfect. I want Lucy close to me, and this town house is sitting here empty. Bada-bing, bada-boom," Jed claims. He jiggles Lucy in his tight grip, grinning lasciviously at her.

He cannot be serious. There are so many reasons why that's a bad idea, starting with . . .

"We don't have a certificate of occupancy . . ." What I really want to say is, *Have you lost your fucking mind?* but I'm aiming for reasonable and legal, both to protect my ass and so I don't piss off my boss.

Jed waves a hand dismissively. "Pshaw, that's only important if someone's *living* here. Lucy's staying on-site as an em . . . ploy . . . ee." Boop. Boop. Boop. He touches the tip of her nose with his thick finger as he drawls out the word and then soothes the tender boops with a kiss.

Holy hell, he's actually paying her to "stay" here, I realize. Jed's balls must be bigger than basketballs, and Lucy must not have the faintest idea what she's walking into with Jed and, more importantly, Chrissy.

I make a note to triple-check all foundation pour sites for any errant disturbed dirt because I'm not going to be the site lead who ends up in jail because someone else—ahem, Chrissy—decided to hide their dead bodies on my job site.

I've worked for Jed Ford long enough to know that arguing with him once he's made up his mind is an exercise in futility. He once argued for weeks about whether we could build a catwalk walkway across a two-story foyer, which would've been possible if he'd been willing to also pay for the support beam to do so. But he didn't want to pay, and I didn't want the walkway to come crashing down on any foreseeable day and time in the future. It'd still taken the structural engineer to squash Jed's idea because he wouldn't listen to me, despite my experience having built hundreds of houses.

And he sure as fuck wasn't smooching and petting his crew and contractors the way he is Lucy. Whether this is her idea or his, this is a done deal, and the sooner I get on board, the better off my life will be. And the less therapy I'll need from seeing Jed Ford's obvious erection in his jeans.

"Uhm, well . . . I'll let everyone know this town house is off-limits so no crew member comes in. Shouldn't be a problem, since it's completed anyway. But better safe than sorry. If you need anything, let me know. I'm always on-site, and Jed can give you my cell number." I nod to Jed, making sure that's cool with him.

"See, it's all good, like I told you," Jed purrs, and Lucy makes some sort of mewling sound that I think is supposed to be cute, but turns my stomach. "It'll be like camping . . . sharing a sleeping bag . . ."

Before I can stop it, I get a mental image of them wrestling in a single sleeping bag like two huge, sweaty wildebeests. Oh my gawd . . . No!

"I'll get going and leave you two to . . ." I trail off and finish, "Later!"

I'm almost free when Jed calls after me. "Hey! By the way, how long you boys got left on the street you're on?"

Boys. Boys?

Annoying but still not worth fighting. "A week, two at most. Wrapping up on the left side of the street, a few things still to do out on the right side. Why?"

Jed's jaw goes tight, and his smile looks forced. "Lucy-Juicy, go looky-wooky at the kitchen again. Make us up a little listy-wisty for the grocery store so that baby-waby has plenty to eat." He rubs her belly fondly. "We can pick up one of those box mattresses too—the ones that unroll and fluff right up—because me and my baby ain't sleeping on the floor."

She groans and laughingly tells me, "This baby makes me so hungry. I'm starving all the time! Craving lime tortilla chips dipped in ketchup morning, noon, and night."

"That sounds . . . disgusting," I admit, and she giggles before bounding off to the kitchen as instructed.

Once we're alone, Jed turns into the surly son of a bitch I'm used to, and I wonder if he's putting on a show for Lucy or if she truly is the only human being in the world who can make him into a normal person. Well, if baby talking, cooing, and lovey-dovey are considered normal.

"Look, Jesse . . . this divorce is gonna be messy as hell. Chrissy is a bit sore with me and being ridiculous. She's threatening to go after the whole damn construction company. My company! And in response, the city won't approve any more permits for us until the division of properties is settled."

Before the ramifications of that sink in, Jed adds, "The last permits approved are for the current street. After that, I'm not sure where we'll assign you and your crews."

"What?" I bark. "We're not finishing?"

"You will," Jed promises me. "Just not right away. I've got to sort the shit with Chrissy out."

That sounds like an indefinite delay if ever I heard one—waiting for Jed and Chrissy to agree on a dispersion of assets? There's no telling how long that could take on a good day, but given the present circumstances and Chrissy's anger, it's going to be a cold day in hell with ice sculptures of pigs flying before we get back to work here.

"What about the people waiting to move in?" I demand hotly.

His brows drop down in confusion. Of course he doesn't give a shit. The people of Cold Springs who need these townhomes are of no concern to Jed. "What about them? They'll buy when we're ready to sell. Maybe in the meantime, the market will go in our favor a bit."

He chuckles, as if that was a good joke. It's no such thing when the entirety of the housing market centers around Ford Construction Company.

I fake a smile, mad that I even have to do so but aware of how important Township is for the entire town. "Sure," I agree tightly. "What about the crews? No pay when there's a pause for an undetermined length of time?"

Jed shrugs like that's a stupid question. "Benefit of having contractors, not employees, right?"

My jaw is so tight that my teeth are in jeopardy of cracking. *Guess it's a good fucking thing I've got dental insurance with my salaried position for Ford Construction,* I think bitterly. My guys won't be so lucky.

Taking my silence as agreement, Jed says, "Good work, boy. Now, if you'll excuse me, I've got a little lady waiting on me."

He skips—or what he probably thinks skipping looks like—out of the bedroom and toward the kitchen. "Jeddie-Weddie is coming, lovebug!"

Blech. I've got to get out of here.

Chapter 11

WREN

I raise my glass of sparkling lime water high in the air. Avery lifts hers, too, while Hazel and Grandpa Joe hold up beer bottles. "To good friends, good food, and good—"

"Fucks," Grandpa Joe finishes gleefully. When we glare at him, he shrugs and explains, "Starts with *f*, and you can't tell me you weren't thinking it."

Avery swats his arm gently. "Nobody was thinking it but you, you dirty old man."

Hazel takes a quick drink of her beer, looking at the ceiling a little too innocently. She definitely was thinking along the same lines as Grandpa Joe. But when she swallows, she laughingly scolds him too. "Yeah, we're not supposed to talk about *s-e-x* because Wren's the only one of us not getting any."

I choke on my water. "What? I am not!" When Hazel grins at me triumphantly, I correct myself, "I mean . . . I am too? Wait . . . what? I don't know if I'm supposed to answer in the positive or the negative here to be right."

"Aren't you supposed to be one of those hotshot lawyers who always drops the Michael at the right time?" Grandpa Joe teases.

"Drop the *mic*, Gramps," Avery amends. "Like microphone, not Mike."

Grandpa Joe guffaws that Avery took the bait of his silly joke and digs into his lasagna. I notice he's using a spoon instead of a fork and holding it fist-style to basically shovel the food into his mouth. It's a definite change in his dexterity, but at least he's feeding himself and has a solid appetite. I'm sure Avery is measuring every bite, monitoring how easily he swallows, and counting every calorie to make sure he gets enough.

I point my fork at Joe, knowing my mom would freak out at the lack of manners, but wanting to prove a point. "And I am one of those hotshot, mic-dropping lawyers. Usually. But I'm a little off my game today, so cut me some slack."

Instead, he tosses me a slice of garlic toast. "I'll cut you some bread to wipe your whiny tears with, crybaby."

He's kidding, mostly, and giving me a hard time so I have someone to rally against. He might be Avery's grandfather, but he grandfathers all of us with a sharp wit, a good heart, and a no-nonsense attitude.

I catch the toast and take a huge bite, chewing noisily and open-mouthed in answer to his prodding.

Carefully, Avery asks, "You okay? You did seem a bit flustered today."

Hazel sputters out a laugh. "Pretty sure you said she was snarling, growling, and snapping at people when you called me today, and declared we needed an emergency girls' night in to save the town from Wren-a-saurus Rex. That's why I'm here. I had to see what had Miss Unflappable all flapped up."

She looks at me eagerly, like that's my cue to spill my guts, but I'm trying to maintain some composure. "It's not client confidentiality, but I can't go around gossiping about Cold Springs residents and their business." But then I drop the customer-service voice to add, "As much as I'd like to, because *dayyyyum*, is there some stuff I'd like to share."

Avery frowns, looking at me with sympathy, but Hazel is unde-terred. "So what I'm hearing is . . . you can't say, but you can't not say either." She winks at me and then tells Avery and Grandpa Joe, "Who's up for charades? Fair warning, I'm fan-fucking-tastic at this game." Hazel doesn't have a humble bone in her body, but she can back up every claim she makes.

Grandpa Joe turns in his chair to face me more fully, ready for the competition. "Game on, Hazelnut. I was playing charades before you were a seed in your mama's womb."

"Grandpa Joe! Eww!" Avery shouts. She's shaking her head and wagging her finger at him like he's a bad dog, but he's grinning with zero remorse and a bit of twisted joy at setting Avery off so easily.

"See, already beat that one because all she'll be thinking about is whether I've lost my marbles. To point, I haven't. They're right in my nut sack for safekeeping. By the way, you girls ever heard of mesothelioma?"

Avery rests her head on her hands, fed up but also completely used to her grandfather's antics. Hazel and I don't bat an eye, also accustomed to his foul mouth and silly jokes.

Hazel takes control of the game we're apparently playing now. "Okay, it's work-related. Blink twice for yes."

I purposefully don't blink at all, not wanting to divulge something that could get me in trouble, but eventually, my eyes dry out, and I blink reflexively.

"Yes! It's work," Hazel shouts.

Avery sets her fork down, giving up on her lasagna. "We already knew that. I saw her on her lunch break, remember? That's when she was all flustered and bitchy."

This game is starting to feel like an interrogation, especially when they're talking about me like I'm not sitting right here.

Hazel shushes Avery, waving a hand at her. "Don't break my con-centration. I'm gonna beat your grandpa's butt at this game and show him who's the charades champion." She stares at me for a moment, then guesses, "It's gotta be the Jed-and-Chrissy fiasco, right?"

I go ahead and blink twice.

And now Avery's attention is piqued. "Or the lawyer," she suggests shrewdly.

I roll my eyes hard.

"Let's come back to that," Hazel suggests. "Stick to one thing at a time because I suspect I've got us a little bit o' intel on that one."

I freeze, staring at Hazel. Working hard to purposefully keep my tone level, I ask, "What do you know?"

Her grin is pure evil. "You tell me and I'll tell you?"

I shouldn't. I know I shouldn't. But of the handful of people I truly trust in this world, three of them are sitting at this table. And if you hold the old adage that if you tell one spouse something, you have to trust the other spouse will know, I'm still good because the other people I trust are my brothers, who happen to be married to Avery and Hazel.

Decision made, I point a sharp nail at each of them. "This stays at this table until you hear it somewhere else. And you never heard it from me. Understood?"

They all nod, and I do a gut check once more to make sure I'm good with what I'm about to do. There's legal and illegal, moral and amoral, and written and unwritten rules. This breaks some unwritten rules, but technically that's it. I wouldn't divulge otherwise, even though I really need to scream and shout, and bitch and moan about this with someone.

"You know about the divorce and why—"

"Everybody does, girl. Get to the good stuff we don't know yet," Grandpa Joe urges. "Before I'm too old to remember it or have to go for a piss and miss something."

I laugh lightly and get to the rest of it. "Chrissy wants the construction company." Their jaws drop as I expected. "That's not even the worst of it. She thinks Jed's hiding money, so while there's a full audit, all construction has to be stopped. No money in, no money out."

Three, two, one . . .

"Township!" Hazel shouts with wide eyes as she realizes what the repercussions of Chrissy's move will be. I blink twice dramatically. "Oh my God! Do they know? Does Jesse know?"

Even mad at him, I've felt like that's been the hardest thing today— not calling him to give him a heads-up. And honestly, probably a fair amount of why I decided to tell Hazel what's going on. She's completely trustworthy, but she's also loyal to a fault to her family. Like "take a bullet, go to jail, provide a false alibi" type of loyal. I can't tell Jesse, but if she accidentally, completely unintentionally happens to share a rumor she heard, then he would be able to prepare a little. He deserves that.

I give Hazel a puppy-dog-eyed look, and she hears me loud and clear. "Ten-four, little buddy. Consider it handled. Sister Hazel's gotcha covered," she says in a CB-worthy voice.

Grandpa Joe knocks on the table. "Is that it? That's the big news? Jed's being handsy with some woman, Chrissy's being grabby with the money, and we'll have to wait a li'l bit for some cookie-cutter houses. I was hoping for some drama. Maybe a family secret or illicit love child. Something real juicy."

"Technically, there is a love child," I whisper. And then I say something I never thought I'd say in a million, bajillion years. "Poor Aunt Chrissy. I can kinda understand why she's going after Jed so hard. Just sucks for Cold Springs."

We go quiet for a minute, letting what this will mean for the town sink in. I'm faster at that process, since I've been ruminating on it for a while now, so I remember something Hazel said. "What do you know about Oliver?"

"The lawyer?" she asks, damn well aware that's who I'm talking about. Her delay is concerning, because Hazel's known for being bluntly up front, regardless of your feelings.

I lift a brow, glaring at her harshly.

She holds my eyes for a long moment and then grins. "Yeah, the lawyer. Oliver, with the fancy-schmancy suits, tight ass, and broad shoulders. Not to mention the sexy blue eyes and hair that Charlene wants to—and I quote—'run my hands through to mess it up a bit because he's a caged tiger waiting for the right woman to set him free . . . *rawr*'—end quote."

Avery laughs, "God help him if Charlene's got her sights set on him."

"I wish," I add. "He asked me out . . . *after* blowing up Township. I mean, I know he's working for his client's best interests, but seriously?"

Grandpa Joe snorts. "I bet a badass like you told him where to fuck around and find out." All three of us look at him in shock at his correct usage of the phrase, and he smiles widely. "See? I'm not *all* old geezer. I keep up with the kids' lingo."

"You're approximately ten percent old geezer," I tell him, pretty comfortable with my math. "And I . . ." I duck my head and mumble, "'Told him to call me."

"What?" Hazel shouts as she slams her palms to the table so hard, the plates bounce. "Please tell me that you did no such thing, Wren Ford." Her eyes are full of fire and directed right into my soul like she's going to fillet and flambé me right here at Avery's dining table.

"Uhh . . ."

Avery jumps in to mediate a battle I didn't know I was entering. "Let's hear her out. I'm sure there's a reason. Other than the caged-tiger thing."

Confused, I clarify. "It doesn't matter anymore. He called me to arrange it, but, uhm . . . he *heard* me, which was awkward as hell, and then sent an even more awkward note."

Blissfully clueless and innocent, Avery echoes, "Heard?"

I look from her to Hazel and then finally Grandpa Joe. Thankfully, he understands more than his granddaughter. "Think I'll visit the little cowboy's room. Yeehaw!" He gets up from the table, but pauses beside me with his hand on my shoulder. "And a 'ride 'em, cowgirl' to you."

I can feel the blood rushing to my cheeks as I flush with embarrassment. Once he's down the hall, I take a steadying breath.

"Oliver heard me with someone else. *Coming.*" I raise my brows to make sure Avery's caught up now, and when her eyes go wide, I know she understands. Finally. "I tried to be quiet and carry on a normal conversation—or as normal as could be—but he knew. The note he sent the next morning made that clear."

I don't know what to expect when I confess that. Shock, horror, embarrassment on my behalf? Avery seems to still be processing as she mumbles, "Why answer the phone *then?*" but Hazel looks to the ceiling and begins whispering. Listening closely, I can make out, "Please let it have been my stupid brother. Please. I don't have time to bail him out for beating the shit out of some rando Wren decided to hook up with."

I laugh bitterly. "Jesse wouldn't beat someone up because I hooked up with them, but it was him."

Avery and Hazel look at each other and then me before busting out in laughter. And then I hear Grandpa Joe laughing in the hallway from where he's obviously been eavesdropping the whole time.

Finally, Hazel manages to get out, "Jesse would absolutely destroy anyone who dared touch you. You're his. He's just been waiting for you to figure that out."

"More like the whole town is waiting for you to figure that out," Grandpa Joe adds, forgetting any semblance of not listening as he comes back in and sits at the table again.

It's my turn to look at them in confusion. "Jesse and I had a thing a while ago, but we've barely talked in ages. I'm not *his* . . . whatever that means."

I don't tell them that my proof is that he called me "baby," the most generic endearment in existence. It's the one thing you call a woman when you can't be bothered to use her name at the most intimate of moments. And I know for a fact that he's called other women that—waitresses, friends, strangers, women he's probably fucked. I've heard it with my own ears, which is why it pisses me off so much.

I know what we had was casual, but when he couldn't even bother to use my name while inside me, it hurt. A lot. And I'm Wren Fucking Ford. I don't do hurt. So I shut down, went distant, and that's where we've been for almost a year.

Until he barged through my door and made me gush like a fucking fire hose while on the phone for a work situation.

And then he did it again. "Baby," my ass.

I blink, coming back from my thoughts to find Avery, Hazel, and Grandpa Joe peering at me with concern.

Hazel leans over to Avery to stage-whisper, "We've been waiting for this moment, but now that it's here, I think this one's on you, girl. I know my limitations, and if I do it, it's not gonna go well."

Grandpa Joe grunts. "Agreed. If she's too stupid to have figured it out herself, someone's gonna need to spell it out *a-b-c* style so she gets it. I thought she was the smart one of your group?"

"Are you talking about me?" I snap. "I'm right here, for fuck's sake."

"Faster," Hazel tells Avery, pushing her on the shoulder encouragingly.

Avery closes her eyes and inhales loudly. This is bad. It's written all over her face and has Hazel shaking in her boots. Whatever she's about to tell me . . . it's bad.

"What?" I demand. I'd rather rip the Band-Aid off than pussyfoot around whatever this is.

But Avery is stuck on gentle mode, like I'm some delicate silk in the washing machine that can't handle a rough toss. "Wren, you know how much everyone in this town loves you—"

I glare at her, not needing some nice-mean-nice sandwich to get to the crux of whatever this is.

Avery makes a sound of discomfort and then spits out, "Have you seriously never wondered why no one, and I mean *no one*, from town asks you out? I mean, you're gorgeous, intelligent, independent, respected, and from a well-known family. The quintessential prom queen, debutante, sweetheart every man dreams about. You're basically the Holy Grail of potential dates. Yet no one asks you out. Or at least no one from here."

I squirm uncomfortably, not wanting to admit that I've definitely thought about that. But only when I'm watching stupid rom-com movies, sipping spiked hot chocolate and eating white chocolate popcorn, alone under a fluffy blanket, and drowning in my feels. And I rarely do that.

Keeping up my tough exterior, I lift my chin. "No, because I know why. I'm driven, focused, ambitious. The level of single-mindedness I have on my career isn't exactly what guys are looking for. Even now, I'm settled in my job, and have more time, but I'm . . . *me*."

I know who and what I am. I knew it already, but I definitely found out in law school. I'm a petite, pretty blonde who men consistently underestimate and want to manipulate, expecting me to look sexy on their arm and make them look good, like I'm no more than a showpiece. When they find out that dynamite comes in small packages and is partnered with an actual brain, high standards, and a backbone, they run.

But that's their problem. I refuse to make myself less because others can't handle me in my natural state.

Hazel grins. "You're not wrong. But that's not why every single man in Cold Springs avoids you like the plague."

"They do not." My brows furrow. "Do they?"

My friends look at me with pity. "Not completely," Avery amends, "just for anything romantic."

"Because of Jesse? Am I a pariah from sleeping with him or something?" A horrible thought occurs to me. "Oh my God, did he give me an STI or something? Do I need to see a doctor?"

Hazel's bark of laughter is rude when I'm midbreakdown. "Birdie, breathe. It's nothing like that. Jesse's just . . . uhm . . ." She side-eyes Avery like she needs help to explain her own brother.

"The lad's in love with you," Grandpa Joe says bluntly.

Time stands still, the only movement is my eyelids blinking, and then I burst out laughing. "No he's not. He's . . . Jesse . . . casual, carefree, no-strings-attached Jesse." They stare at me blankly, so I keep going. "He won't even go out in public with me without all of you going along too. Because I'm diluted a bit that way, not such a strong dose."

Somewhere along the way, my laughter at Grandpa Joe's outrageous claim turns to an ache in my chest. The spot where a little bit of hope used to reside.

The fling Jesse and I had was ongoing for a while, long enough that I truly thought it had developed into something deeper. But that was my mistake. I was the one who fell for Jesse, he was the one who would ditch me to go out with the guys. I put up with it longer than I should've, but eventually, I had to give myself an ultimatum. To save myself. One last try, one last invitation to go to dinner after so many before, and as simple as that request was, he still ran.

Even then, I'm ashamed to say, it wasn't enough to destroy that hope. I didn't go home. I went to Puss N Boots. I'd needed to see with my own eyes . . .

"This is stupid and you know it," I tell myself. But I don't restart the car. I have to do this or I'll never let it go. "Fuck it."

I get out of my car, scanning the parking lot as I walk to the door of Puss N Boots. But the audience for my humiliation isn't out here, they're inside. I open the door and step into the busyness of a Friday night.

I make my way to the bar as quickly as possible, using my small height to stay invisible in the crowd of people. I find a line of sight to the pool tables, and my eyes are drawn to him. Jesse's reigning over the table like the king he is. His dark hair is mussed, his smile is surrounded by scruff, and his eyes are bright as he talks and jokes with the guys from work. At least he told the truth about that.

But they're not the only ones Jesse's playing with. There's a group of women playing at the next table, but also watching Jesse with sly grins. One of them approaches him, and I hold my breath, hoping he tells her to fuck off. Hoping he tells her he's taken.

That's not what happens.

She leans in to him, flirting. I don't need to hear her to know that. I can tell by her mannerisms—her smile, the way she's messing with her dark hair, how she looks at him. The next thing I know, Jesse is stepping over to the table with her and then, standing behind her, with her hips pressed back against his, he helps her line up a shot. A few strokes and the balls fly across the table and into a pocket.

She jumps happily, her squeal of delight audible even from here, and Jesse . . . smiles. She hugs him in her excitement, and he says something, but I'm too far away to hear and can't read his lips because they're buried in her hair. But I can read his intentions because I've been that girl—pressed to Jesse, him whispering in my ear, and breathing me in.

I escape to the bathroom, not wanting anyone to see the tears I'm barely holding back. In the stall, I wipe my eyes and blow my nose, scolding myself for my own stupidity for falling for him. I'm about to step out when the bathroom door opens and voices echo around me.

"He is so hot, Raelynn. You're such a lucky bitch," one voice says.

"I know! And you should hear his voice—all rough and sexy. 'Good shot, baby.' Uhh, I almost came right then and there."

That moment is when any last hope I harbored died a painful, quick death. He called her "baby." And with two syllables, I shut down completely.

I waited for Raelynn and her friends to leave the bathroom and then made a run for it, straight to the door, into the parking lot, and back home.

And that was when I finally let myself cry.

"Wren?" Avery says gently. "You okay?"

I can feel the burn in my eyes again, but I refuse to let anyone—even Avery, Hazel, and Grandpa Joe—see me tear up over something that happened long ago. "I have to go. Thanks for the lasagna, but I—"

I don't pause as they try to stop me. I basically run for the door, waving off their apologies the whole way.

"Wait . . . Wren . . ."

"It's fine. I'm good." If only that were true.

"You sure as fuck aren't. What the hell happened between you two?" Hazel demands.

"Nothing. I'll talk to you later." Much, much later when I have myself back under control.

I'm climbing in my car when I hear Hazel's exclamation, "Well, shit! We fucked that up."

Chapter 12

JESSE

I can't go back to the job site after that conversation with Jed. We're dead in the water, and after this week, my crews are going to be scrambling for cash flow to make ends meet at home. All because of a divorce.

It's ridiculous. It's infuriating. And I feel like it's my fault, or at least my problem to fix for my guys.

I need to do the one thing that always helps me think—play a table or two, alone. It'll help me process and come up with a plan before word gets out so I can come to my guys with a solution, not just a problem that'll implode their wallets.

At Puss N Boots, Charlene greets me with her usual flair and flirtiness, but I put her off politely. "Beer, burger, no bullshit."

Maybe it's my stellar personality, or more likely, my grunting caveman ways, but she smiles happily. "You got it, honey-baby. Coming right up."

It's early enough that the table in the back corner is vacant, so I rack the balls, grab a cue from the wall, and line up my opening shot. The *crack!* shoots out along with my breath, and balls scatter across the table.

I do it again and again, letting my mind clear of everything but the next shot as I clear the table. At some point, Charlene silently sets a pitcher of beer and a cold mug on a nearby table. A few minutes later, she delivers a burger too.

But I keep playing.

One game. Two games. Three games. I lose track of how long I play. At some point, I eat the burger and drink a beer. The restaurant fills up as people get off work and want to grab dinner or play a game themselves. I ignore them all, and thankfully, no one approaches me. Until two guys come up who I have to talk to.

"What'd that eight ball do to you?" Wyatt Ford asks, helping himself to a glass of my beer.

Wyatt's married to my sister, Hazel, and for some strange reason thinks her special brand of batshit crazy is charming and adorable. They literally met when she attack-jumped a guy who'd turned into a sore loser after a pool game. Wyatt intervened, pulling her off the guy's back and getting yelled at for his efforts. But that sketchy meeting somehow resulted in Wyatt falling in love with her, and now my sister is his problem.

I look up from my shot to meet Wyatt's eyes. "Looked at me wrong."

And with that, I make the shot blind without glancing back down at the ball. I don't need to follow it to the pocket to know it sunk cleanly.

Wyatt chuckles and leans over to his brother, Winston, who's wearing his sleeping son in a baby carrier on his chest. "Looks like someone's in a piss-poor mood."

"Don't say *p-i-s-s* in front of Joe." He covers the baby's ears even though he spells out the not-cussword and the boy's so deeply asleep there's a puddle of drool on Winston's shirt. "You good, man?" Winston asks me.

Winston's a good guy, even if bringing a baby to Puss N Boots is . . . weird. I worked with him quite a bit when he was an architect at Ford Construction Company, working for his uncle. But he escaped and started his own design firm, married the girl of his dreams, and they have a baby named after Avery's grandpa Joe, who has taught his namesake wayyy worse words than *piss*.

"Nah, I'm fucked. Royally fucked." They don't deserve to get hit full force by my ugly attitude, but I've been holding it inside for so long that Winston's kind question pops the top and all my anger rushes out like a beer shotgun. "But not as bad as the guys. Did you know Alan's wife is expecting again?"

Crack. Crack. Crack.

I keep shooting as I wait for his answer.

"Meredith? She doing alright?" Winston's trying to figure out why Alan's should-be-happy situation has me trying to kill billiard balls.

"For now. Not that your uncle gives a rat's ass."

That's the missing piece they need. There's no love lost between the Ford boys and their uncle, who nearly destroyed their dad and Cold Springs in one fell swoop.

"What'd he do now? Other than get his mistress pregnant, lie to his wife, and steal more oxygen than he's entitled to." Winston could list off more wrongs Jed has done, but he's already rolling his eyes and shaking his head at the latest round of misdeeds.

I lower my voice to keep what I'm about to say between us. The last thing I need to do is start a panic in town. "Chrissy's going after the company, which means it's frozen. No construction after the existing permits expire or are completed."

The Ford brothers understand construction and permits, with Winston being an architect and Wyatt having done quite a bit of specialized historical woodwork restorations on old homes. But apparently, they didn't know about Jed and Chrissy's issue.

"She's what?" Winston balks. "No way."

"Straight from Jed's mouth," I counter. "Have you met the new woman?" When they shake their heads, I fill them in. "Young, blonde, pregnant. She calls him Jeddie-Weddie and they baby talk to a disgusting degree."

"Jeddie?" Winston says.

"Weddie?" Wyatt finishes.

I nod. "And Lucy-Juicy."

A collective shiver runs through all three of us. "Let me in for the next game. *I* need to hit something, too, after that," Wyatt says, putting a dollar on the rim of the table.

I hand it back. "Keep your money. Game's on me."

I clear the table, and Wyatt racks the balls. We play for a while before Charlene risks coming over again. She sidles up next to Winston to make cooing noises at Joe, who's waking up from his nap, and then says, "Hey, honey-baby, good to see you. That one needs a friendly face." She lifts her chin toward me. "Getcha anything?"

"Fries, please."

Charlene starts to leave, but looking at his phone, Winston calls her back. "Can we get a fresh pitcher too? The girls are incoming."

I make one more shot, the striped twelve ball sinking easily. "Let me finish running this and I'll get outta your way. Need to get home and figure out if I can slow down construction enough to get the guys paychecks for a while longer. Even one more week is something."

Winston nods approvingly, understanding that I'll take a hit for any delays, but it's worth it if the crews get paid. That's what being the boss is about. Not the dismissive shit Jed said before selfishly focusing on himself.

Wyatt glances at his phone, too, and grimaces. "Afraid not, man. The girls are coming for you. And if you say I warned you, I'll tell Hazel you're the one who taught Lester to tell her 'you look like bullshit' and let the hell rain where it will. Namely on you."

Lester is the foul-mouthed parrot Hazel inherited along with Gran's house. He's a riot and a really quick learner. It took only one visit, a plate of scrambled eggs, and a picture of Hazel to teach him to say that to her and only her. But that was months ago, so I guess Wyatt's been banking that tidbit to lord over me until the right time.

"Fuck, man. Why're you going straight for a kill shot?" I frown at him and then realize, "Why's Hazel mad at me? I didn't do anything to piss her off."

As I say it, I search my mind. It doesn't take much to piss my sister off, but I can't think of anything. I helped at Mom's bakery last weekend so Hazel and Wyatt could go to Newport, I didn't leave the toilet seat up when I visited last time, and I've caused zero trouble at Puss N Boots. There's nothing else.

Winston pipes up. "My guess? Something from girls' night in."

"What's that?" I ask dumbly.

"Avery called an emergency meeting tonight. Made cookies and lasagna because she ran into Wren earlier. Said she was shooting daggers at everyone who dared to look her way. That's why I've got Little Man." He pats Joe's butt and starts bouncing as the boy wiggles happily in his carrier. "And got kicked out of my house tonight."

"Same," Wyatt agrees. "What'd you do to Wren?"

Oh, shit. Hazel's not mad at me for something I did to her. She's mad because of something I did to Wren. "Later," I tell them, holding up two fingers and beelining it for the door. The last thing I want to do is talk about Wren . . . with anyone. But especially with Hazel.

I almost make it.

The door opens right in front of me. "Going somewhere?" Hazel purrs, her arms crossed over her chest as she glares into my soul. When I open my mouth, she adds, "I don't think so."

Yep, I thought I was fucked before. But now? I don't know what's worse than that, but that's what I am. I consider pushing past her, but even Avery—sweet, kind, gentle Avery—is lined up shoulder to shoulder with Hazel. A death squad of two against me.

I've already lost the battle, so I let them frog-march me back to the table, where Wyatt and Winston are doing their best not to laugh at my predicament.

Hazel pins Wyatt with a glare. "Why was he leaving in such a rush?"

Whoops, he's busted.

Deflect, distract, disengage. "I was on my way to tell you that Wyatt's the one who taught Lester the 'you look like bullshit' thing."

My hope is that by throwing Wyatt under the bus, I can keep Hazel's attention on him and I can make a run for it.

"Oh, he did, did he?" Hazel sings at her husband. But he's not quaking in his boots like he should be. Instead, he full-on laughs and points at me.

"You actually think she believes you? Dumbass, she's letting you think that so she can be mad at you again later when it oh-so-shockingly comes out that you're the one who did that. She's saving it for a future ass-kicking. Your ass, not mine."

No way. She totally believes me.

But when I look at Hazel, she's now glaring at Wyatt for spilling her top secret strategy. "Wyatt! Don't tell all my secrets or you'll be sleeping on the couch tonight!"

"Where I hear you've done more than sleep," I add because he's not the only one telling secrets. I know too much about that couch, their dining table, and Wyatt's workshop behind the house.

Charlene drops a pitcher of beer and a basket of fries on the table and tells Hazel, "I know it's your night off, but can you take care of this yourself?" She points to our little group. "I've got a group over there that might make my month of tips if I play my cards right."

She slides her eyes to the right, and we follow to see a pair of pool tables surrounded by rough-looking guys who seem to be doing their own low-key pool tournament.

"Ooh, think they'd let me play?" Hazel wonders aloud, seeing dollar signs.

Charlene gives Hazel's butt a friendly smack. "Girl, you know better'n to pull shit like that. Don't mess up my good thing."

Where Hazel sees potential pool buddies, I see potential problems. Bunch of guys, drinking, competing, a cute waitress . . . this could go south quickly. "Charlene, you need help with anything, you holler at us, 'kay?"

Charlene's eye roll is epic. "If I can't handle a tableful of tourists who wanna play a li'l pool and drink a li'l beer, I've got no business being here. Besides, I've got Robbie on speed dial." She means Officer Robbie Milson, who she's *friendly* with when the mood suits them both.

She floats off, dancing through the tables easily, and leaving me the focus of the death squad of two again.

Surprisingly, Avery fires first. "I thought Wren knew about how you feel and she was the one who didn't feel the same?"

Nope, not doing this. She said "feel" twice in one sentence. That's two too many times, especially after my day, when my emotions are riding too close to the surface. "Can we not talk about how she figured out that she's about fifty levels outta my league? I really can't today."

I don't see it coming. I didn't see Hazel move, but suddenly she's beside me and smacks the hell out of the back of my head. It's a move she learned from a show Mom watches while she's working in the early morning at the bakery. She calls the head slap "the DiNozzo."

"Ow! Fuck!" I hiss, rubbing my head. "What the hell was that for?"

Hazel's eyes narrow as she silently stares into my soul for an uncomfortably long moment. Finally, she says, "I knew you were a dumbass, but Wren's the smartest person I know. Yet somehow, you're both stupider than a drunk city boy in a dog-sledding race."

"What?" I sputter. I'm not insulted in the slightest, but I am mad on Wren's behalf.

Hazel's on a roll, though. "She told us about the phone call eargasm *thing*, and then when I asked who it was—"

I interrupt to declare, "She's not fucking around with anyone else." I do know that much for sure.

I give Wren her space, and I'm trying to give her time to realize that no one will take care of her like I will, even if I'm a dirty, semibroke construction guy who's got too many scars, shitty tattoos, and a foul mouth. But even with that time and space, I keep careful track of who she talks to, who she hangs out with, and what's going on with her. Careful in the sense of discreet enough that she doesn't know, and staying on this side of legal so that Officer Milson doesn't have to make a visit to tell me to back off.

"No shit, Sherlock. But she thinks you bailed on her, said something about you not wanting to be seen with her? And had no idea that you've basically told the whole town that if anyone fucks with her, you'll destroy them. When Grandpa Joe said you're in love with her, she laughed. A lot. She has *no idea*."

Every word is a bullet straight into my heart, shredding it to pieces as I try to make sense of what Hazel's saying.

How could Wren not know that I'm fucking gone for her and have been for ages? She seriously laughed at me?

I snort bitterly. "Yeah, I know. I'm not worthy of *the Wren Ford*, but a little respect would be fucking nice."

Hopefully, the anger in my voice covers the hurt I've been stockpiling away for a year. Hazel knows me too well, though, and can see through my bullshit any day, any time. "Pull your head out of your ass. I don't know what happened, but she laughed—" I try to interrupt again, but she gives me a glare reminiscent of Mom's and I shut up. "And then her eyes went all hazy like she was somewhere else. Before we could ask what she was thinking, she ran out so we wouldn't see her cry."

That stops me short. "Wren was crying? Why?"

Hazel almost slaps my head again, but Avery answers first. "Because of you, Jesse. I know you're hurt, but so is she."

I think I would've preferred the smack, because Avery's gentle words are a punch to my gut. Wren's hurting? Because of me? I've done everything I can think of to make this easier on her. I've stayed away, I haven't put pressure on her. And I've been doing my best to get better for her, hoping that eventually, I'll be a man she could be proud of.

Wyatt puts his arm around Hazel's shoulder, backing her up or holding her back, I'm not sure which. But his voice is threaded with a promise of his own. "Fix this. Wren's been through some shit and deserves to be happy. And she's better than all of us put together—no offense, Avery—and if you fuck her over, I will feed your body to my wood chipper." It's his version of a brotherly love threat.

"None taken," Avery answers, lost in little Joe's baby coos as he realizes his mama's here. "Auntie Wren's the best, isn't she? Oh, yes she is. Not as cute as you, though, Joe-baby."

Avery's baby talk is much more tolerable, but I still need to get out of here. I have a lot to think about.

I am so fucking confused.

This whole day has sucked ass. And not in the good way. I can't do anything about Jed's asshattery, but Wren and me? Yeah, I can do something about that shit.

Chapter 13

WREN

I hear Jesse's truck pull up out front, the door slam, and his boots crunch through the gravel before clopping on the steps outside. The doorbell rings at the same time he knocks, and I admit to myself that I'm hiding from him when I seriously consider not answering the door.

He knocks again and yells through the door, "Wren. Open the door. I know you're here."

Of course he does. My car's right out front, and the lights are on. But I can play possum, and maybe he'll think I'm already asleep.

No, that's useless. He'd probably show up at work tomorrow and I'd have to deal with it then.

Resigned, I blindly fluff my hair and rub under my eyes to make sure there are no mascara smears before going to the door. I open it a crack, standing behind it. I'm wearing a huge forest-green T-shirt that I hope he doesn't recognize because I totally swiped it from his place and sleep in it more often than I'd care to admit.

"We need to talk," he grits out.

I'm shaking my head before he gets the words out. "Not tonight, Jesse. It's been a long day, and I want to go to bed."

"Get in the truck." He points at the jacked-up monstrosity behind him like I don't hear it *glub-glub-glubb*ing ten feet away. I know from experience that you can hear it from a half mile away when he *really* winds it up.

I dig my bare feet into the floor as I huff out a disbelieving laugh. "I'm not going anywhere."

"Remember, I tried to play nice," he warns. Confused, I stare at him blankly one second too long, and he nudges the door the rest of the way open, bends down, plants his shoulder at my waist, and scoops me into the air over his shoulder.

In shock, I scream while simultaneously pounding on his back and flailing my legs, but he holds me securely. "Put me down! This is kidnapping!"

He spanks my ass, his hand hitting half bare butt and half T-shirt where it's ridden up. And then I'm wiggling to try to keep the whole world from seeing that my panties have shifted up my crack. And I'm not a thong girl. I invest in good-quality undies that stay where you put them and don't crawl into places they shouldn't be.

But I don't think Kim Kardashian and her designers at SKIMS tested a caveman's carry for the stay-in-placeability of their products. To note: they fail, and I will be writing a scathing review.

Pounding his back, I exclaim, "You did not just do that!"

In answer, Jesse spanks me on the other cheek, then shuts my front door. "Keep at it, and I'll do it again."

That's the final straw. I kick and flail, scream and scratch, not giving two shits about the hour or what my neighbors will think.

"What in the heavens—" I hear Roxy who lives next door exclaim as she opens her door.

Upside down and trying to get my hair out of the way, I plead, "He's kidnapping me! Call Officer Milson!"

But she smiles and leans against the doorframe, casual as can be. "Oh, hey, Jesse! Hey, Wren! You two have a good night." And with that, she shuts her door.

"Are you kidding me?"

Jesse opens the passenger door and heaves me into the seat. Pissed off, but physically okay, I cross my arms and glare at him with every ounce of anger and hurt I possess. I expect him to be mad, too, but he looks at me with surprising softness in his brown eyes and cups my jaw, which is clamped shut and jutted forward stubbornly. "We're gonna get this shit straightened out, I promise you that. Give me a minute, 'kay?"

He buckles me in, carefully making sure I'm safe before closing the door on me. I consider making a run for it as he walks around the front of the truck, but I'm stuck in place. Not by the seat belt, but by my own deep, dark, hidden desire to finally know what the hell I did wrong, other than be me.

Is it needy? Yes. Am I mad at myself for wanting to know? Also yes. Do I say, *Fuck it, that's his problem* and get out of the truck? No.

Because I want to sort this out too. It might be the only way I'll be able to move on.

As he gets in and pulls out of my driveway, I swear I see Roxy's blinds move like she was watching the whole show. "FYI, I'm going to kill your sister."

"Don't say that out loud," Jesse says, sounding softly amused. "It makes it premeditated murder. You lawyer types know that."

Is he joking at a time like this? I turn my head slowly to give him shit, but his eyes are focused straight ahead on the road. With every streetlight we pass, I get a quick glimpse of his profile. He hasn't had a haircut in a while, and the ends of his dark hair are starting to flip up in the back in the way that makes me want to twirl them. His jaw is set as stubbornly as mine, but covered in dark scruff that I know firsthand leaves lips and thighs deliciously raw. The short sleeves of his shirt have pulled up over his biceps, revealing the line of his tan and . . .

Is that a new tattoo? Was that there when I barged into his house?

I try to remember, but admit to myself that I was a little distracted by his man nipples and work-honed abs, and didn't look elsewhere.

I can't see the whole thing, only the edge of some black lines peeking out, but the idea that someone else has seen his body since I last did washes through me painfully. Even a tattoo artist. She was probably gorgeous, with purple hair, dimple piercings, and tattoo-covered skin that Jesse traced with his tongue after she left her mark on him with permanent ink.

A growl rumbles in my chest, and I have to remind myself that it's none of my business. Despite what Hazel and Avery said tonight, what Jesse does or who he does is not my concern. I jerk my eyes back, forcing myself to stare out the window at the passing town.

It doesn't take long for me to figure out where he's taking me. We've been here before. In fact, at one time, I thought this was "our place." Jesse and I never went out. We'd meet at his place or mine, whichever was more convenient. Sometimes, one of us would bring food if we were hungry, but it was never like a date.

Until here.

Jesse did a small side job for someone well outside the city limits and found a creek down a dirt back road where he could fish. He told me he wanted to show it to me, and we came out here a few times, and though we had sex on a blanket on the shore, it felt different. It felt *more*.

We'd talk, sit and watch the sun set and the moon rise, and hold hands while we walked up and down the bank of the creek. He said it was so I wouldn't fall in the sometimes-sticky mud, but in my head, it was because he wanted to touch me, even when we weren't fucking.

And that's where he's taking me now. To the place where I stupidly fell in love with him.

"I'm not sleeping with you," I announce, for his benefit and mine.

I feel the weight of his gaze when he turns to look at me. "I have no intention of *sleeping* with you tonight either. We need to talk," he repeats.

We fall silent for the rest of the drive. I don't know about him, but my mind is racing. I need to prepare my opening statement, arguments, and closing statements so I'm not caught by surprise with whatever he wants to say. He wants to talk? Fine, *I'll talk*. But Jesse has no idea what's coming for him.

When he pulls off the dirt road and puts the truck in park, I don't move, but he still says, "Stay there. You don't have shoes on."

He gets out, grabbing the thick moving blanket he keeps in the back seat of the truck, and then disappears for a moment. As he steps behind a tree, I murmur, "Whose fault is that?"

He comes back a minute later and opens my door. I've already taken my seat belt off and considered using it to choke him, but when he turns around and gives me his back, I do exactly what he wants me to do. I hop on, piggyback-style.

This is ridiculous. You are Wren Fucking Ford. What are you doing?

But that's the pain talking and I know it. I don't want to have this conversation because while I've been mentally preparing for what I'm going to say, part of that process is acknowledging what the other person will argue to plan effective rebuttals. In my head, I've heard Jesse explicitly say that I'm too cold, too work-oriented, too ballsy . . . too not what he wants. And even imagining it hurts. Especially since there's no denying it. It's all true.

But that stupid little shred of hope has been resuscitated by Grandpa Joe's words. *The lad's in love with you.*

There's no way. I know there's no way or we wouldn't have spent the last year apart. But that stupid sliver is so loud. Why are hope and hurt so powerful?

Jesse squats down so I can step onto the blanket easily, and I sit down. I stretch my legs out in front of me, but that feels too nakedly vulnerable, so I fold them in front of me instead and sit up straight. All it'd take is a little "om" and I'd be ready for a yoga class.

But there's no inner peace to be found here tonight. I think, at best, I can hope for brutal honesty.

Jesse pulls off his boots and sits down beside me, as if this were just a regular picnic or some casual stargazing. He stretches his legs out long, not naked at all in his work-distressed jeans and bright-white socks that I know are pulled up under his jeans. The first time I saw him in boxer briefs and tall socks up his muscular calves, I'd laughed. I don't know why it'd been unexpectedly funny. But it'd come to be an oddly sexy look—on him.

Yeah, I'm not exactly your typical lingerie girl. I want panties that cover my ass and apparently have a thing for boot socks on men. But the heart wants what it wants.

"You said you want to talk, so talk," I tell him. It's one of the oldest tricks in the book. Don't show your cards until the other guy does. I'll make adjustments on the fly to my opening statement based on Jesse's, and then I'm responding only to the specific questions asked of me without revealing things I don't want to.

Jesse rubs his feet together, cricketing he calls it, something he usually does to calm down, which tells me he's angry, or irritated at least. The only sound is sock-on-sock friction and the racing beat of my own heart in my ears.

Finally, the full weight of his gaze lands on me. "Hazel and Avery came to Puss N Boots and gave me hell after your girls' night in. They told me some shit that has me confused."

That sounds like an accusation, like this is all my fault.

"And that gives you the right to kidnap me? So I can help you get unconfused?" I counter snarkily.

He cuts his eyes over knowingly. "You came with me willingly, and we both know it."

I don't answer because I don't trust that I can lie convincingly. If I'd really refused to go with Jesse, he would've put me down. But I didn't. I made a show of fighting him. I *hrrmph* and he nods.

"Good, now that we've addressed that, let's get to the real stuff." That's all the warning I get before he dives into my heart. "Why were you crying?"

Instantly, silent tears streak down my cheeks again, and I'm thankful for the darkness surrounding us so that he can't see my weakness, because this is not who I am.

But he knows. Somehow, though I don't make a sound or move a muscle, he knows.

His strong arms snake around me, and he pulls me sideways into his lap in one smooth movement. I'm like a doll to him, but his touch is gentle as he swipes my tears away with his thumbs. "Why, Wren?" he whispers in a gruff voice.

This is not how this is happening. He wants to talk? Then he can talk. I'm not revealing myself to be told outright that I need to tone it down a notch. Instead, I go on the offensive. Wiggling violently, I push at his chest to put distance between us. "Stop manhandling me and demanding that I tell you things." Climbing out of his lap to kneel on the blanket, I snap, "If I'd wanted to have this conversation, I would've bitched you out a year ago. But I've been doing really well at not telling you off like you deserve."

At this point, I'm doing as much talking with my hands as I am my mouth, but at least I hold back from slapping him.

"Same!" he shouts back. "This has been a long time coming, so let's do this. Go ahead and say that I'm shit who's not worth your time and you were slumming it with me." He moves to his knees, too, spreading them wide and getting even louder. "Go ahead, Wren. Do your worst. I fucking need it." He grabs his shirt right over his heart, pulling at it with furor. "Maybe then I'll finally find a way to not love you. Bitch me out with all you've got."

How dare he? He treated me like an interchangeable hole to fuck, not using my name, leaving as soon as we were done, and going straight to another woman. I felt—no, I *still* feel—like I was simultaneously too much and not enough. And now I find out that he's actively told people that I'm his, like I'm a *thing* he can put up on a shelf for later, when and if he decides he wants me.

Furious, I let loose. "Love me? Do you even know what that means?" I snort derisively.

"More," he demands, waving his hands in a gimme motion before resting them back on his thighs. "More." He's snarling like I'm the one hurting him.

"This is not love." I point from him to me. His lips twitch, not a smile but something bordering on it, and I reach a new level of rage that completely breaks down every filter I possess. "You called her baby barely thirty minutes after fucking me!" I scream, my voice cracking with emotion.

"What?" he asks, suddenly sounding stunned. "Who?"

His confusion only makes it worse. Laughing bitterly, I ask, "It happened so many times, you don't even know what I'm talking about, do you? Let me refresh your memory. Her name was Raelynn. Or at least the one I know about, but it sounds like there were more." I narrow my eyes accusingly, though I admit, "That's my bad. I knew who you were, I knew what we were, but to have it thrown in my face fucking hurt."

"I have no clue who this Raelynn chick is, but you're right about one thing. Who I am and who you are." He acts like that makes sense, but it doesn't. At all.

"Want me to remind you? That last night, after we—" I can't say it, but he knows what I mean. "I asked if you wanted to get dinner *again*, and you went to play pool with the guys *again*, so I followed you. I know it's stupid and childish, but I did. I saw you flirting with her, saw you two hug, and I heard her in the bathroom." I throw my voice high, mimicking what I heard that night but adding my own sarcastic bend. "He's so hot! He told me, 'Good shot, baby!' and I nearly spontaneously orgasmed right there. Oh, Jesse!" In my own voice, I spit out, "Fucking asshole."

I flip around, sitting on my ass again with my legs askew, and feeling spent. I don't do this much emotion in one fell swoop. I'm about control, planning, and cerebral endeavors. I was raised to smile while the world burned, never showing reactions. Certainly never this. Not violent, emotional dumping.

But here we are.

Jesse doesn't move other than closing his eyes. In the moonlight, I can see the set of his jaw and the shallow rise and fall of his chest. And then his head dips. For a moment, I think it's all sinking in for him as he remembers what I'm talking about.

Until he starts laughing mirthlessly.

His deep chuckles echo across the creek, disturbing the birds who've already bedded down in their nests for the night. They screech back, and Jesse looks up, and though I can see the brightness of his white teeth, it's more of a snarl than a smile as he shakes his head. He runs his fingers through his hair and says, "You're jealous? You? You're jealous." He sounds incredulous at the very idea, which, for the record, is completely reasonable even if we weren't exclusive. Nobody wants to feel interchangeable or unvalued, and that's exactly how I felt. A few more chuckles boom out, but these sound choked, almost emotional, and he looks up to the sky. "Fucking hell."

"Are you laughing at me?" I snap.

"No, I swear I'm not. It's just . . . you, Wren Ford, are jealous, over some girl I can't even remember. That's hilarious," he manages to get out around his bitter laughs.

"Why?" I slam my arms crossed over my chest and glare at him. I probably look like a pouting child, but I can't find the emotional space to care.

Jesse leans forward, putting his hands on the blanket so he can get right in my face. Nose to nose, breath mingling, he speaks slowly and clearly, "Because I have been in love with you for so long that I haven't so much as looked at another woman since well before the first time we fucked."

I make a noise, beginning my next argument, but he's succeeded in blanking my entire brain of any actual thought or words, a feat I didn't think possible given that I typically have entire monologues running in the background of my mind.

"You . . . what?" That's it. That's all I've got. I need him to explain what he said again because that makes zero sense to me.

His lips land on mine, soft and sure, and in total shock, I freeze like a deer in headlights—eyes open, mouth open, and breath held. I'm trying to jump-start my brain to decide how I feel about this and analyze what's happening, but after the smallest, quickest taste, he pulls back and murmurs, "Not yet."

It seems like he's talking to himself, not me. But the kiss makes me pliable, and curious.

He sits down in front of me, pulling my V'd legs over his out-stretched ones, until we're so close that one tug of a zipper and a little lift could have me impaled on him. Not that I'm thinking about that. Nope, not a bit, not remembering how he always stretched me and filled me just right and it's been so long since I've had that. Not thinking about that at all, because there might not be much physical space between us after he gets us arranged the way he wants, but there's an entire emotional void filled with hurt, pain, and I'm beginning to think a lot of misunderstanding.

"The last time we fucked, let me tell you what I remember," he starts, and though I'm not sure I want to hear this, I don't stop him. "That was around the time Alan and Meredith were going through it and we were damn near life-boating him home every day after work. She was gone a couple of nights a week, and Alan would've been alone. We didn't trust him not to drink himself stupid, so when she was gone, we rallied for him. That night, when I told you I couldn't get dinner because I was meeting the guys for pool? It was for Alan."

I have no idea what he's talking about, but I believe him. There's pain and history in his words, an entire story I don't know. "Are Alan and Meredith okay?" I ask gently.

I can feel his relief when he smiles widely. "Yeah, they're great. Meredith's healthy now, so they're using Alan's medical insurance for something much better—their baby."

"That's awesome. I'm happy for them." I truly am, and if what Jesse's saying is the truth, all those declined dinner invitations that I threaded through with so much meaning actually meant something else entirely. That Jesse is a good friend. "You weren't telling me no because you didn't want to be seen with me?"

It's a dangerous question, entirely too revealing of my insecurities and fears, but Jesse laughs like I'm teasing him.

"Woman, you could ride me down the middle of Main Street like your damn pony if that's what you wanted. I would be proud to be seen with you if you could get off your high horse for a fucking minute."

Anger rises instantly at being called "snobby" in a roundabout way, but something else he said comes back to me. At the moment, I'd gotten stuck on the "love" thing he said, but there was more. Pointing back and forth between us and figuring it out as I go, I say, "You think . . . that I think . . . that I'm better than you? You said I was slumming it with you, but I don't think that at all."

"How could you not? You're Wren Ford, and I'm . . . this." He throws his hands out like I'm supposed to see something that I'm entirely blind to.

"This?" I place the tip of my nail into his chest and push him back a bit until he rests on his hands behind him, but he's lifting his chest, wanting more of my touch. "You mean this man—who works hard, who cares about his family, and would do anything for the people important to him? This man with eyes I want to drown in, a filthy mouth I want to drench, and a body I want to mark all over. The man I dream about every time I wear his shirt to bed, touch myself, and whose name I say every time I come. Is that the man you're talking about?"

His breathing is near panting as I tell him what I see when I look at him. But I'm not done. If this is it, so be it. I'm throwing down the gauntlet, and he'll either rise or fall to the wayside, but at least then, I'll know where I stand.

"I'm Wren Fucking Ford, and if you can't handle that or I'm too much for you, then maybe you're not the man I think you are, Jesse Sullivan."

Chapter 14

JESSE

What the fuck?

My head is screaming. She's not ashamed of me, she's hilariously jealous of some other woman I couldn't give a shit about, and she thinks that *I* don't want *her*.

How did this get so fucked up?

I have no idea, but I'm gonna unfuck it right now.

I sit upright and wrap my arms around her waist tightly, not letting her move an inch. Quietly, so it's just the two of us, I vow, "I think I'm the only man who can handle you full throttle. And God knows, I want to. Give me your worst, and I'll show you my best."

She smiles, and I feel ten feet tall that I did that. That smile is mine, I fucking earned it.

She lays her arms over my shoulders, holding me just as tightly. "And what'll you do with my best?" she challenges.

"Try my damnedest to keep up," I answer honestly. Before she can muster up a comeback, I take her mouth desperately, stealing her breath to give myself life, because without her, I've been a zombie going through the motions. With just the tiniest taste, I remember how good she feels and come back to life, needing her because she's everything.

I squeeze her hips through her shirt, wanting to make sure she's real and not another figment of my imagination, because I've had this exact dream dozens of times. I nip her lip, drawing a squeak of surprise, and I sigh happily, "You're real."

Wren isn't someone who lets things happen to her. She's a full participant in every moment, and she nips me back, demanding more and more from me. Our kiss catches fire, taking us from the uncomfortableness we've been in for so long to a more familiar place, but this time, there's an honesty and a vulnerability in it for us both.

I tease along the hem of her shirt, not breaking our connection until the last moment before I sweep it over her head. She shakes her head to free her hair down her back, and I twirl a lock around my finger. I pull ever so slightly, waiting for her full attention. When her eyes meet mine, I stare into hers as I release her hair to trace my fingertips along her collarbone, down her sternum, and tease over the fullness of her breast. I've barely touched her, but her nipples pearl up as she arches for more.

Cupping the soft, heavy weight, I brush my thumbs over her hard nubs, rubbing them in small circles that pull a groan from Wren's throat. "More."

I don't need to be told twice. I duck my head as I lift her slightly so I can take her breast into my mouth. I suck gently at first, but then I feel her nails on my shoulders, and I moan at the sharp sensation. She knows what that does to me, so I answer her silent request and take a deep draw with my teeth pressed to her sensitive flesh. Wanting to worship all of her, I repeat the move to the other breast, giving them equal attention.

Slowly, I let her body lower, savoring every inch of contact as I press kisses along her breastbone, up her neck, and along her jaw. Her hips roll against my cock, which is trapped behind my zipper. Even so, I can feel the delicious heat of her core, so I push and pull her against me to hit her clit just right.

Lauren Landish

"Use me, Wren. Fucking use me," I tell her. I purposefully say her name, the word *baby* all but eliminated from my vocabulary because of her feelings about it.

As she writhes on me, I watch her in all her glory—head thrown back, eyes closed, and mouth open to let little whimpers escape. She's gorgeous, and I'm the luckiest bastard on the planet. A woman like Wren doesn't let just anyone witness her most vulnerable moments, but she's decided to allow me to see her this way. I don't take that lightly. I never have, and I'll never not be amazed by her passion.

She's getting close, her breathing hitching every other second as she works us both, and her pleasure takes my own higher. Suddenly, her focus redirects to between us where she fumbles with the button of my jeans.

"Thought you weren't *sleeping* with me," I tease, but there's enough hunger in my tone that it's obvious I'm on the edge of control.

"Shut up and fuck me, Jesse. I need it."

I yank my shirt over my head and undo my jeans myself to speed things up, shoving them down as much as I can with Wren on top of me. I do the same with my underwear to free my cock. And then I realize . . .

"Shit! I don't have a condom. Don't carry them, since I haven't needed one."

Her lips twist wryly. "Well, I don't have one, since I was kidnapped half-ass-naked."

I let the tip of my cock bump against her clit through her panties, and we both groan. It's not what either of us wants, but it's enough. It'll have to be. I do it again and again, her panties getting slicker and my cock leaking precum until she's slipping along my length easily.

"I'm clean, protected," she tells me with hazy eyes. She doesn't ask, but I know she wants to hear it.

"Me too. I haven't been with anyone since us. I swear."

She pulls her panties to the side and together, we guide each other right to the precipice of greatness. This time is different than every other, and when Wren lowers herself onto me, taking me fully in one stroke, I bury my face in the hair at her neck and breathe her in. Sunflowers and vanilla, the scent that's quintessentially Wren. I think it's her shampoo or maybe something she puts in her hair, or fuck, for all I know, it's her natural smell, but it releases a tension inside me that I never knew existed until she took it away.

As I hold steady deep inside her, her pussy quivers, massaging my length with her hot, wet heaven. "Fuck, I've missed you."

I roll my hips the tiniest bit, staying buried as I thrust into her. She pushes me back, and I lay down on the blanket, letting her ride me. She braces herself on her knees with her hands on my chest, and I can feel the half-moon marks she's making. I welcome them, want them, needing her to leave some trace that she's deemed me worthy again, if only for a moment in time.

As she bucks her hips, impaling herself on my cock again and again, her breasts sway above me hypnotically. I grab them, kneading the flesh roughly, and Wren's head falls forward, followed by her body going lax. She loses her rhythm, focusing on the pleasurable torture I'm giving her nipples—plucking, pinching, and then gently teasing the oversensitive nubs.

But that's not what either of us wants. I let my hands drop lower, popping her ass sharply. "Keep going," I command.

I help, though, slipping my hands beneath the fabric of her panties and spreading my fingers wide to hold each cheek in my punishing grip. I want to leave my mark, too, ten little reddened circles to remind her who owns her pussy. I guide her so that she's slamming down, taking me in so deeply that I'm afraid I'm hurting her, but the echoing sounds that fill the night are full of her desire for more.

If that's what she wants, I'll give it to her. I lift my ass, giving her all I can as I buck up to meet her downstrokes. Together, we find a rhythm. "There you go, fuck yourself on my cock. Take whatever you need, it's all yours. I'm yours."

She cries out into the night, the moon and me the only witness to her coming again. I feel her juices dripping down over me, running over my balls as the pulses of her pussy massage my length.

"Please, Jesse. I want it, want you," she gasps. "I want to feel you come inside me."

Oh, fuck. We've had sex dozens of times, but that's something we've never done. And I want that badly. I want to paint her insides with my cum, claim her from the inside out. Right now and forever.

I hold her hips tightly, not letting her move an inch and taking charge, though she's above me. I chase my own orgasm, pumping into her. In response, I feel her inner muscles squeeze, milking me for it. I grunt as I explode, filling her with jet after jet of my hot cream.

Spent, I collapse to the blanket, holding Wren tightly against me to place a gentle kiss to her forehead. As the sun starts to lighten the sky to a faded purple, I wish we could lay here like this forever, but I know we're both expected at work in a couple of hours. Life doesn't stop because we're figuring our shit out.

Taking a deep breath, I stroke her hair, asking playfully, "Wanna get breakfast?"

Wren looks up at me, one perfectly done brow arching sharply. "I can't go walking around town in a T-shirt and bare feet." She wiggles her toes, pointing toward the green shirt that's lying in a heap on the edge of the blanket.

"Now who doesn't want to be seen with who?" I tease, testing our comfort level.

She pushes at my chest, scolding me. "Shut up!" But she's smiling.

"Where'd you get that shirt anyway? It's like, ten sizes too big for you. And if it was some other guy, lie to me so I don't have to kill anyone with my bare hands today. I've kinda got a death-wish list going and shouldn't add to it until I mark someone off."

Wren laughs, which is a good thing because it was a joke . . . kinda. "Duh—it's yours. I might've borrowed it from your place once upon a time, which is not stealing because I was only borrowing it and totally planned to give it back. Someday. Maybe."

"That's not my shirt. What do you mean you took it from my place?" I repeat, thoroughly lost. And then, with the rising sun, I can see the shirt more fully and recognize it. "This is Alan's. He must've left it when he crashed on the couch. Have you been wearing this thinking it was mine?"

Oh, shit! What she said flashes across my mind.

"You sleep in this? Wear it when you touch yourself?" I grit out through clenched teeth.

Wren's eyes go wide in horror and thankfully, she looks at the shirt with disgust. "Oh my God! That's not yours?" She scrambles back like it's a snake that might bite her, so I treat it as such.

Grabbing it between my thumb and index finger, I hold it out so it can't attack either of us. "No! Bad shirt!" I tell it, copying the tone we use with Lester when he does something wrong. "Bad!"

With that, I fling it to the closest tree. To be clear, Hazel doesn't do that to Lester, though he'd probably do better than the shirt, which lands high on a branch, getting stuck and waving like an unwanted flag.

Wren laughs at my silly antics, but then her jaw drops. "Oh no! What am I going to wear home? I can't walk to my front door naked! I'm not looking to catch a public indecency charge. That's a class-A misdemeanor in this state."

"You can plea it down to a class B," I tell her, waiting for the recognition to cross her face before I hold up my shirt. "Kidding—maybe. You can wear this. Though I admit it needs a good wash." I sniff it, thankful that it's not as bad as I feared after a day's work. "Sorry about that."

She doesn't seem sorry in the slightest, pulling it over her head and wiggling it down over her body. She even presses it to her nose. "Smells like a sexy man who's been working hard."

"You pronounced *hog sweat* wrong," I tease lightly, "but I'll take it."

"By the way, while we're clearing some things up, I'll need your tattoo artist's name, phone number, and location." She's aiming for a casual, no-big-deal tone, but I know her too well, and now that I know she's got a jealous streak as wide as mine, I can hear it loud and clear. I don't know how I missed it before.

"Sure, his name's Corpse. He's over in Newport. Wyatt told me about him. You looking to get inked?"

"No, I—" She shakes her head. "Never mind. Let me see."

I shift so she can see it in the dawning light. "What do you think?" I hold my breath as I wait for her verdict.

It's a small bird, done in a photorealism style, just above the tan line on my right biceps. There are branches below its clawed feet where it's resting, but only for a moment before it flies away. It's by far the best tattoo I have. I wanted something special for this one and didn't sit for it until I found an artist who could do it justice.

"It's pretty. Even more so now that I know a guy named Corpse did it," she admits. "I'm not up on my ornithology, what kind of bird is it?"

"A wren."

"Oh!" she exclaims after a moment, her hands covering her mouth as the meaning hits her. "Are you serious?"

I shrug, not sure if she's pleased or pissed yet and hedging my bets. But she leans over to place a soft kiss to my arm, right over the bird's head.

"Does that mean you like it?"

She nods, and I feel her smile against my shoulder where she's laid her head. "Good, her name is Wren Fucking Ford for an amazing woman I know. Did you know wrens are badasses?" I don't wait for her to answer, sharing what I learned when I went searching for just the right image of a reddish-feathered bird. "They're tiny but fierce, loud to the point of being mouthy, and smart as hell. They claim all the space around them, not giving a damn about what other birds are around, and are aggressively territorial."

She laughs, and I risk my life by asking, "Sound like anyone you know?"

"Maybeeee . . . ," she drawls out, holding her thumb and finger a tiny inch apart.

I reach out to move them a good three inches apart. "Me too. She's perfect, just the way she is."

Chapter 15

WREN

"Morning, Joanne." I greet her as I pass by on the way to my office, hurrying because I'm a bit late after my night "sleeping" by the creek. I swear I'm walking the same as always, not skipping with happiness or bowlegged from hugging Jesse's hips, but Joanne's mild smile instantly morphs into something much more curious.

"Well, gooood morning to you, Wren." What should be an easy, standard greeting that we exchange daily has numerous questions intertwined into it today.

"Uh, thanks." I keep my pace, not wanting to answer any of the things she wants to ask. She calls my name and I speed up a bit, my short legs fueled by avoidance to move as fast as they can. "Lots to do today, can't talk. Sorry!" I call back over my shoulder.

"But—"

I open my door, planning to escape to the relative safety of my office, but realize too late that I should've listened to Joanne.

"Good morning, Wren." Oliver is sitting in my office, making himself at home in one of my chairs with an ankle resting on the opposite knee. He lets his eyes drip over my body from head to toe. I feel naked even though I'm dressed professionally in a knee-length skirt, short-sleeve blouse, and ankle boots. His lips curl up into an appreciative smile that feels like a physical touch. And not in a good way. "I hope you don't mind that I stopped by without calling. We have some things to discuss, and in-person seemed . . . *preferential.*"

I would've gone with *painfully uncomfortable* given my desire to slam the door shut, run back down the hall and out to the parking lot, and drive away to anywhere there's not a near-stranger who heard me orgasming looking like he wants an up close and personal repeat performance.

But, you know, that's just me. To-ma-to, to-mah-to.

Fighting my fight-or-flight instinct, I move around my desk, giving Oliver a wide berth, or as much as I can in my overgrown coat closet of an office. I sit down, hiding behind the breadth of fake wood as I put my purse in a drawer for safekeeping. "It's fine. Did you find out something about the construction company's financials?"

It's a straightforward attempt to stick to a professional topic, one I pray works.

"Yes, actually, but about the other night—"

Shit.

I interrupt to make one last-ditch effort to avoid this topic. "I'd like to apologize for any misunderstanding. I was distracted and should've given more attention to our conversation," I say evenly.

Oliver's grin grows, and there's no question, I'm out of luck. But Mom didn't raise a little bitch, so I lift my chin, ready to take the hit.

"Distracted? I'll say your focus was centered exactly where it should've been. I know mine was." He shifts his hips as he uncrosses his legs, spreading his thighs to emphasize his point. His dick might as well be pointing right at me from behind his tailored slacks.

I have to address this or we're never going to work together effectively, but it's a delicate dance so I don't piss Oliver off. That won't serve the people of Cold Springs or get Township completed on schedule.

Meeting Oliver's eyes directly, I quit tiptoeing around and bluntly say, "A friend came by. I shouldn't have answered the phone for obvious reasons. It was unprofessional of me, and I would very much like to get back to dealing with the Ford divorce and Township's construction."

I don't apologize. Apologies are sacrilege in the law community, a binding admission of wrongdoing and a submissive showing of your neck, both wrong in virtually every scenario.

He eyes me carefully for a long moment, then nods. "I'm looking forward to working together closely on this." There's still a thread of inappropriateness to the simple statement, but given how over the line I went, baby-stepping it back will have to do. But then he adds, "Just a friend?"

Sigh. I'm not sure how to answer that. Jesse and I are definitely way more than friends, but even with all the emotional dumping last night, we didn't exactly define our situation moving forward.

The pause without an answer tells Oliver everything he thinks he needs to know. "I see. Well, while he's certainly a lucky man, he's a stupid one."

"Excuse me?" I say sharply.

Oliver shrugs, unconcerned that I'm offended at his assessment. "If someone is lucky enough to be your 'friend' and be granted access to touch you in a way that drew those sounds from your sweet mouth"— his eyes drop to my lips and his tongue slips out to wet his own as though we're about to kiss even though there's a desk between us—"he'd have to be stupid to not make it crystal clear how special you are to him."

Whoa. Oliver's voice has gone deep and rough, aiming for raw sex appeal and hitting that target dead center. But I'm not interested, not in him or the compliment.

"I'll be sure to pass along that sentiment," I reply. He's completely serious, but keeping it light seems like the best strategic move, and I'm definitely not explaining the history between Jesse and me. It's none of

Oliver's business, and I'm still figuring it out for myself as I untangle things and what they might mean with the new insight I have now.

He answers my tiny smile with a broad one of his own. "You do that. If I'm not overstepping too much, I'd also suggest that you should consider if someone like that is worthy of you. In the small amount of time I've gotten to know you, it doesn't seem like you suffer fools lightly, but here you are without an answer on whether this man is a mere friend or more."

He shrugs like he shared something casual, but it's actually a heavy and astute observation that I probably should put some thought into. Later, not when Oliver's sitting in front of me, watching my reaction. And with Jesse, since it concerns the both of us.

"Noted." That's all I allow, but he seems to think that he's struck a nerve, given the cocky look of victory in his eyes.

"Good. Should we discuss the case, then?"

He's directing us back to the conversation I wanted to have in the first place, but rather than feeling like a win, it seems like he's controlling the situation now. It's frustrating, but I'm not going to argue when we're moving back to my target.

"Yes, let's. How's the financial audit going?" I ask. "I think we can both agree it'd be great to continue construction at Township."

One of the things Jesse and I discussed this morning was the shit show happening out at Township, with permits and with Lucy moving on-site. It'd been news to me that Jed was even here, since I still haven't heard a word from him or his lawyer. That's starting to worry me more and more. And having his mistress in the model home? There are bad ideas, and then there's that degree of utter stupidity. Not that that surprises me from Jed. Jesse did tell me that he can keep the guys busy for another week or so, but after that, it'll be a full stop. Neither of us wants that. Cold Springs doesn't want that either.

Oliver's jaw goes tight as he clenches his teeth together. *Hmm, seems like I'm the one who's hit a nerve now.* "The audit is going much more quickly than anticipated. For all Mr. Ford's shortcomings, recordkeeping doesn't seem to be one of them. His bookkeeper is meticulous."

"In other words, you found nothing. Jed's not hiding money, is he?" I surmise. Oliver won't say that straight-out, but the dip of his chin is answer enough. "That's good, though. It means they can work through the division of assets and we can proceed with Township."

"If only it were that easy," Oliver replies sadly. "I'm afraid cases like this are never quite that open-and-shut. Of course, if they were, I wouldn't have a job. I've got to do what's best for my client and what she wants, you understand that."

"I can understand having Chrissy's best interests in mind, but keeping construction going so that Township can turn a profit seems like that *would* be to her benefit." I know that's not all Chrissy wants, but a chunk of change can soothe a lot of anger. Chrissy can spend her time drying her tears with twenty-dollar bills while she sits at the spa for all I care.

"It would be, in a lot of ways. But there's a lot to consider," Oliver says cryptically.

I'm not sure what he's talking about, and before I can ask for clarification, my phone rings, echoing in my desk drawer. "Excuse me one moment," I tell him as I'm pulling my phone out. I glance at the screen and see Jesse's name.

Nope, not answering that with Oliver here. That seems like asking for trouble. I let it go to voice mail, but it starts ringing again immediately.

Oliver glances at the phone, and though he can't see the screen, his smile is knowing, like he can guess who's calling. "Go ahead. I know I invaded your morning."

But he doesn't move to give me any privacy. *Dammit.*

"Hello, this is Wren," I answer in my customer service voice, hoping it's enough of a clue for Jesse to realize I'm not alone.

"Hey! Crazy question for ya . . . do you know where that Oliver asshole is right now?"

I cut my eyes to Oliver. I don't have it on speakerphone, but Jesse is screaming so loud that there's no way Oliver didn't hear the question.

"Depends on why you're asking," I answer carefully. "Am I going to need bail money?" I'm half-serious, and it seems warranted to warn Oliver to stay away from Jesse a bit. For both their sakes.

There's a loud ruckus of noise, and I hear Jesse shouting to someone on his end. "I fucking know it! Robbie's on his way!"

"Robbie? What's wrong?" My heart is racing instantly. Why does Jesse need Officer Milson?

Jesse growls and says, "Find The Asshole and haul his ass out to Township. Chrissy's gone psycho out here."

"What's she doing?"

There's another round of shouting, and the line goes dead. With wide eyes, I look at my phone to double-check that it didn't just cut out, and then to Oliver, who's standing. "Heard enough. Let's go."

"I'll drive. C'mon!" We rush down the hall, scaring the hell out of Joanne, who screeches and tries to reprimand me like a child. But I wave her off, yelling behind me, "Tell Ben the shit's hit the fan and I'll be in touch."

He'll know that means I'm going to handle it. I just hope I can.

As soon as we get in my car, Oliver is dialing Chrissy on repeat to no avail. By the fifth time I hear the "leave a message" greeting, I think we both know there's no stopping whatever's happening until we're there.

I press the pedal a little more, glad my car's peppy and that I know these roads like the back of my hand. I try to figure out what the hell Aunt Chrissy could be doing that could possibly make Jesse so desperate that he's looking for Oliver, but I can't come up with anything.

As I turn into the Township development, I see what Jesse meant when he said "psycho," but even seeing it with my own two eyes, I don't believe it.

The first house in the subdivision is under a one-woman attack. The windows are busted in jagged lines across the front, the brick is crumbling in some sections, and the garage door has neon-pink spray paint reading "whore" on it. And that's on top of Chrissy's SUV parked sideways in the middle of the tiny lawn.

"What happened?" Oliver murmurs.

"Guessing Chrissy reached the 'hell hath no fury' phase." It's not a helpful observation, but it does seem to be true.

Chrissy is behind the wheel of a big piece of equipment, some sort of bulldozer type thing with a caged cockpit and forks on the front. It jerks a bit as it revs up, but I'm honestly a little impressed that she got the thing running and moving. She's heading for the front door.

"Knock, knock. Avon calling, bitch!" Chrissy shouts maniacally.

Jesse is waving his arms, his cap in his hands, like he's trying to distract and redirect a raging bull without standing in front of the charging machine. "Chrissy! What the fuck are you doing? Stop!"

She completely ignores him, and I get the sense that Jesse's already said that a few dozen times. He sees Oliver and me running up and shouts, "Lawyer Man, get your client before she kills someone!"

Oliver watches shrewdly, but makes zero move to do anything about the damage Chrissy's inflicting on the home.

"Worthless." Jesse's judgment does seem fairly accurate when Oliver starts texting on his phone. Meanwhile, Chrissy's made her way to the front door and is ramming it wildly, leaving big gouges in the surface and knocking over the shrubbery in the front flower bed. She's letting out some sort of battle cry that sounds like a mix of banshee and overly dramatic Siberian husky.

"Come out and face me like a man, Jed! Oh, that's riiiiight. You're not one without your little blue pills!"

Damn, Chrissy's telling all of Jed's business.

She's made her way through the door, though, and is attempting to use the front steps as some sort of ramp to get into the foyer of the townhome.

"What can I do?" I ask, willing to jump in to save someone . . . or something.

Jesse looks past me with relief. "There's Robbie. Just stay back so you don't get hurt."

The sirens on the car whoop once, enough to get the small crowd's attention, and Robbie gets out of his patrol car with his hand on his hip like we're the danger. "What seems to be the problem?"

Jesse takes the lead, shoving his cap on his head as he explains. "Chrissy came out here, ranting about Jed's mistress living in one of the town houses. She started destroying it with anything she could get her hands on." He throws his hands wide, indicating the current condition of the house. "That place was one hundred percent done, and now look at it."

He sounds both sad and mad about the home's needless destruction.

Robbie nods and cautiously steps over, near where Chrissy is digging the forks of the machine into the siding after giving up on the front door. "Hey, Chrissy, need you to stop this nonsense so we can have us a civil conversation, m'kay?"

He barely raises his voice, but is doing that authoritative thing where he's standing with his feet wide and his hands on his belt, expecting respect.

Is he for real?

Chrissy is red-faced, sweaty, and wild-eyed. Civility and logic have left the building as far as her brain's concerned. She's not gonna blink and suddenly realize that she should listen to someone, least of all a man, regardless of whether he's wearing a uniform or not.

But maybe she'll listen to me.

Before I take a handful of steps, Jesse tries to stop me, but I push him off with a vow that I'll be safe. I might not have authority like Robbie, but I do have a big mouth and enough attitude to get loud and brash. "Aunt Chrissy, what the hell are you doing?" I screech.

She glares at me long enough to say, "She's living here."

I already knew that, but shocked, I ask Jesse, "Is she in the house right now?"

That alone takes this from destruction of property to potential attempted murder.

"No," he sighs, "not this second. But there's a hundred thousand dollars' worth of materials she's blowing through, not to mention the skid steer she's driving like she stole it."

Robbie seems to think that's a valid argument until Oliver finally looks up from his phone. "Technically, she's destroying her own property. The company, and therefore its assets, are in both Mr. and Mrs. Ford's names, so she's welcome to do with it as she pleases."

Robbie tilts his head, mulling that over. "I reckon that makes sense." To Jesse, he holds up his hands and says, "Please don't come at me, man. The law's the law."

Jesse looks like he's still contemplating going after Robbie. At a minimum, they're going to meet at the pool table to settle this. But for now, Jesse surrenders.

"That's some bullshit and you know it," he tells Oliver, pointing a dirty finger at him. "Stay away from our construction zone and keep Chrissy out of it too." He gives one last look at Chrissy and walks away, muttering, "No helmet, no leg protection, no eyewear, and when she gets fucking hurt, who do you think they're gonna come after? Me! Well, fuck that!"

To the crowd of guys, he hollers, "Show's over. She's allowed to do a full demo if she wants, I guess."

There's a displeased rumble through the crowd, and Jesse adds, "We've got work to do if you want to hit your hours this week. We'll work around her if we have to."

That's another straw on the camel's back for Chrissy, and she wails, crying loudly and sloppily, as she tries in vain to get the machine to go through the front door of the town house again. "Yeehiiiii," she shouts as she makes contact.

I think this time she might actually get through.

Chapter 16

JESSE

News of Chrissy's breakdown and deconstruction beats me to town, and Puss N Boots is already packed to the gills with people gossiping away about it. That all stops when I come in.

"Shhh, Jesse's here."

"Did Chrissy really kill Jed's new woman and bury her in the concrete of one of the town houses?"

"I heard Robbie arrested her and she's at the jail tonight, waiting for a transfer to Newport Hospital for a psych eval."

What? I shake my head at the crazy paths the gossip vines can take. Holding up my hands, I try to calm the chaos so I can set the record straight. The last thing we need is people thinking Township is haunted by Lucy's ghost. There would be tents outside the front gates with T-shirts for sale faster than you can say "Area 51."

"Nobody died, nobody was buried in concrete, and nobody got arrested." Instead of being good news, a groan of disappointment goes through the room.

"Well, what happened, then?" a voice calls out.

I climb up on the bar and shout, "Hey!" Still not getting silence, I whistle loudly. Once I have all eyes on me, I explain, "Jed was letting

Lucy stay at Township as 'security.'" I don't do the air quotes, but with my intentional drawl and raised brows, everyone knows what I think of Jed's plan. "Chrissy found out. I guess you could say she came out to evict her—"

"*Preeetty* sure you mean kill her," someone hollers.

I clear my throat, impatiently waiting for silence again. "Evicting someone was apparently her right, since she's part owner of the whole development. Or so her lawyer and Officer Milson say. What matters is that all the damage is fixable and you've got my word, it'll be perfect before it's sold."

That development might be Ford Construction's, but everyone knows I'm the man building it, and my reputation for solid, quality work is unquestioned. I won't let Jed and Chrissy's divorce battle royale jeopardize that.

Aunt Etta comes out from the back, frowning deeply. Every single one of those lines on her forehead represents a whack she's given my ass when I was a kid. All completely warranted. "Jesse, what the hell are you doing on my bar? You'd best getchur ass and those dirty boots down from there right this minute if you know what's good for you."

She might as well be the principal breaking up an after-school fight, because everyone scatters like roaches, quickly going back to their pool tables and dinners so Etta doesn't yell at them too. I jump down, my boots echoing loudly on the wood floor. "Sorry! Wanted to explain once and be done. It's been a long-ass day."

I grab a towel and a spray bottle to clean the bar off myself, looking for Aunt Etta's acceptance of my apology. She narrows her eyes, and with a flip of her dark braid, she disappears into the back again, and the whole room releases a collective breath. That hair flip of hers is deadly if you're standing too close, but oddly, seeing it usually means that you've passed one of Etta's tests and she's leaving you to whatever nonsense you're up to.

Lauren Landish

I look around for an open table, but it's the blonde waving me over that finally brings a much-needed smile to my face after this shitty day.

"Hey!" I groan as I collapse into a chair beside her.

"Good speech." The compliment is accompanied by a wry twist of Wren's lips and a small golf clap.

I thank her by pulling her chair between my spread legs and throwing an arm over the back. Leaning in, I pause for the tiniest of moments to whisper, "Hi."

Not waiting for an answer, I meet her lips with mine for a hello kiss. It feels natural, like we've done it a hundred times before, and in some ways, we have. But not like this . . . not as a gentle reconnection after both of us having especially bad days.

And not in front of the entirety of Puss N Boots on a busy night.

"Wooo, hell yeah!"

"About"—*clap*—"damn"—*clap*—"time"—*clap*.

There's also a chorus of hoots and hollers that don't have words, but all mean the same thing—our town is happy for us.

I can feel Wren shrinking away from me at the newfound audience, but we're not doing that. Not when I finally have her. I chase her mouth, kissing her deeply as I hold up a middle finger to everyone else.

There's a bit of laughter, but all my attention is centered on Wren and her reaction. She doubts my desire to be seen with her? After this kiss, she won't. There won't be room in her beautiful mind for doubt. Only pure certainty that she's mine and I'm hers.

Finally.

She surrenders to the moment, to the kiss . . . to us. And only then do I release her. Though I add a couple of soft, smacking kisses before pulling back completely.

"Hi yourself," she answers dreamily. The look on her face is exactly what I've imagined—her guards down, her eyes soft, and her lips lifted in a blissed-out smile. Not many people are lucky enough to see Wren

144

this way, so I appreciate the gift she's giving me by letting me behind the walls of her hard shell.

I relax back into my chair, but keep my arm on the back of Wren's, claiming her. And for good measure, I pull her legs over my thigh, letting her calf brush against my cock. "I'd ask how your day was, but I think I have some idea."

"Screw that." Wren bumps me with her shoulder and grins. "I wanna hear how that played out before I got there."

"You and everyone else," I tease. "I don't know how Chrissy found out, but she showed up and commandeered that skid steer. Nearly ran Roscoe over because he was trying to talk some sense into her, and when he knew she was too far gone, he couldn't get outta her way fast enough. I was just glad Lucy wasn't there. I don't know what Chrissy would've done."

"Or Jed," she adds.

I shrug. "Nah, he deserves whatever's coming his way."

"Yeah, no love lost there on my side either. But that'll help with the workload, right? Keep your guys busy for a while longer?"

I side-eye her and whisper hotly, "Did you do that? Tell Chrissy about Lucy so that my crews could work?"

The timing is suspect, but damn if I wouldn't be shocked as shit if Wren did something like that. It's out of character for her, but she's also willing to do just about anything for the people she cares about.

"What? No!" she exclaims in surprise. "Wait . . . did you?"

I snort. "Hell no, it's a good idea, though. Too good for me." We look at each other, both working out who might've done something that diabolically brilliant.

"Etta?" Wren suggests quietly, looking over her shoulder like my aunt might pop up out of nowhere to overhear her.

I whisper in Wren's ear, "If so, we'd best shut our mouths about it or she'll tell Tayvious not to feed us."

Wren grins widely and whispers back, "Good thing I already ordered nachos, then."

Delighted and starving, I pat my hollow belly and groan, "Fuuuck, that's why I love you. Always thinking ahead."

Her eyes drop, but I can see her brows furrow as her mind works at something. I give her a minute, and then she asks, "How did I not know?"

"What?"

"I feel stupid," she confesses. "Everyone else knew this big thing, like it was some secret the whole town was in on, and now I'm rethinking every conversation I've had, every look people have given me, and it's all . . . I feel stupid. And that pisses me off." Her pity party doesn't last for long, turning to frustration and anger.

"No, no, no . . . Wren, that's on me. Put that on me." I pat my chest forcefully, making a few deep *thumps* in the process. "I didn't go around telling everyone to keep this from you, but they could see the way I watched you, the way I wanted you. They wanted us to have our time, when it was right. Like now. They're happy for us."

She looks around the room and granted, there are more than a few eyes turned to us, but it's not in judgment. "I still feel stupid."

I can't help but chuckle at her pouty tone. "Birdie, the absolute last thing anyone would ever think about you is that you're stupid. You're smarter than damn near everyone in town, and probably most folks in the state. I bet Ben thanks his lucky stars every night that you decided to stay here, and I don't know what I did in a previous life to be rewarded with the slightest bit of you, but I'm so fucking glad I did it."

"Excuse me, lovebirds. Here's your nachos." Charlene sets the heavy plate, piled with chips, in the middle of the table and refills Wren's water glass. "Jesse, you want a beer?"

"Make it a pitcher. We've got incoming . . ." I lift my chin toward the door where Wyatt, Hazel, Winston, Avery, and my mom are coming in. "Better go ahead and bring more nachos, too, because we ain't sharing these."

Charlene winks and runs off, calling out, "Daisy Sullivan, you'd best keep that baby away from me. That shit's contagious and this baby factory is closed, ya hear me?"

My mom laughs, holding Winston and Avery's son out like a monster that's going to get Charlene. "Get her, Joe! Git'er!" When they surround our table, my mom tells Hazel, "You hear that? Babies are contagious. You wanna hold him?"

She holds Joe out, and Hazel takes him easily, cooing, "Just because you come with every single body fluid known to man, that doesn't mean you're contagious, does it? You snot, drool, pee, and shit on everyone and we think it's cute as can be, don't we? But you're not fooling me, man. Grandpa Joe's been teaching you, hasn't he?"

Hazel winks at the baby like she's in on his game plan of cuteness. Credit to Joe, he babbles and grins, *goo*-ing at the words.

Wyatt takes the more direct approach. "Daisy, I'm not having mini-Hazels running around until I know how to handle the full-size one I've got."

"Hey!" Hazel balks, but we all know Wyatt has a valid point.

Mom laughs. "Good luck with that, then. Guess I'll have to count on Winston and Avery for more grandbabies."

Technically, we're not related to either Winston or Avery, so their baby—or babies as the case may be—wouldn't be Mom's grandchildren. But no one would dare tell her that. Family is more than DNA sometimes.

They pull chairs from here and there, joining us. As soon as she's got her butt in a chair, Mom looks from me to Wren and back, measuring the distance between us, which is basically none. It's obvious that things are different now. Mom's smile beams as she clasps her hands below her chin. "For real?"

"Smooth, Mom," I scold her dryly. "Real subtle." But I can't be mad at her. Mom listened to me rant and rave in the early days when I was hurt bad by Wren not calling me back, and has been there to help me stay steady in the months since. "Long story short, I was crazy for her, she was crazy for me, but we're shit communicators and in our heads too much. We fixed that last night."

Mom holds her arms out to us, jumping up and rushing around the table to fold Wren into a hug. "Welcome to the family! I always knew he'd win you over."

"Jeezusss!" I hiss. "Maybe don't make it seem like I'm such a loser."

But Wren's laughing at Mom's exuberance and hugging her back, though with considerably more reserve. "Oh, you hush, Jesse. Let a mom be happy for her kids." I think she means Hazel and me, but Mom kinda takes on a caretaker role for everyone in town. Primarily through their stomachs, since she makes the best pastries around.

"Thanks, Ms. Sullivan," Wren tells my mom.

"Daisy . . . or Mom?" she suggests instead, flashing puppy-dog eyes of hopefulness at Wren.

Surprised, Wren stammers out, "Uhm, thanks . . . Daisy."

As Mom sits down, pleased as punch with herself, she lets out a whooping noise. "Whoo-wee, that was the good news I needed to hear 'cuz I don't know about you, but I had a helluva day."

Wren and I look at each other and share a private grin, both certain that nothing could top our day.

"Chrissy Ford came on in to the Bakery Box, in the middle of my morning rush hour, and started measuring walls like she was gonna rip them down, right then and there." She waits for our gasps of surprise and anger but keeps right on rolling. "I told her to get out of my shop, and she started some song and dance about how she's gonna get the building in the divorce and is thinking about what she might want to do with it."

Jed Ford, and apparently Chrissy, own buildings all over Cold Springs, including the one where my mom's bakery has been since the day she opened the place. Her apartment is upstairs, too, so Chrissy trying to do something with the building would affect Mom's work and home.

"You have an airtight lease in place, right?" Wren goes right for the legal solutions, sticking with what she knows.

Hazel and I run a different path. "I know what she can do with it," I say. Hazel finishes with the line Aunt Etta taught us. "Shove it right up her ass and whistle a tune."

Mom waves us off from hunting Chrissy down and answers Wren. "Yes, I do." To us, she says, "No need for that. I know a thing or two about a thing or two, so I told Chrissy that she might want to concern herself with bigger fish than my little bakery." She smiles evilly, and almost as if she's changing subjects, she says, "Pregnancy cravings are a bitch. It's a good thing I've got Donny doing some deliveries around town these days."

Wait.

Is she saying . . .

"Mom, did you tell Chrissy about Lucy being at Township?" I shout.

She preens a bit, brushing her hair out of her eyes and looking innocent as can be, something she most definitely is not. "Maybe I did. Maybe I didn't. I've got no love lost for either Jed or Chrissy, so they can stay the hell out of my bakery and my business."

"Do you have any idea what your little distraction led to?" I demand, my palms slapping on the table.

Mom pauses at that, her eyes cutting around the table as she realizes that she might be out of the loop, which is a bad place to be in a small town. "What?"

"Chrissy came out there and destroyed the town house Lucy's been staying in. Luckily, she wasn't inside, but the building is fucking destroyed. I'm gonna have to rebuild the whole thing." I'm furious again. Not at Mom, though I'm irritated with her, but at the whole situation.

Wren puts her hand on my cheek, forcing my eyes to hers. "Hey, it's okay. It's more work for Alan, and all the guys. In fact, maybe we should do a little late-night demo out there ourselves to keep you busy."

She winks comically, her lashes fluttering down over her cheek. The joke surprises me from Wren. She wouldn't dream of actually doing anything that illegal. My sister, on the other hand . . .

Keeping my eyes locked on Wren, I point a finger at Hazel. "No." She whines, but used to it from a lifetime of her drama, I easily ignore it to press a sweet kiss to Wren's lips. Quietly, I murmur, "Thank you. But let's leave the criminal trespass and vandalism for another day."

"Heard. You're not saying no, you're saying no for now. I gotchu," Hazel answers, swinging V'd fingers from her eyes to mine.

Avery's been quiet, but at that, she touches her nose with the tip of her finger. "Not it for bail."

Wyatt chuckles. "See, Daisy. We can't have grandkids because we're literally taking turns on who's gonna bail Hazel out *this time*."

He's joking, mostly. Hazel hasn't spent a day in jail in years, and the last time was for a fundraiser for the high school where the bail money went to the girls' volleyball team. But I sure as shit used that picture of Hazel in an orange jumpsuit for Christmas cards that year and have it printed on a T-shirt to wear when she pisses me off.

I throw a twenty on the table. "We've had a long day too. Think we'll head out."

I hold Wren's chair as she gets up and wrap her hand in mine as we head to the door.

Tayvious pops his head through the window to the kitchen. "Bye, Jesse! Bye, Wren! You two are cute as a couple of frenchie puppies ready to go sniff each other's asses!"

Tayvious's loud comment draws everyone's attention our way again, but having learned their lesson the first time, most folks just offer up a small wave and go on about their business.

Chapter 17

WREN

"Not wanting to step on your toes here, but I want to see what this jerk's got up his sleeve too. Especially after that bullshit Chrissy pulled," Ben tells me. He looks out the window with narrowed eyes, and to a bystander, it'd almost seem like he's mentally fading away. But Ben's mind is sharp, and he's likely playing out scenarios the same way I've been doing since this meeting was called.

Three hours ago.

Divorce is typically a slow endeavor. Divorce with contentious parties? Even slower. But when my phone rang this morning, Oliver was downright snippy with me, demanding a sit-down with all parties today.

Luckily, the conference room is available because the book club group was willing to reschedule this week's meeting—with a reminder that they want any shareable details first—so Ben and I are sitting here, waiting for this circus to get started.

"Let them show their cards first," Ben reminds me. "You did us right with that contract, so whatever dodginess they've got in mind for each other should slide right off us like shit off a duck's back."

"Unless they pull out of the whole build project," I suggest. "They're obligated to finish phase one, but they can delay the rest indefinitely if the divorce stays unresolved." That's my main fear, and Francine's too. We want Township for Cold Springs, so in some ways, Jed has us by the short hairs and he knows it.

"If they're hustling like this, I don't reckon it'll be unresolved for long."

Joanne pokes her head in the door. "Should I get coffee or water for the table?"

"It ain't the pope coming and this is no friendly meet 'n' greet. If they're thirsty, they can get a drink out of the water fountain in the hall." Ben's crankiness is warranted. I've got a matching case, but we need to hide it a bit better until we find out what's going on.

"Thanks, Joanne. We're good for now," I tell her, much more kindly.

A few minutes later, I can hear the *click-clack* of shoes coming down the hallway. "Showtime," Ben says.

I plaster a politely blank expression on my face and stand as we wait for the door to open. Jed and his lawyer, Robert Jenkins, come in like this is their meeting room, making themselves at home on the opposite side of the table.

Jed's lawyer is exactly what I expected. His personality enters the room almost before he does—big, bold, brash, and smarmy in an expensive suit. I could've guessed Robert Jenkins was an attorney without seeing his business card. He's probably the type that, when he's not defending assholes in messy divorces, does cable TV commercials promising you millions for that rash you got with your last visit to the doctor's office. Not the one you got treated . . . the other one.

"Good to meet you. Ben Norton?" Robert holds his hand out to Ben, ignoring me completely. I'm not surprised. He probably thinks I'm an assistant or someone equally beneath him.

Ben shakes Robert's, but also adds, "This is Wren Ford, Cold Springs' attorney."

Robert's eyes ping-pong from Ben to me, almost amused. Does he think Ben is kidding?

Lauren Landish

I hold my hand out, waiting with a mild version of my resting bitch face. I'm naturally a fairly smiley, happy person, and one of the first lessons I learned in law school was to fix my face. It's a skill that's been useful over the years, especially when people underestimate me.

Like Robert Jenkins is doing right now, shaking my hand the way you might placate a toddler who wants you to bow because they're a real princess. If he tries to pat me on the head, I swear he'll come back with a nub.

Uncle Jed doesn't bother shaking my hand, but rather goes straight for the family connection. "Hey, Wren, I haven't seen you in a bit. How's your mama doing? She still dragging Bill to those yoga classes?"

He chuckles, elbowing Robert like, *Can you believe that?* Jed might be my uncle, but Mom and Dad aren't close with him anymore and haven't been in a while. For living in a small town, we basically see Jed at Christmas and maybe the occasional run-in at the coffee shop or gas station.

Jed thinks that's my mother's doing, but the truth is, Dad feels like he finally escaped Jed's shadow and has no interest in going back into the dark, much preferring the light. He and Mom have created a lovely life in their retirement, with yoga dates, a book club, and babysitting for Winston, taking Joe as much as they can. They're happier without Jed in their lives, and so am I.

If we can just get Township done, hopefully I won't have to deal with him anymore.

"They're enjoying retirement." A simple, truthful statement that ignores his implication that Mom somehow holds Dad's balls in her purse.

We sit down, and after a few awkward minutes of silence, Oliver and Chrissy arrive.

Chrissy came dressed to impress, in a black pencil skirt that fits her like a second skin, a black blouse that hugs her breasts, and black heels. Her hair and makeup are pristine, and I wouldn't be surprised if she

154

had them professionally done this morning. She looks nothing like the crazed, wild woman who destroyed a town house yesterday, but rather a refined, pulled-together woman who will give Jed and his lawyer a run for their money.

The atmosphere chills instantly as Jed glares at Chrissy, and she feigns indifference.

Oliver pulls out a chair for Chrissy, and she perches on it delicately. "Hello, Wren, Ben," he greets us as he sits down comfortably.

The difference in approaches is apparent from the jump. Robert feels big and important, and I'd bet he is accustomed to people fawning over him. Oliver's already been working with us and is relaxed and friendly, going so far as to shoot me a more-than-familiar smile. Ben and I are stuck in the middle, not giving two shits about the divorce other than how it affects our town.

"Let's get this done." Robert's opener is cold and mechanical, but Oliver responds in kind, pulling a thick manila folder from his briefcase.

"I'm keeping the house," Chrissy declares.

Jed scoffs. "Over my dead body."

"Well, you'd best get to dying, then, because I'm sleeping there tonight. Alone."

Ding, ding. Fight!

And so begins an hours-long fight for every penny, property, and even a coffeepot that apparently is a bone of contention between the two of them. I feel like a voyeur as I watch them reveal secrets no one outside their marriage should know, like that Jed sings while he shits every morning, waking Chrissy up with his off-key warbling of seventies rock hits, and that Chrissy has a bad habit of picking her nose until it bleeds.

"We'll see about that," Chrissy sneers about Jed's claim that he's taking his truck.

Jed mocks Chrissy, "Oh, you think so?"

"You have no idea what I can do," Chrissy threatens. "I already shut down your stupid development, didn't I? And got you out of the house? And took my share of the bank account? You don't know what I'm capable of."

Boiling bunnies maybe?

"I guess we'll see about that, won't we?" Jed throws Chrissy's words right back at her, and they sound significantly more concerning coming from him. She's wild and out of control with hurt, but Jed's shrewd and calculating. And obviously planning something.

Nothing has been decided, only battled over. I didn't expect them to negotiate a list of his and hers today, they're just sparring and feeling each other out, but finally, we get down to the nitty-gritty that matters—Ford Construction Company.

Oliver flips to a new page in his folder. He glances at me, and for the first time since they entered today, I can see sorrow in his eyes. It's only a flash before he returns to his cutthroat persona, but concern bubbles up in my throat. "We've had our financial auditor estimate the value, but concede that you will likely want to do the same, considering the significant assets."

Jed scoffs and Robert clears his throat, pointedly silencing his client, before nodding at Oliver to continue.

"We propose that personal assets be divided seventy-thirty, in Ms. Ford's favor, in light of Mr. Ford's obvious and incontestable activities outside of the marriage. In addition, professional assets will be divided seventy-thirty. While we concede that Mr. Ford has run the day-to-day operations of their marital business, it was Ms. Ford's initial investment that started the business, and she has been an active and equal participant in the business all along, providing support that allowed Mr. Ford the freedom to work as he desired."

Holy shit! Chrissy really is planning to take Jed to the cleaners. A seventy-thirty division of all assets? I'm no fan of Jed's, but that's punitive by definition.

"You think you're equal in my business?" Jed sneers at Chrissy.

She smiles coldly. "Honestly, considering it was my inheritance that funded your little Bob the Builder dream, I'd say *more* than equal."

Jed nearly comes across the table at her, but stops halfway to plant one hand on the surface and point at her with a thick finger. "You bitch. No matter how miserable I was, you never gave a shit. Just wanted me to fund your shopping sprees and spa days. And now you're pissed that I'm finally happy."

Chrissy doesn't so much as blink at his angry outburst, but rather coldly answers back, "Happy with *her*? She's a baby, Jed. Of course she thinks you're some knight in shining armor and you're going to have this *oh-so-perfect little family*, but I bet she feels differently when her knight can't afford a pot to piss in, hates children, and is too old to get it up without a blue pill."

Oooh, snap! Chrissy and Jed are hitting low and hard.

I'm on the edge of my seat, morbidly curious how he's going to reply back to that, but Robert forcibly pulls Jed back to his seat and leans over to whisper in his ear. I can't hear what he's saying, but Jed is turning redder by the moment, mostly because I don't think he's breathing in his effort to bite his tongue.

Keeping a straight face, I look to Oliver, who's holding out a staying hand at Chrissy's. He looks . . . pleased? This must be some sort of bluff on their part, a negotiation tactic to get the ball rolling in Chrissy's favor, which isn't unusual. Start at seventy-thirty, Jed counters fifty-fifty, and they settle at sixty-forty, which still nets Chrissy more than she probably expected from Jed.

Robert gets a nod from Jed, and leans forward to look at his phone screen. Typing on his calculator app, he repeats, "We've looked over your financial auditor's evaluation." Type, type, type. He holds up the calculator, showing the number to Jed with raised brows. When Jed doesn't react, Robert finishes, "We agree to its contents."

That alone surprises me. Even if he's not hiding money, I figured Jed would want to undervalue some things and overvalue others. It's a common tactic in contentious divorces so that one party gets more than their "fair share," and totally something Jed would do.

"Okay," Oliver agrees slowly. His answer is solid, but his shoulders have inched up a bit. Why is he nervous? It's his idea.

"Agreed." Robert's single word sets the room ablaze.

"What?" Chrissy squawks.

"What?" I hiss.

Ben makes a gurgling noise that has me worried for a second.

Even Oliver seems shocked, but maintaining professionalism, he holds his hand out to shake on the deal.

Robert grins. "Ah, ah, ah, not so fast—"

Thank fuck. There's got to be more to this, because otherwise, Chrissy just became the CEO and owner of Ford Construction Company and the person I'll have to deal with for Township. And as bad as Jed is, Chrissy is . . . Chrissy.

"With one consideration. Jed wants to retain the ownership of the name Ford Construction Company, with no noncompete to enforce."

"Wait. What?" Chrissy demands. "It's my company. That's what you just agreed to."

Jed smiles now. "You buy out my share and you get the company . . . *assets*. The Ford name is mine, and I won't have you doing business as me, trading on the success I've built." He stands, and Robert mirrors him. With an evil grin, Jed slides a whole ring full of keys across the table, pinging right into Chrissy's chest because she's not remotely prepared to catch them. "Good luck."

"We'll be in touch," Robert tells Oliver. The two men exit, both with matching shit-eating smiles that terrify me, and Chrissy looks at Oliver in confusion.

"That's good, right? I got it all?"

Oliver frowns. "Yes, but it's way too easy. I'll read through the settlement carefully to make sure there are no surprises."

Chrissy quit listening after the "yes" and is basically jumping around the conference room like she's won the lottery. "Let's go, Ollie! We've got celebrating to do! Champagne's on me!"

Oliver stands, still looking concerned as he gathers his papers.

"Looking forward to working with you on Township, Wren." Chrissy's statement might as well have swept my feet out from underneath me because it definitely steals my breath.

"Whaaat?"

But Chrissy's gone, quickly tippy-tapping down the hallway in her excitement and taking my pride in Township with her.

My first big contract deal for Cold Springs has turned into a clusterfuck of explosive proportions. There's no way Chrissy can finish out the development, completely clueless about not only how to build a house, but how to run a business. I don't know what Jed actually does all day, but he's got more experience at it than Chrissy does.

"Wren—" Oliver says quietly. "Can we talk about this?"

I drag my eyes back to him, anger turning my gaze icy. Holding up a hand, I tell him snidely, "Don't. Whatever's best for your client, I know."

"Yes, but I never thought . . ." He glances to Ben, who's sitting silently by my side cataloging everything he sees and hears. I don't need to look to know what's on Ben's face—complete blankness. Not because he hasn't figured out there's an undercurrent of something else going on, but because he's holding judgment until he's compiled all the facts.

Fact number one—Oliver should've followed his client, but he's still here to talk to me.

Fact number two—the request to talk about this sounds more like a date than a work thing.

Fact number three—I sound like a scorned woman.

"It's fine. Go with Chrissy, read the settlement, and we can set up a meeting to discuss Township moving forward," I add. "The book club already reserved the conference room for tomorrow morning, so it'll have to be after that." Crisp, clipped, and professional is my goal. I'm not sure I hit it, but I for sure land somewhere around bossy bitch.

He straightens his back and schools his face, leaving without another word.

"Sooo, that went well," Ben says sarcastically.

"It's not what you think," I rush to reassure him.

He guffaws. "Girl, I think it's exactly what I think . . . that man has more than business on his mind where you're concerned." He dips his chin, staring at me from above his glasses and daring me to disagree. When I stay silent, he continues, "I thought I heard you and Jesse were finally figuring things out?"

Yeah, like the whole rest of the town—everyone but me—apparently Ben knows about that too. "We are."

"Well, it sounds like you got plenty of other stuff to figure out. What do you think about Chrissy running the Township deal?"

"She doesn't know her ass from her elbow, couldn't run a 'boss babe' business with a step-by-step instruction manual, and will, no doubt, do something that'll ruin Township. So it's up to me to figure out how to stop that from happening."

"How d'ya plan to do that?" Ben's lips are twitching as he fights to hide a smile at my sudden urgency.

"Research. The lawyer's best offense, defense, and friend. The answer is in the law." A professor in law school said that, and it's always stuck with me. This time, I add my own supplement to the saying, "Or in the contract."

Ben lets that smile loose. "Well, you'd best get to it, Nancy Drew. Sounds like you've got a mystery to solve—how to prevent the destruction of Township."

Chapter 18

JESSE

I haven't been to Bill and Pamela Ford's home since Winston's wedding. And that was as a helper for my mother, not as a guest.

I hoped that the next time I came here, it would be at Wren's invitation to have dinner with her parents. I'd get dressed up, shake her dad's hand and give her mom a bouquet of flowers from the grocery store, and we'd sit down to a fancy meal where I'd prove to them that I'm the right man for their only daughter.

Unfortunately, that's not how tonight's gonna go.

I ring the bell, thankful I at least had a clean T-shirt in my truck. Still, I give my pits a sniff to make sure the extra layer of deodorant I slicked on is doing its job.

The woman who answers the door smiles warmly, not seeming to care about my rough appearance. "Ah, Jesse! Good to see you!" Maria gathers me in her arms, patting my shoulder in welcome. "Your mama is already in the dining room with the others."

Maria usually comes into Puss N Boots on Sundays with her friends from church, and I'm sometimes there running a table or grabbing a bite. But she's also one of Mom's regular customers, so I see her at the Bakery Box pretty often when she comes in for her favorite BDSM cookies. Though she won't order them with the shortened nickname, instead preferring the long version—bacon, dates, sugar, and maple syrup cookies.

"Dining room?" I repeat, patting my belly. I came straight from work, following the instructions in Wren's group text, which was basically come to the Ford house ASAP. 911. and nothing more. I'm not sure what's going on or who else is here, but my Spidey-Senses tell me this can't be good because Wren doesn't ask for help.

Period.

But she has, from people she trusts. And it means something that I'm on that short list.

"There are snacks in there already," Maria assures me. When I give her a puppy-dog look, she laughs and squeezes my biceps appreciatively. "And I'll bring in dinner shortly. I know a boy like you can't live on char-tooter-y alone."

I laugh at her intentional mispronunciation. "Thanks, Maria."

"You'd better get on in there, but don't be a stranger around here, m'kay?" She pats my cheek with affection and a fair dose of *don't screw this up.*

The dining room has been converted into a war room of sorts. There's a dry-erase board covered in what I'm guessing are legal cases because it says things like "Jones v. City of Marshall." All of Wren's generals are pulled together into some mismatched Scooby-Doo gang.

Wyatt and Hazel, Winston and Avery, my mom, Bill and Pamela, Grandpa Joe and his namesake, Aunt Etta, Ben Norton, and Francine Lockewood. Everyone's sitting around the table, staring at a screen or nose buried in a book, though it looks like Grandpa Joe is drawing in the book he's holding. If Francine catches him defacing a book, she'll have him cleaning bookshelves over at the city library. You don't fuck with books on Francine's watch.

Not wanting to interrupt everyone, I go to Wren's side first, admiring her concentration as she reads the thick tome in her hands. She's beautiful. Her hair is pushed behind her ears, her green eyes scan left to right, and her lips are parted slightly. I wait for her to reach a pause point in her reading, and when she glances up, likely feeling my eyes on her, she smiles brightly. "You came."

"Of course I did. Tell me what you need me to do."

"Kiss me first," she commands with a tiny, flirty smile.

"Gladly," I growl as I crowd into her space, smooshing the book between us. I bend down to meet her lips with mine, and she kisses me back with confidence. It's over too quickly, but I can feel the stress in her body relax ever so slightly.

Knowing she needs more to fuel whatever's going on, I crack open the Naked Mighty Mango I grabbed from the store on my way over and hold it out to her. I might not have gone all the way home to shower or change, but I sure as shit got Wren a drink. While she takes a long pull, I make a quick stack of cheese and crackers, not for me, but for Wren. I'd bet my left nut—which I'm seriously attached to—that she hasn't had a bite to eat. She's too focused on whatever's triggered this little study group. I'm desperately curious what that is, but I trust that she'll explain when she's ready.

I hold a cracker stack in front of her, and she nibbles it from my hand without pausing in her reading. "Fank whu," she mutters around the mouthful.

"What else?"

"Grab a book, use the index to look for those cases"—she points to the list on the side of the board—"read those sections, see if it has anything to do with company ownership changes during a contract period or anything else that seems relevant."

"Yes, ma'am," I rumble, smiling widely. I'm not smart the way she is. Hell, no one is, but she trusts me to help with this, the same as everyone else. I grab a medium-size blue book and sprawl out in a chair, but find eyes looking at me from every direction.

To no one's surprise, Hazel is the first to speak. Stage-whispering to Avery, she says, "Are we all supposed to pretend that we didn't see him waltz in here and go all caring, sweety-sweetums and Wren *not* rip him a new one? It's kinda ruining both their reps."

"Someone sounds jealous," Wyatt teases his wife, exponentially increasing his odds of sleeping on the couch tonight. Those odds get even worse when Hazel cuts her eyes his way and instead of cowering, he glares right back like, *Did I lie?* and adds, "And if I did that, you'd do a lot more than rip me a new one, so don't give me shit for throwing food at you from across the room and hoping it lands somewhere that'll feed you or distract you from killing me."

Thankfully, he says it all with the utmost love for my psycho sister or I'd feel compelled to defend her, which would be hard as hell because he's totally right. There's independent and then there's Hazel. Of course, she learned from the best examples in Mom and Aunt Etta.

My dad died when I was a kid and far too young to take on a man-of-the-house-type role. Instead, what I grew up with was women who didn't need a man in their life. I learned that women are stronger than almost any man, smarter than anyone gives them credit for, and all-around amazing creatures. I have the utmost respect for them.

But Hazel is talking smack about Wren, and that I won't stand for.

I put the book in my lap, protecting my important parts, and tell Hazel, "Don't give Wren shit when she's doing this to save your ass. She's taking care of us, so I'm taking care of her."

I point at Wren, and though her eyes are cast down at the book, her lips tilt up in a small smile so I know she's listening.

"You don't even know what we're doing here, since you were late," Hazel argues accusingly.

"Don't need to know. Wren's been tied up in the divorce deal and has all of us here, so something's obviously gone way off the rails. This is about that, so ipso facto, it's for Cold Springs. And all of us. Even you, Miss I Don't Need Nothing or No One."

I've been fighting with and for my sister since we were kids, and it's made us both stronger in the long run. And closer. No one can give her a hard time like I can, or I'd skin them alive, and I know she's the same about me. So though everyone else is holding their breath, waiting for an explosion, I'm grinning at Hazel like I just took a chomp out of the last Popsicle in the freezer, suffering through the instant brain freeze because I know she won't get one.

"Ipso facto?" she echoes. "What the hell have you been watching while you've been pining away for Wren? *Jeopardy!*?" A tease and a secret reveal, but one I don't mind.

"Anything that'd get me through until I got another shot with her," I confess easily. There's no need to hide it. Everyone in this room already knows it.

"Aww," Avery sings with teary eyes, burying her nose in baby Joe's hair.

Mom's grinning like she's planning our wedding cake, and Bill and Pamela Ford are looking at me like they've never seen me before. Hopefully, I'm exceeding whatever judgment they're passing.

It's Wren who gives me the best response, though, coming over to where I'm sitting and gesturing at me to move my book-protective cup. When I do, she climbs into my lap, sitting sideways with her legs over the arm of the chair. She places a quick peck to my cheek and smiles at me in a way that could make the whole world seem perfect even if it was ablaze.

"What was that for?" I ask, ready to repeat whatever it was if it gets me sweet kisses like that.

"For kidnapping me," she answers easily. And though she smiles as she goes back to reading, her parents and brothers are eyeing me with unspoken, curious threats. One, what does she mean by kidnapping? And two, if I hurt her, the next place I rest my head might be six or ten feet underground via my own crew's excavator.

But I can take it. For Wren.

"By the way, I'm Bill. This is Pamela," Wren's dad says finally.

Shit. I probably should've shaken their hands or something, since this time I'm not here as the help. Awkwardly, I lift a hand their way. "Uhm, nice to meet you. Again? I'm Jesse."

Pamela grins, though, waving a dismissive hand at me. "Oh, we know exactly who you are, dear. And I remember what a help you were for Winston's wedding. I think we're just a little surprised at our rather prickly daughter's reaction to you."

Instead of seeming put off, she's smiling like I'm a magician who pulled a rabbit out of a hat.

Wren snaps her fingers and points at the book in her hands, and we all get the message to get back to work.

I look at the index in my chosen book, find the listed page, and start reading. I have no idea what all this legal mumbo jumbo is, but construction shit? I got that part down. Thank fuck, because I'm three books in before I know it, and my eyes are crossing from reading the unfamiliar words and phrases. But Grandpa Joe is snoring loud enough to wake the dead, so at least I'm not the most useless in the room.

Avery is dancing around with baby Joe, trying to put him to sleep like his namesake, while writing on the dry-erase board as we find things to note. "Guys, I think we should try to consolidate this because we're starting to repeat information."

Wren looks up, scanning the board quickly. To my dismay, she climbs out of my lap and walks over to the board. "Okay, let's see here . . ."

What happens next, I can't describe because Wren, Ben, Bill, and Francine start talking lightning fast with words that are totally part of the English language but make zero sense to me in the order they're saying them.

At one point, I ask, "Is Chrissy really gonna get the business? I mean, she can wish in one hand and shit in the other, and see which fills up faster, but she's not really going to get it, is she?"

Wren frowns sadly, filling me in on what I missed by being late. "Jed gave her the keys. He gave in, only arguing for his name. He said it's so she doesn't sully his name, but . . ."

Bill pops in. "It's so he can throw out a new shingle and compete with Chrissy. That's how he is. He's going to take whatever money he gets, start a new business, and then take complete and utter glee in driving her into the ground. It's a way to punish her for daring to question him and leave him."

Damn. I might say some shit about Hazel, but it's all in love. Bill talks about his brother with no love lost between them.

"Has anyone else met Lucy?" When everyone shakes their head, I offer, "It was weird. Jed and her were all baby talk and lovey-dovey. Suuuper handsy in the most disgusting of ways. But in a weird way, he seemed . . . happy?"

Bill scoffs. "Yeah, I feel for her, whoever she is. She's a new plaything he can control."

"Family drama aside, I need to protect Cold Springs from this. What's our best play?" Francine poses the question to the room at large, not just the smarties who've been talking through legalese like it's a kiddie book.

"It's still Jed's company until the divorce is final. What if we delay it a bit, get those boys back to work, and get Township all sewn up?" Grandpa Joe pipes in, apparently following the conversation despite his snores.

"Yeah! We could tie Chrissy up with legal stuff until Township is done," Avery echoes.

Hazel laughs evilly. "Or literally tie her up in a barn somewhere until Jesse's done. I've got rope and could borrow a barn, no problem. How long do you need?"

I shrug as I do the mental calculations. "At least a month, maybe closer to two, to finish the bulk of it. We've got three more streets, but the last one at the back of the development is shorter because of the pond." In my mind, I'm already making a cut list of what I'd need. "I could push the guys. Most of 'em would be good with sunup to sundown for a short time if it meant big paychecks, piling in the overtime. I'll warn them that after this build-out, jobs are in question, though, so nobody goes out and plops the cash down on a new truck or some shit. And materials were ordered in bulk when we started, with a delivery schedule per street. I could see about moving up those dates. As long as the weather holds, I can get it done."

"Jesse—" Winston knows how much work I'm talking about. He's been eyeball deep in Jed's operation before, and understands the scope of work a development like Township requires. "You really willing to do that for Cold Springs?"

"Hell no," I answer, shaking my head. "But I'm willing to do it for Wren. She said this contract is important to her, so if I need to turn myself inside out so that it doesn't fall apart, I will."

Wren drops the book she's holding to the floor and strides directly toward me. One hand on each arm of the chair, she bends down to meet my eyes. "You are an amazing man, Jesse Sullivan." And then she kisses me solidly.

I can't believe we were so stupid for so long, her worried she's too much and me sure that I'm not enough. We couldn't have been more wrong. Because together, we're perfect, and she can use my rough edges to polish the shine of her diamond all she wants.

"That's really sweet and all," Francine says, "but I also don't want a whole development speed built that's going to give our residents problems later. No offense, Jesse." I dip my chin, understanding her concern and that it's not a slight of my work. "What if we rewrite the contract with Chrissy? We could add in some clauses to our favor."

Ben and Wren have some sort of sidebar conversation that I don't get, and after a minute, Wren says, "We agree. I'm going to have to work with Chrissy and Oliver to revamp the contract. That also means that all construction is going to have to stop, because the deal they're built under is no longer in place."

She looks at me apologetically, but it's not me who needs an apology. It's my crew.

"Effective when?" I grit out. She's doing what she has to do, but I've got an entire site and a bunch of guys I'm responsible for who she's affecting in the worst way.

"Uhm . . . as soon as I tell Jed and Chrissy that their contract with the city is under reconsideration."

I nod, furious even though I understand. "Gimme till Monday, at least. Please. I can have the guys bust ass tomorrow and all weekend, working overtime. We'll get as much done as we can, so the guys get a little cushion and we clear out some materials so they don't go to waste before this gets straightened out."

"I can do that," Wren agrees, looking at Ben and Francine for consensus.

I stand and take a deep breath. "I gotta go, then. I'll let the crews know, but I want to spend some time out at the site tonight making a plan of attack."

Wyatt and Winston rise too. "We'll go with you and help. If nothing else, we can help set up materials so they're ready to roll in the morning."

I shake both their hands appreciatively. "Thanks, the pay is zero dollars an hour, but I'll order us pizza later. Overtime's a beer at Puss N Boots."

"Deal," Wyatt says.

Winston kisses baby Joe on the head and then Avery. He points a finger at Grandpa Joe, instructing him, "Take care of my girl and my li'l man for me."

Grandpa Joe couldn't do a thing but press his emergency alert button if something went wrong, but Winston respects him and his place in their extended family unit.

I wrap my arms around Wren, and she presses her palms to my chest. "I'll talk to you later, Birdie. Maybe set your meeting for as late on Monday as you can?"

She smiles and curls her fingers, digging her nails into my flesh through my shirt. It's all the answer I need, and I have to swallow the growl that threatens to escape. I think her dad would have my hide if I made those kinda noises with his little girl, no matter the fact that Wren likes them. As evidenced by her sweet smile turning sly. I bend down as she raises up to her toes and our lips meet in the middle. It's a goodbye for a few days while we both bury ourselves in work, and a promise to bury ourselves in each other after Monday.

With that, me and Wren's brothers head out.

"Never thought I'd see the day," Winston says in the driveway as we head to our individual vehicles. He's got some sort of SUV with a high-safety rating, a total Dad-mobile, while Wyatt drives a truck. It's nothing like mine, though, which is beat up from job sites and hauling materials. Wyatt's truck is fancy and shiny, only used for carrying an occasional small custom furniture piece in Bubble Wrap and soft blankets or towing a trailer with more of the same.

"What?"

"Some guy actually being worthy of Wren," Winston answers. "Really never thought it'd be you." He's grinning as he says it, likely thinking he's teasing, but it cuts deep.

"Me neither," I growl. "Let's go. I've got a fuckton of work to do."

Chapter 19

WREN

This weekend has sucked.

First, I thought I'd be alone the whole time while Jesse's working at Township. And I really wanted to see him. But instead, my front door might as well have been a revolving door.

Mom and Dad came to see me, wanting to talk about Jed, the contract, and what I suspect to be their real reason for coming, Jesse and me.

Then Ben and Francine stopped by. They at least stayed on topic, giving me all sorts of advice and ideas on what to include in the new contract. But I had to shut down Francine's hopes of adding in a way to attract migrating ducks to the pond. "They're awful for the bank's soil erosion, can pollute the water with foreign algae, and most importantly, they already have migration plans in place, so drawing them off-path can lead to them being lost." She'd cried about the poor, lost duckies while Ben and I drafted a few clauses about signage instead.

Hazel stopped by to bring food from Puss N Boots to stock my fridge and pastries from Daisy's bakery. She also gave me the scoop from Wyatt about working on setup at Township with Jesse, so I was glad to hear that.

Despite the cupcakes and flatbread pizza from Hazel, the whole weekend had been rough. Today's not going to be any better.

Sitting in the conference room again, with Ben at my side, I have a sense of déjà vu. "What do you think?" he asks.

"I'm expecting an explosion from Chrissy, because she has no idea how to run a company so it probably hasn't occurred to her that in changing ownership, the existing contract is null and void," I reply reasonably. "And I think Jed's gonna laugh his ass off. Maybe offer to complete the contract with his new company if Dad's right about his plans."

"Yep," he agrees. "But you're ready."

The vote of confidence is kind, and appreciated, but deep down, I wish Jed and Chrissy could just hold out for a couple of months until Township is finished. Then, none of this would be necessary.

That's actually my first option to present. It makes the most sense and serves them both well financially, while keeping Cold Springs' best interest at the center of the deal. Not that either of them cares about that. But it's a last-ditch effort before we go whole hog on the contract with Chrissy.

Oliver and Chrissy arrive first this time. Chrissy's smiling, further assuring me that she has no idea what's going on. Oliver's smiling, too, but that seems to be directly related to me. "Hi, Wren. Wasn't expecting to see you again so soon, but this is a very pleasant surprise."

He pulls a chair out for Chrissy, guiding her to sit across from Ben, and then sits directly across from me. His blue eyes dance as he takes me in, and I feel like he could probably accurately describe me to a sketch artist or draw me himself. It's a bit unnerving.

"Jed and Robert should be here any minute," I answer, avoiding Oliver's greeting.

"Already here," I hear from the doorway. Jed's coming in, but Robert's nowhere to be seen, and he's not a guy you'd miss. When I look at Jed questioningly, he explains, "Ain't paying that guy to sit here and listen to her bullshit. Told him I'd call him if I needed him."

Oh-kay, that's like Lawyer Bad Idea number one, but it's Jed's prerogative.

Jed sits down and crosses his hands in front of him. "So what's this all about?"

That's my cue.

"After our meeting, I did a bit of research. You see, Cold Springs' contract for Township's development is with Ford Construction Company as it existed at the time the contract was signed." I glance to Jed, whose eyes look smugly knowledgeable. He anticipated this, I suspect. "Though it technically was a jointly held asset at that time, I think we can all agree that our negotiations and discussions were solely with Jed."

"Only because he didn't let me—" Chrissy's outburst is cut short by Oliver placing a hand on hers, silently telling her to let me finish.

"And if there are to be any changes to ownership of Ford Construction, then the contract, in its existing state, is null and void. And will need to be redrafted."

"What do you got in mind?" Jed drawls, leaning forward in interest. "Are you suggesting that this development might go up for bids? Say . . . to a newly formed construction company with proven ownership?"

Looks like Dad was right. He knows Jed's plays before Jed probably even thinks them up. Chrissy, however, doesn't have that skill.

"What? No! It's mine! You said so. Township and the construction company are mine!" Chrissy won't be stopped this time, ranting and slamming her palm against the table sharply and pointing at Jed, who's grinning like he's the smartest player at the table. Normally, he might be right. But not today.

Not with me here.

"What are you proposing?" Oliver asks, ignoring Chrissy's bellowing and Jed's gloating. He seems markedly less happy now, frowning and looking at me through narrowed eyes. He knows I've got the advantage here, despite Jed's and Chrissy's caterwauling.

I flip open my folder to the page with the bullet points I've laid out, discussed with Ben, and gotten approved by Francine. I don't need to look at it, but it's all part of the show. "Putting our cards on the table, our priority is Cold Springs and getting Township built expeditiously to provide affordable, quality housing for our residents. We understand that your primary goal may be slightly different, especially now. However, we'd like to propose that we maintain status quo on the company, the development, and the contract for the short period of time until Township is completed."

Chrissy's listening carefully, but I guess I used too many big words, because she spins to look at Oliver. "What does that mean?" she demands.

Keeping an eye on me, like he's trying to read my mind, he leans over to inform Chrissy, "They want you and Jed to stay married so there's no division of assets until Township's done."

I dip my chin, relaying that that's exactly what we'd prefer. "According to the original plans, the timeline to completion is pretty reasonable. And it seems those could even be pushed up to a faster pace if materials are available for delivery. We're not asking for much, just a couple of months maybe."

"How do you know how quick my guys could get it done?" Jed asks shrewdly.

Shit. I wouldn't have any way of knowing that . . . except one. And I'm not looking to throw Jesse under the bus.

"Given the hold on permits, it seemed prudent to ensure the letter of the law is adhered to on-site, so I spoke with the job site manager." See? A perfectly reasonable, professional, and legal reason for me to know that.

"You mean you fucked Jesse and got some pillow talk outta the boy?" Jed's accusation isn't said with vitriol, but rather, admiration.

"Knew you took after your old Uncle Jed. Anything to seal the deal, right?"

He chuckles as though that's some sort of compliment. Inwardly, I think he should be glad that I don't have anything sharp or pointy nearby, while outwardly, I intentionally drop my practiced smile and let him see the hard-nosed bitch he's dealing with. To his credit, Jed moves back two inches, showing some sense of self-preservation.

"You can't do that!" Chrissy shouts. To Oliver, she asks, "She can't do that, can she? It's illegal or collusion or something." I think we're all surprised Chrissy even knows the word *collusion*, but to be clear, it's not.

"She can, and it sounds like she did," Oliver says in a flat voice. Why is he making it sound like while what I did is legal, it's somehow wrong for Jesse and me to have a conversation? It's not like he has any say-so in who I talk to. Pillow or otherwise. Did he think his little "think about it" recommendation was going to have me telling Jesse to fuck off and fall into his arms instead?

Not wanting to get sidetracked, I clarify, "For a couple of months, can we consider things staying as they are, at least business-wise? Get Township completed, sell the units—which we all know will happen quickly—and then the divorce can be finalized however you see fit, with the division of profits and company addressed then?"

Chrissy looks at Jed. "Would that mean more money?"

She totally means would *she* get more money, and the fact that she's asking Jed speaks volumes to how little knowledge she has of their finances. I honestly want to shake her and ask how she could be so stupid as to allow a man like Jed to keep her so blindly ignorant to their entire financial situation. Everybody who shares finances with someone should know the ins and outs, down to the details. It's fine if one partner pays the bills and whatnot, but the other party should know if all's well or you're swimming in debt at the least. Chrissy probably doesn't know if she can afford to buy a Coke at the grocery store or buy the whole grocery store itself. It's ridiculous.

"I'm not waiting," Jed declares. "Lucy and me are getting hitched before Jed Junior's born, so I want this shit handled now."

"Married? Jed Junior?" Chrissy echoes vacantly.

Smiling as he twists the knife, Jed tells her, "Yep. Jed and Lucy Ford, and little Jed Junior."

Jesus. Could he be any more evil? Chrissy's not the best, but she doesn't deserve that, for fuck's sake.

She sits with it, numbly staring at him as it sinks in and then . . .

Chrissy hurls herself across the table, kneeling as she lunges for Jed with clawed hands. "You sonuvabitch! I'm gonna kill you and your whore!"

It turns into more banshee screeches while Ben and Oliver try to pull her back. Jed simply scoots his chair back from the table, baiting Chrissy more, likely hoping she'll fall to the floor at his feet.

"We're gonna be one happy little family," he says gleefully, egging Chrissy's breakdown on. "Probably send out Christmas cards with matching pj's and a cute nickname like hashtag-FordFam. Maybe start us up one of those family InstaTok accounts."

"Shut the fuck up, Uncle Jed!" I shout, not giving a shit about professionalism when this meeting has turned into a three-ring circus. "Shut *alllll* the fucking way up!"

Oliver finally manages to pull Chrissy off the table and to her feet, but she looks utterly defeated. The anger and hurt of a moment ago have completely petered out, leaving her empty and probably exhausted.

"Chrissy, go home and let me handle this. This is what I'm here for," Oliver instructs her stonily. Chrissy obediently turns to leave, and I think her head only stays lifted and her shoulders back from years of practice. Otherwise, I think she'd be curled up with her arms crossed and eyes dropped to the floor.

Once she's gone, Jed claps his hands once sharply to get everyone's attention. He's got a wide grin on his face, though I don't think he stopped smiling once through Chrissy's attack, either, and says, "I'm open to renegotiating that contract with my new construction company as soon as I get the paperwork filed."

Is he for real right now? Honestly, if I could let the whole development go to salt, I would, because I don't want to work with Chrissy or Jed. Him, because he's a narcissistic jerk, and her, because she's clueless. But I have to, for Cold Springs.

I rub the bridge of my nose as I take a deep breath, mulling over my thoughts to see if there are any other angles I can play. But when I find none, I glance at Ben to be sure he's come to the same conclusion. He stays stoic, not giving me a hint of his thoughts either way. It's another test. Not if I know what to do because we've already discussed that at length, but of whether I'll do it even when it's the best of two excruciatingly bad choices.

Being a lawyer is not always about right and wrong, but sometimes of defending the least wrong.

"Moving forward with the divorce now, then, and giving Chrissy ownership of the existing company and contracts, means that the development stays with Chrissy as you agreed to," I tell Jed. Turning to Oliver, I continue, "However, the contract will not be a simple matter of find and replace the name of the company. We'll need to go through it with a fine-tooth comb to reflect the new ownership and her skills, or lack thereof."

"I can do that with you on Chrissy's behalf," Oliver offers a bit too quickly. "We can start tonight after I meet with my client to discuss today."

Shit. Of course he's happy about the whole thing. Beyond working up a new contract being a side gig for him with Chrissy, and therefore, worth at least a couple dozen more billed hours, he'll be spending at least a chunk of those hours with me.

I'm not new to someone pursuing me. But when it's a professional relationship, it's wrong, or dangerous at the minimum. And I'm exploring things with Jesse, and don't want to jeopardize that. I wish Oliver would get the hint!

Jed balks, likely thinking he had this in the bag. "If you have to rewrite the contract anyway, why not do it with me?"

"Because you threw the keys to Chrissy, gave her the land and development, and don't have your shit straight. Need any other reasons?" I snap. I've never spoken to him this way, not even when he was screwing my dad over. I was the good daughter, quietly taking care of things like always. But I'm done with Jed and his assholery. He literally uses everyone, every chance he gets, and then somehow thinks he's still the hero we all love and adore.

He's not.

And maybe, if I can work this contract with Chrissy right, I can tweak a few of the details in Cold Springs' favor somehow. That's my focus now. Not Jed's delusions of grandeur.

Jed pushes back from the table, blustering as he stands abruptly and digs a finger into the tabletop. "Young lady, I've done more for Chrissy and Cold Springs than anyone else ever has. I don't need you telling me how to handle my business—family or otherwise."

He glares coldly at me, likely thinking I'm going to back down like the little girl he sees me as.

I'm no such thing.

I stand, too, but maintain an even voice. "Your relationship with Chrissy is none of my business, except when it affects the town I'm duty-bound and heart-driven to protect. This is just the latest way you've tried to destroy it, and we all know it. I went to bat with Francine as we made the difficult decision on whether to allow Township to happen with you in the first place, but we gambled on you for our citizens' sake. I won't make that mistake ever again."

I gather my papers, quickly tapping them on the table and shoving them into their file folder before pinning Oliver with a sharp gaze. "Six o'clock. This conference room. I'll be starting the contract, with or without your input."

With that, I leave the three men staring after me as I strut down to my office and close the door behind me. Only then do I take a breath.

To quote Hazel's filthy mouth, "Fucking fuckity fuck."

Huh, she's right. That does feel a little better. I sink into my chair, slumping down so my head rests on the back and I can stare at the ceiling. I trace over the dark spots in the drop-down tiles, trying to find some sense of normalcy. But like so many things, I think it's all gone.

I pick up my phone and dial the one person I've been wanting to see all weekend, but really don't want to talk to now.

"Hey, Birdie," Jesse answers. He sounds tired, even though he tries to insert some energy into his rough voice.

"Hi," I reply, a faint smile breaking through the weight of my worry.

It's all he needs to know what happened. "They didn't agree to delay the divorce, did they? And you're going to rewrite the contract with Chrissy as boss."

"Yeah. I'm starting now so I can get it done as quickly as possible for you, though. Well, for you and Cold Springs." He knows what I mean. If the contract's under negotiation, all work stops, and his guys are going to be impacted most of all. "Were you able to get a lot of hours over the weekend for them?"

"As many as I could."

It feels like there's this big *thing* floating between us now. I'm the one stopping his work, but I have to. It's my job to. Somehow, our responsibilities to the town are at odds with each other, putting us on opposing sides, even though we both want what's best for everyone— building Township.

"That's good," I say, knowing it's not good enough. "How's Alan's wife?"

"Due any day now. Need to make sure they keep their insurance updated while we're on a work stoppage, I guess."

I can hear the scratchiness as he rubs his hand over his unshaven face. I hate that I'm causing him more stress. Well, not me *exactly*. Technically, I guess it's Jed's fault. But right now, in this moment, it sure feels like it's mine.

"Glad she's doing well. Let me know if I can help."

Is that what we've become in one phone conversation? Polite, meaningless pleasantries. If this can set us this far off course, maybe . . .

No. I stop the thought before it fully forms. Jesse and I are getting our chance now. And I won't let Jed's wandering dick fuck that up. Not for me, and not for Jesse.

I quickly add on, "I really missed you this weekend. I was working, but what I really wanted was to be with you. Wrapped in your arms, pinned underneath you, or just cuddled up next to you."

Sounding much more like himself, he growls, "Missed you too. Was too tired to even jack off to thoughts of you, but I sure as shit had 'em as I fell asleep." He chuckles, deep and sexy, and things start to feel right again. "Had some real good dreams about you, though. Wet ones."

"Such a charmer," I tease. But he knows I'm charmed by his raunchy flirting. Always have been, always will be.

Too soon, we say goodbye as I promise to get the contract done as quickly as I can. "I know you will, Birdie. In the meantime, think I'll see if Mom needs any help at the bakery or go give Etta a run for her money on a table or two."

After we hang up, I sit in silence, staring at my phone. Jesse is a good man. Things are falling apart for him, at least temporarily, but he's worried about his crews and Alan's wife, and he's going to spend the spare time taking care of his family. How could he ever have thought I would think he was anything less than awesome?

Before I get back to work, I call Mom, too, apologizing for having to cancel our Monday night dinner. "I have to get this done. Sorry, Mom."

"Honey, I understand when work takes priority. I was a mayor's wife for more years than you probably remember. But I'm guessing this means the meeting today didn't go well?" She sounds sorry even though it's not her fault.

My sigh is full of the weight of the world. "Definitely not. Chrissy tried to attack Jed, like, literally on the table, lunging for him. I probably should've called Officer Milson. But before I could do that, I was yelling at Uncle Jed to shut the fuck up."

"You did not," she whispers in shock.

I nod, though she can't see me, and say, "I did."

I'm expecting her to be disappointed in me for losing control and letting my professionalism slip. But Mom gleefully says, "Ooh, I bet that felt good. I've been wanting to tell that man off for most of my life at this point." We both laugh, a common bond through our hatred of the man who almost ruined our family. "Are there video cameras in that conference room?" she asks through her giggles.

"I wish! I'd watch it on repeat just to see Jed's face go slack in shock. I could almost hear his thoughts—" Mimicking Uncle Jed's drawl, I say, *"Whuut? Nobody speaks to me like that, young lady."*

"Stop it! I'm crying over here!" Mom exclaims, still laughing hard. "Oh my goodness, I'm going to miss you for dinner, but that was worth it just to hear that story. You can bet I'm gonna be telling it at yoga class tomorrow."

"Mom, isn't yoga supposed to be all Zen positive vibes? Not taking pleasure in someone else's pain?" I don't really care. I'm just giving her a hard time.

"Laughter yoga is a thing, dear. It's good for the soul," she informs me. "And I can't think of a better person for this to happen to than Jed."

We say our goodbyes, and though I'll miss our dinner, the phone call was the little pep talk I needed.

Chapter 20

JESSE

It's been less than a week since I've held Wren in my arms. The long weekend of three days, plus the three days to get us midweek, and those have been filled with texts and phone calls. They've taken some of the edge off. But I want to hold her, kiss her, fuck her. No, I *need* to.

She's working, I remind myself for the kajillionth time. *Trust her, her work, and that she has your back and is doing the contract as quickly as she can.*

It's not enough.

I grab my phone, sending her a text . . . Thinking about you. Missing you lots. I add a heart emoji, wishing I was better at writing poetry or something flowery to send. But I'm pretty much stuck at *roses are red, violets are blue, bend over girl, I wanna fuck you* and that's not exactly what I'm trying to express here, even though it's true.

Staring at my screen, I wait for the three little dots or an emoji. Something, anything, but it doesn't come.

She's busy.

Grumpier than I was before I sent the text, I rack up another round on the table I've basically owned every evening this week. Helping Mom means I'm done by noon, two at the latest. After that, I'm left to my own devices.

There's not enough lawns to mow, horses to feed, or shit to shovel to keep me and every guy on my crew who's looking for handyman work busy, though Aunt Etta said her barn hasn't been this clean in decades. Which is quite the compliment, considering she usually cleans it herself and spoils her horse, Nala, like the queen that she is.

"I can't keep doing this." Roscoe's been complaining every hour, on the hour, but keeps agreeing to another game every time we clear the table. "How long is this gonna take?"

"About twenty minutes, give or take. Depends on how long Tayvious takes with my basket of fries."

Roscoe grunts. "You know I ain't talking about the table. I mean this whole contract business. I need to work."

"You and me both!" a guy at the next table interjects. I look over and see Seth, one of the electrical crew leads, sharing a pitcher of beer with his crew.

"Yeah, me too," one of them adds.

"I know, guys." I'm trying to show them that I'm on their side. Guys like us are men of action, and days of sitting on our asses aren't good for our bodies or our brains. "I'm going stir-crazy, too, but we have to be patient. The contract's underway, but Chrissy's . . ." I trail off, not wanting to say what I really think of her. I don't have any problem with women being in charge—hell, I like it in certain situations—but Chrissy has zero business sense and even less knowledge about what we do, so she's holding up the process.

"A bitch," another voice finishes.

Someone else adds, "I heard she was walking around downtown like she didn't have a care in the world. Shopping and eating lunch, not giving a single shit about my rent being due next week or Larry's kid needing insulin. That shit's expensive, ya know?"

"Is anyone surprised that she's prissing around like things are hunky-dory while we're worried about bills?"

"You know I ain't surprised at shit. That woman's always rubbed me the wrong way. And that's saying something because there ain't supposed to be a bad way to rub." The sex joke falls flat, a rarity with a group of rough, filthy-mouthed, laboring guys.

"Jed was an asshole, but at least he let us do our jobs, paid on time, and stayed out of our way," Mike says flatly.

Roscoe can't keep quiet about that, though, not that he's ever had much of a filter. "He's the one who fucked us over in the first place, though. All he had to do was stay married for two months till we were done, and then him and Chrissy could fight to the death in one of those octagons and sell tickets for all I care. But could he do that for the guys who've killed themselves over the years for him? Fuck no."

"I'd buy a ticket for that show," I confess and then burst out in laughter when I actually picture it. "Can you imagine? Chrissy bitching about breaking a nail and Jed huffing and puffing just from walking to the ring, but throwing his hands up like he's already a winner anyway." I lift my hands in a V and silently roar the way Jed would.

"They'd end up rolling around on the mat, and Chrissy'd end up on top, sitting on his face. And Jed'd be hollering because he 'don't do that' like a pussy. She'd snarl out, 'I know' on account of them being together so long," Mike adds, coming around to the shit talking about Jed and Chrissy.

Before long, we're all laughing at the ridiculous idea of them fighting like that. It's a much-needed break from the stress we're all feeling.

"Wish he coulda kept his dick in his pants in the first place," Seth offers. "That woulda solved all this too." Seth's a good guy, been married to his wife for less than a year, and probably can't imagine cheating on her or how ugly a marriage can get after decades of bitterness and resentment. I hope he always keeps that innocence. The rest of us aren't so naive.

Roscoe barks out a rusty-sounding chuckle and slams the cue ball with a punishing stroke that belies his age. Balls go squirrelly over the whole table, and when not a single one finds its way to a pocket, he perches on the edge of a stool with a rumble of mutters under his breath. "Go ahead, Jesse. I'm done with this shit anyway. Tomorrow, I'm gonna go into Newport and see if they've got any day laborer jobs."

Seth offers, "I'll go with you, man."

"Me too," another voice says.

"Can someone pick me up? Wife's keeping the car to run the kids to school."

My whole crew is falling apart in front of me. These guys are gonna go to Newport, find jobs, and when Jed and Chrissy finally get their shit figured out, I'm going to be down valuable guys and left holding the bag. This whole house of cards is crumbling, and time's running out.

"I understand, guys," I say slowly, hoping to save what I can. "But when this contract's figured out, I'm gonna want each and every one of you back on the job site. We've got work to do, work for Cold Springs. And I ain't got time to train rookies on your jobs and have them redo everything three times to get it right. I need you, ya hear me? So go fuck around in Newport with some annoying gigs so you can pay your bills, but don't get used to day jobs where you're your own boss. Your asses are mine as soon as I say so."

I'm not a poet, and I'm also not that great at pep talks, unfortunately. But hopefully, they understand I'm coming from a good place.

"Is there anything we can do?" Mike asks me. "Can you talk to Wren?"

I shake my head. "I have. She's doing her best, working with that Oliver asshole all day. Did I mention I hate that prick?"

It's a rhetorical question, but they all laugh. "A time or two . . . hundred," Roscoe teases.

Mike corrects him, "More like thousand."

"Shut up, assholes," I growl, knowing they're probably right. "You'd be pissed, too, if your girl was hanging out all day with a guy like that. You should see the way he looks at her. Makes me want to punch that smug smile right off his face." Even thinking about it makes me angry again.

The guys chuckle. "We can tell."

Seth suggests, "You should go see her. Do the whole surprise thing. Girls love that."

It's my turn to chuckle. "Wren's not like your wife, man. She'd bitch me out for interrupting her work. Work she's doing for us, remember?" But even as I say no, I'm considering it. I'd get to see her, check how things are going on the contract, and show Oliver that I'm around, even when I'm not around. The idea has merit.

"Take food when you go," Roscoe advises wisely. "Caffeine, chocolate, and cock. The three *c*'s. You can't go wrong with that combo."

Or maybe not so wisely, but he does have a point. I'm sure Wren hasn't been taking care of herself the last few days. She's driven and focused, which means things like food and sleep fall by the wayside, especially with something this important. And that's where I come in.

"Hey, Charlene," I call out as she shuffles past us, staying busy with the weekday crowd. When she pauses, I ask, "Can I get those fries to go? And add a bowl of chili?"

"Sure thing, honey-baby. You want 'em disco-style?" she asks, referring to the smothered mess that somehow became known as disco fries. When I shake my head, she pops her gum and nods. "Okay. Gimme two shakes and I'll get that boxed up for you."

She winks and is gone in an instant, and the guys lose interest in my love life for the moment, returning to chatting about jobs and organizing their trip into Newport tomorrow.

When Charlene comes back a few minutes later with a brown bag, she says, "Gotchu all set with a spoon if you wanna eat the chili, and a tray of fries if you wanna pour the chili on top. I put a little cup of the sprinkle cheese and snuck you a little bit of the queso too." She places a finger in front of her lips like anyone gives a shit that she gave me some queso on the down low.

Trading the bag for a twenty, I tell her thank you.

The guys cheer as I head out to see Wren, "go get her, man!" and "good luck!" coming at me from all sides. And just as importantly, a reminder that they're all counting on her to get this contract on the books so we can get back to work.

I throw them a two-fingered wave and head out on my mission.

The drive over is quick, and I head inside without pausing to reconsider the intelligence of this action. Joanne's long gone, so I walk down the hall toward Wren's office, but hear her laughter coming from the conference room.

I freeze, eavesdropping without even choosing to do so.

"Oh my gosh, you're the worst," she says, laughing again.

"You love it and you know it," Oliver answers, sex in his voice.

My nerve endings alight with jealousy, making my whole body hot. I shouldn't have come. I should've trusted my first instincts and stayed away to let Wren work. I can see that now. Because I'm standing in the hallway like a chump, holding food and worrying about a woman who's ten levels above me and doesn't need a damn thing from a man like me.

"Stop it," Wren says in a high-pitched voice. Maybe later I'll hear something else in that tone, but right now, it sounds like fear.

I don't think. I bust through the door, commanding forcefully, "Get the fuck away from her!"

Wren and Oliver look up in surprise . . . from where they're sitting side by side at the conference room table, completely professional and not at all in danger of crossing any boundaries.

"Jesse!" Wren hollers, her hand to her chest in surprise. "What the hell?"

For his part, Oliver grins like I'm a complete dumbass. Which I am. But that doesn't make me any less pissed about it.

"Sorry, I heard you scream 'stop it' and thought the worst," I admit.

"I would never," Oliver snaps, offended by my implied accusation.

I glare at him, fairly sure he would. Maybe not assault someone—that's a special type of asshole—but a little pressure here, a bit of fake charm there? Yeah, he's that type. "Wasn't willing to take that chance with Wren," I answer hotly.

"You'd think if you were that worried, you would've stopped by last night or the night before that," he speculates. "I don't think it was concern for Wren that had you barging in like some out-of-control, raging bull, but rather concern for yourself. Your jealousy got the best of you and made you think I was charming the pants off your girl, literally or metaphorically."

He makes it sound like I'm a juvenile, irrational child, but he pulls at his collar, and I note that despite his argument to the contrary, he's lost his tie, his top two buttons are undone, and he's rolled up his sleeves to reveal muscled forearms. It could be a bit of relaxation after long hours of working on a contract, or it could be getting comfy to break down Wren's typically well-honed defenses.

"No one charms Wren. She's too smart for that and will see right through your bullshit."

"She's also right here, watching you two measure your dicks like that'll decide something when it most definitely won't. You, read over that clause again." She points at Oliver. "You, come with me." That one was to me.

Wren stands, and I realize she doesn't have on shoes, probably having kicked them off under the table after the long day. She passes Oliver on her way to the door, and he makes it a point to look at her ass in her tailored slacks and shoot me a grin, knowing I can't do anything about it without pissing Wren off further. But he doesn't know me that well.

"Fuckin' asshole," I growl, stepping closer to the table, dropping the bag of food, and rearing back for a perfect punch.

Unfortunately, Wren steps in my way to stop me. But not before the smile melted from Oliver's face and he scooted back from the table quickly, damn near running from me. "Crazy bastard," he mutters.

But we both know who won that nonfight. Only one of us backed down, and it sure as shit wasn't me.

I hold an arm out in invitation for Wren to leave first, keeping my eyes on Oliver. Before I turn to follow her in her barefooted steps, I pause for one quick second . . . just long enough to leave a little present behind. I send a silent vow of thanks to Tayvious for the greasy fries earlier, because they allow me to crop dust Oliver and then leave him to stew in it.

I can hear him coughing as I follow Wren into her office and can't help but feel a little victorious. Is it immature? Yes. Do I give a fuck? Absolutely not.

I close the door behind me, preparing for Wren's wrath. I deserve it. I interrupted her work, I didn't trust her, and I probably jeopardized the contract. "Give it to me," I tell her. "All you got."

She stares at me, her green eyes deep and unreadable for two seconds, and then she launches herself at me so hard and fast that my back slams into the door. I catch her ass in my palms as her legs wrap around my waist and her arms go around my neck. Burying her face in my neck, she whispers, "I've missed you so much."

Well, hell, seems like I'm not the only one who was feeling lonely with all this work keeping us apart.

I grip her ass a bit tighter, and fight to find her mouth as she squeezes me tight. "I missed you too," I say between kisses. "I texted you, but you didn't respond."

She nips at my lip playfully. "Too busy. Contract." Her explanation is choppy, but given the way she's kissing me back, I don't mind a bit. "You brought me food?"

Huh, guess Roscoe wasn't wrong about that. Even if there's no caffeine or chocolate. But I know Wren, and chili is one of her love languages. "Yeah, knew you'd need it," I explain as I lay a trail of kisses down her neck to the point where it joins her shoulder. I lick in the tiny hollow there, and she shudders.

"You're jealous because I'm working with Oliver?" she asks, her hands shoved into my hair and nails scratching my scalp deliciously. She also doesn't make jealous sound as bad as Oliver did. In fact, Wren sounds . . . turned on?

"Fuck yeah, I'm jealous. He's getting your time, and I want some of it. Some of you. Because you're mine, Wren." The possessive claim is growled against her skin as I squeeze her tightly and bury my nose in her hair. I let my teeth graze over the sensitive skin of her neck, and she moans, deep and throaty.

I whirl, pinning her against the door for another kiss. I try to use it as leverage so I can get one hand between us, but Wren wiggles to get down. I let her feet touch the floor, and she drops even lower, sitting on her shins on the cold floor. "Wren?"

But she doesn't answer, at least not aloud. But her hands are doing plenty of talking as they brush over my thick cock. The zipper of my jeans is uncomfortably tight, and when Wren releases the button, the zipper shoots down on its own. I sigh in relief, but immediately groan when her hands cup me and she brushes over the top of my cock through my underwear.

"You're already leaking," she whispers, grinning up at me.

"Fuck yeah, I am. I've been leaking for days, wanting you. This bitchy mouth, your tiny hand, that tight pussy." I run my thumb over her bottom lip roughly, smearing whatever lipstick she had left from the day.

I want to ruin her the way she's ruined me. Make sure that she doesn't even notice other men or their flirtations. Because she can't help it, men are going to see her and want her.

But she's mine. My Wren.

She yanks my underwear over my cock, freeing me fully, and looks up at me with eyes as bright as the rarest emeralds. "They're yours."

She licks a swirl around the tip of my cock. Even the slightest touch feels so good, and my eyes squeeze shut as a groan escapes. "Ssshh," she admonishes me sharply, her hands going to my thighs with her nails digging in the tiniest bit. "Be good."

"Fuuuuck, Wren," I whisper, trying to be quiet even though I don't give a shit if anyone hears me. It's her sounds I'm possessive of.

She takes me deeper into her mouth, sealing her lips around my length and finding a pace that quickly takes me higher. I'm not surprised that she knows exactly how to work me, and I'm so on edge, I'll blow in just a few strokes of her sweet mouth.

I grip her hair in one hand, holding the back of her head against the door, and brace myself with my other hand on the wooden door too. Wren wraps her hand around the base of my cock and lets me fuck her mouth with long, slow strokes that hit the back of her throat.

"Yesss," I hiss when she swallows involuntarily, her throat massaging my head. I stay there, deep in her mouth, teasing over her throat and watching her carefully. Her eyes start to water, but she's sucking me as she swallows. I know what she wants, and I want to give it to her. "You ready, Wren?"

She mumbles something I can't understand, but her nod is loud and clear.

I go a little faster, a little deeper, whispering to her, "That's it. Take all of me, swallow me down. You look so fucking pretty with my cock in your mouth." Her green eyes peer up at me, begging me to do it, and the next time she swallows, it sends me over the edge. I groan as hot jets of my cream pulse down her throat, and she swallows over and over until she can't keep up and gags a little. But she doesn't lose any and goes right back to licking me clean, wanting every drop.

"Get up here," I order her, wanting to give her as much pleasure as she's giving me. I help her rise from the floor and undo her pants as quickly as I can. When they fall to the floor along with the panties I shove down, she steps out of them, and I spin her around. I bend her in half, letting her forehead rest against the door as I wrap an arm around her waist. I bend over, too, but I lay my cheek on her bare ass, letting my palms trace appreciatively over her soft skin.

I move lower, dipping my finger into her slick folds. She arches her back for more, and I circle over her clit gently a few times before tapping it quickly in succession. I find a rhythm that drives her crazy—three long, slow circles followed by a flurry of taps like I'm her own personal ten-speed vibrator.

Like me, she's on the edge quickly. Her hips are bucking reflexively, and her knees are shaking as she searches for the release I want to give her. "Are you gonna come for me?"

She nods jerkily.

"Keep it quiet. You don't want the whole office to hear you coming for me, do you?" I don't think there are many people still here at this hour. Maybe a few here and there, but most importantly, there's one man a couple of doors down who I don't want to hear Wren. Now that she's mine, her sounds are mine, and no one gets to see or hear her in that primal state but me. It's a trust she places in me, and I'll guard her at her most vulnerable of moments.

She makes a choked noise, holding back as fresh juices coat my fingers in pulsing waves. I keep my attention on her clit, helping her ride out her orgasm as long as possible, and holding her tight at the waist because her knees are bending more and more, threatening to give out beneath her.

When she shudders a final time, I stand and look around. We've joked before that our height difference makes things interesting sometimes, but when we're laying down, we can align however we need to. But there's nothing to lay on in here, except . . .

I pick Wren up and carry her over to her desk. Shoving my jeans and underwear down to my thighs, I guide her to bend over her desk.

I lean over her, my cock notched right at her opening, and whisper in her ear, "I'm gonna fuck you right here, and then when you're working, you're going to randomly remember what we did and get horny for me. Every time you do, I want you to tell me right then. Call, text, send a fucking smoke signal, I don't care. I just want to know that you're remembering the filthy things we did in your office. Understand?"

As soon as her chin lowers in a nod, I slam home. She's wet and ready for me, but taking me all at once is a shock to us both. She grunts, trying to stay quiet, and I praise her, "You feel so good, Wren. Look so beautiful with me stretching your sweet pussy."

She sighs happily, wiggling beneath me, and then commands, "Fuck me, Jesse. Like I'm yours."

Goddamn, her mouth. She likes my dirty talk, but fuck if she can't nearly send me over the edge with one word.

"You are mine," I remind her with deep, powerful, bonding strokes.

I grab her hips, tilting them up even more, and her tippy-toes leave the floor. Her legs flail a bit, looking for an anchor, and she finds my legs, wrapping around them with her own and locking her feet behind my calves.

I think we're still being quiet, but I've honestly forgotten to give a fuck when Wren is writhing beneath me until there's a knock on the door. Though I don't want to, we freeze.

"Wren?" Oliver calls out.

Fuck that guy.

I start to slide in and out of Wren slowly, fucking her as I feel her go extra slick again. I lean over her, gripping her hair in my fist to turn her head. Meeting her eyes, I warn, "Get rid of him or I'm gonna answer the door with my dick out. Let him see me covered in your sweet honey so he knows you're mine and I'm yours, and he'll never get at this beautiful pussy."

She must see something in my eyes that says I'm dead fucking serious—which I am—because she says, "Uhm, Oliver—" Her voice cracks, and she clears her throat roughly before trying again. "Hey, can we continue this . . . *ungh* . . . tomorrow? *Mmm.*"

She's doing her best, but I'm intentionally making it hard on her, rolling my hips to hit the front wall inside her at the right angle as I slip in deep with each stroke.

"Yeah, see you in the morning," he says slowly. I can hear the anger in his voice, but he's not my concern right now.

I wait a second to give him time to walk away and then let loose on Wren. She's on the edge again, so close to falling apart, and I want to give her that. I want to feel her release every control she holds so tightly and fly, her pussy sucking another orgasm from me as she does it. I thrust into her hard. Deep. Fast. She's losing control and reaches for my hand, placing it over her own mouth to help her stay quiet. I press harder, watching carefully even though I know she can breathe through her nose, and keep my pace.

It only takes a few more strokes for her to spasm. Her nails dig into my hand as she holds it there even tighter, muffling her cries of pleasure. I do my best, gritting my teeth and trying to hold in my grunts as I come with her. Her pussy quivers around my cock, pulling my cum from me, as we ride out the high together.

Reality seeps in slowly as Wren untangles her feet and reaches toward the floor. I release her mouth and hips, straightening my legs, which are suddenly threatening to seize on me. I slip out of her, and though I mourn the loss of being inside her, as I stand up straight, I hiss, "Shiiit."

Wren giggles quietly as she adjusts, too, stretching her arms over her head and reaching as high as she can. Her breasts lift enticingly in her shirt, and I realize that I didn't even touch them. Instantly, I vow to show them extra attention next time. Maybe see if I can get Wren to come solely through nipple play?

Challenge gladly accepted.

"I think we're made for bed sex, or couch sex, or floor sex. Something where we can align our parts without you crouching down and me arching my back like I'm in a contortionist yoga class."

"Wall sex. I can hoist you up, pin you, and then go to town," I suggest as another alternative.

The easy joke eases the transition back to the reality of what we just did in her office. "Do you think he's gone?" she asks, not needing to explain who she's talking about.

"I didn't hear his footsteps, so he might be out there right now listening to us talk about his little dick and shitty personality."

Wren's eyes fly open wide. "Jesse!"

"Or he might be wearing loafers that don't make noise on the floor," I admit.

That seems to soothe her, and she moves toward the door to grab her pants. She shakes them out a couple of times, sending her panties flying across the room. Finishing my own button and zipper, I snatch them out of the air and hold them up, swinging them from a fingertip. "Did you want these?"

"Toss them here," she orders.

"Yeah, no," I answer as I stuff them in my back pocket. "Think I'll save these. I'm sentimental like that." She doesn't believe me, thinking I'm going to jack off with them later, but I really do want to keep them as a souvenir of our time in her office.

This office is where she's going to do big things for Cold Springs and for herself, becoming the attorney she wants to be. And as cheesy as it is, I want to remember that . . . with red, no-show hipsters that have Wren's scent on them.

"For real?" she challenges, but when I lift a brow in answer, she smiles and pulls her pants on commando. "I'm going to die when I take these to the cleaners. Uhm, yeah, Ms. Maldonado, there's a sex stain in the crotch of those. Do you think you could treat that without ruining the fabric?" But she doesn't sound mad, just a little embarrassed.

"I'll buy you a new pair if that's better?" I offer.

She looks at me in surprise, her head tilted like I'm a puzzle she's trying to figure out. "You would, wouldn't you?"

I shrug. "Yeah, if you don't want Ms. Maldonado knowing what a sex-starved maniac you are."

She laughs. "Or maybe I'll tell her that you're a panty thief."

"Yeah, you go ahead and do that and see who's more embarrassed, me or you. Here's a hint . . . I don't give two shits what Ms. Maldonado thinks of me, and I've definitely been called worse than 'panty thief,'" I tell Wren.

Deciding she's already lost this fight, she redirects. "Did you say you brought chili fries?"

In awe at how fast her mind works when mine is still going, *Goooooood . . . happyyyyyy*, I blink and remember. "Yeah, I did. So you'd have something to eat, because I figured you wouldn't have." She blushes a little, her pink cheeks telling me that I'm right. "Come on, I'll take you home and while you eat, I'll run you a hot bath. That always makes things better."

"You take baths?" she asks as we walk down the hall the few doors to the conference room. There are a few papers and a manila folder sitting there, along with Wren's laptop, but no bag from Puss N Boots.

"That asshole took your dinner!" I shout, pissed off anew.

But Wren laughs and tells me, "It's okay. I've got takeout in the fridge at home from last night. I'll eat that, but I still want a bath."

"Deal."

Chapter 21

WREN

Jesse was right. This bath is exactly what I needed, even if I feel guilty that he's sitting on the cold floor of my bathroom while I'm scrunched down to get the hot water up to my chin. But like he said, he wouldn't fit in my tub anyway, especially at the same time as me.

"How's the contract redo going?" he asks carefully.

It feels like dangerous territory. We both want what's best for Cold Springs, but it definitely seems like we've landed on different ways to get that.

"Meh," I answer with a shrug. "It's not as cut-and-dried as I think it should be. There's no need to rewrite the whole damn thing. A lot of it should carry over with minimal review and approval, but Oliver is dissecting every single word like he's getting paid per letter."

"Or by the hour," he suggests, and I nod, knowing he's right. "Plus, the more difficult the process is, the more time he gets to spend with you."

"I am pretty awesome," I allow, "but it's not really like that. We talk about the contract ninety percent of the time, what to eat for lunch for five percent, and random bullshit the other five."

Jesse's dark brow raises doubtfully. "I'm not saying you're encouraging him. But he's after you. Just know that."

I'm quiet, considering his words. Working with Oliver has been interesting. He's sharp and understands the legal nuances of writing a contract to equally benefit both parties. That's a good thing, but it's also a double-edged sword. If he were a dumbass, I could steamroll over him and favor Cold Springs. Not that I'd do that . . . explicitly. But a little here and there? Absolutely.

Instead, I'm arguing for every little detail.

Which makes me wonder if Jesse might be right. Is Oliver arguing simply to draw this out . . . either for financial gain or for me? The money seems more likely for sure, but I won't say he hasn't been friendly, occasionally bordering on a bit flirty, while we work. I just ignore it for the most part and stick to the work at hand, but maybe that's not the best strategy.

I've gone quiet, and Jesse hands me the glass of sparkling water he poured for me while the bathwater ran. I stare into its clear depths, watching the bubbles rise to the surface.

"Do you know why I don't drink?" I ask, suddenly curious if he knows.

Jesse drinks beer when we go to Puss N Boots, and he always has a six-pack in his fridge, but somewhere along the way, he noticed that I don't drink. Ever. So he's never offered me beer or wine, never questioned why I get tap or sparkling water, never made it a thing at all. Most other women crawling into a hot bath after a long day would probably take a glass of wine with them, but here I am . . . with my sparkling water.

He shrugs nonchalantly as he says, "Figured it had to do with your dad."

I look at him in surprise before narrowing my eyes. "How do you know that?"

"I grew up in a bar, seen more drunks than I cared to. Seen their families too. There's a way they watch them, like they're waiting for them to fuck up. You do that with your dad sometimes. It could've been for another reason, but back when Winston was getting married . . . the day we met—"

"And I thought you were the caterer," I finish, knowing where that sentence goes from our relentless teasing.

But Jesse shakes his head. "Before that. I was in the house, bringing in the cupcakes for Mom, and I walked past the living room dozens of times. People don't notice you when you're doing shit like that. It's like you're invisible. Anyway, I saw your dad sitting in there alone, and he seemed melancholy. I would've chalked it up to the wedding, like the bittersweetness of your kid getting older, but it was the way he was staring at the glass in his hand that struck me. I'd seen it before. So, when I noticed you didn't drink and saw the way you take care of your family, I figured that was why. You can't be responsible for everyone else when you're not stone-cold sober, can you? And they need you."

He's remarkably spot-on, on every account.

Except one.

"They don't need me so much anymore," I admit, with more sadness than I thought I'd feel about it. "For a long time, I was struggling hard. Going to school, coming home, doing internships, keeping up appearances, and all the while, my family was falling apart for one reason and one reason only. Uncle Jed."

"Hate that motherfucker," Jesse spits out, rallying to my cause without even understanding why.

I smile softly. "He had Dad all tied up in that deal here, the one he ended up building in Brookstone, and Dad knew it was a bad deal but couldn't get out of it. He took to drinking, trying to soothe his soul, but he'd sold it to the devil. It wasn't until that whole thing blew up and Jed slunk away to lick his wounds that my dad got better. He quit drinking, quit his job as mayor, and started hanging out with Mom. They're doing really well now."

My smile grows as I think of all the happy moments they've had over the last few years.

"But you still remember. Still want to be ready if they need you to catch them when they fall," Jesse guesses. "Does it bother you that I have a beer or two sometimes? I can stop if it does."

The offer is kind and shows how sensitive the heart that beats in his tattooed chest can be. "No, no. That's not why I mentioned it," I tell him. "It's because of Jed. I know you're disappointed that we're having to redo this contract and Chrissy's your new boss, and I guess I'm worried that maybe I could've done more to get them to stay together for a few months. But I have so much hatred for Uncle Jed that I don't know if I did my best."

I didn't even realize I was carrying so much guilt about that until the words tumble out. But now that I hear them, I can feel that ugly darkness deep in my heart.

Could I have done more?

There's always something else to try, another angle to play, another negotiation to offer, but when Jed said no, I let him walk away without another word.

Jesse scoffs, grinning at me in that sexy, sideways kinda way he has. His hair falls forward, into his face, but he leaves it, letting one dark eye peer through the curtain of hair. "You're amazing, you know that? I don't know all the details, but I've got a pretty good idea what it took to get the Township contract with Jed done in the first place. But you did it, with heart and grit. And a helluva lotta brains. You, Wren Fucking Ford, the badass city attorney for Cold Springs. Jed's some sort of big bad guy in your mind, but you negotiated the shit outta that deal. You won't do any less for this one, and nobody wants you to. We want you to do what you're best at, working for the people of Cold Springs."

He pauses, and I swear I can see him forcing the words off his tongue, "Even if it means working with The Asshole."

"He's not that bad," I argue. "You two might even be friends if you talked to one another."

Jesse looks doubtful, but offers, "Yeah, maybe we could play a round or two of pool. Winner gets first punch."

I laugh, knowing as well as he does that he'd win. "Okay, maybe not."

We talk about the guys he's seen over the last few days and how everyone's getting nervous about their jobs. "They're going to Newport," he admits at one point. "I just hope I can get them back when the time comes."

His eyes go vacant for a moment, and I think he's planning through how that could play out if he does lose some crew members permanently. Reaching up, I take his hand. "Someone pretty awesome told me to do what I'm good at, so maybe you should keep doing that too."

His eyes drop to my breasts, which are quickly becoming exposed as the bubbles disintegrate. "I know one thing I'm good at that I didn't get to do earlier."

Dirty-minded boy.

Good thing I love it.

But first . . . "You're good at taking care of your guys. Chrissy is going to be an absolute shit show. There's nothing I can do about that. But you can be the buffer between her and your guys. You might have to become an operations manager or something, even."

Jesse nods thoughtfully, and I feel like he's letting my words sink in and really considering them. But he also asks, "Is she really that bad?"

The scrunchy face that accompanies the question says he doesn't really want the answer, but I don't sugarcoat things.

"We spent three hours arguing over whether the electrical lines could be run underground or if they had to be run on poles. She completely didn't understand that was a nonnegotiable . . . because the freaking electricity is already on-site and run throughout the property."

"You didn't," he argues disbelievingly.

I nod my reassurance. "Yep, all because she didn't like the aesthetic of wires in the air. So she wanted them rerun underground so she didn't have to see them."

"Shiiiit, maybe I'll go to Newport tomorrow too," he laughingly suggests. He's not doing any such thing. The other guys will, but Jesse will remain true to the bitter end. I just hope that's not sooner rather than later with Chrissy at the helm of the ship otherwise known as Chrissy's Construction, with a heart over the *i* in Chrissy.

And unfortunately, I'm dead serious. It's one of the company names in consideration. I'll save that one for later. Jesse's had about as much as he can take right now. Still, I think about him drawing little hearts on his paperwork every day and giggle.

"Someone's getting a bit too cold." Jesse rises from the floor, grabbing a fluffy towel as he does. He holds it out wide as I stand from the lukewarm water, and quickly wraps me up in it, rubbing me gently to help me dry off.

In the bedroom, he pulls back the blankets and gestures for me to get in. "I need pajamas or I'll freeze."

"Not with me behind you." He grins devilishly.

"You're staying over?" I ask, hearing the hopefulness in my own voice.

"Couldn't kick me out now if you tried. Get into bed while I go warm up your leftovers. Dinner in bed, and then you need some sleep." He points at me and then the bed, allowing for no arguments.

Not that I want to argue. A bath, dinner, and sleep sound like heaven right now, and I'm one for three as of yet.

"Yes, sir," I snap jokingly, not used to people telling me what to do or taking care of me. But I kinda like it . . . from Jesse.

"Careful, Birdie. You start that shit and there's no telling when you'll get to rest," he warns. His dark eyes have gone instantly molten, promising all sorts of naughty fun. I'm heavily considering starting that shit right now, but a yawn escapes, and Jesse's brows knit together in concern. "Bed. Now."

He guides me to lay down on my propped-up, freshly fluffed pillows, and places a quick peck to my forehead. "Back in a second," he tells me, nearly running for the kitchen to heat up the leftovers.

But even that's too long, I guess, because I fall asleep before he gets back. I dream that he strips down and climbs into bed with me, arranging us into big and little spoons, with me as the little spoon. I think I argue about wanting to be his jet pack, but he chuckles and tells me to go back to sleep. All I know is I sleep well, warm and safe wrapped in Jesse's arms.

Chapter 22

JESSE

I don't know the number on my phone, which usually means it's a spam call. I go to hit "Decline," but for some reason, it accidentally answers. Rolling my eyes at my fat-fingering and already annoyed at the interruption to my not-at-all-busy day, I say, "Hello."

"Jesse?" a female voice says.

Trying to figure out who it is, I carefully answer, "Yeah?"

"Oh, good. I need you to come in around ten so we can go over a few things."

She pauses like I'm supposed to agree, but considering I still don't know if this is the blood bank asking for a pint, my doctor's office, or the bank wanting me to sign some shit, I don't agree to anything. "Who is this?" I demand instead.

"Oh." Whoever she is, she's definitely not happy that I don't know. If I hadn't been so hung up on Wren for so long, I might be worried it was an old girlfriend chasing me down, but that ship sailed long ago. "This is Chrissy Ford, your employer and boss."

I swear to God, she says it like she's explaining that she's the queen of England and I should properly worship her existence, even through the phone.

Is she seriously going for hoity-toity snobby when I saw her screeching and destroying property days ago? And I've spent my whole life hearing about what pieces of shit Jed and Chrissy are from Aunt Etta? And she's putting my job site on pause, making it so my crews are struggling to pay their bills?

Yeah, I'm not really feeling her "bow down to me, peasant" vibe. I'm more in the "bitch, please" camp.

"'Sup?" I mumble, purposefully sounding too casual and disrespectful in order to get under her skin.

"Excuse me?" she snipes back. But something must make her rethink the locked-and-loaded rant she's ready to unleash on me, because she makes an audible *hmmph* sound and then starts again. "Jesse, this is Chrissy Ford. I want to meet with you this morning to go over some Township details."

That was too easy. The guys are going to eat her alive if she gives in like that every time.

"Okay. Can't do ten, though, make it eleven," I reply. "At the trailer at Township or the main office?"

I have jack shit to do today and could meet her anytime, but I'm being intentionally ornery to further test her because it's fun. I grin as I glance down at my sock-covered feet propped up on the coffee table next to my protein shake. After seeing Wren off to work with breakfast in her belly and a lunch in her bag, I've already come home, worked out, showered, and gotten dressed other than my boots, which are stored by the door to keep my place clean. My big plan for the day is to head over to Aunt Etta's barn to stay busy and productive. There's always something to do over there, and if not, I can bother Wyatt. His workshop is behind Gran's old house, and running saws at a hundred decibels is a good way to mentally unwind.

"Eleven is fine. The main office," she clips out.

"'Kay. I'll be there." *Click.*

I hang up the phone, taking twisted glee in irritating her. Yeah, she might be my new boss, but right now, she's the boss of nothing. She's got no crews, no jobs, no contracts, and no right to call the shots. Jed's awful, no doubt about that, but I could respect that he left us alone and I didn't have to deal with him. Hopefully, after a little meet and greet, Chrissy will be the same.

If not, we'll have to teach her how we do things around Ford Construction Company, or whatever the hell she's gonna call it now.

If I'm going to the main office, there's one thing I need to do first—stop by the Bakery Box. If I don't bring cupcakes to Maggie, she's likely to skin me alive, and I'd prefer to not be turned into a warning story for what not to do when you visit the main office.

I throw the lid on my protein shake and yank my boots on. I start my truck, loving the loud engine rumbles, and wave at Mrs. Capshaw's front window. It doesn't seem like she's watching right now, but she hates my truck and its "needless noise pollution." Of course, she pretty much hates everything.

Once downtown, I find a parking spot and walk the few doors down to Mom's bakery. The bells jingle as I open the door. "Welcome to the Bakery Box," Mom says automatically, and then she looks up. "Oh, hey!"

Her smile is home, this building almost as much so. The pine floors are shiny, probably freshly mopped mere hours ago, and covered with knots and nail holes that show their age. The glass display cases are full of delicious treats, and though the menu board on the wall lists out the details of Mom's specialties, most folks order based on which one looks the best. Mom calls it "ordering by eye." I call it "get in my belly!" appeal.

"Hi, Mom. I've gotta go into the office, so I wanted to grab a few treats for Maggie and them," I reply. "Whatever you think they'll like, because it sounds like Chrissy is over there acting like the queen herself."

"She is not!" Mom says, shaking her head. She disappears beneath the counter, her hand reaching into the case. "I swear, she's a real piece of work. Always has been, always will be. Can't believe she's gonna be my landlord now. No telling what crap she'll try to pull . . ."

While Mom rants, I look around the bakery. Hazel helps Mom several days a week, bouncing between the Bakery Box and waiting tables at Puss N Boots, and while I help when I can, I'm usually relegated to the kitchen to deal with Helga, Mom's favorite and temperamental industrial mixer. I haven't been up front in a bit, and my detailed eye scans for potential things to take care of. The paint seems okay, the tables are in good repair, but there's a light bulb in one of the ceiling fixtures that's out.

"Want me to change that real quick?" I offer.

Mom reappears like a weird version of Pop Goes the Weasel and looks to where I'm pointing. "Hmm, hadn't even noticed it yet. Nah, let's do it after hours so we don't make a mess with the ladder and stuff." I make a mental note to do that next time I'm here before opening, because she'll forget about it, too focused on new flavor combinations and recipes to try.

She closes up the pink-and-white-striped box she's filled. "Put two of Maggie's favorite Buttery Nipple ones in there, a My Milkshake Brings All the Boys to the Yard cream-filled one, two Chocolate Orgasms, and a new one Hazel named—FAAFO. She said it means 'fuck around and find out'?" Mom's brows lift, double-checking if Hazel is pulling one over on her, because it wouldn't be the first time Hazel's done something like that.

I laugh and agree. "Yeah, that's what FAAFO means." I repeat it the way she did, like it's an actual word—*fayfoh*. Already knowing the answer, I ask, "Who's that one for?"

"Queen Bitch herself, of course. Maybe don't tell her the flavor combo?" Sparkles of wickedness shine in Mom's eyes, and when I open the box to peer inside, hoping for a hint, Mom fills me in. "It's based on this cupcake show I saw on Netflix one day, where they had to do two flavors that don't make a lick of sense, but still taste delicious together. That one's grapefruit jalapeño."

I legitimately cringe, revolted at the very idea. "That sounds disgusting."

Mom frowns severely, and if I was closer, I think she'd smack me for insulting her food. I hold up my hands, making it clear that I'm not trying to catch her hands. She settles, soothed by my silent apology. "I know! People love it, though." She shrugs like she doesn't understand it either. "The sour is this brightness, then heat is deeper, and it's all soothed by the cream-cheese frosting."

It still sounds absolutely awful, but I have the wherewithal to fix my face and hide my thoughts.

"You want one to go?" she offers.

I shake my head quickly. "Nah, thanks, though. Got my protein shake in the truck. I'm a growing boy, ya know?" I pat my flat belly, knowing Mom's not fooled a bit.

"Speaking of growing up—"

Shit. I walked right into that one. Hell, I lobbed the verbal ball into the air for her to spike it back at me. "Yeah?"

"How are you and Wren doing with this whole contract deal? You two are just getting yourselves sorted, and I don't want this to . . ." She stops and shakes her head. "Nope, not putting that into the universe. You two turn to each other, even when things get hard. Promise me that."

That's Mom's advice about everything. Put good out and the universe will respond in kind. Of course, none of us remind her of the time the universe fucked us all over and took Dad away. Instead, we go along with her positive vibes, which are salted by the occasional FAAFO. It's a good balance.

"We will, Mom," I assure her. "We're doing okay, just missing each other because she's working nonstop and I'm not working at all. I'm not exactly a 'sit around and twiddle my thumbs' type."

I'm not a "spill my feelings" kinda guy, either, but moms are built different. They know their kids, or at least mine does. And she hears the undercurrent trying to pull me down in the simple statement. "You're not working because your company is going through rough times. It's got nothing to do with you or your value. You men always tie up all your identities in your jobs. What you do is not who you are, Jesse. Who you are is a kind, caring, hard-working, patient man who loves with a fierceness I've only seen in one other man. Your father."

I grit my teeth together, swallowing the shit that she's stirring up in my insides. We don't talk about Dad much, not anymore. It's not painful exactly, but it's been a long time since he passed, so it doesn't always seem relevant in the here and now. But it's part of what shaped me into who I am, both his presence and his absence.

"Pretty sure you're the fiercest person I know, Mom." It's the truth. She's tough and strong, but manages to be soft and kind too. Hazel and I got the tough and strong parts, but are covered with spikes to keep people at bay, unlike Mom, who's never met a stranger she couldn't turn into at least an acquaintance.

"Well, if that's so, then don't you be arguing with me, mister. Wren doesn't think any less of you. She never did—*which I told you*—and she doesn't now just because Jed and Chrissy are going through *Divorce Court* drama."

I want to hear her, believe her. And I'm doing my best to stay busy, keep distracted, take care of everyone else, but deep down . . . I'm worried. What if this contract rewrite takes forever? I can't do a damn thing about it, but I still feel like I'm letting my guys down with every passing day. And Wren might not think less of me, but she's still this shining star of brains and beauty, and I'm a too-rough guy who's good with his hands. When I'm idle, what can I offer her? A great fuck and a shoulder to lean on? That's not enough for a woman like Wren.

I think that's why I keep getting struck by these fits of jealousy. I want her so much, want to build a life with her, want to have a forever with her. But Oliver the Asshole is this bright example of everything I'm not, being shoved in my face over and over. He's smart in a way I can never be, able to relate to Wren on topics I can't even pronounce, and though I hate to admit it, he's a good-looking, fancy-dressed guy who's someone you'd expect Wren to be with, a.k.a. not a grunting caveman who can build her a house from the ground up and start a fire to grill some meat, like me.

"Well, shit," I hear Mom say from a distance. Blinking, I come back from my own whirling thoughts to find her digging in the display case again. She comes up with one of those FAAFO cupcakes in her hand. "I thought I was giving you a pep talk, but I can tell by the way you're gritting the teeth I paid the orthodontist to straighten that it didn't work. So now I'm going with Plan B . . . open."

She holds up the cupcake, which looks like a vanilla cake covered in orange-and-green tie-dye frosting with a sugared grapefruit gummy in the center.

"No, thanks, Mom. I'm fine," I stammer, willing to do anything, say anything . . . as long as I don't have to eat that thing.

"Too late. You *fay-foh'd* and now you're gonna eat this. You need a spark to go off to the meeting with Chrissy so you're not all *wah-whiny baby, woe is me*. Be the badass you are, go in there, and tell her how this new company is gonna work." I nod, thinking that sounds okay. Good, even. "And that starts right here."

She holds the cupcake right in front of my face, and I can smell the sourness. I shake my head, refusing, and Mom glares at me, her head tilted a bit threateningly.

Okay, just a little bite. How bad can it be?

I open to nibble at it, and Mom forcefully shoves the whole thing into my mouth, getting frosting from my nose to my chin. "Mahm!" I say, or try to say around the mouthful. I can't even chew. I'm just moving my tongue around and swallowing to keep from choking. But eventually, I get enough down that I taste the cupcake. It's . . .

"Not bad actually," I admit in surprise. "Is there jalapeño jelly in the middle?"

She nods, pleased with herself. "Sweetened with agave nectar."

"Huh, who'd've thought?"

"Me," Mom says dryly. "And that's why you should listen to me. About Wren and about Chrissy. Now go before the sugar wears off."

I grab the box of packaged cupcakes and a handful of napkins, cleaning my face as I make a run for the door. "Bye, Mom! Thanks!" I hear her muttering something about stupid protein shakes, but she throws up a wave goodbye. "And I'll get that light changed later!"

The drive over to the main office is short, but I slam down the rest of my shake, wanting to have some protein in my belly with all that sugar. I should've planned what I want to say, but I'm more of a pants-er, as in, seat of mine, than a planner anyway. At least when it comes to meetings.

The headquarters of Ford Construction Company, or whatever Chrissy's gonna call it now, is a simple suite in a nondescript building. The brown stucco looks bland and forgettable, and the single glass door has black film to keep the sun out and a white vinyl sticker with the company logo. It definitely doesn't showcase what we can do, design-wise or build-wise.

The inside isn't much better. Cubicles with movable walls, cheap carpet, and stark white walls make the space feel temporary and almost scammy. For someone so concerned with appearances, it'd seemed odd that Jed didn't do more with the office, but when I asked him about it once, he said that he wasn't putting money into a space no one sees.

Realistically, I decided he was putting the money into his own pocket.

At the front desk, Maggie looks grumpier than a mama bear chasing her cubs out of the water for the tenth time this morning. "Uh, hey, Maggie! I brought goodies," I tease, holding up the box and hoping it'll gain me entrance without getting my head bitten off. "Mom put in two Buttery Nipples for you. A matching pair."

I wiggle the box in front of my chest, shimmying my shoulders a bit. Thankfully, it pulls a small smile from the woman who's put up with more of Jed's shit than anyone else, probably including Chrissy herself.

"Thanks, Jesse. I need these," Maggie says, sounding exasperated and not waiting a second to dig into the box. She pulls out a cupcake with a tan caramel areola on butterscotch-schnapps frosting and takes a big bite. Moaning, she mumbles, "Gah, these are sooo gud."

I grin, glad that I could bring a little bit of joy to her day. I lean on the counter to whisper, "What's going on? I got a call to do The Bitch's bidding today?"

Maggie giggles, sounding much younger than her fiftysomething years. "She's got ants in her pants, probably realizing that she doesn't have a clue."

She gives me a knowing look as she takes another bite. I think she's thinking like Wren, that I could have the run of the place if I play my cards right. But I shrug noncommittally. "Jed didn't either. We all know you run the office and I run the job site. Who needs 'em?"

"Ain't that the truth?" she agrees wholeheartedly.

Once upon a time, I think Jed hired Maggie to answer the phones or something equally low-key. But over the years, she's become the true star of the show behind the scenes. You need to know the budget? Ask Maggie. Want to order materials? Maggie. Got an issue with your paycheck? Maggie . . . well, she has a payroll company that does most of the work now, but for a lot of years, she was the one printing every check. Just about anything that actually makes the company function? Maggie does it or oversees the person who does.

I didn't even realize how much she does until Winston was singing her praises one night after he started his own firm. He needed to hire help and couldn't figure out how to post a job for "Maggie."

"She driving you crazy yet?" I guess.

"A little, but I can understand it. Taking over operations of this scale isn't for the faint of heart, and she's got not a lick of business sense in her head. Add on that she's got trust issues and it's a recipe for disaster. I'm doing my best to show her a little at a time so she doesn't get overwhelmed, while trying to keep things going." Maggie takes another bite of her cupcake, and I wish I'd brought her a coffee too. It sounds like she needs it.

"Are you telling me that's what I need to do too?" I hope that's not the case. I'm not gonna hold Chrissy's hand while she figures out the difference between a two-by-four and a two-by-six. And if she wants to be on a job site, she'll have to recognize that I'm in charge there, for everyone's safety.

"You'll figure out what works for you and her. You did with Jed, and I know the two of you were like piss and vinegar." Maggie's being kind. Jed and I nearly had some rip-roaring battles back when I first got promoted to job-site manager. He had other guys who'd give in to his blustering and bellowing. I was not one of them. But he learned that his reputation went up when I was the man on the job because I don't do shit work. It's done right or not at all.

Chrissy opens a door at the back of the space. "Jesse?"

I flash a charming smile to Maggie and remind her, "Make sure you get that other Buttery Nipple. You know you need a pair."

"Already got that set," she assures me as she laughingly shimmies her shoulders, "but you know I'll get my cupcakes too."

Walking to Jed's . . . no, Chrissy's office . . . feels weird. There's a knife dangling over all of our heads, and while what Maggie said is true about giving Chrissy a little grace, Township doesn't have time for that. We have materials en route right now, and we're not ready for them.

"Hey, Chrissy. I brought cupcakes from Mom's bakery for the office." I don't tell her that there's a special one just for her, as much as Mom would've liked for me to. I'll leave it to chance, especially since it was surprisingly pretty good.

"Thanks. I want to talk about Township."

Chrissy sits down behind Jed's big desk, looking small in the large chair that Jed filled out. I make myself at home in one of the other chairs and wait for her to make the first move.

I'm expecting her to ask questions about deadlines, designs, and maybe some delivery dates. But that's not at all what she asks . . .

"Does it have to be those tacky little town houses?"

"Uhm, what?" I'm sure I misheard her. I had to have. I try to think of something else to ask, but what comes out again is, "What?"

She wiggles her chair back and forth, not quite spinning but going right to left and left to right, as she hums thoughtfully. "I don't know. They're just so . . . *boring*. And didn't seem particularly well-built. Like they'd probably fall apart in a windstorm."

"One held up to you trying to drive a skid steer through it. That stunt of yours only cost us into five figures to fix. You know, *no big fucking deal*." Is sarcasm the ideal way to talk to my new boss? Probably not. Do I give a fuck? No. Especially when she's insulting the workmanship of my guys and me.

"Touché. I was mad," she offers by way of explanation, like that makes it all okay.

"Lady, you were wild and out of control," I declare, stopping short of what I want to say only by a hairbreadth. "And your actions put the entire site at risk. My site, my crews, and that won't happen again." If nothing else, I want to make that crystal clear. And you can bet I'll be documenting it in writing later to cover my own ass.

Her cheeks go red, but I'm not sure if she's embarrassed or angry with me now. "Sorry," she bites out.

The bitchiness still doesn't tell me which way she's leaning, but if she's mad at me now, this work relationship is only gonna get worse. And so help her if she comes after me like she did that town house or Jed. I won't be nearly as nice, and she will end up in the back of Officer Milson's cruiser when I press charges.

Having apparently made the only amends she's going to make, she goes back to talking about Township. "The ones that are built are fine, I guess, but can't we do something? What about if we combined some on the back streets or something to make them bigger? Or did some beautiful colors on the outside so they're not all sterile and white? We need to add some *pizzazz*." She moves her hands through the air like she's drawing a rainbow or some shit, and I wonder if she's always this annoying. "What do you think?"

I think it sounds like someone's been on Pinterest a bit too much and is distracting themselves from not knowing a thing about the business with pretty details that don't matter a lick.

"I think that's stupid as hell," I say honestly. This is a test of how we're going to work together. Or not.

Chrissy's smile falls instantly, and her mouth drops open in offense. "Excuse me?"

I lean forward in my seat, putting my elbows on my knees to look directly into Chrissy's eyes. "Look, I'm gonna be honest with you, and I hope you can appreciate the gift that my honesty is. Not because my opinion is worth shit, but because I've got experience you don't, and you pay me to give it. And seeing as this is our first meeting, we need to set some ground rules."

I'm a good boss, but I'm also a no-nonsense bastard, and Chrissy needs to know that.

Her response is to blink blankly.

"As far as Township is concerned, it's a done deal," I tell her sternly. "The plans are drawn, the plots are surveyed, and the materials are ordered. The contract needs to be re-signed, the permits approved, and then we'll get the crews back on-site to finish it as quickly as we can to open it up for sales. Changing it midbuild is a waste of time and resources that'll only cost money in the long run. Money you don't have right now."

Chrissy falls back in her chair, crossing her arms and glaring at me. I can almost see the pouty Karen coming out of her. "How do you know what I have?" she challenges.

I rise from my chair, having gotten what I need. "If that's all you got out of what I said, then I know everything I need to. Good luck."

She makes a sound of annoyance, and when I glare back, not budging, she rolls her eyes.

"Fine. Finish it how it is or whatever." She waves her hand dismissively.

But that's not it.

I sit back down. "Look, I'm your best manager on the sites, and my crews are the best. Treat us right, listen to us, and we'll keep working our asses off. If not, I hear there are other construction companies starting up in the area that we could all go work for."

Her eyes shoot daggers, and if this were any other situation, I bet she'd be demanding to speak to my manager. Bad news for her . . . she's my boss. "Is that a threat?"

I meet her gaze, chill as can be. "Nope. A promise. We're not the ones proving ourselves to you here. You gotta prove yourself to us, because you can betchur ass that Jed's gonna try to poach off every good worker here as soon as he's got his ducks in a row. Starting with Maggie and me."

I don't have an ego issue, and I'm not being dramatic when I say that. I've seen it happen time and time again. Hell, even a few of my quality guys quit when Winston left Ford Construction. Not to work for him, since he does more architect design work than construction, but because they didn't want to do the cookie-cutter shit Jed builds. Construction is a big world, but it's about as inbred as it comes, and skilled tradespeople can write their own ticket in a lot of ways.

Her expression morphs to terror. "Oh my God, is he already doing that? He can't do that, can he? This is my company. He said so."

"He hasn't reached out to me. Yet. But I want you to understand the situation here. Don't fuck up a good thing because you think construction is about deciding between shades of pink for the town houses or whether the flowers out front should be perennials or annuals. That ain't what we do, and it's not what you do if you're running this company."

"Sounds like you want to run it," she mumbles.

I shake my head vehemently. "Hell no. Office work ain't my gig. But you got someone who thrives in it. Treat her right, pay her at least double what you think she deserves, and maybe . . . *maybe* she'll save your ass."

Chrissy looks past me, out to where Maggie's sitting and eating her second Buttery Nipple, and I can see that she's getting it now.

I stand again, deciding this went better than I thought it would. A helluva lot better than when I first started working with Jed. Maybe there's hope for Chrissy yet. "I'll let you get back to it. Keep me updated on the contract negotiations. The moment you sign, I'll be waiting in Bea's office to file the permits so we can get back to work."

She follows me out to Maggie's desk and offers a sincere thanks to the both of us. "No problem, Chrissy. Hang in there. Maybe don't commit any felonies for a few days, and do normal divorce celebration shit like drink too much wine, sell your ring, and fuck a younger guy."

I almost say I know someone for that last idea, but I like Mike too much to screw him over that way. Chrissy laughs, and when she does, I can see the haze of hurt drop away for a split second. For all her bitchiness, I think she's going through a lot she never planned on, and maybe Maggie's right about giving a little bit of grace.

"Every good divorce starts with cake. Try that tie-dye one out. It's Mom's new recipe," I tell her, shooting Maggie a quick wink of "watch this."

Chrissy goes right for it, carefully pulling the cupcake from the box. "Ooh, it's pretty!" she squeals before taking a delicate bite.

It doesn't matter. There's enough sour and spice to getcha even with a nibble, and Chrissy's eyes go wide and her mouth drops open, showing the half-chewed food. "Aahh! I wadn't 'pecting . . . ooh!" She chews a little bit, unsure but starting to get the sweetness. When she swallows, her eyes are a little watery. "Wow, that was not what I thought it was gonna be."

"What flavor is it?" Maggie asks, eyeing the large chunk in Chrissy's hand warily.

"FAAFO," I tell them. "Grapefruit jalapeño."

"That sounds awful," Maggie says bluntly, wrinkling her nose.

Chrissy holds it out. "It's actually good now that I know what it is. I just wasn't expecting it. You wanna try?"

Maggie shakes her head, but I add to the sales pitch. "Mom shoved one in my mouth this morning. It's pretty tasty."

Still not sure if I'm pranking her like I was Chrissy, Maggie takes a teeny bite from the other side from Chrissy's. She looks prepared for it to taste like medicine or ass, but she brightens quickly. "Huh, who'd have thunk it? Your mom is so amazing. Creative and talented, a deadly combination."

"I'll tell her you said so." I wave as I walk toward the door. "Bye, ladies."

If they can get the contract done and Chrissy can keep from doing anything stupid, this might actually work out.

Chapter 23

WREN

This is never going to work.

The contract is nearly done, which should be a good thing. Two signatures—Francine's and Chrissy's—and we can get to work at Township again. But getting to this point has shown where Chrissy's priorities lay, and her lack of experience shows.

After arguing with Chrissy about the electrical lines for hours and getting that sorted, and then getting past the aesthetic changes she wanted to make, denying almost all of them, we finally got down to the nitty-gritty of the actual legal aspects of the contract, which left Chrissy bored and needing even the simplest of things explained. And to be honest, that's Oliver's job as her attorney, not mine.

At that point, Oliver suggested she stay away for the remainder of the contract discussion and let him work on her behalf. That was remarkably helpful because, since then, we've made major progress.

Thanks to Oliver's bullheaded negotiations stopping me at every turn from adding clauses to financially favor the city, the contract is pretty evenly matched as far as favoring Chrissy or Cold Springs. I wouldn't admit it aloud, but that part has been a tiny bit enjoyable, reminding me of strategy sessions and head-to-head debates in law school. What we've come up with is similar to the contract the city held with Jed, with a few changes to reflect that Chrissy's new ownership is unproven, so she'll be subject to frequent check-ins by city inspectors, multiphase deadlines, and meetings with the city development board.

But though the contract is rock-solid, it all centers on Chrissy making good business choices and correctly overseeing a huge build, things she has basically zero chance of doing. And that's going to affect Township and Cold Springs.

Closing my eyes, I tilt my head to the right and left, stretching my neck after staring at my screen for so long. This conference room is starting to feel like my second home, and my body is paying the price of playing hostess to Oliver with ordered-in lunches, chairs that are fine for a meeting but not to sit in all day, and fluorescent lights that buzz with a low hum that started driving me crazy hours ago.

Suddenly, I feel hands on my shoulders, massaging the tight muscles, and Oliver rumbles quietly, right in my ear, "Tense?"

I jerk away in surprise as my eyes fly open. Stonily glaring at him, I say, "No. I'm fine."

Oliver falls into the chair beside me, so close that his thigh touches mine. I shift, crossing my legs away from him. "Guess we should get to the two last clauses?"

That's all we have left—review the final page, do our individual read-throughs, and pass the contract on for signatures. "Actually, I was hoping you'd allow me the pleasure of using your brain," he says, turning the charm up to one hundred and smiling like my brain isn't all he wants. "You know, for fun."

As an attorney, I know better than to blindly agree to anything. Especially with another attorney. "What do you have in mind?"

He glances at the flashy watch on his wrist and says, "It's late, and we've been at this for days. On top of that, I've been working on the divorce decree in the evenings. You could say I'm burning the Benjamins at both ends." He chuckles at his own joke about his hourly rate, which I'm sure is astronomical. I can't imagine how much he's charging Chrissy for on-site, twenty-four-hour, personal attorney services. Whatever it is, there are probably extra line-item fees for hotel, food, and per diem too.

Considering I'm a salaried employee of the city, he's making significantly more than I am just sitting here. Which I'm sure is why he does what he does, but money isn't why I'm a lawyer. "Mm-hmm," I answer, not cracking a smile.

"I was hoping you might give the decree a once-over for me? Confidentially of course, but strictly off the books. No responsibility, no blame, and no credit." He winks like that's somehow a favor . . . to me. "I've been staring at it so long, I'd like to be sure I didn't miss anything, especially given Jenkins's reputation."

Curiosity is the polite term for nosiness, so I'll admit that I'm curious as hell about what's in that divorce decree. But not enough to spend hours staring at a contract tonight, poring over it when I've already been doing that all day on another contract. Plus there's the complication of Oliver himself. "I don't think that's va good idea," I say gently.

Instead of taking the refusal politely, he doubles down, speaking more forcefully. "You're not understanding. I would really appreciate it if *you'd look this over*. Make sure there's nothing *unexpected*."

Is he speaking in code or something? Given the pointed look in his eyes, I'd say so. "Just say what you want to say," I tell him bluntly.

"Oh, it's just that I find Cold Springs to be such a surprising town. I wasn't sure I'd like it when I came here, but there are so many interesting properties and people."

It feels like I'm translating Lassie's barks. *Is Timmy in the well? Rrruff, rrruff. Good girl.*

Cold Springs. Interesting properties. People.

Oliver knows how to pique my interest by playing to the thing I care about most—this town. And Jed owns at least half of it—commercial buildings, undeveloped land, and Township. If there's something I should know about so that I'm able to protect Cold Springs, I have to do whatever's necessary to find out.

"Fine," I say carefully, "but to be clear, this is a professional courtesy. Nothing more."

He smirks doubtfully at my clarification, but nods in agreement. "Thank you so much. I really appreciate it. We can look at it over dinner? There's a steakhouse downtown where I've been working every night. It's delicious, has impeccable service, and dinner will be on me. Well, on Chrissy technically, I guess. I'll meet you there at seven?"

It's not what I wanted to do tonight, but I'll do it for Cold Springs. Still, I remind myself to be careful. Don't be the cat and get killed by your curiosity, professionally speaking of course.

※

I knew what steakhouse Oliver was talking about as soon as he said "downtown." There are only two true steakhouses in town, one's a chain out by the highway into town that serves charred leather most of the time, and the other one is Bernard's Chophouse. It's as close to white tablecloth service as you can get in Cold Springs.

It's been a while since I've eaten here, but at one point, I was a regular. I'd sit and be quiet, remember my manners, and smile politely while Dad held dinner meetings as mayor. He'd discuss things that went way over my head or that I didn't care about, but over time, I started to listen, started to care, and started to learn.

Coming in tonight reminds me that I should possibly treat myself to this place more often. "Wren Ford? Is that you? Goodness gracious, I haven't seen you in ages." Bernard's greeting is exuberant and welcoming, complete with cheek kisses. "Rose, get Miss Ford a table!" he tells the hostess standing at the front podium. "The best we've got!"

She looks at me questioningly, and I hold up two fingers. "Table for two, but I'm not sure if he's here already. Oliver Laurent?"

Rose's face doesn't move, but interest blooms in her eyes. "Oh, Oliver's already here. He's sitting at his usual table. This way."

He's been in town for a short time, but apparently has a "usual table"? I guess he really has been working here in the evenings.

Before Rose leads me away, Bernard says, "Will you allow me the honor of providing you and your guest with a chef's choice tonight?"

He's smiling kindly, excited at the idea, and I nod in concession. "That'd be wonderful. Thank you."

I follow Rose to Oliver's table, which is beside a window that overlooks the downtown square and has a lit votive in the middle of it that gives a glowing light. Oliver stands when he sees me, moving to pull out my chair, but I hold out a hand. "No worries, I got it."

I don't want this meeting to be misconstrued in his mind. We're discussing a case, a contract, work, work, work. And nothing more. Despite the ambiance, this is not a date in any way.

Rose doesn't look convinced of that at all, and when she looks from me to Oliver before turning away, I'm tempted to explain what's going on here. Otherwise, the town hotline is going to be blazing about my romantic interlude with the out-of-town hottie, and word will get back to Jesse in an instant.

To that end . . .

I pull out my phone, telling Oliver, "Give me one second. I need to send a quick text."

> I'm having a completely professional meeting at Bernard's with Oliver to discuss the divorce decree. Don't freak out when the gossip starts. And do NOT come fuck me on the table where everyone can hear, ya caveman. Do that later. Your place. Nine o'clock?

I hit "Send," and Jesse responds back less than a second later.

Deal. How about my dining table instead?

Along with the text comes a selfie of Jesse. He's at home, working out judging by his shirtless and sweaty state. His dark eyes pierce into my core, even through the picture.

Oliver clears his throat, and I glance up to find him watching me with a hint of a smile. "I'm guessing your friend isn't so stupid after all?"

"He never was," I answer bluntly. I don't need Oliver's opinion on Jesse and me. I send a heart and a fire emoji back and slip my phone into my purse. "Let's get to the divorce decree?"

"Oh, would you like to look at the menu first?"

I push at the leather-bound book in front of me. "No need. Bernard said he'd do a chef's choice for us if that's okay?"

He blinks, obviously surprised. "It seems you're more of a regular here than I am."

I shrug. "Once upon a time. The decree?"

Oliver picks up a manila folder from the table and hands it over to me. While I open it and begin to read, he simply watches me.

At first, it seems like a pretty standard intro, lots of first party this and second party that. I skip down to the part pertaining to Ford Construction Company to make sure that what we've been planning for Township is feasible and correct, and find it pretty straightforward.

"The division of the company looks good, all things considered," I tell Oliver.

He nods and picks up his wine. Against the glass, he murmurs, "Check out page fifteen," and then takes a sip.

Okay, now we're getting somewhere. This must be what he wants me to see about the decree. I flip to page fifteen and start to scan.

It's a list of properties held by Jed and Chrissy Ford, and their dispersions under the settlement. The primary one that I care about is the land under development at Township, but there are several others. I scroll through them, seeing that Oliver and Robert have allocated some properties for each of their clients.

"How did you decide which properties Chrissy would keep versus Jed?" I ask, still reading the list that continues onto page sixteen.

"Negotiated individually, one by one, based on property values and equity," he answers tiredly.

"I can imagine what a long, arduous process that must've been. Actually, I can't, nor do I want to," I joke.

Bernard interrupts my reading to deliver two plates of filet mignon, baby red potatoes, and a creamed spinach that's my absolute favorite. "I remember how much you enjoyed it," he says, smiling when he sees my food happy dance. "The filet has a plum and pink peppercorn sauce, which we've paired with a Malbec wine I think you'll enjoy." He looks at Oliver's glass. "Would the gentleman like the Malbec as well?"

"No, thank you. I'm good with the Cab," Oliver answers.

Bernard inclines his chin, but looks at me with slight offense in his eyes like, *Can you believe that?* I suppress a giggle and tell Bernard thank you.

The decree is forgotten for a moment as we begin to eat the delicious dinner. "Bernard was the only chef here for a long time," I explain to Oliver. "It was by reservation only, prix fixe menu, and you had to be prepared to wait for your meal. But several years ago, Bernard began loosening his grip on the kitchen. He's mostly front of house now, but he still designs the menu, creates the recipes, and has his hand in the kitchen. He can't let it go."

Oliver tastes the sauce delicately and frowns in surprise. "That's unexpectedly good."

I swallow my own bite of filet and then take a sip of water, leaving the Malbec untouched. I won't drink it, but I didn't want to offend Bernard. "It's not Tayvious's chili nachos, but it'll do."

It's barely a joke, but Oliver laughs fully. "I thought you were crazy, but those were so good. I'm going to dream about that chili-cheese combo when I'm gone." I smile, glad that he tried them, because I'm still pretty sure nachos are not his style at all, but Tayvious can convert even the most high-strung into a cheese-guzzling whore with his nachos. Oliver isn't done, though. "They're not the only thing I'll miss."

The humor has left his voice, turning it smoky and deep, and his eyes stare into mine with heat. I'm 100 percent sure that works for him 99 percent of the time. Too bad for him, I'm the one-percenter.

I've known guys like Oliver. Hell, I've dated them. And while, on paper, we should be a good match, they're not it for me. Guys like Oliver do nothing besides turn me into a frosty, strategic, analytical robot, which is great in a courtroom. Not so great in the bedroom or in a relationship. They're the wrong man for me, no matter how much they wish they were the right one. And they usually assume they're the catch I've been waiting my whole life for, as though law school was merely a way to narrow my dating pool.

"We should get back to the divorce decree," I say flatly, letting my bitch face loose as I stare at him, devoid of all emotion. I don't want to lead Oliver on, and I don't feel like I have in any way. I've been honest that I have another person in my life, and I shouldn't even have to do that, considering our relationship is predicated on a legal issue and related to a contract only. "Page sixteen."

I begin reading again, the paperwork in my left and my fork in my right as I multitask my way through a working dinner. As my eyes scan line by line, I'm surprised at the number of properties Jed owns. It seems like there are some missing? I pulled a list on my own weeks ago to facilitate the divorce process, and I glanced over it, but admittedly didn't study it thoroughly. I didn't think it would matter . . . not like this.

"It says here that Jed is keeping the building at the corner of Main and Second Street?" Not able to see the paperwork, but probably having a significant portion memorized from the hours spent preparing it, he nods with certainty. "Right, but what about the building next to that?

Where the antique store is?" I point out the window to the storefront whose sign is lit even though they closed hours ago.

Oliver looks where I'm pointing, but shrugs. "That's everything in Jed and Chrissy's names, both as co-owners or individually. Do you think there are properties missing?"

The answer is yes. Saying that aloud without proof is akin to slander. "I don't know," I venture. "When are Jed and Chrissy due to sign this?"

"We've got three days of review before the hearing with the judge. Why?"

I glance down at the page again, feeling a gnawing sense of concern in my gut. I remember the slick, wily, borderline illegal ways Jed tried to ramrod his previous development through approvals. With Township, he's been better. Or has he?

What if that's one instance of doing the right thing in an entire clusterfuck of wrongs? A way to visibly repair his reputation while continuing on with his bullshit behind the curtain?

"Can I keep this copy? I promise to keep it safe and confidential, but there's something I'd like to look into if you don't mind?"

Oliver has no reason to let me take this copy. It breaks several ethical codes, and puts both of us at risk with at least the state bar association. And though we've been working together well on Chrissy's contract with Cold Springs, Jed is my uncle, after all. A shitty one who I hate, but my uncle nonetheless.

But after a quick consideration where Oliver scans my face with soft eyes, he agrees. "Safe and confidential."

We finish our filets, and too excited to get to work on this new puzzle my brain is taking apart and examining, I barely take two bites of the chocolate mousse Bernard brings out.

"Shall we?" Oliver asks, holding out an arm as we leave the table to allow me to walk in front of him.

After a quick promise to Bernard to come back soon, I walk with Oliver into the cool night air. The downtown council has done a great job making the square a destination. There are small, warm lights criss-crossing the streets, benches line the cobblestone sidewalks, and large pottery displays filled with seasonal flowers are at every corner. There's soft music playing from an ice-cream shop a few doors down and people walking hand in hand, enjoying the evening.

At my car, Oliver pauses and looks down at me. Usually, I hate being short because people think it makes me cute. I've literally been told I'm "fun-size" like a Halloween candy bar or "pocket-size" by people who think that's a compliment somehow. Right this moment, I'm glad there are several inches between Oliver's face and mine, because I've seen that look in his eyes.

He wants to kiss me.

I step back, adding more space between us. "Thank you for dinner. I'll get back with you about the decree."

Polite manners plus professional focus equal an all-business me that I hope he can respect. But he lifts his hand, gently brushing my hair behind my ear to whisper, "You are an amazing woman, Wren Ford."

I flinch and push his hand away. "Oliver. Don't."

It's the most forward he's been, but also the bluntest I've been, and I feel like things have been building to this point for weeks.

He licks his lips, and I can almost see him erecting walls around himself, ones I welcome and appreciate because they belong there. I've certainly got mine up and fortified. "Sorry. I got carried away for a moment."

"Apology accepted. This time only." It's a threat and a warning wrapped into one. "I'll see you tomorrow morning to finish the Township contract."

He nods silently, obviously upset—with himself? With me? I don't care, I've got a dining table, a hot guy who is my type, and a property list I want to research waiting on me.

Minutes later, I'm pulling up to Jesse's house, where the front porch light is on and through the blinds, I can see the flashing lights of the television. Jesse must've been watching or listening for me because as soon as I step up to the door, it swings open before I can even knock.

Though he's still shirtless, it looks like he's showered since his work-out selfie, because his dark hair is slightly damp, and he's wearing low-slung pajama pants with . . .

"Are those hot dogs wearing party hats?" I wonder out loud as I point to the cartoons all over his legs. I read the multicolored words splashed all over the pants, and my wonder turns to hilarity.

WELCOME TO THE SAUSAGE FEST!

I giggle at the silliness, but Jesse's in no laughing mood. His eyes are dark as midnight as he smirks at me in that sexy, bedroom way that drives me crazy. "Hey, Birdie," he grumbles. "Fuck, I missed you."

That's all it takes. I'm a puddle, standing on his front porch with big news I wanted to share about the oddities in the divorce decree. But now I can barely remember my name.

This is what I want. A man who wants me, not for the boxes I check, but because I'm a blend of just-right and all-wrong. A man who doesn't want me to be less and thinks my "too much" is the perfect amount. I thought that wasn't Jesse, but it turns out I was so wrong. He's exactly that man. The one who challenges me and isn't afraid to call me on my bullshit, but also sees that sometimes I need a safe space to crack the strong, independent shell I wear as armor and be taken care of.

Stepping inside, I curl right into his chest, my head fitting there perfectly. Smiling against his skin, I sigh, "I missed you too."

He places a soft kiss to the top of my head as his arms wrap around me, and after a moment of connection where we end up swaying together, I feel like I can relax enough to breathe again. He makes the day melt away until the only thing that matters is him.

No, us.

"Get in here and tell me about this meeting with The Asshole," Jesse says as he pulls me in and takes my purse. He sounds more annoyed than jealous, even rolling his eyes sardonically. "And I'll tell you about my meeting with Chrissy."

"Later," I argue, shaking my head as I take his hand and lead him toward the kitchen. "First, I was promised an up-close-and-personal look at your dining room table. I hope you're hungry."

I throw a sexy smile over my shoulder as I raise a questioning brow. As if the growing "hot dog" in Jesse's pajama pants isn't answer enough. "Fucking starving for you. Always."

He has me naked and spread-eagle on the table in seconds, sitting in one of the chairs like I'm his gourmet dinner, though I don't know that I've ever seen him attack a meal with as much gusto as he does me. Not even Tayvious's infamous chili cheeseburger, which would be an understandable and allowable exception for anyone who's ever had one.

I lose track of how many times his devilish tongue makes me come, demanding one more from me with my clit between his teeth and my ass sitting in a puddle of my own making as he holds me in place with a tight arm pressing down over my hips. I don't think I can do it again, but Jesse knows my body almost better than I know it myself, and I shatter violently, bucking and writhing with a scream choked in my throat and my nails digging into his shoulders.

"You're so fucking beautiful right now," he murmurs once I regain consciousness. His head is resting on my inner thigh, leaving beard burn I know I'll feel tomorrow, and I can sense his eyes looking up my body as his fingers trace pathways over my other thigh.

I can't help but giggle a little bit. I don't feel beautiful. I feel like an absolute mess—hair in knots at the back of my head, eye makeup running, mouth dry but skin soaked, and I can't catch my breath. I lick my lips and look down at Jesse. "Thank you."

Chapter 24

JESSE

"Doo doo-doo-doo, doo-doo-doo-doo," I sing, doing my best to imitate the *Mission: Impossible* theme song, dramatically making my way down the hallway. I press my back to the wall, looking behind Wren and me for any tails we might've caught along the way. "Coast is clear, let's go."

I peel myself off the wall with a dangerous grin and grab Wren's hand to encourage her toward our destination—the property tax office.

Wren's heels *click-clack* noisily, and if we were actually on a top-secret mission, they'd garner way too much attention, and her laughter would surely get us busted. "Sshhh," I hiss, glaring at her offending heels. "Before I banish those to the bedroom!"

"You're the one who'll lead people to ask questions we don't want to answer," she teases back. Her smile says she's having fun being silly, though.

We need it after this morning. We spent the hours as the sun came up curled together in my bed, talking through the drama of our individual days. She was surprised when I told her how bluntly aggressive I was in my meeting with Chrissy, but understood the strategy of setting the stage for our new working relationship. But neither of us was surprised at Jed trying to pull a fast one in the divorce decree. I think we'd be more surprised if he didn't do something shady.

Wren hasn't let me see the decree, claiming confidentiality, which I understand, but she's sure the property list is incomplete. Her doubt in it is enough for me.

That's why I called Maggie this morning and asked her to meet us for this hush-hush meeting too. She's entirely trustworthy and has had numerous opportunities over the years to prove that, to the point that if Jed was doing something sketchy, he must have hidden it from Maggie too. For example, she had no idea about the affair with Lucy. But if anyone knows about Jed's properties, it's her. Jed wouldn't know how to file his nails, much less ownership papers with the county.

Of course, that's what lawyers are for, but there's always a trail. Always.

And hopefully, Maggie is a bloodhound.

One more corner and we'll be there, but before we can make the turn, someone else comes around it and nearly runs right into us. "Oh! Sorry," Bill Ford says, stopping short and looking from Wren to me and back. His smile falls slowly, turning to suspicion. "What are you two up to?"

"Hi, Dad. What are you doing here?" Wren asks, ignoring his question. "It's like old times, seeing you around the halls here." She smiles as though remembering happy times when Bill was the mayor and Wren was interning with Ben.

Rather than going down memory lane with her, Bill narrows his eyes. "Good try, but I taught you that trick. Now, what's up?"

Wren laughs, the sound a bit forced and high-pitched, and bats her lashes a bit.

"Immune to that one too. Ask your mother." He tilts his head, enacting the Dad Glare 5000 to silently pull the answer from Wren.

But she's a pro, able to keep her mouth shut even when it's her own father demanding answers. "Nothing to worry about, Dad."

The Wrong Guy

Concern instantly furrows his brow, and she reassures him again. "I promise. We're good."

Still not sure, he searches her face before turning to me. "Don't let this one get you into trouble, Jesse." His lips tilt up the tiniest bit in a grin. "It's hard to keep up with the big monster inside her."

His gaze turns back to his daughter, pride beaming on his happy face. It's good to see on him after that quiet, sad moment before the wedding, and I can see where Wren gets her confidence from. It was poured into her by her parents from a young age. Her dad doesn't tell me to protect his little girl like some parents would, but rather warns me about her badass nature like it's the best compliment he can give.

"I wouldn't dream of trying. I just make sure she's got a good place to come back to after she fights the town's battles." It's the smallest hint of what we're doing. I feel like he deserves that.

He makes a grunting noise of approval and steps aside. "Well, I'll leave you to it. Let me know if I can help with anything." He starts to walk past us but stops. "Oh, also . . . call your mother. She knows how busy you are, but she's missed your Monday night dinners."

"I will," Wren vows. "I have too."

Making our way around the corner, we find the tax assessor's office without running into anyone else.

"Uh, hi?" Christiana utters when we sneak inside, shutting the door behind us quickly.

Wren told her she needed to meet this morning, but not what it was about. Maggie sitting in a chair makes the topic pretty clear, though.

"Hi, Christiana, Maggie." Wren sets her bag on the floor, taking the other chair in front of the desk. I offer a wave and lean against the door to keep anyone from interrupting us. This is Wren's show, I'm basically a bouncer to keep it on the down-low.

"Jesse, you've got my hackles up with curiosity. Now, what's this all about?" Maggie asks. "And it'd better be good, since I had to tell Chrissy

233

that my hot flashes got the best of me and I'd be working from home today, naked with cool towels on my neck."

I could've gone my whole life without that image in my head, but it's too late now. "You could've said you had a flat tire, a headache, or any one of a dozen other things," I reply. But when she gets up, threatening to leave, I backpedal. "Thanks, Maggie. It's important."

Looking pleased with herself, she sits back down, turning her attention to Wren, who delicately explains that she needs the property records for Jed, Chrissy, Jed and Chrissy, and Ford Construction for the last thirty years, choosing her words with the legal ramifications in mind.

"Can you search for those in particular?" she asks Christiana, who's already typing on her computer.

"Yeah, that's an easy database search and public records. Do you want the ones currently held by them or ones held by them at any time?" she asks.

Wren's eyes go sharp. "Any time."

"Guessing you want me to verify them or something?" Maggie offers. She's a smart cookie and pretty easily puts together what her role in this could be. When I nod, Maggie's lips press together into a flat line. "I gotcha, whatever you need. I know you'd do the same for me."

I absolutely would.

A few minutes later, Christiana has pages and pages of property information printed, and Maggie is starting to read through them. "What am I looking for?" she asks absently, reading each page.

Wren opens the manila folder she's been holding and swallows thickly. "I need to compare that list to another one."

"You wanna tell me why or what lists we're comparing?" Maggie asks, feigning indifference.

Wren shakes her head and starts at the top. "3854 Allens Avenue."

Maggie grabs a highlighter and runs a line through that address, the marker squeaking loudly. On and on, they do this, until Wren runs out of addresses.

"What about these other ones?" Maggie asks.

And that's the answer she needed. There are properties that should be on the divorce decree but aren't. "Can we look up the history of those individually?"

Maggie reads them out to Christiana, and she begins typing again. "That one sold in 2015. Next?"

That's how several go, and then Christiana says something none of us expect. "Wait. You said 90888 Millview Street?" Maggie nods, and Christiana looks up. "Wren, you want to look at this?"

Pointing at the screen, her eyes are wide in shock. Wren gets up and goes around the desk to see what Christiana's found. She reads the screen and huffs out an ironic laugh. "Jed, you are such a motherfucking asshole."

"What?" I ask. "What is it?"

"The property," she says deliberately. "It's in Lucy Blivings's name."

A bomb might as well have gone off, because we're all dead silent. "Seriously?" I echo. "Why would Jed do that? Putting property in Lucy's name seems premature, right?"

Wren looks around the room, judging each person's trustworthiness again before she speaks, still keeping it general enough to have plausible deniability if called on it. "Someone might do that to hide property so it's not included in a divorce."

The ramifications of that sink in. "Shiiiit, what do you want to do?"

Still thinking, she mutters under her breath, "I wonder if Lucy even knows?"

Maggie sighs heavily and reveals, "I'd bet not. He forged Chrissy's signature once to set up an LLC, and when I questioned it, he told me to just do the notary stamp." She slows down, making sure we understand how offensively bad this next part is. "Because it was 'financial stuff above my head' and 'I shouldn't worry.'" She rolls her eyes. "As if there was anything he ever did that was over my head. I swear, the man can't add two plus two sometimes. But I didn't do the notary then, and didn't do the one a few months later to move the properties back into Jed's name."

"How do you know he did that, then?" I ask.

Maggie's answer is simple. "I basically ran the company."

Wren's quiet for a long moment while Christiana and Maggie check the remaining properties. There are several that have legally and correctly sold to others, but there are five in Lucy's name, all high-value properties.

I watch as Wren's stress level climbs, her eyes going flinty and hard as she stares at the decree in her hand. Finally, when they're done confirming ownership of all the properties, we look to Wren for guidance.

"I need to talk to Lucy," she says finally.

I hold my hand up, ready to make her smile. "I have an idea for that."

◈

"Cupcakes or cookies?" Mom asks as soon as Wren and I walk through the door at the Bakery Box. Food, especially sweets, is her love language, so she instantly tries to feed us.

"Maybe later," I tell Mom. "First, we wanted to talk to you about something."

She grins maniacally and starts clapping. "Of course I'll do the wedding cake. I've already been thinking about it. How about a twist on a hummingbird cake? I can do a rum soak on the pineapple and candy the pecans with cinnamon sugar. I think it'll be perfect for you . . . a little sweet, a little sour, and a little spicy."

My head drops, my chin hitting my chest as my eyes close. I cannot believe her. She's gonna have us married before we get out on a real date with me picking Wren up, taking her to dinner, and back home. One large breath for calm and sanity, and I pin Mom with a glare.

"Whatever's going on in your head, shut that shit down. That's not why we're here."

Mom's jaw drops as she makes a sound of displeasure. "Don't talk to me like that, Jesse Sullivan. I brought you into this world, and I can take you out . . . and I don't mean to dinner, young man." Her head's swiveling, and her expression has taken on that "try me" threatening vibe that all moms magically master on day one. She's the one trying to marry me off in record time, yet somehow, I'm the one in trouble.

Wren's fighting back laughter, barely succeeding at keeping her lips pressed together.

"Sorry," I say just to move on. "Mom, focus. Remember when Chrissy came in here snooping around, you said that you knew exactly where to send her because Lucy placed a delivery order?"

She's slow to answer, looking at me like I might implicate her in a felony crime if she answers that question honestly. Or maybe she's just still pissy about me calling her out. "Yeaaah?"

"Is Donny still delivering pregnancy treats to her? Where is she now?"

Mom huffs out a laugh, her face morphing into something akin to offense. "Not like you suddenly decide, midpregnancy, that something else is tastier than my Blue Balls lemon-blueberry cake pops."

I look to Wren, silently asking if she's sure of her plan. This could backfire big-time, and if it does, she'll be the one in trouble. And Jed will most definitely pursue every legal avenue to make Wren pay. Hell, I wouldn't put it past him to use some illegal options too.

But badass that she is, she steps right up to Mom's display case. "Can I send a batch of Blue Balls to Lucy, please? I have a private note to include. Inside the box, where only she'll see it."

"Oh, shit, Wren. Are you sure about that?" Mom asks, looking extremely uncomfortable with the idea.

Wren nods. "Yes, ma'am. Completely sure."

Mom leans to the right to look around Wren and meet my eyes. "Jesse, if you don't marry her, I will. Let me box up some balls and call Donny for a special delivery!"

Mom seems almost giddy about the whole thing now that she's seen Wren's game face. But I've known all along that my little bird is awesome. That's why I've had so many doubts, because Wren is the woman so many people want, the total package of brains, beauty, and the perfect amount of crazy to keep things interesting. And though I'm not chopped liver, there aren't a whole lot of guys who'd live up to being at Wren's side long-term. She shines so bright, which can be intimidating as fuck, but I want to support her in that. Hell, I'll do what I can to help her shine even brighter if that's what she wants.

I just hope that after all this is over, she doesn't realize that I'm just a dirty guy who works with his hands, hasn't read a literature book since high school, and is too possessive to be totally sane, and decide that I'm not good enough for her.

While we wait for Mom to work her magic, I wrap my arms around Wren's shoulders and pull her back to me. "So how do you feel about hummingbird cake?" I tease. "Remix style?"

She laughs quietly, probably so Mom doesn't hear her. "I figured you'd be more of a 'classic vanilla cake' kinda guy."

I chuckle, too, but go dead serious when I tell her, "I'm a whatever the fuck you want if I'm lucky enough to get a ring on your finger, Birdie."

She goes silent and frozen in my arms instantly.

Fuck, man. Way to scare the shit outta her.

But it's the truth.

Chapter 25

WREN

"Anything else, Ms. Pamela?" Maria asks Mom as she does a last-minute check over the charcuterie board and needlessly readjusts the pitcher of sweet tea and glasses.

Mom looks to me for the answer. "This is your show, honey. You need anything?"

"A Xanax?" I suggest, half-serious. But what I do is take Jesse's hand for support. He entwines our fingers, then lifts our hands to place a soft kiss to the back of mine. It'd be sweet and romantic, except for the wink and cocky grin he shoots me.

He's not being arrogant about himself, but rather is that confident in me. Even if what I'm about to do is by far the most dangerous, and potentially the stupidest, thing I've ever done, he'll cheer me on if I want to do it. Because it's also the right thing to do, and if it costs me the career I've worked years to achieve, then I'll lose my license with a clear conscience.

Mom's brows shoot up. "Uhm, if you're serious, I do have one." But even as she makes the offer, she looks like she's sorry she did. "Not sure that's a good idea, though."

I force a smile to my face to ease her nerves. "Kidding, Mom." Trying to exude calm, I tell Maria, "We're fine. Thank you."

"Okay, good luck, *mija*. You use that brain of yours, and be smart." She cups my cheeks in her hands, almost nose to nose with me, as if she can will it so. I nod, only able to make a tiny movement, and she releases me. She makes a clucking sound with her tongue that somehow sounds like concern and love rolled into one. "I'm off to feed Leo dinner. If you need something, ring me."

She takes off her apron as she walks to the kitchen, muttering in Spanish so quietly and quickly that I can't catch a single word. But it sounds like a prayer for me. Maria doesn't know what's going on tonight, but anything that has Mom and me riled up isn't good in her book.

We sit in awkward silence for a few minutes, and then the doorbell rings. "I've got it," Mom tells me, virtually running for the door. I hear her greeting whoever's arrived first. "Come on in the front room."

I hold my breath and squeeze Jesse's hand. This could be it, the fire lighting the fuse.

Etta comes in with Mom at her back. Etta's smiling, but gives me shit. "Hey, girl, am I early for the start of the show? Does that mean I get to watch the previews and get a sneaky-peek at what the hell you've got going on?" She scans the room like a bogeyman might jump out at her.

"No previews, I'm afraid. But there's pepper jack cheese and tiny toast. And some of Daisy's Blue Balls." I point to the table with Maria's prettily arranged spread.

"I leave blue balls everywhere I go," Etta quips back, pushing her hair behind her ear. I don't think I've ever seen it down. She almost always has it in a braid, and if not, it's wrapped up in a bun on top of her head. She picks up a cake ball and a napkin before sitting in a chair, seeming more refined than usual. She's wearing cutoff jean shorts and boots, looking like exactly what she is . . . a country woman who owns a damn good bar, but there's an attempt at fanciness in the way she's moving and sitting.

Chrissy arrives next, looking comfortable with an invitation from Mom until she sees Etta. "What's going on?"

"We're waiting on everyone to get here, and then I'll explain," I tell her. She sits down but is looking at Etta warily.

For her part, Etta says, "Heard you went for a little joyride and did some heavy-duty property destruction?" Chrissy's eyes fall in embarrassment until Etta adds, "Good job. I went for putting Coke in his gas tank. I was too young and stupid to be creative back then."

Chrissy raises her gaze in surprise. "That was you? He loved that car!" she says reflexively. But a second later, she laughs. "He *loved* that car! You have no idea how many times I heard him whine about the engine blowing up out of nowhere."

The two women seem to bond over some decades-old revenge that they now both appreciate.

Maggie arrives next, waving to Chrissy uncertainly. "Thanks for having me, Pamela."

I know they've met at various Christmas parties, but Mom and Maggie are basically acquaintances connected by Two Degrees of Kevin Bacon—my dad and Jed.

There's a quiet knock on the door, and I meet Mom's eyes. But before she can go, Jesse hops up. "I've got this one."

I sit frozen, listening as I hear Jesse say, "It's fine. I promise. Just come on in and listen. You can leave anytime." Lucy must agree, because she appears in the doorway with Jesse behind her. Her eyes go wide at seeing the congregation of women all staring at her, and she takes an involuntary step back, bouncing into Jesse's chest.

"Oh!" she exclaims.

Jesse steps away from her, holding his hands out peacefully. "Not holding you hostage. Just standing here," he chuckles, trying to put her at ease. "You're all good here."

But Lucy's eyes have landed and locked on to Chrissy, whose anger is beginning to burn hot again.

"What are you doing here?" Chrissy demands, her tone as icy as her gaze is ablaze. She stands, her hands fisted at her sides and teeth clenched.

Fearing a catfight between the two, I stand, playing hostess, though it's my mom's home. Holding out my hand, I say, "Lucy, I'm Wren Ford. Nice to meet you."

She takes my hand, shaking hesitantly, but keeps her eyes on Chrissy, not forgetting her question.

Etta pipes up, "Welcome to the Jed Ford Support Group. Thought we'd go ahead and start your initiation ceremony. You brought the rubbing alcohol and tattoo needle, right?"

"What?" she balks in fear.

"Aunt Etta, don't." Jesse's warning is fully ignored. "You're gonna scare her."

Etta doesn't seem the least bit apologetic, but she does explain, "We're all victims of Jed, one way or another. And Wren's got something to tell us. You can go if you wanna, but I'd listen to her if I were you."

With that, she pops a Blue Ball in her mouth. Somehow the gesture gets through to Lucy, who visibly relaxes a notch.

"Are those from the Bakery Box?" Lucy says suddenly, her focus zeroed in on the treat Etta just ate. Before anyone answers, she's grabbed one and is sitting in a chair, nibbling at the blue-dyed white-chocolate covering like it's the most delicious thing she's ever had and glaring around like one of us might rip it from her hand. I swear I can almost see her mind impersonating Gollum . . . *my precious*. "Mmm, these are so good. I crave them like an addict." Realizing how that sounds, she widens her eyes in horror. "Not that I . . ."

"We're all addicted to Daisy's balls," Etta assures her. "My sister has a way around the kitchen." Her pride is obvious and endearing.

I figure I'd better get started before Lucy finishes her treat and makes a run for it. "Ladies, thank you for coming. Like Etta said, we all have some connection to Jed." Out of the corner of my eye, I see Lucy place her hand on her round belly.

"Some of us more recently than others," Chrissy snipes, throwing shade at Lucy.

Lucy returns fire, shooting eye daggers at Chrissy. "Maybe if *some* of us had a connection with him, he wouldn't have looked for connections *elsewhere.*"

This was a horrendously bad idea. They're less than a blink away from going at each other, and given Chrissy's recent antics, I'm not sure Lucy is safe. I'll never forgive myself if she or the baby gets hurt because I invited her here.

Mom is probably the only person who can say this without consequence, so thankfully, she jumps in. "Chrissy, you haven't liked Jed, much less loved him, in years. So what if someone else is washing his dirty underwear? What do you care?"

Her voice is sharp, piercing through the cattiness.

Etta shudders. "And sucking his balls." To Lucy, she says genuinely, "I hope for your sake, he's discovered the art of manscaping after all these years." She plays at picking at her teeth like she's got a hair caught between them, tutting. "That's one of the reasons why I like the younger men. These days, they're all smooth as a dolphin's butt."

Jesse coughs, looking disturbed at the very idea of his aunt with some bare-bodied young stud, and Maggie holds out a glass of tea to him.

He takes the tea gratefully, swallowing a healthy amount. "I'm good. Just gonna pretend the last ten seconds were a fever dream and didn't actually happen. Carry on."

He waves a hand at us, specifically at me, begging me to direct this conversation where it needs to go and not to whatever else Etta might share.

"Some connection to Jed—" I repeat louder, gathering everyone's attention. "He's my uncle. Mom's brother-in-law, Etta's ex-fiancé, Chrissy's soon-to-be ex-husband, Maggie and Jesse's soon-to-be ex-boss, and Lucy's current . . . boyfriend?" I offer, not sure of the title they're going by.

"Her Jeddie-Weddie," Jesse reminds me, cringing.

Lucy cuts her eyes to Jesse and then back to us to dramatically hold up her hand, flashing a rock so big, I'm surprised she can lift it without a crane. "Fiancé," she gloats proudly.

"Girl, we ain't happy for you," Etta laughs when Lucy's brag falls flat. "We feel sorry for you because the next support group meeting is gonna be when Jed's cheated on you. It's what he does, because his ego needs all the stroking it can get. And the only thing worse than stroking Jed's ego is stroking his di—"

I cut her off, "Divorce!" Etta beams triumphantly, and I consider that she's being outrageous to get me to hurry up with whatever I've got planned. Maybe even to take the pressure off me a bit. She's a skilled people reader as a bartender, so I wouldn't put it past her. Though the alternative, that she's enjoying fucking with me, is equally likely. "I mean, I've been working on behalf of the city on the Township contract. As part of that process"—I school my face as I lie because what I dis-covered wasn't through that deal at all, but I can't and won't share that I've seen the decree, because that would get myself and Oliver in trouble with the ethics board—"I pulled the tax records for all properties owned by Jed, not only currently but at any time in the last thirty years."

"Those are public records?" Mom asks. She knows the answer to that question, but is giving me an opportunity to state it for everyone else.

I nod in agreement. "Completely public, available at the tax asses-sor's office any day, any time. There's even a website you can search."

"The current ones will change as soon as the divorce is final," Chrissy informs me, as if I don't understand what a division of assets is.

"Right. I know you and Jed have agreed to a split of properties and assets. But I think it's worth each of you looking at these reports." I pull the printouts from a folder and set them on the table.

Maggie takes a slow, deep breath and then mutters so quietly, I'm not sure I heard her or if I imagined it. "Page four."

Chrissy gets there first and scans down the page. When she sees Lucy's name, she pauses. "You've got property here? I thought you were from Brookstone?"

"I am," Lucy answers, not understanding what Chrissy's asking. But when Chrissy holds up the paper, pointing to the listing of property owners, Lucy's eyes go wide. "What's that?"

The surprise and confusion on her face is all I need to know that our suspicions are right. She has no idea what Jed's doing in her name.

I can lead them to it, but I can't draw the conclusions for them without going way out on a limb over lawyer-infested waters that'll eat me quicker than any shark would. But Jesse can say things I can't. He's under no obligations, legal or ethical, to not hypothesize about property records.

He must feel the weight of my gaze, because he meets my eyes with a questioning look in his dark ones. *Do you want me to step in and help you?* his eyes ask. Any other time, the answer would be a resounding *no* and likely even a ranting diatribe about being able to save myself. But this time is different. I need to walk the tightrope of what I'm allowed to do and what needs to be done.

"You thought Jed was hiding money in the company," he tells Chrissy. "Turns out, he's hiding property in your name," he tells Lucy. "Under false pretenses, likely forging your signature so he could move property under your name and it wouldn't be caught in the divorce settlement. My guess is that he plans to move it back into his name as soon as the divorce is final."

"What?" Lucy says quietly as her eyes jump around the room to each person. I think she's hoping someone will tell her that's not true.

But Maggie nods pretty convincingly. "He tried it before," she admits, before telling Chrissy specifically, "and I refused."

Situations like this are where Mom shines, and she sits down next to Lucy. "I'm sorry. It's what he does. He uses people, manipulates them without concern for anything other than himself. He almost killed Bill, running him into the ground with his lies and exploitation. He destroyed his own brother's career and almost his life, and then blamed us. We were left to rebuild—our relationship, the town, and the town's trust in us. And Jed went on like nothing had happened, completely uncaring of the destruction in his wake."

Her eyes flick to me, and I know she's talking about when I became city attorney. There were people concerned because of my last name, especially when one of my first deals was Township with Uncle Jed. People thought I was a plant for him, someone who'd sign off on his shit no matter what. Fortunately for Cold Springs, I'm the exact opposite and don't trust Jed at all, because he's proven time after time that he's not trustworthy.

Lucy nods woodenly. Her eyes have gone vacant as she stares at the coffee table, but I don't think she's actually seeing anything. Not even the Blue Balls. She's lost in her mind, thinking and processing.

"I was a waitress, barely making ends meet," she whispers. "Jed came in one day, and we hit it off. He became a regular, and the next thing you know, we're . . ." She looks at Chrissy apologetically and explains, "I knew he was married, but he took care of me. I wasn't hungry, my bills were paid, and he bought me nice things. Things I'd never had before."

"He can be charming when he wants to be," Etta offers kindly.

But Lucy shakes her head. "He's not charming. It's fake, a mask he puts on, and I know it, but it's better than where I was."

"Lots better now," Chrissy says cynically. "This property's tax appraisal is in the seven figures."

Lucy huffs out a laugh. "But it's not mine. He's using me like I'm using him. Should've known. That's what men do."

She sounds more bereft than I expected. I guess, like everyone else, I kinda thought she was either a careless homewrecker who stole a married man from his marriage or a naive pushover seduced by Jed's charms, whatever those might be. But it seems like she's simply a woman in a rough situation, with some painful history, who was willing to do anything to make a better life for herself.

Even if what she had to do was . . . Jed.

"Actually," I say, "regardless of how you received them, right now, you are on record as the sole owner of several properties in Cold Springs. If you were interested in doing something with them . . . say, moving them into an LLC or selling them, I might know a lawyer who could help with your properties." I choose each word carefully, not giving legal advice, but making sure that Lucy understands what I'm saying.

"You. Own. Them," Chrissy utters, realizing what I mean first. "They're yours. And *he* doesn't know that *you* know, so you can do *whatever* you want with them." Her glee is bordering on madness as she considers Jed truly losing everything.

"You could do a lot with seven figures," Etta suggests casually, popping a cheese-and-cracker combo into her mouth. "All of which involve a nice life for you and your baby, and none of which involve sucking Jed's dick."

And there it is. The opportunity that Lucy has. She can legally take the money and run, or she can stay.

"Are you really in love with Jeddie-Weddie, Lucy-Juicy?" Jesse asks from the doorway, where he's been leaning and silently observing. "If so, go home, tell him you know . . . or don't, and live your life with Jed Junior, nose kisses, and baby talk. If not . . . if he was a ticket out? There ain't no shame in doing what you gotta do to get by. And that's true for what you've already done and what you do now."

"Someone pretty smart once told me that you choose your life every day." Chrissy looks to Etta with sadness shining in her eyes. "I wasted a lot of years making that choice by default, not actually deciding." She goes quiet for a moment, but there's more on the tip of her tongue. "I guess I did decide, I just didn't want to admit it. But you have the chance now, while you're young. Don't waste your life on Jed Ford, honey. He's not worth it, I swear."

Lucy stares at Chrissy, Etta, and then Jesse for a long moment before her eyes fall to the floor, seemingly contemplating Mom's rug. I'm holding my breath, scared that she's going to tattle on me . . . to Jed, to the city council, to the bar association. I've been careful with my words, but that doesn't mean they won't launch an investigation into my behavior. When her eyelids fall closed with a heavy sigh, I'm sure I'm done for. But when she lifts her gaze, cold resolution burns in the blue depths. "Can I talk to that lawyer you said you could recommend?"

Surprised, I answer, "Yeah. Absolutely. I'll call him right now."

I pick up my phone and step into the foyer, leaving Jed's trail of women to talk among themselves.

"Unless city hall is being overrun by picketers again, there is no good reason for you to interrupt my nightly news and Samuel Adams, Wren," Ben declares when he answers the phone.

"No picketers. But I do have a bit of an emergency. Can you come over to my parents' house? Now."

"An emergency? A legal emergency? I don't know many things that'd qualify for that, but you've got my interest piqued, and that's hard to do for an old guy like me."

"Well, hopefully you're an old dog who doesn't mind learning a few new tricks, because this one's a doozy. Do you need me to send someone to pick you up?" Jesse's followed me into the foyer and holds up his hand, volunteering, when he hears my question.

"Nah, truth be told, I'm out of my damn beers. Been messing with my routine all night," Ben confesses. "Already pulling my shoes on and heading that way. You wanna give me a hint what I'm walking into?"

Behind me, I hear a hard knock on the coffee table and Mom says, "I hereby call to order the inaugural meeting of the Jed Ford Support Group." And then the women giggling together as one.

I'm glad they're not in danger of killing each other anymore, but now, I'm kinda worried they might kill Jed. Literally or figuratively, or both for all I know. There's a lot of years of hate, revenge, bitterness, and more sitting around that coffee table, being fueled by sugar and cheese.

"You wouldn't believe me if I did. You'll have to see it with your own eyes," I tell Ben.

When I hang up with him, Jesse crowds into me. He's looming over me, creating that protective bubble where only we exist. His smile is a bit crooked as he looks down at me, twirling a lock of my hair around his finger. "You are amazing, Wren. I can't believe you pulled that off with those women in there. That brain of yours is so fucking sexy."

He presses a sweet kiss to my forehead that shouldn't make me buzz, but definitely does. I shrug humbly. "I didn't do much. There wasn't a lot I could legally say."

Jesse chuckles. "You didn't have to say much. You set it all up perfectly, like one of those domino chain-reaction deals, and then you tapped the first one and watched your masterpiece take shape. You play so fucking dirty, but in the cleanest way possible."

The compliment warms my heart. Not just that he values what I do, but that he sees the precision it takes to do it. Because he pays that much attention. "Thank you," I tell him softly. "And thanks for understanding what I couldn't say and doing it for me."

"Anytime," he vows seriously. "I've always got your back."

Chapter 26

WREN

The courtroom is packed. Normally, family court is never like this. But this divorce is affecting the whole city, and Cold Springs has turned up in force to find out who's getting what. Some of them are worried about their own leases and want to know who's going to be getting their monthly rent checks. Others are just nosy as hell.

And some of us are hoping that their dominos fall as intended.

I'm sitting with Jesse on a hard wooden pew. His arm is thrown over the back, allowing me to get closer to his side, so our thighs are pressed against one another. With a quick scan of the room, I can see Etta, Mom, Dad, Daisy, Maggie, Francine, Ben, Wyatt, Lucy, and several city council members who are "friends" of Jed's.

And of course, Jed and Robert Jenkins are up front, sitting opposite Chrissy and Oliver.

"Nervous?" Jesse whispers into my ear.

Silently, I look at him, letting him see the freak-out I'm holding at bay in my eyes. When he nods and squeezes my shoulder, I let the veil fall back over my expression. Resting Bitch Face is apropos for the courtroom, especially when I'm here to represent the city's interests if needed.

Judge Hobner bangs his gavel on the wooden desk and warns the gallery, "I know this divorce is a big deal to some of you, but I won't have any tomfoolery in my courtroom today. The only people I want to hear from are Mr. and Mrs. Ford and their representatives. Understood?" He points with the gavel, and everyone quietly nods agreeably, not willing to get kicked out before the good stuff happens. "Good. Now, let's hear whatcha got. Mr. Jenkins?"

"Your Honor," he starts once he's stood, "with the advice of counsel, Mr. and Mrs. Ford have reached an agreement on the dissolution of their marriage and dispersion of assets."

"That true?" Judge Hobner asks Oliver.

He stands quickly. "Yes, Your Honor."

"Alright, lemme see it, then."

Robert approaches the bench—which is just an oversize desk on a small riser—and hands over a manila folder before returning to Jed's side. Judge Hobner opens it and starts to read, his brows climbing closer to where his hairline used to be with every line.

"This says that Mrs. Ford is to receive approximately *seventy* percent of the marital assets?" Judge Hobner chokes slightly, glancing up to make sure that's not a typo. When neither Robert nor Oliver corrects him, he continues, seeming stunned at that figure. "That works out to be the family home, several bank accounts, her vehicle, and a laundry list of properties that I'm going to assume you've both verified. Is that correct?" he asks, dropping the paper to the desk heavily.

"Yes, Your Honor," Robert intones flatly.

With his confirmation, the gallery gasps in surprise. People from town had no idea that was even a possibility and are whispering to one another with shocked expressions as they look at Jed's forlorn expression, which is absolutely an act to play the victim to Chrissy's moneygrubbing.

Judge Hobner bangs his gavel again. "Order, order. I warned you. If necessary, I'll make this a closed proceeding."

No, he won't. Judge Hobner is enjoying every second of this. He's a small-town, family-court judge whose most exciting days are adoptions, divorces, and child-support hearings. Something this salacious, with him at the helm as the big man in charge? He's eating this shit up. But throwing around his power—and his phallic gavel—is par for the course.

But his words have the intended effect, and the gallery quiets. A little.

He picks up the decree and begins to read again. "Okay, as to Ford Construction Company—" Judge Hobner stumbles over his words and jerks his eyes up to Jed. "Is this right?"

"Afraid so, Your Honor," Jed responds.

I can feel the audience leaning forward, eager to hear what's so unusual in the decree.

The judge tilts his head in disbelief, but keeps going. "The Ford Construction Company will also be divided seventy-thirty, with a specific list of properties and assets to be allocated there as well."

A murmur works its way through everyone in the room, but this time Judge Hobner doesn't try to stop it. I think he understands that no one can be quiet after hearing that.

Oliver stands. "Your Honor?" He waits for the judge's permission to speak and then says, "Please note the clause stating that Mr. Ford retains the usage rights for the name Ford Construction, and there will not be a noncompete in place. Additionally, we've included a copy of the corporate name-change filing, setting up the existing company as CDF Construction." Thankfully, she decided to go with a more respectable name, not Chrissy's Construction.

Oliver sits, giving Chrissy a reassuring nod.

"Let the record reflect those clauses and addendum," the judge tells the court reporter. To the two people sitting on opposite sides of the courtroom, he advises, "This is one of the most one-sided divorce decrees I've ever seen, and leaves Mrs. Ford with a significantly larger portion of the marital assets. Is this agreeable to you, Mr. Ford?"

As Jed rises, he shoots a wounded look at Chrissy. "Yes, Your Honor. I've done some things that Chrissy didn't deserve, and now . . . I just want us both to move on. I want my own life"—he turns to smile at Lucy, who lays a hand on her belly but doesn't return the smile—"and I want Chrissy to be happy in hers."

"Jesus, it's getting deep in here," I hiss in Jesse's ear, and he chuckles softly. "You know as well as I do that Jed doesn't think he's done a damn thing wrong. Ever. But saying I traded in my wife of thirty years for a younger model doesn't exactly set you up to be the bastion of respectability for the town, does it?"

"And you, Mrs. Ford? I take it these terms are agreeable to you as well?" the judge asks.

Chrissy nods, not even rising to answer.

Judge Hobner takes one more glance through the decree, holding several pages up at a time as he scans again and again. "Okay, your funeral," he tells Jed. "Divorce decree accepted as presented. Case closed."

And with a sharp bang of the gavel this time, everything changes.

"It's done?" Chrissy asks Oliver, wanting to be sure before she gloats.

Oliver grins, probably congratulating himself on the big win. "Yep, it's finalized."

"Woo-hoo!" she screeches, losing any and all attempts she was making at being well-behaved. "Fuck you, Jed!"

The shout is full of relief and joy. And freedom after years of being under Jed's thumb. The gallery is talking among themselves, some even laughing, despite Judge Hobner banging his gavel repeatedly at Chrissy's outburst. "Quiet down!"

But no one pays him any mind, in shock at Jed's capitulation to his now-ex-wife.

Jed turns around and reaches out to Lucy, who stands to step forward. It's the only thing that could get this crowd to focus, as they look to Chrissy for her reaction to the two lovebirds.

The air thickens with anticipation, but rather than Lucy consoling Jed, she walks the few steps to Chrissy's side.

"Oh, shit," someone says.

"Here we go," someone else adds.

I swear there are probably betting odds—in Chrissy's favor, she's shown her crazy quite a bit lately and Lucy's pregnant; in Lucy's favor, youth and that mama-bear instinct.

The two women stare at each other for an awkwardly long moment where we all hold our breaths, and then they . . . hug. Tears of happiness stream down both of their faces as they laugh, and Chrissy exclaims, "We did it!"

"What?" Jed blusters, jumping up from his seat. "What's going on?"

Lucy looks at Jed, letting the adoring veil drop from her gaze. "I know."

Two simple words, but with them, everyone realizes there's more going on than a simple divorce today. Even Jed.

He smiles sweetly at her, his tone pulling somewhere between pure innocence and lovesick teenager. "What do you mean, Lucy-Juicy? You know what? That I'm divorced and we can get married now?"

He's trying hard to set the narrative and remain in charge, but it's not working.

"I know you hid properties in my name," Lucy tells him flatly. Jed's eyes jump to Chrissy, afraid for her to hear that intel, but Lucy's got that too. "She already knows. We all know."

"We?" Jed echoes as his brows slam down in confusion.

This is it. I squeeze Jesse's hand so hard I'm probably breaking bones, but he doesn't stop me. He's watching my dominos fall with me, proudly anticipating that I've set each one perfectly and in awe of how my brain works.

One at a time, women stand from the gallery and step forward to join Chrissy and Lucy . . .

Etta, with a shit-eating grin that says she's really enjoying this.

Mom, with a politely bland expression.

Maggie, seeming nervous but standing with the other women anyway.

"What the hell is this?" Jed demands as he shoots up from the table, eyeing each woman with undisguised hatred.

"Jed Ford Support Group," Etta informs him. "We're thinking of getting T-shirts with 'JFSG' on them, but we can't agree on a mascot yet. I'm team hippo, happily living life and lying in wait to strike when the opportunity presents itself. But for obvious reasons, Lucy's not on board with that right now." Etta pats Lucy's belly like a proud aunt. "She's team honey badger, which, to be honest, we're probably gonna go with because who's gonna tell the pregnant woman no? Not me for sure."

Jed lost track of what Etta was rambling about somewhere around "Support Group" but zeros in on her touching Lucy's baby bump, and realizes that he's at a disadvantage. "What did you do, you crazy bitch?"

"Moi?" Etta answers, a hand to her chest. "Wasn't me . . . *this time.*" She grins evilly, fully admitting that she's fucked with him in the past.

Trying to regain control, Jed aims for the one person he thinks he can still sway. "Lucy, what have these women filled your mind with? They're bitter, old hags who're jealous of you and would lie to hurt me. You know that, right?"

Lucy doesn't believe him for a second. "They're smart, kind women with beautiful spirits that you tried to break. But you fucked up with me." She pauses, letting him wonder how badly he's misjudged her before dropping the bomb. "I'm a survivor. I've fought for everything I've ever had, scraped by when others wouldn't, and done some distasteful things to get by."

"Is she talking about Jed?" someone whispers loudly.

Jed's face is getting ruddy as it finally starts to sink in that he's fucked up. Majorly. "What did you do?"

"I sold them," she says simply.

Jed takes a heavy step toward her, and Robert, to his credit, holds his client back. But Jed still shouts at her, "You can't do that! Those properties are mine."

Lucy shrugs. "I was advised that the properties were in my name, and therefore, rightfully mine to do with as I saw fit. So I sold them. Alternatively, if they were under my name through some sort of false pretenses, charges could be pressed. What's more important to you, Jed? Your money or your freedom?"

I honestly think that might be a hard decision for him. But Robert can see the writing on the wall and whispers in Jed's ear through gritted teeth. Jed nods to answer whatever Robert asks, and receives an eye roll in response.

"Dumbass," Robert says, which is probably not his professional opinion, but correct regardless.

"Who? Who'd you sell my property to?" Jed demands.

"I believe you mean *my* properties," Mom answers, smiling like the beauty queen she once was. She once received a Miss Congeniality sash, but that was long before Jed almost took Dad from her. Now, she's more Miss Consequences, and I'm loving it because Jed deserves every bit of this after a lifetime of ruining others for his own gain. "I thought it'd be fun to piddle around with a few rental places, so when the opportunity came up, I couldn't resist."

I stifle a giggle. Mom's making Jed's significant property assets sound like a little side hustle, which pisses him off even more.

"Those are my investments," he snarls at Mom. I don't think he's ever considered her a risk or a danger in any way. She's the Junior League president, library volunteer, mom type who simply existed as a useless footnote to his brother. She's beneath his business-minded, long-game-focused way of using people to his advantage. But that's where he's wrong.

"Those are for our future, for Jed Junior," he appeals to Lucy, not giving up.

She rubs her belly affectionately. "Good news, then. They'll be used to create a life for him. One where he doesn't have to struggle, but also one where he doesn't have to lie and cheat."

"I'll take him from you. Sue for full custody," Jed declares maliciously.

The whole gallery gasps at the vitriol in his voice, surprised that even he would sink so low as to use an innocent child to get his way.

But Lucy doesn't let it faze her. "You're a manipulative bastard with no money, who never wanted a child. I will be a loving mother who provides not only financial support, but emotional support to the child I've always dreamed of. I won't keep him from you, but I'll be honest with him about who you are and *who you are not.*"

He can sense that he's beat. It's written in the angry scowl lines that crease his face. But he's not a man who admits defeat, even when he's been outplayed at every angle . . .

In an attempt to get divorced quickly, he gave Aunt Chrissy more than her fair share, thinking he had an ace in the hole. He gave her what he considers to be the worthless part of the company, keeping his name to trade on, but his reputation is getting more sullied by the minute. He used Lucy to hide assets, thinking she'd be none the wiser or, worst-case scenario, he could sweet-talk her if she did find out. But she not only found out, she took advantage of the situation. He thought he was trading up from the wife he had it easy with to a younger, more exciting version only to discover the new woman isn't nearly as naive as he imagined. Even the past he thought he'd outrun has come back to haunt him, with Mom and Etta both playing a part in his downfall.

Digging deep for bluster, he points a finger at Chrissy and snarls, "This isn't over."

It's telling that he's mad at Chrissy and not Lucy, and I wonder if somewhere in his cold, dead, manipulative heart, he did once care for her in the only way he knew how. But she deserves better. She always has, and now she's beginning to realize it.

Despite Jed's proclamation to the contrary, this is over. The divorce is final, the properties transferred ownership this morning, and the company paperwork for the new name is filed and approved. He's done.

My final domino has fallen.

Jed storms out of the courtroom, and chatter begins almost immediately as people give their take on what just happened with the soap-opera-worthy drama that played out in front of a good portion of the city.

Belatedly, Judge Hobner knocks his gavel on the desk again. "Quiet. This isn't the only courtroom we've got in session today." But he doesn't seem to be that concerned, because he returns to listening from afar.

Etta's ready for this. It's not her first rodeo with town drama, and she knows what to do. "After-party's at Puss N Boots. You buy a drink and a burger, and the fries are on me," she calls out. Then she points at Judge Hobner, calling out, "Tom, you come on by and your meal's on me. Sorry for taking over your courtroom today."

It's a prime example of why Etta's beloved in Cold Springs. Free fries and a chance to gossip? You could sign more than half the town up for that easily. Plus, a little bonus for the judge who got a little RickRolled today by having his domain unexpectedly used as a stage instead of a divorce court.

The crowd begins to disperse, racing to Puss N Boots to get a table most likely, and I stand as Ben comes up to shake my hand. "Good work, young lady."

"You too, old man. You thinking of taking up real-estate law in your retirement?" I tease, only half-kidding. He did an amazing job pulling together the contract to sell Lucy's properties to Mom in record time.

"Hell no. That was a onetime deal for a friend." His smile is warm, not that of a mentor and mentee, but of friendship, and I feel like I passed a final test with him.

"Thanks, then. I promise not to interrupt your Samuel Adams sunset again if I can help it," I vow, hoping I can keep the promise. "But you keep that mind sharp. You never know when I might need someone to bounce ideas off."

Chrissy and Oliver are walking to the exit, and she stops to hug me. "Thanks, Wren. I couldn't have done it without you."

Oliver looks like his flabber's been gasted, eyes sliding from Chrissy to me and back again. "You? How did you—"

But Chrissy cuts him off. "Come on, Ollie. Champagne's on me, and fries are on Etta. I wanna get there before they run out of Tayvious's ketchup. That stuff is delicious."

She shoos him out the door with her, but he glances back at me, mouthing, "Later?"

Jesse chuckles from beside me. "Fucker don't give up, does he?"

I look down to discover he's stretched out, both arms laid over the backrest of the bench, looking comfortable as can be on the hard wood.

"Jealous?" I tease, knowing he is. But also, that he has absolutely nothing to be worried about.

Instead of answering the question, he says, "Hey, did I tell you about that new waitress over at the deli? Her name's Drew, and she makes the best homemade pickles I've ever had in my mouth." His lips quirk as his dark eyes pin me, daring me to deny that him mentioning another woman bothers me.

I bend down to get right in his face, putting my hand on his chest and digging my nails in ever so slightly. "I don't share. You're mine."

He moves quickly, his hands cupping my face and holding me nose to nose with him. Where I was the one in control, now he is. "Birdie, you've been mine long before you even knew it. Had me stalking you all over town for months and threatening to beat the fuck outta anyone who looked at you sideways. And I sure as shit don't share."

He kisses me with heat, his tongue slipping in to taste mine.

"Oh! Excuse me," a voice says.

I jerk, but Jesse takes his time, not done kissing me yet. After a quick succession of smacks, he pulls back with a sexy smirk.

I look behind me to find the court reporter grinning as she gathers her stuff. "Don't mind me. Just heading out for the day."

"Us too," Jesse answers, standing and taking my hand.

As we walk out of the courtroom, I say, "Tell me more about Drew and these pickles."

He laughs loudly. "She's sixty if she's a day, and makes pickles from scratch. Says she's been doing it since she was a kid, canning cucumbers from her grandma's garden."

I lift a brow in concession. "Fine, you got me. But I think I'll stop by for lunch one day this week. Just to check these *pickles* out."

Chapter 27

Jesse

I don't think I've ever seen Puss N Boots this busy, and that's saying something considering it's the only place open late on Saturday nights, and we once had a whole town protest relocated here for a strategy session. But those crowds have nothing on this.

I hold Wren's hand tightly, keeping her behind me, as I push into the crowd to join the celebration and make a path for her.

"Jesse! Over here!" a voice shouts, and I turn to see Wyatt holding an arm up. I give him a nod and start making my way in his direction, guiding Wren along with me.

"Hey, guys!" There are no chairs, but we pull up to stand next to the tall table. I pour myself a beer from the pitcher already sitting there, and ask Wren, "Want a water? I'll go up to the bar and get it."

She shakes her head. "I'll wait a bit. I'm too excited. If I drink anything, I'll probably have to pee."

Her nose-wrinkling grin is adorably cute, which is not a side she usually shows. It makes me happy to see her so happy.

"How'd it get so wild in here?" I ask Wyatt. But he shrugs and points to Winston, who's got baby Joe in a carrier again, bouncing and patting his butt. Beside him, Avery is bouncing in sync, probably not even aware that she's doing it without a baby in her arms.

"Cold Springs hotline went crazy after the courtroom drama. Dad called me, I called Wyatt. I think Charlene called everyone." He gestures to the room at large. "Probably hoping for some good tips."

"Thinking Hazel had something to do with that," Wyatt interjects, pointing at the bar where his wife is climbing up to address her customers. "I wonder if she's gonna dance again."

The last time Hazel climbed up there, it was to dance at Avery's makeshift bachelorette party. So it only seems fitting for her to do it for a divorce party, I guess. But shouldn't Chrissy be up there too?

Hazel lets out an earsplitting whistle, and everyone immediately looks her way. Someone hollers, "Damn, Hazel. Think you split my eardrum."

"Boo-hoo, Carl," she shouts back, not sorry at all. "Listen up! You've got eyes, you can see we're busy, so don't be giving Charlene and me shit about your beer. Tayvious is doing the best he can, too, so you'll get your burger when it's good and fucking ready. Anyone who asks me about fries ain't getting a single one. *Capisce?*"

It's a good thing my sister waitresses at Aunt Etta's place, because she'd be fired from anywhere else on her first day. But here, she fits right in, mostly getting her sass from Aunt Etta anyway.

Winston asks Wren, "You really get Mom to buy some of Jed's properties?"

"Maybe," she drawls out, looking guilty as can be. "Mom didn't need much convincing, though . . . or so I 'heard.' I think she was pretty excited at getting one over on Jed to begin with. The fact that it's the properties he wanted to hoard away and steal from Chrissy? Even better. I'm in total support of Badass Mom."

"Me too," both brothers tell her quickly, not wanting to risk unleashing Wren's wrath on them. Pamela might be coming into her own, but Wren has always been the unexpected assassin—her beauty lulling you into complacency before she slices and dices you. Usually in a courtroom or over a negotiation table, but I wouldn't put it past her to have some hidden tricks either. Ones I can't wait to discover.

"And Chrissy got the company, house, and bank accounts," Wren summarizes, reporting facts instead of bragging, which is what she should be doing. "And the contract for Township is a done deal," she tells me.

I nod. "Already called Bea. Told her I'd see her first thing in the morning to submit a bunch of permits and to be ready for speedy approvals."

Wren waves at someone and then says, "I see Lucy over there. I want to check on her, make sure no one's being rude about the whole Jed thing."

"I'll come with you," Avery offers. "It'd be nice to make a mom-friend so I have someone to talk to about baby poop and teething drool."

Wren's nose scrunches up. "Yeah, I love you and Joe, but I don't want to talk about bodily fluids. Come on," she tells Avery, and after she leans in to give me a quick peck, the two of them are off.

No sooner than they're gone, the guys lean in. "You and Wren good?" Wyatt asks.

Winston's grin is pure devilment. "I want to hear the story of how you went from her stomping out of here to kill you to oh-so-casually kissing you goodbye just to walk around the room."

"I have a very particular set of skills," I brag.

"That's my sister you're talking about," Wyatt quips automatically, and I give him a dirty look.

"Yeah, I know, asshole. Payback's a bitch, ain't it?" I tease, glad that he's the one dealing with my sister now, because Hazel's a lot on a good day. On a bad one? I'm man enough to admit that I do my damnedest to stay outta her way.

I find Wren again and track her around the room, watching her shine as she chats with people, accepting congratulations and thanks. Only then do I answer their original question. "Yeah, we're real good actually."

I can't stop my smile from beaming. I probably look like a stupid, lovesick puppy, but I'm happy.

I've got the girl. The one I've obsessed over, and she's apparently been crushing on me too. And we're going home together tonight to fall into bed and each other.

I've got the job I enjoy. My guys will be back to work within days, and we'll finish Township for Cold Springs.

I've got a boss who's going to be better than Jed, hopefully. At least she seems willing to listen and didn't fire me outright when I was brutally honest. That goes a long way in my book.

My family is all safe and content. Mom's happy with the bakery, Etta's happy with Puss N Boots and her horse, whose stall is clean enough that I would sleep in there without a second thought.

And Etta's . . . talking to Mike? Fuck. I mean, fuck no. But even that bad idea can't get me down tonight. Not when Wren is nearly floating around the room on cloud nine.

Soon, she's with Avery and Lucy, and though she's semismiling, I can tell they must be talking about something gross because she also seems a bit horrified.

I chuckle as she excuses herself and walks away from them with wide eyes and a face screwed up in disgust.

Only to be stopped . . . by Oliver the Asshole.

My feet start moving before my brain makes the decision, and behind me, I hear either Wyatt or Winston, not sure which, mutter, "Oh, fuck, here we go."

But I'm not going over to start shit. Wren can talk to him, politely tell him good job on the contract, and then say goodbye because that douchewaffle's leaving town. Tonight, if I have anything to say about it.

I don't say a word, people just move out of my way, probably because my eyes are locked on Wren, measuring her fake smile and watching it fall by increments. Something's wrong, and I need to get there. Now.

There's a tall guy in my way who must mistake my mission focus for him, because he posts up and grunts, "What?"

"Move." I push past him, bumping his shoulder with mine, not out of anger but lack of space in the crowded room. And once I get past him, I see . . .

Oliver move in to kiss Wren.

Time slows as their lips meet, his hands on her face as he tries to take the kiss deeper.

A hush falls over the room. Or at least I think it does, because the roar in my ears is so fucking loud, I can't hear a thing. But I can sense eyes on me, and there's suddenly plenty of room for me to move as people get the hell out of the way.

My fists are clenched at my sides, but I'm not holding back. I'm preparing.

There's no need to, though. Right as I get close enough, Wren pulls out of his grasp, rears back, and throws a solid right cross to The Asshole's nose. There's a popping sound, and blood gushes everywhere, down over his mouth and dripping to his probably stupid-expensive dress shirt as he collapses forward, clutching his nose and muttering in shock.

"What the fuck are you doing? How many times do I have to tell you no? I've tried polite, I've tried blunt, and now I'm trying this." Her voice cuts through the crowd as she reads Oliver down, and though my instinct is to step in to protect her, she doesn't need it. She's doing fine on her own. Better than fine actually. "Let me be clear. Our relationship was professional, only professional. You are not my type, no matter what you'd like to think. My type is the monster of a man standing behind you, holding himself back from killing you."

Oliver's head jerks, sending blood droplets all over Aunt Etta's wood floor. His eyes are fear-filled as they land on me. And instead of taking the L and running, he stands up to face me.

Game fucking on. I've been wanting this for weeks.

But he doesn't try to fight me. No, he shouts, "She hit me! That's assault! You all saw her! Look at my nose!"

I grin at the nasal whininess the blood's added to his voice.

Hazel arrives, stepping between Oliver and me with a pool stick at the ready. I've seen her beat the shit out of guys with one before, so I know she's not fucking around. She's also holding me back, protecting me from charges, not protecting Oliver from a beatdown. Wren steps around Hazel and comes to my side, where I welcome her with an arm around her shoulders. I take her hand, press a soft kiss to her red knuckles, and whisper, "You okay?"

My eyes plumb deep into hers, asking if I can beat this guy up for her.

"I'm okay. He's not worth it," she tells me. I'm disappointed I can't unleash on Oliver, teach him a lesson about not taking a no the first time. It's maybe a bit hypocritical considering the lengths I went to for Wren. But I held myself back, letting her have space until she came to me. I didn't force my way into her life, even though it damn near killed me.

"Assault, you say?" Hazel echoes. "Anyone see an assault?"

Avery raises her hand, and though her voice is quiet, she's sure. "I did." Oliver's smug grin is blood tinged until she adds, "I saw him sexually assault Wren and her defend herself."

"What? No!" he shouts, the grin falling as he looks around.

"Me too," someone else says.

"Yep, that's what I saw."

There are several nods, too, and Oliver realizes that despite his fancy clothes, fancy law degree, and fancy entitlement, he's not going to win this one. Not in our town and not with our Wren.

"Maybe we should call the police," he suggests snidely.

There's a booming laugh from a few tables away, and the crowd parts, revealing Robbie. "I'm already here, and that's what I saw too."

Charlene is at Officer Milson's side, and I'm betting he was deep in *conversation* with her when things went down and didn't see a thing. But he's got Wren's back.

We all do.

"You wanna press charges, Wren?" Robbie asks conversationally. "I think Judge Hobner's on call for criminal court overnight, and he's three sheets to the wind over there after that stunt you pulled today, so it'll be tomorrow morning before I can get your boy arraigned. A night in the clink might do him good."

Oliver spits a bloody bit of saliva to the floor at Hazel's feet, and there's a gasp of horror. Oliver doesn't know what the hell he's done. Wren's one thing, my sister's another. And then I'm the one holding her back. "You're not going to jail tonight, Hazel. He ain't worth it."

"Wren is," Hazel argues. She's not wrong, that's for sure. But Wren has it under control.

She bends down and swipes her red-nailed fingers through the grossness on the floor and then walks up to Oliver. It's the hardest thing I've ever done to let her step closer to that asshole again, but I wanna see what she's gonna do as much as everyone else.

And this tiny spitfire of a woman, who oozes brains and beauty, pats Oliver's cheek with his own spit. Hard. "You forgot something on your way out," she tells him, her entire demeanor gone dark and deadly. "So . . . bye."

He flinches, thinking she's going to do more, so when her hand drops and her lips quirk up in triumph, he's embarrassed again. "You people are fucking crazy," he tells the room at large.

As he's nearly running for the door with his tail between his legs, Tayvious calls out, "Hey, I made you a real *special* Fat Pussy. Did you want it to go?"

We laugh. Nobody wants one of those special burgers. Tayvious wouldn't disrespect his own food by spitting in it, but there's no telling what he did do to it.

It breaks the mood, and with Oliver gone, everyone starts talking about Wren. "I thought for sure it was gonna be Jesse who punched that guy."

"Me too. Here ya go."

Money's being exchanged all across the room, apparently most folks losing their bet on me losing my cool over Wren and beating up Oliver.

I escort her back to the table, keeping her tucked in at my side like someone else might have a go at her too. Charlene brings a whole bottle of hand sanitizer and a pitcher of ice water. "For your hand," she tells Wren, sounding experienced with bar brawls. "No telling what a slimeball like that has, and you don't want to get an infection."

"Thanks," she tells Charlene, already swishing the lube-like fluid over her hands. To Wyatt, she says, "And thank you for teaching me to throw a solid punch."

He tries to play it off with a casual shrug, but looks pretty pleased with himself. "That's what brothers are for. Just remind me not to piss you off."

Wren looks at me, and what the rest of the bar thinks or says doesn't matter. My world's this woman, and how much she means to me.

"You okay?" I ask her, pushing her hair behind her ear so I can see her eyes better. That's my primary concern. Wren. My world.

She nods slowly, her eyes filling with fire. "Fucker was shocked that I pulled that off at court today. Literally asked if Ben helped me, and when I said it was all me, he had the audacity to look impressed. 'You?'" She throws her voice, not deep, but high and whiny, which makes me chuckle. "He tried to tell me that we'd make a good team and he'd be willing to put in a good word for me back at his firm, but I'd have to pay my dues. Like I didn't know what that meant. Entitled prick."

Her rant has us all fighting back grins.

"Fuck, you're sexy," I tell her. It's probably not the right thing to say. I should be sweet and romantic, or take gentle care of her after such an upsetting event. But that's not what I see. She's not some delicate bird who needs protecting, or at least she's not right now. Wren's strong, puts up with no shit, and literally holds no punches. And it's sexy as hell. Later, if the high wears off and she needs someone to take care of her, I'll do that too.

But right now, she's fierce and proclaimed to the whole town that I'm her type. Her man.

"Let's get out of here," I suggest quietly into her ear so only she hears me. While I'm at the side of her neck, I breathe her in. Her sweet essence is there, which only makes her badassery that much more exciting.

Her gaze drops to my lips, but she wiggles her finger to ask me to come closer. In my ear, she purrs, "I need you to get him off me. Claim me as yours again because that's what I am."

Holeeee fuck. I grab her noninjured hand, and wave to the guys and Avery. "Gotta go."

They laugh, and so does Wren until I'm dragging her out of Puss N Boots.

Behind me, I hear someone say, "Official time: five minutes, fourteen seconds. Pay up."

Apparently, everyone was betting on how long it'd be until I hauled Wren out of here to fuck her senseless. I'm not offended in the slightest. Rather, I'm impressed I made it five whole minutes.

Chapter 28

WREN

Jesse rushes me to his truck, buckles me in, and runs around to get in the driver's seat. I watch with a laugh trying to bubble up at the urgency in his every movement. But when he pulls out of the lot, spinning gravel under the tires, and grabs onto my thigh, the humor evaporates, replaced with heat.

"Your place or mine?" he demands.

"Yours. It's closer," I respond. But I'm not waiting that long. I reach over the console to run my hand up his jeans-covered thigh until I reach his cock, which is quickly thickening. I cup him through the denim, feeling powerful when he shifts in his seat to spread his thighs for more of my touch.

The truck roars as he speeds up, and by the time he's pulling into his drive, we're nearly on two wheels. I guess it's a good thing Officer Milson's back at Puss N Boots, along with the entirety of the town. He runs around to get me, but I hop down on my own.

"Get inside unless you want me to fuck you on the front lawn," he growls sexily. I squeal and make a run for the front door.

Mrs. Capshaw's door opens. "What's with all the racket out here?"

"Sorry!" I yell to her. Then I hiss at Jesse, "Just gonna go have sex! Hurry up!"

The door opens and we virtually fall inside. Jesse slams the door behind us, not giving Mrs. Capshaw a chance to bitch more.

I start yanking at Jesse's shirt, needing his skin. But it's too slow for us both, and when he shoves my hands away to rip his shirt over his head, I do the same with my own. I get the buttons undone in record time and then reach behind my back to undo my bra. My breasts fall free, and Jesse cups them instantly.

His thumbs brush over my sensitive nipples, which pearl beneath his touch. Heat zings through me straight to my clit, and I moan at the delicious heat building there.

"Yeah, do that again," Jesse orders, wanting my sounds of pleasure. He pinches the hard nubs sharply, and I cry out at the pleasant pain. I float as Jesse picks me up in his powerful arms, swept away in the feeling. A second later, I'm flying through the air to land on his bed. I writhe against the scratchy sheets, enjoying the sensation.

Jesse follows me to the bed, aiming for my breasts. He takes one into his mouth, sucking hard as his tongue circles my nipple. When he releases me, his teeth run over my skin, triggering all the nerve endings. I scratch my nails up his back until gooseflesh breaks out and then let my touch glance over the muscles of his shoulders.

I push at his chest, wanting space between us so that I can get the rest of my clothes off. Jesse stands beside the bed, watching as I kick off my heels and shimmy my pants off, leaving me in only my panties.

"These are your sexy ones." The heat in the words washes over me as he slides them down my legs.

I know they are. Not only are they some of my sexy panties, they're Jesse's favorite ones. I wore them on purpose for good luck today, hopeful that things would end up exactly as they are. Naked with Jesse.

There's only one thing missing.

"Need you. Now. Fuck me, Jesse."

Instead of unbuttoning his own jeans, he drops to his knees on the floor and pulls me to the edge of the bed, burying his face in my core. I slide my hands into his hair, holding on for dear life as he devours me. It's such an onslaught, I can't tell what's tongue, teeth, or mouth because my entire pussy is going liquid for him.

As good as it is, I still feel empty without him inside me. I buck my hips, riding his mouth. "There you go. Use me," he praises.

"Fingers," I beg.

I only have to say it once and Jesse slides two fingers into me easily, going directly to impaling me with them hard and fast. "Yes," I hiss. He knows my body, knows how to get me there quick and how to draw it out. This time, we're going for coming fast.

It's only seconds until the throbbing pulses send me into the darkness behind my eyes. Sparkles flash there like fireworks, but the real show is happening between my legs where Jesse's humming against my flesh.

When I can pry my eyes open again, I reach for him. "C'mere."

He pulls away from me with a glossiness over his lips that he swipes away with the back of his hand. He's quick to kick off his boots and undress, climbing over me on the bed. Propped on outstretched arms, he hovers above me, and I reach between us. When I wrap my hand around his thick, hard cock, his eyes flutter and he groans low in his throat, the feeling of being powerful surging in me again.

I stroke him, up and down, with my fist getting tighter and then squeezing over the tip. "This cock . . . mine. Your heart . . . mine. You . . ." I pause, waiting for him to open his eyes. Deep in their darkness, there's still a tiny shred of doubt.

Doubt and hope, two sides of the same coin. And what took months from us because we didn't just talk about what we wanted. I won't make that mistake again. Dropping all my own guards and being vulnerable is scary, but it's the only way to get what we both want.

"You . . . mine. Because I love you." The three words are weighted with a question. I've never said them to anyone before and deep down, I think I was waiting for Jesse to say them to me first. But I can see the relief wash through him as my truth settles into those cracks caused by doubt. He's enough for me.

And I'm not too much for him.

We're perfect, and together, we're even better.

Looking between us, I guide him to my entrance, and he moves his hips, teasing us both. "Wren . . ."

It's hard to drag my eyes back up to his, but I do it. I'm rewarded by him slamming balls-deep into me and falling down to pin me to the bed with the length of his body. I spasm instantly at the pleasurable invasion. It's exactly what I need.

His mouth goes straight to my ear and he growls, "I love you too. I've loved you for ages."

No, that's what I needed. And he knew it.

He takes a big breath and then pours himself into me, thrusting and rolling his hips to fill me over and over. I'm stretched delightfully, but want even more.

I wrap my legs around his waist, locking my feet to hold him deep inside me, and take control. Jesse lets me, holding himself still while I fuck him. He flashes that cocky smirk. "Fuck, you're so damn sexy. Don't stop. Never stop."

I don't think I could even if I wanted to. And when I dig my nails into his back for leverage to keep him locked against me, he throws his head back, the tendons in his neck standing out in stark relief. "Yes," he groans.

I can feel the heat of his cum filling me in pulsing jets. He takes over, stroking into me hard and fast, but pulling back slightly to meet my eyes. His brow furrows as he fights to maintain our gaze, and the deep intimacy I see there coupled with the rough fuck is more than I ever dreamed. Using my inner muscles, I squeeze him, wanting to prolong his orgasm, but it sends me into another as he rubs over my clit.

"There you go, come for me, Wren. Take my cum, take me . . . all of me."

Jesse rolls us over, staying inside me, and I collapse on top of him with limbs askew. Panting with my cheek pressed to his chest, I smile. "That was . . . wow."

"Yeah, you are." I'm too exhausted to lift my head, but I can hear the humor in his voice.

"Not too bad yourself," I tease.

He's so much more than that. He's everything. He's perfect. He's the right man for me. It just took a while for it to be the right time for us. But now it is.

Now, it's our time.

Epilogue

JESSE

"How's the new addition going?" Hazel asks over dinner.

Wren shrugs. "Loud?"

I laughingly tell Hazel, "It's going great. Should be done in three weeks or so."

After we eloped, Wren and I decided to move into her house because she didn't want to leave her neighborhood and Finnegan, the community cat who's been staying at the neighbors' house most nights now. I honestly thought Wren was fucking with me when she said she had a cat because I'd never seen the damn thing. But he's real, he's a jerk, and he likes to hide in the bushes, only coming out for food. To me, that does not equal a good pet, but Wren disagrees. Either way, I moved into her place and there's a new guy at work who needed a place to stay, so he's renting my house.

We also decided that adding a few hundred square feet to the back of the house was a good idea, and I've been working on that renovation after hours.

"And there's no specific reason as to why you're doing that?" Hazel's like a dog with a bone on this one. She decided that the only reason

Wren and I would go for a quick wedding and then immediately start building is because Wren's pregnant.

Which she's not. Yet.

We eloped because, as Wren describes it, "My brothers' weddings were absolute circuses, and I'm not doing that."

She wanted quiet and intimate, and I wanted to give her whatever she wanted. So a short trip to an island paradise later, we came back married. Not Mr. and Mrs. Sullivan, since Wren kept her own name, but she's mine all the same. And I'm hers.

"No babies," Wren answers.

Lester only hears one word, though—"babies." Hazel's gray parrot intones like a zombie, "Baby birds yummy."

It's a trick Hazel taught him and something he usually only says when eating eggs, but I guess the wording triggered him. Or he's asking for eggs. Or he's being a dick, which is the most likely scenario.

"What about you?" Avery asks Hazel, not letting her escape unscathed by suspicions. "We could use another member in our mommy group."

Hazel gets up from the table, shaking her head as she pulls cupcakes from one of Mom's boxes. "Nope, not yet. Lester's all the baby I can handle. Isn't that right, sweet boy?" she coos to the demon pigeon.

"You look like bullshit," he answers, and I choke on my beer. Wyatt chuckles at my reaction, which is fine as long as Hazel doesn't kill me and feed me to Lester as punishment for teaching him that.

The mommy group Avery's talking about is her and Lucy, who ended up staying in Cold Springs. She's become another member of our little group, and has been taken in by our town as the catalyst for change after what she did to Jed.

It was weird in the days following the courtroom soap opera. Jed tried to throw his weight around the way he always had, pulling strings here and greasing palms there, but no one really gave a shit. All his power was taken away. But the best part was the power he'd given away because he was so arrogant that he thought he knew better than everyone else. Wren taught him that his cockiness was sorely misplaced, even continuing to field his phone calls about how what she did was illegal, ethically bankrupt, and morally gray for weeks after the divorce was final. And she shut him down every time, telling him that she'd happily take on his lawyers again if he'd like, which he didn't. Last I heard, he was living in Newport, where he founded his new company.

I lost a couple of guys to him, but the majority stayed with me as site manager and Chrissy as the owner and CEO of CDF Construction. It helps that Maggie is now COO and largely in charge of how things are run on a day-to-day basis while Chrissy does . . . whatever Chrissy does with her time. Actually, it's Friday night, so I think she's at Puss N Boots, singing karaoke. She likes "These Boots Are Made for Walking," and does a decent job strutting around the stage area, which is just a section of floor where they push the tables out of the way.

"How is Joe?" I ask Avery, hoping to take the heat off me.

"Grandpa or baby?" she asks, but answers anyway. "They're both fine. Home with two different sitters tonight. Ironically, I had to tell them both about diaper changes. One because he's got a little rash, and the other because he does not have shingles and there isn't a rash on his taint." Avery rolls her eyes at Grandpa Joe's susceptibility to TV commercials, which have apparently moved on from mesothelioma to shingles vaccines.

Wyatt sets his Chocolate Orgasm cupcake down. "Can we not talk about taints while I'm eating a chocolate cupcake, please?"

Wren grabs the treat from her brother's plate. "Doesn't bother me. Your loss." She promptly takes a good-size bite from it, leaving a bit of icing at the corner of her mouth.

I grab the seat of her chair, pulling her over to me with a grin. "My gain," I say before kissing the edge of her mouth, right over the icing. I let my tongue slip out to taste it. "Yummy. More please."

"Man, I lost my cupcake, my sister, and my appetite," Wyatt complains.

Hazel plops into his lap. "But you got me, so winner winner, chicken dinner."

"Funny," I say, "I got your cupcake, your sister, and a damn good appetite." I throw one arm over the back of her chair and adjust my cock with the other.

Winston joins in, taking his brother's side. "That was wrong, Jesse."

My Wren decides to add, "But he's oh so right."

Yeah, I am.

ABOUT THE AUTHOR

Wall Street Journal, USA Today, Washington Post, and #1 Amazon bestselling author Lauren Landish welcomes readers into a world of rock-hard abs and chiseled smiles. Her sexy contemporary romances—including her wildly successful Bennett Boys Ranch books, the Truth or Dare series, and the Big Fat Fake series—have garnered a legion of praise. When Lauren isn't plotting ways to introduce readers to their next sexy-as-hell book boyfriend, she's deep in her writing cave and furiously tapping away on her keyboard, crafting scenes that would make even a hardened sailor blush. For all the updates and news on her upcoming books (not to mention a whole lotta hunks), visit www.LaurenLandish.com.